F
MEA

WATERFORD CITY AND COUNTY LIBRARIES
WITHDRAWN

D0585037

Web of Deceit

Also by Glenn Meade

Brandenburg
Snow Wolf
The Sands of Sakkara
Resurrection Day

GLENN MEADE

Web of Deceit

WATERFORD CITY AND COUNTY LIBRARIES WITHDRAWN WATERFORD MUNICIPAL LIBRARY

Hodder & Stoughton

Copyright © 2004 by Glenn Meade

First published in Great Britain in 2004 by Hodder and Stoughton
A division of Hodder Headline

The right of Glenn Meade to be identified as the Author of the Work has been
asserted by him in accordance with the Copyright, Designs and Patents Act 1988

1 3 5 7 9 10 8 6 4 2

All rights reserved. No part of this publication may be reproduced, stored in a
retrieval system, or transmitted, in any form or by any means without the prior
written permission of the publisher, nor be otherwise circulated in any form of
binding or cover other than that in which it is published and without a similar
condition being imposed on the subsequent purchaser.

All characters in this publication are fictitious and any resemblance to
real persons, living or dead, is purely coincidental.

A CIP catalogue record for this title is available from the British Library

Hardback ISBN 0 340 83540 0
Trade Paperback ISBN 0 340 83554 0

Typeset in Plantin Light by Palimpsest Book Production Limited,
Polmont, Stirlingshire
Printed and bound by
Mackays of Chatham Ltd, Chatham, Kent

Hodder Headline's policy is to use papers that are natural, renewable and
recyclable products and made from wood grown in sustainable forests.
The logging and manufacturing processes are expected to conform
to the environmental regulations of the country of origin.

Hodder and Stoughton Ltd
A division of Hodder Headline
338 Euston Road
London NW1 3BH

With love to my fellow 'Waltons' –
Tom, Diane, and Elaine.

PART ONE

I

At 3 a.m., in New York, Jennifer March came awake in the dark, sensing a presence in her bedroom.

A storm raged outside, lightning flickering beyond the window, the rain lashing down in torrents. When she opened her eyes she was already frightened, and suddenly aware of two things: the roar of the storm and the terrifying feeling that there was *someone* near her. Perspiration beaded her face and her breath came in short, rapid throbs. As she pulled back the covers and started to get up off the bed she saw the figure of a man dressed in black standing over her. '*Don't move,*' he ordered.

Despite the warning, Jennifer struggled in panic, but the man slapped her, a stinging blow across the face. '*Stay still!*' A flash of lightning flooded the bedroom and she glimpsed the intruder's face.

He had no face.

He wore a black ski mask, piercing dark eyes visible through the slits, and he held a butcher's knife in his leather-gloved hand. When Jennifer went to scream the man's other hand went over her mouth. She cried, curled up with fear, and her nightgown rode up her legs. Carefully, the man placed the knife on the night stand. Jennifer suddenly felt a hand crawl over her flesh as the man forced her legs apart. '*Stay still or I'll cut your throat!*'

Jennifer March was petrified. The man unbuckled his trousers, moved on top of her and entered her savagely. The pain was terrible. She was more frightened than she had ever been in her life and there was something animal and repulsive about what the man was doing, but she was so caught up in the horror of what was happening to her that she didn't dare move. While the storm raged outside the man grunted, taking his pleasure.

And then suddenly it was over. The man sat up, took his hand off her mouth, but Jennifer was too traumatised to scream as he picked up the knife from the night stand and the bloodied steel flashed. She sobbed. 'What . . . what are you going to do?'

'*Kill you.*'

Jennifer March screamed . . .

2

She woke with a scream, clutching a pillow to her chest. This time the wakening was not a nightmare, but for real. Panting with terror, she gulped air.

Jennifer March let go of the pillow and threw back the covers. She switched on the bedside light, fumbled out of bed, and moved over to the window. Forcing herself to breathe more slowly, she became aware of the harsh murmur beyond the open window. Rain. Heavy, incessant torrents that hissed out there in the coldness of the stormy night.

Staring out, she saw nothing, no silvery lunar light to comfort her, just black icy rain sluicing the glass, washed by a ragged wind. Lightning flashed and a chorus of thunder rumbled. New York was asleep, the entire East Coast bathed in stormy darkness, but she was wide awake, her soul swamped by heart-thumping fear and a terrible anguish. As always, the dream came to her during a storm. And as always, it was so real it distressed her.

Like a sleepwalker, she moved out to the apartment hallway, stepped into the bathroom, grabbed the towel from the ring and dabbed perspiration from her face. Then she found her way to the kitchen, switched on the night light over the cooker hob, took a bottle of water from the icebox, poured a large measure into a tall glass, and clinked in some ice cubes. She took a long drink, then padded back to her room and sat on the bed. Her back to the wall, she placed the ice-cold glass against her forehead, stared at the pale green numbers on the digital clock on her night stand: *3.05*.

Almost without thinking, she found the sleeping pills on the night stand, thumbed open the plastic bottle and popped two in her mouth, washed them down with another mouthful of water. She didn't like taking the pills, but knew she had to now. She wanted sleep, and without the torment of her dreams.

The condo in Long Beach, Long Island, was a one-bed, with a pleasant living room, a kitchenette and a tiny bathroom. On a clear day she could see across the inlet to Cove End, her parents' house: it was deserted and forlorn, a grey-and-white-painted colonial property with its own waterside dock. She had moved to the apartment hoping to make a fresh start, unable to live in the house any more, but really she hadn't made any kind of start at all. She was forever trapped in her past, bound by its chains. The nightmare still came. The memories still haunted. No matter what she did to try to forget, they still came back. And she knew why. Sometimes dreams were all she had. All she had to remember the life she had shared and lost with her father and mother, and the sacredness of their lives together.

But sometimes those dreams disturbed, brought her horror and grief, and tonight they had her in their grip and wouldn't let go. Which was why she knew she needed to hear a human voice, needed to know she wasn't alone, know that she was connected to another living being.

She peered again at the illuminated clock on the night stand: 3.06. She knew there was only one person in the world whom she could talk to about her despair in the middle of the night, or at any other time. She picked up the phone, laid it beside her, punched the back-lit numbers on the keypad. Seven miles away in Elmont, Long Island, the line rang for a couple of seconds before a man's sleepy voice answered. 'Hello?'

'It's me.'

'Jennifer? Are you OK? Is . . . is everything all right?'

Mark Ryan's voice came awake. She could sense his concern. 'I'm sorry, Mark. I know it's been a little while, but I didn't know who else to call.'

'It's OK, Jennifer. I'm here for you.'

'I woke you.'

'It's all right. I only got to bed a little while ago.' He laughed softly. 'Usually I'd sleep through an earthquake, but I guess I must have been half awake.' A rustle of sheets; he was sitting up in bed. A loud crack of thunder made Jennifer jump. Mark said, 'It sounds like a terrible night out there.'

'It's pretty bad.'

'I guess you were dreaming. Is that why you rang, Jennifer? You were dreaming?'

'It was the same dream. I could see him in the room. He was so real, like always. And my imagination always makes it worse in the dream. I always imagine that the intruder really did succeed in raping me.'

'You're just upset, Jennifer.'

Her voice broke. 'At times it feels like I've cracked, rent down the middle. Tonight's one of them, Mark. I guess I still miss them so terribly, feel lost without them. I used to think it would get easier with time. But it doesn't. It's been two years, but sometimes it's like it all happened yesterday.'

Mark listened, then said softly, 'I know it's not easy, Jennifer, and anniversaries can make us sensitive, especially tragic ones. It gets like that for all of us now and then. But you have to realise that the man isn't going to come back. Not ever. Please understand that.'

She heard the words, let them comfort her as she looked over numbly at the rain sheeting down. A few hundred yards across the wet, stormy inlet Cove End would be smothered by the cold, tarry darkness. Once it had been a warm and welcoming house that had held so many good memories, but not any longer.

'Are you still there, Jennifer?'

'I'm still here.'

'Your mom wouldn't want you to be like this. She wouldn't want you anguished and upset, even on her anniversary. So what I want you to do now is lie down and close your eyes, just try to sleep. Will you do that for me, Jennifer?'

'I took some pills, I feel sleepy now.'

'How many pills did you take?'

'Two.'

She heard the hint of relief in Mark's voice. 'Well, no harm there. Right now you need them. Will you be OK? Are the pills really working?'

'I think so.'

'How about I call you tomorrow, or you call me, whenever you feel up to it or you want to talk?'

'That sounds good.'

'Goodnight, Jennifer. Try and rest.' There was a tiny hint of laughter in his voice, deliberate, as if to try to ease her out of her anguish. 'If I was there, you know, and we had that kind of relationship, I'd offer to rock you to sleep.'

'I know. Goodnight. And . . . and thanks for listening, Mark. Thanks for being there.'

'What's a friend for? We've known each other a long time. Rest now. I'll talk to you soon.'

The last words he said were 'Take care', and then the line clicked.

Silence now, but for the silken lash of water drenching the window and a distant growl of thunder. When she finally put down the phone, Jennifer March lay on her side, her hands under her head like a child, staring out with misted eyes at the dark rivers of rain washing the glass, until finally the velvet grip of the drug took hold and numbed her. Caught there, in the narcotic no man's land between wake and sleep, she knew in her heart that no one could really help her. No one could ever really help her but herself. Someday, somehow, she had to learn to live in peace with the demons that haunted her soul.

Right now, she knew that was impossible, but at least the masked man wasn't there any more and the nightmare was gone. At least there was that. And then the sleep she had longed for finally came, her eyelids flickered, and Jennifer March surrendered herself to what remained of the night.

3

Nadia prayed for it to be over.

If she survived these next few minutes, she would live. If not, she was dead. She anxiously clutched the baby to her breast, and held on to the hand of her two-year-old daughter. The airport was noisy and crowded. It was her first time in JFK and she was frightened, even though the men had told her what to expect. She felt perspiration dampen her face, rivulets of sweat running down the back of her woollen dress.

She was twenty-three, with soft blue eyes and an innocent face, which was why the men had picked her. Her daughter Tamara had her mother's looks, a perfect little round face and wide, innocent eyes, and Nadia loved her very much.

It was a difficult life in Moscow. Hard to make a living with eight million people in the streets. Hard to survive in a small room on the fourth floor of a tenement apartment block, with no hot water and the rooms infested with rats and insects.

Nadia Fedov wanted a better life for her daughter. The girl wasn't going to end up like her mother, working in a nightclub that was no more than a brothel; wasn't going to have brutal, drunken men abusing her body for a handful of roubles. She was going to have clean sheets and hot water, a nice apartment in a good neighbourhood and nice children as friends. These were the things Nadia wanted for her daughter. She looked down at Tamara. The child was tired now that the excitement of the eight-hour flight from Moscow was over, her hair tousled. She rubbed her eyes.

'Can I sleep soon, Mama?'

'Soon, Tamara. Soon.'

Nadia rocked the baby, wrapped in a blue blanket, and looked up at the Immigration desk ahead of her. There was just one person in front of her now, and she waited anxiously at the yellow line marked on the floor.

'*Try not to be afraid,*' she told herself.

Her passport was an excellent forgery, undetectable, the names of the children entered on the document, the US visa stamped on one of the pages. Suddenly it was her turn and the Immigration officer in the dark blue uniform beckoned her forward. She complied and handed over her passport and the landing card she had filled in during the flight.

The man examined her passport and looked at her face. Then he ran the passport over some kind of scanner, before he looked up, holding out his hand. 'Tickets, please.'

Nadia handed him her airline tickets. The officer examined them, then looked back at her. 'You're staying fourteen days in New York City?'

'*Da.* Yes.'

'At this address?'

'Yes.'

'These your children?'

'Yes.'

The officer strained over the high desk to get a good look at Tamara, then winked down at her. Tamara smiled back, shyly clutching her mother's dress. The man said, 'Pretty girl.'

'Yes.' Nadia smiled back nervously. The man was nice, not as she had expected. He glanced briefly at the baby, wrapped in a blanket in Nadia's arms, then stapled part of the landing card on one of the pages of her passport, stamped it, and handed it back along with her tickets.

'Thank you, ma'am. Have a nice stay in New York.'

But it wasn't over yet. Nadia retrieved her suitcase from the carousel, paid for a luggage trolley, and approached US Customs, pushing the trolley with one hand, the baby still cradled in her free arm, Tamara holding on to the trolley. Nadia felt terribly scared, her heart pumping hard inside her ribs. She rocked the swaddled baby in her arms and whispered, 'Sleep, Alexei. Sleep, little one.'

She saw the Customs desks ten metres away, a couple of uniformed officers standing around. An automatic door led out to the arrivals area, and she thought: *So close to freedom. So close to having all the things I want for Tamara.* She kept telling herself that everything would be OK, but her body felt as if it were on fire. The men had told her that sometimes Customs didn't stop you, sometimes they just let you pass through. *Above all, don't look at them, try not to catch their eye, or look scared or suspicious. These men are trained to smell fear the way a hound smells a fox. Just behave like any normal passenger, with nothing to hide.*

Nadia tried to remember all these things, but it was difficult as she wrestled with the luggage trolley and held on to the baby. As she approached the desk, she noticed that most of the passengers were passing through freely, and the Customs officers hardly seemed to be bothered stopping anyone. She saw one of the officers look at her and tried not to catch his eye, pretending to attend to her baby, rocking the child in her arms and whispering, 'Sleep, Alexei.'

She was walking right by him now but the man didn't stop her, and she felt overcome with relief.

'Is this your luggage, ma'am?'

As she made to step towards arrivals, another Customs officer suddenly put a hand on her trolley. Nadia's heart was pounding. '*Da,* my . . . my luggage.' *Try not to look nervous.*

'Step over here, please.' *If they stop you, do what they tell you. Look calm, like you've nothing to fear.*

But Nadia felt terribly afraid. She pushed the trolley over to the desk, and her legs felt like jelly. The man lifted her suitcase off the trolley, laid it on the metal desk and said, 'Would you open the suitcase, please.'

Nadia fumbled to get her bag open, holding on to the baby, getting flustered, guessing that the man sensed her unease. She finally found the key. Still holding the baby in her arms, she made to unlock the luggage, her hand shaking a little, but the Customs man said politely, 'Here, let me do that for you.'

He opened the suitcase and searched her belongings. Cheap clothes and underwear for her and Tamara and the baby. A small gift-wrapped box tied with a pink bow was nestled among the clothes, and it caught the Customs officer's attention. He put it aside, then went through the rest of her things quickly and thoroughly. When he had finished searching the suitcase, he picked up the gift-wrapped box. 'What's inside here, ma'am?'

'A gift. For my cousin.'

'What kind of gift?'

'A scarf.'

The man shook the box. It didn't rattle. He studied Nadia intently, looked at the baby in her arms, then down at Tamara. Finally, he looked back at Nadia. 'Which flight did you arrive on, ma'am?'

Nadia read the flight number on her tickets and said the numbers slowly. 'The flight is from Moscow. I arrive just now.' She rocked the baby, trying to soothe her own nervousness.

The man frowned a little and said, 'Is your baby OK?'

Nadia shook her head. 'It was a long flight. I don't think he is well.'

The man looked at the box in his hand, as if trying to decide what to do next, then he said, 'Would you mind stepping into the office, please.'

'But my baby, I think maybe he needs a doctor . . .'

'This won't take a moment.'

The man pushed her trolley over to an office door. Another Customs officer joined him, opened the door for them. The second officer was a woman. Petite, pretty, dark haired, Mexican blood in her veins. The tag over her left breast said her name was Reta Hondalez. Nadia felt sick inside. It was hot in the small office. She clutched Tamara's hand; her daughter looked on wide eyed, puzzled as to why these people wanted to speak to her mother.

The man laid the box on the table, while his female colleague stood to one side. 'I'm afraid I need to open this, ma'am. Do you have any objection?'

'Pardon?'

'It's OK that I open the gift?'

Nadia nodded, trying not to tremble. 'Yes, you can open it.'

While his female colleague watched, the Customs officer carefully undid the pink bow, peeled off the wrapping paper, and opened the box. He found a cheap, patterned nylon scarf among the wrapping paper. He carefully searched inside the box but found nothing else. He looked a little angry, his face flushed, as if he was upset at not finding anything, or had made a mistake. 'May I see your passport, please.'

Nadia fumbled in her handbag and found her passport again, almost dropped it in the process, but the officer caught it. He studied the pages. 'These are your children?'

'Yes, it's in my passport.'

'I know it's in your passport, but are these your children?'

'Yes.'

'How old is the baby?'

'Three weeks.'

The officer looked at the bundle in Nadia's arms. Nadia said quietly, 'He hasn't been well. The long flight . . .'

'So you said. We won't detain you any longer, ma'am.' The officer came round from behind the desk to hand back her passport. He looked down at the baby, wrapped up snugly in the pale blue cotton blanket, its face serene, its eyes closed.

He hesitated, then some instinct made him reach over and touch the baby's cheek. He paled, his face shocked as he stared back at Nadia, his eyes telling her what she already knew.

'Ma'am, this baby's dead.'

The 113th Precinct in New York's Queens district is located in a drab, pale brick building on Baisley Boulevard. The precinct covers the sprawling borough of Queens, and also one of the world's busiest airports: JFK International.

Jennifer March parked her blue Ford sedan on the street

outside and went in through the main entrance. The desk sergeant and a couple of uniformed officers were attending to a line of waiting people, but the sergeant looked up instinctively when he saw the young, attractive woman with the leather briefcase come towards him. She was in her late twenties, pretty, with dark hair, and she wore a neat, navy-blue two-piece suit that hugged her figure. The sergeant gave her a surly look that suggested he wasn't pleased to see her. 'You back with us again, Counsellor March?'

'I guess it's your warm welcome that just keeps me coming back, Sergeant. Is Mark Ryan around?'

'He was heading towards his office last time I saw him.'

'Thanks.'

The cop grunted a reply and Jennifer walked to a room down the hall and knocked on the door. A voice said, 'Come in if you're good looking.'

She stepped into a tiny, cramped office with drab grey walls. Paperwork littered the desk and a plainclothes officer sat behind a computer typing up some notes from a sheaf of papers, sipping coffee from a plastic cup. He smiled boyishly. 'That's the first time I hit pay dirt all week. Hello, Jenny.'

Detective Mark Ryan was in his middle thirties, dark haired, with an easy, likeable manner and cheerful green eyes. He came round from behind the desk and kissed Jennifer's cheek. 'What are you doing here?'

'Nobody else was available so they asked me to cover the Nadia Fedov case.'

'You going to be her attorney?'

'That's what the Federal Defender Division pays me for, and she's entitled to a lawyer, Mark. I've got some free time before the presentment in court later this afternoon so I thought I'd talk with her. And seeing as I didn't get all the details, I was kind of hoping you could fill me in.'

'Sure, Jenny, no problem, and it's good to see you, anyway.' Ryan's smile became a look of concern. 'How've you been since the other night?'

Jennifer touched his arm. 'Fine, Mark. I appreciate you

listening, I really do. You're the only person I could call. One of the few people I know who'd understand.'

Ryan nodded. 'Like I said, what are friends for? You want some coffee before we start?'

'Thanks, but I've got another appointment after this, so I'd like to get on with it.'

'Does the Federal Defender Division always work its attorneys so hard?'

Jennifer took a notebook and pen from her briefcase, smiled back as she glanced at the paperwork-littered desk. 'You seem pretty overworked yourself.'

Ryan made a face. 'Tell me about it. By the way, in case you're wondering how your client ended up being held here and not at the Federal Detention Center in Brooklyn, they were overcrowded and had no female spaces available, so they asked me to hold her temporarily at the precinct.'

'It figures.'

Mark sat on the edge of his desk and gestured to the chair in front. 'Take a seat.'

Jennifer sat. Ryan put down his coffee. 'I was working with a DEA task force at JFK this morning when the girl was arrested by Customs. She came in off an Aeroflot flight from Moscow with a three-week-old, dead baby boy in her arms.'

'And?'

'The infant's body had been cut down the chest cavity and sewn up. When Pathology did their stuff they found five pounds of heroin sewn inside.'

Jennifer turned pale. Mark Ryan looked at her. 'Are you OK?'

'Yes, I'm OK.'

'You sure you don't want a glass of water or something?'

'No, I'll be fine. How long had the child been dead?'

'About sixteen hours, give or take an hour. The fight takes over eight hours. Allow another hour at most from the time she stepped off the plane at JFK, and another three before the autopsy was done. Which means the infant was dead about four hours before the woman left Moscow.'

'Was he murdered?'

'The medical examiner suspects the child probably died of natural cases, but I haven't got the full report yet. And all the internal organs had been removed, so it may be difficult to tell exactly.'

Jennifer was still pale as she shook her head. 'I thought I'd heard it all. But that's probably the most despicable, horrific thing I've heard in a long time.'

Ryan said quietly, 'I know, it sounds callous beyond belief. But that's the kind of scum we're dealing with here. Narcotics smugglers. I've heard of it being done in the Far East, but I've never come across an actual case. They get a dead infant from a morgue, or wherever, and before the drugs run they remove the organs, treat the body with formaldehyde to preserve it, and then sew up the narcotics inside. The woman kept the corpse well covered during the flight, hardly let it out of her arms.' Ryan paused, then added gravely, 'The people behind this, if you can call them people, have no qualms or morals about doing something like that. There *are* evil people in this world, Jenny.' He hesitated again, looked at her. 'But then you know that.'

Jennifer felt ill. 'What about the young woman?'

'She's twenty-three, a Russian citizen. It turns out the passport she had was a fake. It was stolen and professionally altered, with a forged US visa. It's pretty good, too. She managed to get past Immigration, no problem.'

Jennifer jotted down some notes and looked up. 'Anything else?'

'She had another child with her. A little girl, two years old. Right now, the girl's being looked after by the welfare office.'

'Was the dead baby hers?'

'No. She claims it was given to her at Moscow airport by a couple she never met before.'

'What about the little girl?'

'She says she's her daughter. Her name's Tamara.'

'How is she?'

'The daughter?'

'The mother, the daughter, both.'

Ryan shrugged. 'The kid's confused and wants her mom. The mother's pretty scared and lost. She knows she's going to be put away for a long time. At times like this, I wish I'd never become a cop.'

'How much were they paying her?'

'She says ten thousand dollars.'

'What else did she tell you?'

'Nothing much. She won't really talk and she asked for a lawyer. She seems pretty frightened about something.'

'You think she was a willing accomplice?'

Ryan shrugged and sighed. 'I don't know. My instinct tells me someone threatened her and made her do it, but who knows? And right now she's not saying.'

'Was she read her rights?'

'What do you take me for, Jenny?' Ryan smiled. 'We've known each other since we were kids.'

Jennifer put down her notebook, looked up and said quietly, 'What's going to happen to her, Mark?'

'You ought to know. She's not a US citizen, so she won't get bail. And innocent or not, she's a runner, and we're talking about federal crime. She carried a forged passport and visa, and used a corpse to smuggle five pounds of pure-grade heroin. That could figure up to ten years in Danbury by my reckoning, and that's if she's lucky. But she's definitely going down, no question. Unless she talks, which I'm guessing she won't. To you, maybe, seeing as you're her attorney, but not to the police.'

'And her daughter?'

'She'll be sent back to Moscow. To relatives, if the kid has any. At worst, she ends up in some crummy state home.'

'Does she speak English?'

'The mother? She speaks it pretty well, and she's bright too, so you shouldn't need a translator. But if you really want, I'll get one.'

Jennifer shook her head and gathered up her things.

The door of the interview room banged shut and Jennifer looked at the young woman who stood up slowly from behind the wooden table. She looked younger than twenty-three, more like eighteen, with soft pale skin and wide, innocent eyes. Her blue woollen dress was cheap and worn, sewn in places, and she had a terrible look of despair on her face, her eyes swollen red from crying.

Jennifer felt sympathy for her, but her desire to offer comfort to Nadia Fedov was tempered by the knowledge that just a few hours ago the young woman was carrying around a dead baby stuffed with heroin. Jennifer didn't know to what extent the woman was involved in the crime, but her naturally sympathetic nature led her to hope she wasn't totally complicit. She offered her hand. 'My name's Jennifer March. I work for the Federal Defender Division and I've been appointed to act as your lawyer. Do you understand what I'm saying, Nadia?'

The girl trembled as she shook Jennifer's hand. '*Da*. I think so. Yes. They told me a lawyer would talk to me.'

'Are you OK?'

Jennifer saw tears well up in the woman's eyes. 'I want to see my daughter.'

'I may be able to arrange that later, but for now we have to talk. Sit down, Nadia.'

Jennifer pulled out a chair from the table and the girl sat opposite. 'I have no money to pay for you.'

'The Federal Defender Division will take care of your legal expenses. They represent, free of charge, individuals who are charged with federal crimes and who are unable to afford an attorney to represent them. In this country, even if you're an illegal alien and have no visible means of support, you're entitled to a lawyer to defend you. Do you understand what I've told you, Nadia?'

The girl nodded silently.

'You were caught with a large quantity of heroin in your possession. And a dead baby that may possibly have been murdered for the purpose of smuggling heroin. Those are very serious charges, so maybe the best thing to do first is simply tell me the truth, what happened from the beginning.'

Nadia Fedov made to speak, then faltered, as if she'd changed her mind.

Jennifer said, 'You have to trust me, Nadia. You have to believe that I'm on your side. Please understand that. Right now, you're facing a federal charge and I'm the only one who can help you. But before I do that, you have to tell me what happened.'

Nadia Fedov bit her lip, then wiped her eyes. 'I work in night-club in Moscow. I have been to college, I have degree in economics, but in Russia life is difficult, and this is only work I can get. Two men who sometimes visit nightclub, they always have lots of money. And they always watch me. Then one day one of them say to me, "How would you like to earn ten thousand dollars?" I asked how. They told me I had to take something to New York City. They would give me a Russian passport for myself and my daughter, with an American visa. I asked what they wanted me to take and they told me it was something important. Ten thousand dollars is a lot of money, and with American visa I can maybe stay in your country, not go back to Moscow. So I say, maybe.'

Jennifer said gently, 'Go on.'

'A few days later, one of the men comes to see me again. He says I must take a dead infant with me.' Nadia Fedov's voice broke, and tears streamed down her face. 'The child would be on my passport. There would be drugs inside the body. I was frightened, and I ask the man where they got the child and he said it was not my business to know. I didn't like to think that a dead baby would be used to smuggle drugs. It was . . . evil, so I told the man, no, I will not do it. Then the men beat me. They said they would harm my daughter, kill her, if I didn't do as they told me. But if I did what they wanted I would receive the money and not be harmed. So I did what they told me.'

'What were you supposed to do with the dead child when you reached New York?'

'Someone would be waiting for me at a hotel near the airport after I come out of arrivals. I wouldn't know them, but they would know me. They would take the baby from me and pay me. After that, I keep the passport they give me, and I am free to go where I want.'

Jennifer sat forward, looked into the woman's face. 'You're telling me the truth, Nadia?'

Nadia Fedov made the sign of the cross. 'I swear it, on my life.'

'Why didn't you simply tell Customs at JFK that you had been forced to smuggle drugs?'

'Because the men said they would find me and my daughter and kill us if I told the police or did anything like that.'

'What were the men's names?'

Nadia Fedov shrugged. 'I don't know. And even if I did, I couldn't tell you.'

'Why? Are you afraid?'

'Yes, I'm afraid. The men said it didn't matter if I was in prison, they would find me and kill me if I talked. Kill me and my little girl.' Nadia wiped her eyes. 'These men, they are very . . . hard. They are evil men. They hurt people, and they enjoy it. I know they mean what they say. They tell me I won't get caught, it's easy for me to do as they ask, because with two children I don't look like I smuggle drugs. But if I am caught, they tell me I am dead if I tell the police anything about them. What they look like, how to recognise them.'

'Why did you first agree to do what the men asked, Nadia? Even though you knew it was illegal?'

Nadia Fedov hesitated, and bit her lip. 'For my daughter.'

'What do you mean?'

'You are an American. You live in a rich country. You don't know what it's like to be poor. To have no money and no hope. To have no life, only poverty and pain. I didn't want my daughter to be poor and to suffer. I wanted her to live. To have a good life, here, in America. But now I will never see her again.'

Nadia Fedov put her face in her hands and sobbed. Jennifer stood, walked round the table and put her arms around her shoulders, held her, trying to offer comfort, but she was inconsolable.

★

Mark Ryan was waiting for her in the corridor. 'Well? How'd it go?'

'She was a dupe, Mark. She was used.'

'The little people always are. The big guys get away with it pretty much every time. I figured from the start that she was a mule. They always use small fry who'll smuggle either for money or because they've been physically threatened, or both. Do you think she'll talk to me?'

'I doubt it. She's really scared.'

'I'm not surprised. She's probably been told by whoever put her up to it that they could have her bumped off in prison if she opened her mouth.' Ryan looked at Jennifer March's face and saw tears in the corners of her eyes. 'Are you OK? You seem upset.'

'I'll be fine. I just keep thinking about that dead baby and the lives of a young woman and her child being ruined.'

Ryan put a hand on Jennifer's arm. 'Hey, take it easy. Remember the first rule, don't get emotionally involved.'

'What about the woman's daughter? Can she see her?'

'I'll see what I can do.'

'Promise?'

'Sure.'

'Thanks, Mark.'

'On a lighter note, how've you been keeping?'

'OK.'

'How's Bobby?'

'Bobby's fine.'

'I've been out to the Cauldwell to see him a couple of times. But it's been a few months. I guess I'm due a visit.'

'He'd like that.'

Ryan hesitated. 'Maybe this is a bad time to ask, but are you free for dinner this week?'

'I'm really sorry, Mark. But just at the moment I'm pretty much up to my eyes with work. How about another time?'

Ryan blushed, gave a valiant smile. 'Sure, whenever. You want some advice? Go home and try not to think about all this. That

21

WATERFORD
No. 0030546 37
MUNICIPAL LIBRARY

woman back there in the blue dress will be doing enough of that for both of us.'

Jennifer went into the women's restroom on the ground floor and tried to compose herself. She had joined the Federal Defender Division's Brooklyn office after she had clerked for a federal judge for six months, and she loved her work, even if sometimes she got to hear horror stories like the one she'd just heard. And she could identify with the young woman: she knew what it was like to be hurt and traumatised, to have your life destroyed by evil, brutal people. She knew it so well – she still bore the scars and the pain had never gone away – so she understood what the woman must be going through.

She knew what all her tormented clients were going through, that was what made Jennifer good at her job. For her, the work was more than just a way to fill the day, it was a calling. It certainly wasn't about money. She earned about a quarter of what her law school classmates earned, those who worked for fancy city law firms. But she *cared* about the downtrodden and the wrongfully accused of this world, and one day she meant to be a successful criminal defence attorney.

She looked at herself in the mirror. She had a vivacious, interesting face. Her hair was dark brown and her skin a soft, creamy white. Her features were regular and fine, with a generous, sensitive mouth and intelligent blue eyes. She had a good figure, curves in all the right places and shapely legs, and she knew she was reasonably attractive to most men. But there was an air of aloofness about her image that even Jennifer sensed. She knew it was part of the protective armour she had worn since her mother's death.

She had lots of acquaintances, a busy social life that revolved mostly around going to the gym and having coffee or dinner with former college classmates, but she had few real friends. She rented her one-bedroom apartment and drove a five-year-old Ford sedan. At almost thirty-one, she was unmarried, unattached, and in love with no one.

She thought: *Maybe I just haven't met the right man?*

But she knew it was much more than that, and her relationship with Mark Ryan was proof, if proof were needed. She'd known him since childhood, when he'd lived across her street, and back then they'd been just enough acquainted to say hello once in a while. He was five years older than her and she'd always liked him a lot, even though she'd just said no to his offer of dinner. He was divorced, charming, good at his job, had a sense of humour and, most of all, he was patient and considerate. Not since Jennifer's late teens had their paths crossed again, until one day three years ago when she was still a law student and Mark Ryan was one of a group of NYPD detectives who came to Columbia Law School to lecture on police procedures. Afterwards, they'd had coffee in the college canteen and she'd learned that he was going through a messy divorce. He had seemed lost and hurt at the time, and more than a little bitter, but even though neither of them had shown the slightest romantic interest in the other that day at Columbia, they had somehow struck up a casual friendship. The friendship had deepened over most of the following year, and though they went for dinner together at least once a month and hardly a week went by when they didn't speak on the phone, that was it: no sex, no intimacy. Mark was a true, dear friend, maybe the closest friend she had, and though she liked him, even felt attracted to him, she knew she was afraid of getting too close to any man.

She remembered two months ago when they had gone to Spaglio's for a dinner date and afterwards in her apartment Mark had kissed her, and she had enjoyed the pleasure of feeling close to him, but as soon as the kiss started to get heavy and he tried to unbutton her blouse, she had panicked and asked him to stop.

As she looked at herself in the mirror she thought: *Maybe it's just me, maybe I'm frigid.*

It had been over two years since she had gone out on a serious date. Apart from Mark, the two casual dates she had accepted from men in the last six months had ended the same way: the guy trying to get into her pants and Jennifer making her excuses and ending the relationship even before it began. When it came to sex, something clammed up inside her.

If she were honest with herself, she had given up on sex. Some things were so deeply ingrained they were like a habit, impossible to break, and she knew no amount of talking or therapy could cure her problem. Therapists were useless. Most of them seemed to have more hang-ups and problems than their patients. And she knew her problem had to do with the trauma of the night of her mother's death, and she could *never* forget that terrifying nightmare. Besides, today was the anniversary of her death, and she didn't want her to be alone.

Calverton cemetery on Long Island was sunny and deserted that afternoon. Jennifer parked her Ford and walked to her mother's grave, carrying a bunch of roses. The inscription on the white marble stone always sent a cold shiver through her heart.

> *In loving memory of Anna March,*
> *beloved wife of Paul March,*
> *RIP*

It had been exactly two years ago, and not a day had gone by when she didn't remember and relive the nightmare of her mother's death and her father's disappearance. Not a single moment passed when she didn't wish them back. Her parents had meant everything to her. Her father had been a generous and gentle man, and her mother everything a daughter could have wished for: beautiful, intelligent, loving.

The grave was tidily kept and she always made sure to bring fresh flowers at least once a week. Standing there in the spring sunshine, Jennifer looked down at the marble slab. But the simple white stone hid so much and said so little, for there was so much more to her parents' past than any gravestone or inscription could ever tell.

Jennifer placed the roses on the grave, then stood back, letting the past wash over her, remembering it all . . .

4

During the first five years of her life, Jennifer saw very little of her father. He was always travelling abroad on business: to Paris, London, Zurich, Rome, exotic cities and strange countries she had never heard of before, and Jennifer missed him terribly.

Paul March was an investment banker, a tall, slim, handsome man with dark, gentle eyes. Jennifer loved the feel of his strong arms sweeping her up, the sense of security he instilled in her when he held her hand or just gave her one of his smiles. She loved his smell, a mixture of deodorant and strong soap, combined with a distinctive odour she later realised was male.

When she was twelve, Jennifer's father joined a small private investment bank in New York called Prime International Securities. Always ambitious, he was keen to make a success of his career. And although his work meant long hours and travelling away from home, he always remembered to send his only daughter a postcard from every new, strange and wonderful place he visited.

'*This is Paris, Jennifer. Isn't it pretty?*'

'*I had dinner by the Trevi fountain last night. Rome is a beautiful city. I'm flying to Switzerland tomorrow and I'll send you another postcard.*'

'*I've bought you a gift in London that you're going to love, my precious.*'

When she and her mother had read the messages, Jennifer always insisted on keeping the cards, as if they were a priceless treasure. She would hoard them in a tattered old cardboard shoe box, and even though they never made up for the days and weeks her father spent away from home, she knew from the words on those simple picture cards that her father was thinking about her, and that reassurance somehow cushioned his absence.

Sometimes, as a small child, Jennifer would sneak into his study and climb up into his chair, because there she felt closer to her father. She would sit for hours, holding on to one of his belongings, a sweater, or one of his shirts or slippers, as she shuffled through the colourful exotic cards, longing for the moment when her father returned. And then the day would come when she'd see her father come up the pathway. He'd be smiling, his arms open, waiting for her to run to them. He always brought her gifts: chocolate from Switzerland, a rag doll from France, a colourful wooden marionette puppet from Italy. But the warm feeling of security Jennifer felt in her father's arms meant more to her than any of those simple gifts.

As Paul March's success grew, her parents moved to a wonderful old renovated house on Long Beach, a waterside property with its own private dock. Though Jennifer's father had prospered, and her childhood was always comfortable, her parents lived simply. Her mother had worked as a legal secretary, but when Jennifer was born she had given up her job to take care of her daughter. Jennifer loved her mother. She had a beautiful face, with high cheekbones and soft blonde hair. Warm and caring and spontaneous, she took easily to motherhood, and as with her husband it was obvious that she loved her daughter very much.

Jennifer always remembered the little things her mother did that made her love her so much. Like the habit she had of baking cookies for her every time it rained. And every so often picking her up from school and taking her on crazy pleasure trips: like a visit to the Natural History Museum in Manhattan, and then afterwards they would go roller-skating in Central Park. Later, her mother's love had always been a source of confidence to Jennifer as she faced the usual hurdles of childhood and adolescence. But although she cherished her mother deeply, Jennifer felt closer to her father. Perhaps because of his absences, he was more of an enigma, and that mystery made her love him all the more.

Though constantly away from home, Paul March would always try to take time off from his busy schedule to spend time with his wife and daughter. Sometimes, Jennifer's mother travelled abroad with her husband, and Jennifer was cared for by a hired babysitter, but to make up for it her parents would take her on long summer holidays. They travelled in America or to Mexico, and sometimes even to Europe, and Jennifer would experience the marvellous places she had seen on her father's postcards: Rome, London, Zurich, Paris.

She could always remember walking over the cobbled streets of Paris with her parents one summer's morning, the sights and sounds and smells of that strange, wonderful city ringing in her ears, and later that afternoon, after a pleasure-boat ride on the Seine and a visit to the gardens of a beautiful chateau, her parents had taken her back to the hotel, all of them exhausted, and Jennifer fell asleep in her parents' arms. The greatest pleasure she remembered as a child was sleeping with her mother and father, feeling warm and comforted, cherished and wanted.

When she was thirteen, her brother Robert was born and she had to endure the fact that she was no longer the centre of attention. But Jennifer didn't mind too much, because Bobby was a good-humoured little boy with a shock of blond, curly hair, who smiled and gurgled a lot and loved to be picked up and played with by his older sister. The only pangs of insecurity she had to endure were when her father held Bobby in his arms, just as he had held her. He seemed to adore Bobby, and Jennifer felt intensely jealous, until her mother explained that her new brother had been an unexpected miracle after years of trying for another child, and that all fathers longed for a son, but that it didn't mean her father loved Jennifer any less. It was something she had to live with, even though she felt that a part of her father's love was gone for ever from her life.

But as she grew older, she began to realise that there was something more vital missing from all their lives. Slowly, imperceptibly, she had started to notice that there were no family photographs from her father's past. Her mother had parents, aunts and uncles and cousins who sometimes came to visit, but Jennifer's father had none.

And her father never mentioned anything about his relatives, no more than he spoke much about his work. It was as if he didn't have a past.

But she learned that he *did* have a past, and it came with a terrible secret.

She discovered the trunk in the attic while her father was in Europe on one of his business trips. She was fourteen and had started to grow into a reasonably attractive young woman; already her legs had taken a stretch, and she was conscious of other changes taking place, though her dental braces and her awkward, changing body always made Jennifer feel ugly when she looked in the mirror, and she hated her image.

That day, her mother had an errand to run and left her alone in the house. Bored, Jennifer had climbed up into the attic, a part of the house she rarely if ever visited. Stuck in a corner was a big old-fashioned wooden trunk. It had a sturdy lock but Jennifer remembered seeing a set of keys belonging to her father, hanging in his study. Curious to know what was inside the trunk, she went downstairs and found the bunch of keys. One of them fitted the lock. When she opened the trunk, she found a file of papers inside.

She thought at first they were old business documents of her father's, but when she began leafing through some of the sheets she realised they were something entirely different. Years later she was to understand that they were copies of legal depositions, the statements made to the police by the victims of one man.

'*Joseph Delgado destroyed my life . . . he butchered my son . . .*'

'*Joseph Delgado stole from my company . . . he's a thief who cannot be trusted . . .*'

'*Joseph Delgado is a killer who deserves to die for his crimes . . .*'

'*Joseph Delgado is a dangerous young man who ought to be put behind bars for the rest of his life . . .*'

There were pages of statements.

Who was Joseph Delgado?

Among the papers in the trunk was what looked like a black-and-white crime-scene photograph. A ghastly picture of a murdered man lying in a filthy alleyway, a knife stuck in his chest, his face contorted in death. It was all too much horror to take in and Jennifer couldn't bear to look any more.

As she started to close the trunk she noticed another photograph lying among the papers. When she picked it up and stared at the image, her mouth fell open in shock. It was a photograph of a dark-haired young man wearing a prison uniform. Someone had written a name underneath in black ballpoint ink: Joseph Delgado.

The face looked disturbingly familiar.

It was her father's face.

The discovery horrified Jennifer. Delgado was obviously an evil man. But her father wasn't evil. She was confused. When her father came back from his business trip, she said to him, 'Who's Joseph Delgado?'

Paul March became suddenly white faced. 'How . . . how do you know that name?'

Jennifer confessed to opening the attic trunk. 'The . . . the man in the photograph, he looked like you, Daddy.'

It was the first time she had seen her father angry, and there was a strange, frightening look in his eyes. He slapped Jennifer's face. The shock of it made her slow to react and she didn't even have time to cry because her father stormed out of the room. Then she wept, her sobs racking her body, and her mother had to console her. 'Why . . . why did Daddy get so angry, Mom? Why did he hit me?'

'You were *wrong* to go through your father's things, Jennifer,' her mother said quietly. 'You must *never* pry into your father's private business in future.'

'But I only . . .'

'*Never*, Jennifer.'

★

It was to be many years before Jennifer went up to the attic again, or pried into her father's private business. And the next time it happened, it was by accident, but the secrets she was eventually to discover were even more disturbing.

By then, she was a grown woman in her twenties. After completing her undergraduate studies in Arts and spending two tedious years working in a Manhattan art gallery, she had finally decided at age twenty-four to study law. She won a scholarship to New York University, and though she had to work painfully hard, it especially pleased her that her father seemed more than proud that she had chosen to study for a law degree.

He himself had remained with Prime and his career had prospered. A year earlier, the company had been bought by a private, offshore investor and soon her father was promoted to vice-president, in charge of the company's top accounts. He was earning more money than ever and had gained more responsibility, but he had grown distant and moody, and seemed unhappy in himself, and Jennifer couldn't understand why.

One day, she passed by his study. A pair of French doors led out to the garden, and the patio beyond had a view of the sea and the tiny private jetty where her father often took Bobby for walks. They would sit on the jetty for hours in summer, fishing and talking until the sun went down. But this day she saw that the French doors were open and her father was sitting alone on the patio in his favourite deck chair, his face buried in his hands. When he looked up, it was to stare blankly out to sea, and Jennifer thought she had never seen him look so deeply troubled, his face a mask of anxiety.

As she walked through the study to join him, she passed his apple-wood desk and saw a grey-coloured metal security box. The lid was open, and the box was empty, but there was a yellow legal notepad and black vinyl floppy disk beside it. She paused and glimpsed the word 'Spiderweb' written on the notepad and below it several illegible paragraphs in her father's handwriting.

Then he suddenly noticed her, rose from his chair and stormed in through the French doors. 'Were you reading my papers, Jennifer?'

'No, I . . . I just came by to see if you were OK, Dad.'

Her father picked up the notepad and disk and placed them in the security box, his tone unusually harsh. 'Those are private papers and none of your business.'

'But I was only—'

'Don't ever do it again, and don't stick your nose where it doesn't concern you.'

He took a silver key from his wallet and locked the security box. His face was flushed with anger, the same kind of anger Jennifer had witnessed when she was fourteen and had confronted him about the attic photograph. But now she was an adult, and yet her father was treating her like a meddling child, and she couldn't understand it. 'Is . . . is everything OK, Dad? You seem upset.'

He put the silver key back in his wallet and led her smartly to the door. 'If you don't mind I'd like to be left alone. I've got a lot of work to do.'

'Dad, I didn't mean to—'

'We'll talk about it another time. Now please leave, Jennifer.' As her father ushered her out of his study, his last words to her before he locked the door behind her were, 'And don't ever pry where it doesn't concern you.'

'But I really wasn't—'

'*Don't*, Jennifer.'

She never would. A month later her mother was brutally murdered and her father vanished.

She would always recall the night it happened. Her mother had asked her to stay the weekend, an offer Jennifer gratefully accepted, and that same evening her father had flown to Switzerland on business. The tiny one-bed Manhattan apartment that Jennifer shared on weekdays with another female law student was claustrophobic and cramped, and she was always glad of the luxury of sleeping in her own room and enjoying her mother's cooking.

But that night, after dinner when she went to sleep, there was a frightening storm raging in the darkness outside her bedroom, lightning flickering beyond the window, a savage wind clawing at the house, the rain beating down in torrents. The noise must have disturbed her because when she opened her eyes she was already terrified, and suddenly aware of two things: the savage roar of the storm and the odd feeling that there was a *presence* in the house.

Jennifer felt uneasy and flicked on the bedside light. Nothing happened. She guessed the storm had knocked out the electricity. She climbed out of bed, pulled on her bathrobe and opened her door. Her parents' room was down the hall, and Bobby's was next to it. As she stepped out into the hallway, she felt a freezing blast of air that made her shiver. She tried the lights on the landing. They were dead. She noticed a window open at the end of the landing, curtains lifting and falling in the ferocious wind. She wondered about the window. Usually it was shut. She thought: *The wind must have blown it open.* Jennifer went to shut it, and a powerful blast of air almost knocked her off her feet. When she finally managed to close the window, the lights in the hallway flickered on a moment, then extinguished. Frightened, Jennifer called out, '*Mom?*'

There was no reply. She opened the door to her parents' bedroom and stepped inside. The room was silent and Jennifer felt terribly frightened. Why didn't her mother answer? For a second or two the bedroom light flickered on overhead, and then a blaze of lightning exploded beyond the rain-lashed window. In the wash of electric blue light she noticed that the bedroom was in disarray. Drawers had been ransacked, clothes scattered on the floor. Blood was spattered on the white carpet and on the walls.

She froze in horror. Another crack of lightning illuminated the room, the intensity of the noise making her jump, and she suddenly saw the bodies. Her mother lay across the bed, savage wounds in her chest, an obscene crimson staining the bedclothes. Bobby lay on the floor near the bed, his body crumpled, blood seeping from a bullet wound to his neck.

For a brief moment Jennifer thought she was having a terrible nightmare, but when she blinked and looked again at the horrific scene, she knew she wasn't dreaming.

As she made to scream a hand clamped over her mouth . . .

It was a man and he was physically powerful. As Jennifer struggled in terror, he dragged her across the landing to her bedroom. When she tried to fight back the man smashed a fist into her face, and when she fell back down he tied a gag over her mouth. The bedside light flickered on and she glimpsed his face.

He had no face. He wore a black ski mask, his dark, evil eyes and mouth visible through the slits, his appearance truly frightening. He held a bloodstained butcher's knife in one hand. 'Stay still, you bitch, and you won't get hurt,' he ordered hoarsely.

The man placed the knife on the night stand. Jennifer saw a pistol tucked into his waistband. She cried behind the gag, curled up with fear, and her bathrobe rode up her legs. Suddenly she felt a hand crawl over her flesh. 'Stay still or I'll cut your throat.'

Jennifer was petrified, and she sobbed as the man forced her legs apart. She was more frightened than she had ever been in her life and she didn't dare move. But as the storm raged outside, the bedside lamp flickered on again and Jennifer glimpsed the bloodied knife on the table and the sight of her mother's blood made her livid and galvanised her into action. She fumbled desperately for the knife and stabbed the blade into the man's neck.

His body jolted and he screamed, his eyes opening wildly behind the mask, then his hand went up to pull out the blade. Jennifer saw her chance to push him away and clambered off the bed and ran to the bedroom door. She raced down the stairs and out the front door into the storm, tearing the gag from her mouth. Rain lashed against her body, the sky exploding with light, but she kept moving, sobbing as she ran.

'*Oh God . . . Oh God help me!*'

The nearest neighbour's house was sixty yards across the

street. Jennifer could just make out the white door in the drenching downpour, the veranda in darkness. Her heart pounded as she looked back and saw the masked man running after her, the bloodied knife in one hand, his other clutching at his wound.

Oh God . . . No!

Forty yards to the door.

Thirty.

Her nightgown flapped around her legs, slowing her down.

Twenty yards.

The rain cut into her eyes and she heard running footsteps behind her, but she didn't dare look back.

He's going to kill me!

Ten.

Jennifer raced up the veranda steps.

She hammered on the door and screamed, '*PLEASE HELP ME! . . . SOMEONE PLEASE HELP ME! . . . HE'S GOING TO KILL ME . . . PLEASE!*'

And then all her senses seemed to go and she fainted.

When she came to she was lying in a hospital bed in a private room. Someone had left the windows open; a soft wind was blowing, the curtains lifting and falling in the breeze. A man came into the room. He was in his late fifties, distinguished looking, with a handsome face and silver hair, and the only thing that detracted from his immaculate image was a slight limp. Jennifer glimpsed a uniformed police officer standing guard outside, before the man closed the door. He said quietly, 'How are you feeling, Jennifer?'

She was still in shock, trembling. 'I . . . I don't know.'

'Jennifer, I'm not sure what to say.' It was obvious the man was deeply upset; he seemed at a complete loss for words and she could see tears in his eyes.

'My name's Jack Kelso. I'm a friend of your father's. Perhaps he mentioned me?'

'No, he . . . he didn't. Are you a colleague?'

'No, but we're good friends, and I apologise for coming here at such a difficult time, but I really felt I had to as soon as I heard what happened. Your mom . . . she was . . . she was terrific . . . a wonderful person.'

Jennifer said hoarsely, 'My mom's dead, isn't she?'

Kelso nodded. 'Yes, Jennifer, she's dead.'

'And Bobby?'

Kelso sighed, his face troubled. 'Bobby's alive. He's in intensive care at the Schneider hospital.'

'Is he OK? Is Bobby OK?'

Kelso hesitated, as if not knowing whether to say it or not. 'Bobby's doing fine, he's going to live. But a bullet shattered part of his spinal cord, and there's been some brain damage. I've been told he's going to have difficulty walking, and maybe talking, but . . . he's alive, Jennifer.'

'*Oh God.*'

'Look at me. He's *alive*, Jennifer, and that's what matters right now.'

In her dazed state, there was the only question she could think of asking. 'Why? Why would anyone want to kill my mom and shoot Bobby?'

Kelso shook his head. 'I don't know, Jennifer. That's where you might be able to help the police. Bobby can't talk right now. He's too traumatised. Maybe he won't ever want to remember. That happens sometimes, especially with young victims of a traumatic crime. But the police say whoever broke into the house maybe stole some jewellery belonging to your mom. They think that maybe she woke and disturbed the killer, and that Bobby tried to intervene, and that's why they were attacked.'

'The . . . the man. He tried to kill me too.'

Kelso nodded, held her hand reassuringly. 'Please don't worry, he won't come back. The police intend protecting you and will have an armed officer outside your room, twenty-four hours. Is there anything you can tell them that might help solve this terrible crime?'

Jennifer shook her head. Later she would tell the police everything she could remember but right now she felt deeply confused.

35

'I . . . I want to go home.' And then she realised she really had no home, not after what had happened there.

'Just as soon as you're well enough, they'll have you out of here, I promise.'

'I . . . I want my dad. When is he coming back?'

'Soon. He'll be back soon, I'm sure.'

She saw something in Kelso's face then, recognised the lie, and said, 'What's happened to him? Why hasn't he called? Have you told him about my mother?'

Kelso stood, and looked uncomfortable. 'The police are still trying to locate him, Jennifer.'

'He's in Zurich, Switzerland.'

'Yes, they know.' Kelso made to leave. 'You need to get well, so try and rest. We'll talk again.'

Jennifer said, 'Something's wrong, isn't it? Something's wrong with my father. What's wrong with him?'

Kelso shook his head. 'I don't know, Jennifer.'

'What do you mean?'

Kelso sighed. 'It seems that the Swiss police checked every hotel in Zurich, without success. Right now, they're not even sure he arrived in Switzerland, and they don't know where he might be. But I'm told that Interpol is doing everything they can to find him.'

'What are you saying?'

'He's vanished, Jennifer. Your father's simply vanished.'

After Kelso had left, Jennifer stared blankly at the walls. She didn't seem to care whether she lived or died. All she could think of was that her mother was dead, her brother might never walk or talk again, and her father had vanished, and the grief that flooded her mind almost smothered her. Her ordeal at the hands of the killer had been terrible, and the police doctor who had examined her afterwards had only made the trauma worse. But her pain was nothing compared to the loss of her mother, the cruel harm done to Bobby, and the confusion she felt on account of her father's disappearance.

She suddenly felt terribly alone and nothing could ease the anguish. She would never hear her mother's voice again, never see her. A little later a doctor and nurse came in. They gave her a glass of water and some yellow sleeping pills and the sedative flooded through her veins.

A police detective had come with her in her car to pick up her belongings and close up the house on Long Beach. It was six weeks after the murder, and she still felt vulnerable. There was no word of her father's whereabouts and the police had informed her that Interpol had been unable to trace Paul March, in Zurich or anywhere else. As Kelso had told her, her father had simply vanished.

She told the detective she wanted to be left alone to sort through her things. Besides, there were personal belongings of her parents she wanted to take with her for keepsakes. 'I'm sorry, miss. I think it would be better if I stayed. You're still upset.'

She looked at him sternly. 'This is my home. Please do as I say.'

He saw the wilful look in her eyes and, not wanting to upset her, reluctantly agreed. 'I'll be out front in the car. If you need me, you call.'

When he left, she walked through the rooms in a daze. Once they had been happy rooms but now they seemed desolate and chilling. Something terrible had happened here and it could never be her home again, at least while her father was no longer in her life. She couldn't bear to go into her parents' bedroom – that would have been too much. The masked man hadn't come back but he lived in her nightmares every single night.

She sat in her father's study chair and looked through all the old postcards he had sent her throughout her childhood. She wanted to cry again but she had used up all her tears. She had noticed that several of the drawers had been disturbed and left half open, and upstairs a number of the bedroom closets were in disarray, as if the house had been recently searched, but she guessed it must have been the police. She opened the French windows and looked out to the jetty and the boathouse and heard the soft sound of the sea. Her father had recently allowed himself a small luxury: an inexpensive second-hand motorboat which he used for sea fishing. Now it languished in the boathouse, and was covered in spider's webs.

She poured herself a glass of her father's Scotch and lit one of his cigarettes. Her parents would not have approved, but there was no one there now to approve or not, and somehow it didn't seem to matter what she did. Carrying her glass, she walked down to the wooden jetty and sat on the edge, near the boathouse.

The tide was out and her feet dangled over the wet sand, a metal ladder leading down. It was spring, the afternoon air still cool, a chilly Atlantic breeze whipping up the white-topped waves far out to sea. The boardwalk was where her father liked to come when he needed to be alone. Some summer nights, lying in her bedroom, she'd hear the hollow echo of his footsteps on the boardwalk as he paced up and down, mulling over some problem or other. And when she was a teenager he would often sit with her and Bobby at the end of the jetty, their legs dangling over the edge, and her father would point out the stars. *'See that star, Jennifer and Bobby? That's Sirius. And that one over there, that's Capella.'*

Then her mother might call him from the kitchen and he'd stroll back up to the house, but not before winking at Jennifer and saying with a smile, 'I'll be back soon, honey. Take care of your kid brother.'

She closed her eyes and cried: she'd never hear those footsteps return. She missed her father's voice, missed his company. She missed everything about him. And most of all, right now she *needed* him to be there. But he wasn't. And all the time that one unanswered question kept coming back: *why?* Why had her mother been slaughtered and Bobby left for dead? Why had her father disappeared and where had he gone?

She couldn't understand any of it. Kelso had said the police had thought the motive was robbery – inexpensive items of jewellery missing from her mother's dressing room suggested theft – but days after the murder Jennifer had been visited again in her hospital room by two detectives from Homicide. They wanted to go over her story once more, wanted to know whether her father had been depressed, taking tranquillisers, or had ever beaten her mother.

She answered no to each of their questions. Afterwards, she had felt sickened when she heard the detectives talking in the hallway outside her room. They talked about her father as if *he* might have been responsible, as if *he* had committed the crimes himself, or paid someone to carry them out. But Jennifer couldn't believe that, not for a moment. Her father wouldn't have attempted to rape and kill her, shoot Bobby and kill her mother, or paid someone to do those terrible things. It was too repulsive even to think about.

Returning to the study, she idly opened the drawers of her father's desk: there were lots of household bills and sheaves of blank typing paper but no sign of the security box that had contained the yellow legal pad. It was nowhere to be found, and as she remembered how angry her father had been she recalled the other incident when she had discovered the trunk in the attic and mentioned the name Joseph Delgado. But she was confused. Had the incident really happened? It was so long ago. Had she imagined the whole thing?

The cigarette made her dizzy. The Scotch made her want to throw up, and the questions and the memories made her grief flood back. She went to the bathroom and took a cold shower, the icy water chilling her skin. When she had dressed and packed, and taken all the photograph albums belonging to herself and her parents, she went back to her father's study and saw the old bunch of keys lying tossed on one of the shelves. Hesitating, she picked them up and climbed the stairs to the attic.

When she opened the trunk it was empty.

Now Jennifer stood in the cemetery, looking down at her mother's grave. Two years ago she had been the only family member who attended the funeral. The service was a subdued affair – a few of her neighbours, a handful of her mother's relatives, some colleagues of her father's whom she had never met before, and Kelso. Even by then, a week after her mother's death, her father had not come back. Not a word, not a line, not a phone call. Ever.

Bobby was too ill to attend the service, and the first time she was allowed to visit him he looked helpless, confined in a wheelchair, tubes in his nostrils and his fifteen-year-old face pale and lost and confused. Kelso was right: Bobby couldn't walk and he couldn't speak. The bullet that had shattered his spine had crippled and muted him. He still had some power in his hands, and a police psychologist had tried to get him to write down what had happened the night of the murder, using pictures and words, but it was obvious Bobby was too traumatised and that he was unable to identify the intruder. Finding his mother brutally slain had disturbed him deeply, and every time the psychologist tried to bring up the subject Bobby withdrew deeper into himself. He never wanted to talk about their parents or about the murder. It was as if he just wanted to erase the whole thing from his mind.

After months of trying to get over her anguish, Jennifer resumed her legal studies. Bobby's injuries meant he had to be taken into permanent care at the Cauldwell home, where she visited him every day, and in their first months of shared grief they had clung to each other with a desperate intensity, Bobby never wanting to let her go when it came time for her to leave.

For it seemed that no matter how hard Jennifer tried she couldn't find any kind of closure. She couldn't bear to live alone in her parents' house but she couldn't bring herself to sell it either, so she paid a local handyman to cut and weed the lawns and tend to any repairs while the property remained vacant. Meanwhile she rented the condo on Long Beach, for she still had an inexplicable need to remain close to the place of her happy childhood, perhaps because she dreamt of the day when her father would return home and together with Bobby they could try to rebuild their shattered lives.

For a long time she wanted to talk to no one and her friends and classmates suffered. She started screening her calls, only returning them when she knew people were out and she only had to speak to an answering machine, and her friends found it impossible to get through to her. Gradually they started to leave her alone, believing that it was the only way they could help her. She learned to keep everyone at arm's length, never allowed anyone to get close enough to break down her defences.

Jack Kelso had sometimes come to visit her, tried to ease her agony with conversation, and he often visited Bobby. But she had learned little about Kelso and he had never fully explained how he and her father had met, except to say that they worked in the same business. Gradually his visits dwindled over the following year, and by then her memory of her father had become a wistful ache. Yet she always hoped that, someday, someone would tell her why the nightmare had happened, and that her father would come back.

For months after her mother's death, the police had occasionally come by to visit her, but only to tell her that their investigation was going nowhere. Did she remember anything else, anything at all, any detail, no matter how small? She told them about the day she had found the papers in the attic trunk, told them of the grisly photograph she had seen, and the name of the man in prison uniform who had looked like her father: Joseph Delgado.

'We'll look into it,' one of the detectives promised. 'See what we can come up with.'

But the next time they visited they confessed they'd still got nowhere. 'The name's drawn a blank. You sure about the name, Jennifer?'

'Yes, I'm sure.'

'We'll get back to you if anything turns up.'

Months passed but the detectives never came back. Some nights she would dream that they would catch whoever had killed her mother and destroyed Bobby's life, and she would be the prosecution lawyer facing the masked man in court, and she'd help send him to the electric chair. It was an absurd dream –

New York no longer sentenced murderers to die in the electric chair – but in her fevered imagination she'd have her revenge. She would watch her attacker squirm and cry for mercy, plumes of smoke rising from his mask as his body burned, until he was finally dead and the grief and anger she carried deep inside her could wash away. And sometimes she'd dream that when the trial was over and the masked man was caught and dead, she would see her father come up the pathway as he did when she was a little girl, and he'd be smiling at her the way he used to smile, and his arms would be open, waiting for her to run to them.

But they were just dreams.

When she was twenty-nine, Jennifer graduated from Columbia School of Law with just enough of a grade point average to scrape through. She had worked hard in her final year, ruthlessly cut herself off from everything and everyone, including her valued friendship with Mark, and tried to concentrate solely on her studies. She knew it was also part of a defence mechanism, that she needed to retreat from the world and immerse herself in work in order to help bury her grief. The little free time she had was taken up by part-time jobs to pay the food and rent bills, to supplement what money was left over from her mother's will, most of which she'd put into trust to pay for Bobby's care at the Cauldwell. After four years of struggle she had succeeded, and the dream of becoming a lawyer finally came true.

But the other dreams never worked out. The police never caught the man who had killed her mother and shot Bobby, and her father never came back.

5

The Swiss Alps

The Romans believed that the spirits of the dead lingered near their tombs – Chuck McCaul had read that somewhere once – but he never would have believed that a ghost was waiting for him on the mountain.

It had started to rain as he drove his hired Renault up the steep rocky track. When it came to an end, McCaul braked to a halt and climbed out. He was twenty-one, fit and muscular, with cropped blond hair, and he had the healthy look of someone who was at home in the outdoors.

Above him towered the craggy peaks of the Alps. The one that interested him was called the Wasenhorn, over three thousand metres high, and it rose like some fossilised dinosaur out of a mist of icy cloud. McCaul went round to the back of the car, unlocked the trunk and began to assemble his climbing gear. Nylon ropes, a collapsible walking stick, crampons for his boots, and a small nylon backpack. He hooked his plastic helmet on to his belt and slung the ropes over his shoulder. This high up, at over a thousand metres, it was freezing, even in spring, the Alps covered in snow. The amount of climbing he was going to have to do today was minimal, a hike really, but it was a tough hike, and he might need the ropes in case he got into trouble.

The western side of the Wasenhorn stood just inside Swiss territory; the eastern part of it rolled down to the Italian side of the border, where McCaul was headed, almost two hours away on foot. At the top of the mountain was a vast glacier of solid ice he would have to cross, but once you got up there the scene was simply heart-stopping.

On a clear day, you could see the rugged tops of the mountains, the deep valleys where Hannibal had crossed with his infantry and elephants eighteen centuries ago to conquer Rome, the craggy Simplon pass where Napoleon had gouged out a million tons of rock to move his vast army south for his Italian campaign. And beyond lay Italy, the mountains rolling down to the warmth of Lake Maggiore, splendid views of hilltop castles, villages and church monasteries that took your breath away.

He locked the Renault, hefted the pack on to his back and checked his watch: 9.52 a.m.

The chill bit into McCaul's bones despite his heavy protective clothing. He had finally reached the glacier, and now he looked down as he paused for breath, the air fogging in front of his face.

Below him lay a deep, long, jagged gully that had been formed thousands of centuries ago, gouged out of the mountain during the Ice Age by shifting rock and debris, a testament to the awesome power of nature. And in the centre of the gully lay the frozen glacier. A solid mass of blue-coloured ice, covered in snow, stretching about a quarter of a kilometre across to the far side.

The sun shone down now, and the combination of light reflecting off the white snow and the pressure of the altitude gave McCaul a slight headache. He put on his Ray-Bans and his plastic safety helmet before he commenced his walk. The metal crampons were attached to his boots to ensure a good grip, and the ice seemed firm underfoot. He started to walk, slowly and carefully. There was nothing but intense white cold and silence all around him, disturbed only by the laboured sound of his own breathing and his feet crunching on the crust of snow. After thirty minutes, he was fifty metres from the far side of the glacier, and he paused again for breath.

The view from where he stood was quite incredible. Far below in the distance lay Italy, rugged, picturesque Alpine villages with red pan-tiled roofs, clinging to the mountain sides as if defying the laws of gravity. With the spring, the glacial ice was shifting and melting, feeding the hundreds of rivers and waterfalls that gushed down from the Alps. It was a hazardous time to cross

44

the glacier, unless you were an experienced mountaineer and knew the route. McCaul wasn't that experienced, although he knew the route, had hiked it once before in late September two years ago on a group mountaineering holiday, but now it was spring and pretty dangerous.

Ahead, he could see a series of narrow slits in the snow. The crevasses were a death trap, deep gashes in the glacier that had been cracked wide open by altitude pressure and cold. Some went down only a couple of metres, others dropped to the very bottom of the glacier, and that might be more than a hundred metres – an abyss. If a guy fell into one of those sons-of-bitches, he might not get out again. McCaul counted three crevasses in all, one after another, each perhaps a metre wide, with maybe a five-metre gap between each of them, which he had to get across.

He could jump all three, one after the other, *no big deal*.

Very carefully, McCaul prodded ahead of him with the tip of his walking stick. The snow appeared pretty solid. The first crevasse was just a couple of steps away. He moved back to take a run. The crampons gave him a good grip, and he could easily get up enough speed to make the jump.

He had run three long strides when it happened.

One moment his feet were on the ice and the next they were stabbing at the air as the ground beneath him seemed to disappear in an avalanche.

Jesus . . . !

McCaul screamed, lost his balance, and plunged into the crevasse.

When he opened his eyes he was lying on his back. The cold was intense. McCaul's teeth chattered, and he felt dizzy. His body felt as if it had been beaten with a sledgehammer and his skull throbbed, but he was still wearing his safety helmet and he guessed it had probably saved his life. He didn't know how deep the chamber that he had fallen into was, but directly overhead he could see the mouth of the crevasse: a jagged, blinding slash of blue sky high above him. It was hard to judge distance, but he figured it was at least seven or eight metres to the top.

Fuck.

Slowly, he moved his arms and legs. Nothing felt broken but he ached all over. He lay on a mound of snow, created by the small avalanche when the mouth of the crevasse had given way, and he figured the snow must have softened his fall. For the first moments of consciousness he was simply glad to be alive, but now he began to panic.

Sweat ran down his face and his heart raced. He knew if he stayed in the crevasse he'd freeze to death. He looked up again at the slash of blue sky. He still had the nylon rope slung around his shoulder. He could probably climb back up, even without the rope, by bracing his back and legs against the walls.

Once his eyes became accustomed to the dimness, McCaul saw that the chamber was faintly lit. The sheer walls of solid blue ice acted as a mirror, reflecting brilliant patches of light down from the sky. Small pockets of darkness existed here and there but the crevasse appeared to stretch endlessly, jaggedly, either side of him.

He exercised his legs, was just getting ready to push his feet against the ice and begin the climb when a dark object inside the crevasse wall directly opposite him caught his eye. He couldn't make out what it was – the thing looked sort of fuzzy – but it appeared to be some kind of rectangular object embedded in the ice.

McCaul frowned and edged closer. All he could make out was a dark form. Curious, he removed his backpack and fumbled for his ice axe. The embedded object didn't appear to be far in. He began to chip away, breaking off chunks of frozen water. He hit something soft. When he prised away the last shards of ice with his numbed fingers he saw it was a canvas rucksack. What was a rucksack doing at the bottom of a crevasse? It looked in pretty good condition, the canvas frozen solid and the back of it stuck like glue to the ice. McCaul got a grip on the canvas, gave a couple of sharp tugs, and the rucksack came free from the ice with a sound like Scotch tape being removed.

Jeez, it felt heavy.

Forget the rucksack, Chuck. Leave it and just get the fuck out of here.

His bones still ached and his legs felt shaky. It was going to be a hard climb to the top. He forced himself against the wall, the backpack softening the pressure on his spine, then stuck out one leg, locked it hard against the ice, then his other leg, and braced himself. Slowly, achingly, he began to climb. He had gone only a couple of metres when he got the greatest scare of his life. He froze, his breath catching in his throat, and he almost slipped with shock and had to brace himself hard against the walls to prevent himself from falling.

Jesus Christ . . . !

He looked straight ahead in horror.

Locked inside the ice, staring out at him like a ghostly apparition, was the face of a man.

6

Italian–Swiss border

The Agusta helicopter descended out of the rain clouds at a thousand feet and circled once before it came in to land.

As the whir of the rotor blades died, Victor Caruso climbed wearily out of the passenger seat. He was a small man in his early fifties, overweight, with a bushy handlebar moustache and penetrating grey eyes, and as he tossed away his half-finished cigarette a squall of wind threw rain in his face.

'A great start to the day,' he called back to the pilot.

'It could be worse, Captain.'

'I doubt it somehow,' Caruso said moodily. 'Not when you're woken at five in the morning.'

As Caruso pulled up his raincoat collar he saw two blue-and-white Fiats parked a short distance away. Half a dozen uniformed men from the local Carabinieri station in Varzo stood around in the rain, chatting and smoking cigarettes. Caruso glanced up at the mountains. Not that he saw much. It was a filthy morning and the view was masked by a swirling mass of thick grey cloud.

A man dressed in a sergeant's uniform and carrying a walkie-talkie came away from the group and approached him. Tall and robust, he had a stubby cigar clenched between his teeth, which he tossed away before he saluted.

Caruso nodded. 'Sergeant Barti, I presume?'

Barti offered his hand. 'Good morning, Captain. Thanks for coming.'

Caruso glanced up at the grey clouds. 'Tell me what's good about it? Yesterday I was in Turin minding my own business, looking forward to my first day off in a month, when some idiot from headquarters phones and tells me I'm being flown up north to the sticks.'

Barti smiled. 'Sorry we've messed up your rest day, but we needed expert help. Do you know this region, Captain?'

Caruso made a face as he looked at the towering crags. 'Better than I should. My father came from the area, and I was posted here once for six months. I still have the corns on my feet to prove it.' The rain was coming down in a fine drizzle as Caruso lit another cigarette in cupped hands and flicked shut his lighter. 'So where's the stiff?'

Barti nodded up towards the mountains. 'Up there, about an hour and a half away, most of it on foot. The weather's too cloudy to use the helicopter.'

Caruso raised his eyes in despair. 'So the pilot tells me. Can't we take a car?'

'I'm afraid only as far as the Alpe Veglia. Then we've got to walk to the glacier. You know the Alpe Veglia, Captain?'

Caruso nodded and sighed. The Alpe Veglia was a huge nature reserve in the Italian Alps, completely closed to traffic, except the four-wheel-drives of the reserve's patrol vehicles. But even they couldn't make it all the way up the steep rock-shale tracks that bordered Switzerland. 'Terrific. So who's up there now?'

'Two of my men. One's a local who knows the glacier pretty well. And there's a forensic pathologist from Turin, an officer named Rima.'

'Vito Rima?'

'You know him?'

Caruso nodded. 'They call him Vito the Vulture. You can always count on Vito hovering around wherever there's a body. So what's happening?'

'We've got the place cordoned off. Not that it matters much, it's as quiet as the grave up there.' Barti jerked his thumb over at the waiting men. 'The others are going to wait down here until we need them. No point in all of us freezing to death on the glacier.'

Caruso sighed again. The last thing he wanted right now was

to go tramping up the mountains in shitty weather; heavy grey rain cloud hung overhead and the air was damp and cold. As he turned back, he noticed a confused look on Barti's face. 'What's the matter, Sergeant? You seem troubled.'

Barti frowned. 'This whole business, it's pretty weird, to say the least. I've lived in these parts for twenty years and I've never known anything like it.'

Caruso tossed away his cigarette and nodded towards the Fiat. 'OK, let's get going. You can tell me on the way.'

It was warmer in the Fiat, but not by much. Caruso rubbed condensation from the windscreen with his finger, made to light another cigarette, then changed his mind. There were two major police forces in Italy, the paramilitary Carabinieri, to which Caruso belonged, and the civil police. The cities and towns were mostly the domain of the civil police, while the rural areas were usually Carabinieri territory, though in reality the work often overlapped. Caruso was attached to Turin HQ, Homicide. The local station in Varzo which covered the area where the body was found had requested Turin's assistance and Caruso had drawn the short straw. Still, it wasn't often you got to investigate the case of a corpse found frozen into a glacier.

He glanced over at the sergeant. 'I suppose you'd better fill me in.'

'We had a call yesterday afternoon from the Swiss police in Brig. A young American climber staying in a local hotel in Simplon called the Berghof reported that he'd found a body in the mountains. Apparently, the corpse was frozen into the bottom of a deep crevasse on the Wasenhorn glacier. The American kid had been walking across the ice when he fell into the crevasse and discovered the body.'

'You said kid. What age?'

'Twenty-one.' Barti half smiled. 'At my age, that's a kid. His name is Chuck McCaul.'

'And what was this Chuck doing up on the glacier?'

'He's a tourist, who likes to hill-walk and climb. It turns out he also found a rucksack lodged in the ice near the body.'

Caruso raised his eyes. 'Did you find anything in the rucksack?'

'The American left it in the crevasse – the shock of finding the corpse. I thought it best not to touch it until you and Rima arrived.'

'Wise. Go on.'

'The Swiss police sent a team up to the Wasenhorn. It turns out the body's on our side of the border. That's when we were contacted.'

Barti paused just as the Fiat jerked over some rocky ground. The vehicle lifted slightly, then settled. Caruso looked out through the drizzle beyond the windscreen. The terrain was rough and desolate. He turned back as Barti continued.

'I sent a patrol up to have a look. The body's locked in solid ice a couple of metres from the bottom of the crevasse.'

'Man or woman?'

Barti shrugged. 'We think it's a man. But the face is distorted behind the ice. It's difficult to be absolutely certain.'

'You're sure the stiff is on our side of the border?'

Barti nodded. 'Absolutely. I double-checked the maps. The Swiss can count themselves lucky this isn't their case and we got the shit end of the stick.'

'Why?'

Barti glanced over. 'There's something pretty strange about the body.'

Caruso made to speak, but hesitated as Barti halted the Fiat. A narrow track lay ahead, a rock-shale mountain path worn by long years of use, and covered in a fine sprinkling of snow. It was impossible for the Fiat to go any farther, and Caruso saw footprints where the others had gone ahead. The cloud and mist had cleared a little, the drizzle had almost died, and beyond lay an incredible sight. Soaring peaks of white-topped, jagged mountains stretched ahead, part of the Alpine range that formed the natural border between Switzerland and Italy. Far in the distance rose the glorious Matterhorn and the majestic Eiger.

Caruso saw a rock-shale path curve upwards, knew it was one

of the ancient mule tracks that criss-crossed the Alps like spider's webs, worn trails that went back to medieval times when smugglers used them to transport contraband.

He looked over at the sergeant. 'You didn't tell me what was so strange about the body.'

Barti jerked on the handbrake. 'First, I think it better if you take a look for yourself.'

7

Near one of the crevasses stood two young corporals. Both wore heavy parkas and boots, and they had a small Primus stove going on which they were making coffee. Cloud wisps swirled around the Wasenhorn peak in the cold sunshine, and Caruso was aware of an immense feeling of the raw, rugged power of nature.

The glacier was a remarkable sight. Hard packed with ice and duck-egg blue in colour, it seemed like a wide, frozen river. Here and there were deep slits in the ice, where giant crevasses had opened up. Beside one of them, a couple of ropes were anchored in the ice and snaked down over the edge. It had taken over an hour of hard walking to reach the site, and by then the sun was shining and the rain was gone. It was a difficult hike and Caruso was fighting for breath most of the way, his legs aching, his feet raw and sore, but he wasn't too exhausted to appreciate the magnificent view. 'Where's Rima?' he wheezed.

Barti shrugged. 'Probably down in the crevasse, examining the body.'

'Find out what's happening.'

Caruso was still struggling to catch his breath as the sergeant went over to the two men. A small blue bivouac tent had been erected near by, and a square had been marked out in the snow, with short aluminium poles planted around the mouth of the crevasse, yellow plastic tape strung between the poles. Barti came back with one of the corporals in tow. 'This is Corporal Fausto.'

The young man saluted. 'Captain.'

'Tell me what's been happening.'

The corporal indicated the crevasse. 'We've marked off the site, as you can see. The pathologist is still down there.'

'The sergeant tells me you know this area better than the mountain goats.'

The corporal smiled and shrugged. 'I used to work out of the local village as a guide.'

'You know the glacier well?'

'I've crossed it many times. It's a scenic route.'

'What kind of people come up here?'

'Tourists, mostly. Italians and Swiss. It's a popular place with climbers and hikers. People get a kick out of walking across the ice.'

'Isn't that dangerous?'

'Not if you know the terrain, or have a guide.'

Caruso turned to Barti. 'I'd like to see the body.'

The corporal led them over to the edge of the crevasse, to where the ropes dangled down between jagged, icy walls. Caruso peered over into a pale blue chamber that got darker the farther down it went. A bend in the crevasse made it impossible to see to the bottom. Barti said, 'It's an easy enough descent.'

'I'll have to take your word for it. Lead the way.'

Barti slipped a harness around his waist, took hold of one of the ropes and lowered himself down. Caruso followed.

It was bone-chillingly cold in the crevasse. As Caruso abseiled down he splayed his feet against the frozen walls. He saw a blaze of blinding light somewhere below and moments later Barti gripped his waist. 'OK, you're at the bottom, let go.'

Caruso let go of the rope and his feet hit packed ice. Round a bend, several metres away, a couple of powerful torches illuminated the floor of the chamber. A thinly built man had a black doctor's bag open at his feet, his breath clouding in the chilled air. He had a grey goatee beard, thick metal-rimmed glasses, and wore a quilted arctic parka and heavy woollen gloves. 'About time somebody decided to join me,' he said sourly. 'I was beginning to think I'd got a contagious disease.'

'How are you, Rima?'

'Cold as an undertaker's kiss. I've worked in some shitty sites in my life but this beats them all.'

Caruso scanned the chamber's icy floor. 'Did you check the ground around here?'

Rima nodded. 'I swept ten metres either side of the body. That's as far as I could move before the walls started to narrow.'

'And?'

'Nothing, I'm afraid, apart from the rucksack the American found.'

'Where is it?'

'Over there.' Rima nodded to a large clear plastic bag propped against the far wall, and Caruso picked it up. The plastic was ice cold and partly clouded. Inside was a canvas rucksack. It felt heavy, appeared in good condition, and had a metal snap lock.

'You didn't open it?'

'I tried, but it's frozen solid, so I thought it best to wait until the officer in charge arrived.' Rima smiled. 'I guess that's you.'

Caruso put the rucksack down. 'OK, let's have a look at the stiff. An accident, you think?'

'Impossible to tell until we thaw him out.' Rima jerked a thumb behind him. 'See for yourself. He's over there.'

Rima picked up a powerful torch and they moved along the crevasse bottom for five metres. Facing the left-hand wall, Caruso saw a portable folding aluminium chair with a canvas seat. To his left, he noticed a small square cut into the ice near the chamber floor. He knelt and examined the area.

'That's where the American found the rucksack,' Rima explained. 'The body's about half a metre above your head, lying almost horizontally, with a slight upward angle. You'll need to stand on the chair to see it.'

Caruso stood on the rickety chair and shone the cone of torchlight on to the frozen wall, then came a moment of pure horror. A man's face stared out at him grotesquely from the ice. '*Jesus.*'

'Kind of gives you the creeps, doesn't it? The ice acts like a deep freeze. I'd say it's kept the body perfectly preserved.'

Caruso shivered as he peered in closer and said to Barti, 'You still haven't told me, what's so strange about it?'

'I checked our records of missing persons, people we know who got lost in this part of the Alps. All were found and accounted for, dead or alive. The Swiss say the same.'

'How far back did you check?'

'Twenty years, the same as the Swiss. And the authorities on both sides of the border keep careful records of anyone who has gone missing in these regions. So it's pretty odd that we've found a body that no one knew was lost.'

Caruso saw that the frozen head was clearly visible, the nose and lips, ears and cheeks, locks of dark-coloured hair plastered across the forehead. He shone the torchlight on the man's face, and it was a disturbing experience. The skin was alabaster white and the eyes were wide open. 'How long do you think the body's been here?'

'I really can't say until we cut it out and I have it on the slab,' said Rima. 'But definitely a long time. Do you know anything about glaciers, Captain?'

Caruso shook his head. 'About as much as I know about women after thirty years of marriage.'

Rima smiled and pointed up towards the gaping mouth of the crevasse, to where a thin slash of piercing white light shone down and reflected brilliantly off the blue walls. 'It's eight metres deep to here, and the body's just over two metres from the bottom. The glacial ice depends on rain and snowfall to refresh it. Year after year it turns to hard-packed ice and builds up. But year after year it also melts and flows down into the valleys.' Rima shrugged. 'At this depth, the body could have been here a long time. Years maybe.'

'I'll take your word for it. Are you through?'

Rima rubbed his freezing hands. 'Almost. The next step is to cut our friend here out of the ice. We'll use a chain saw.'

'I'll need to talk to the American. Where is he?'

'One of my men is picking him up from his Swiss hotel,' Barti explained. 'I've arranged for you to have the use of one of the offices in our station.'

'Good. Have all the necessary photographs been taken?'

'Sure, we've got everything we need.'

Caruso took another look at the entombed face, shivered, and stepped down off the chair. 'OK, I've seen enough. Let's get back up.'

The office in the small Carabinieri station in Varzo overlooked a tiny square. Caruso sat at the desk near the window, where he had plenty of light, and picked up the plastic evidence bag. He slipped on a pair of disposable rubber gloves and removed the heavy rucksack. The ice had thawed, and the canvas was wet and soggy.

His curiosity had been gnawing at him during the entire journey back to the station, and now he felt small tinglings of excitement spreading through his hands and feet. He pulled out his Swiss army penknife and tried to force open the snap lock. It wouldn't budge. He picked up the internal telephone and called the desk. 'Do you have a large screwdriver?'

'*Sir?*'

'This is Caruso here. I need a screwdriver. A sturdy one.'

'I'll see what I can find, sir.'

Five minutes later there was a knock on the door and a corporal appeared with a large, ferocious-looking screwdriver. 'Will this do, Captain?'

'If it doesn't, I'm going to need dynamite. Thank you, you may go.'

Caruso used both the knife and the screwdriver this time, jamming the rucksack between his legs and levering the lock. It took a lot of effort but on the third try it snapped open. He lifted the flap and a strong smell of canvas wafted out.

He peered inside and saw a jumble of clothes: an overcoat, a suit, a shirt and tie and patent leather shoes among them. At the bottom of the pile he saw a Browning automatic pistol and what looked like a slim, black leather wallet. The pistol looked in good condition, hardly any sign of rust. He removed the wallet and placed it on the desk, then he slipped the penknife blade into the pistol's trigger guard, laid the weapon down beside the wallet, and stared thoughtfully at the entire contents of the rucksack for several moments.

Finally, he picked up the wallet. Very carefully, he slid the blade of his penknife between the covers and prised it open. To his surprise, it wasn't a wallet but a passport cover. As he began to separate the pages there was a knock on the door and the corporal put his head into the room. 'Signore McCaul is here, Captain.'

'Give me five minutes, then send him in.'

Caruso sat on the edge of the desk and looked at the young American seated opposite. Chuck McCaul was clean cut, fit looking, and seemed like the well-mannered type. His eyes were fixed on the rucksack contents lying on the desk. 'You found that stuff in the rucksack, sir?'

'*Si.*'

'Can I look?'

'Yes, you can look. But please don't touch.'

McCaul took a particular interest in the pistol. '*Jeez*, way out, man.'

'Pardon?'

McCaul half smiled. 'I meant that it's pretty remarkable, sir. The whole damned thing. The body frozen into the glacier. The gun and document wallet. All pretty strange.'

Caruso nodded. 'Yes, it's certainly that. And who knows what else we may find when we examine the body. But you must forgive my English, signore. I don't get to practise very often. Tell me please how you found the body.'

'But I already told Sergeant Barti.'

'Please tell me.'

McCaul told him. Caruso listened, then said, 'You must have been frightened, no?'

'With respect, sir, the truth is I almost fucking shit myself.'

'You're also very lucky that you got out of the crevasse alive. Did you find anything else besides the rucksack?'

'No, sir.'

'You're certain?'

'My father's a private detective. I wouldn't lie about police evidence, sir.'

Caruso nodded, certain the young man was telling the truth. 'I'm sorry for taking up your time, but I wanted to speak with you myself. And now, I won't keep you any longer. When do you leave Switzerland?'

'I don't fly home for another four days. Is that it, Captain?'

'*Si*. That's it.'

McCaul stood. 'You mind if I ask a question?'

'Of course not.'

'What's going down?'

Caruso frowned, looked at the floor, then up again. '*Scusi*, but I don't understand.'

McCaul smiled. 'I meant, what's the story? Who's the guy in the ice?'

'I cannot confirm his identity until we examine the body. But according to the passport I found it seems he was an American named Paul March.'

8

New York

Leroy Murphy leaned his burly, six-feet-six black frame over the wheelchair and gently removed the Sony CD headset from Bobby's ears. They were in the conservatory of the Cauldwell home, the doors open, a cool breeze blowing into the hot room. Jennifer, Bobby and Leroy, the male nurse, wearing his whites with short sleeves, the material straining over his powerful physique as he leaned over, the skin on his thick arms as black as tar against the soft white cotton.

Bobby sat in the wheelchair, head to one side, saliva running down his chin. Jennifer leaned over and wiped it away with a paper tissue. Then she took a comb from her bag and combed Bobby's hair where the wind had lifted it.

Leroy said, 'OK, man's had enough attention. Looks like he's ready to rock. Quiz time, Bobby. Take a little break from Michael Jackson. Bobby likes Michael, don't you, man?'

Bobby nodded. Leroy smiled. 'Bobby here's an honorary brother. Man knows more about music than anyone I know. That right, Bobby? And we're gonna show Jenny, ain't we?'

Bobby gave a lopsided grin and nodded again, as Leroy placed the open notepad on Bobby's lap and handed him the ballpoint pen.

'That's my man. Song called "Closer Than Close". Gimme the singer, gimme the year.'

Bobby gripped the pen hard between his thumb and fore-finger, then scrawled across the page. '*Rosie Gaines.*'

'Tell me *when*, man. Don't let me down, now.'

Bobby wrote: '*1997.*'

'You're my man. Tough one coming. Coolio had a number

60

one that stayed in the charts four weeks the same year. Gimme the song. Impress sister Jenny.'

Bobby hesitated for a moment, his face twisted in concentration, then he wrote on the pad and gave a tiny grin of triumph. Leroy checked the answer, slapped a big, meaty leg. 'Man, you're a walking archive, you know that? Got a memory better than a damned elephant.'

He ruffled Bobby's hair, stood, ready to leave, and looked across at Jennifer, his broad, friendly face grinning from ear to ear. 'Man never lets me down, not ever. Could win himself a *big* quiz show. Cars. Holidays. Lots of dollars. Me, I'm gonna be his manager.'

Jennifer touched the male nurse's hand, felt the gentle strength of the man. 'Thanks, Leroy.'

'Any time.'

It was sunny in the conservatory, and very quiet, the lawns beyond the glass rolling away to a thick bank of pine trees and a pond in the near distance. A breeze blew in across the Spanish tiles and ruffled Bobby's hair again. Jennifer leaned over, patted it down. 'So, how are you doing?'

Bobby gave a nod and rocked back and forth in his wheelchair. He was seventeen, but he looked a boyish fourteen, with his thick dark hair and pale, milky skin. He was always shy, even as a kid, except now and then when a fiery temper erupted, a temper that had more to do with frustration than mood. Sometimes Jennifer thought about all the things he might have been if his life hadn't turned out the way it had. Right now he'd be in high school, he'd have a girlfriend, he'd be living an ordinary life, but she had to push those thoughts away. Bobby was alive, that was what was important, and they still had each other, except today Bobby seemed distant.

'You miss me?'

Bobby nodded.

'Leroy tells me you haven't been eating too well in the last few days. Is everything OK?'

Bobby looked uncomfortable. He turned his face away and strained in the chair, as if something was on his mind.

'What's wrong, Bobby?'

Bobby picked up his notepad, laid it on his knee. In the last year he had learned to use sign language, and of necessity so had Jennifer, because mostly now Bobby signed his response, but whenever he was upset or angry, for some reason he still preferred to use his notepad and write his reply. The memory game he played with Leroy was just something to keep his mind busy, because Bobby had a terrific memory and had always loved music, even when he was a baby. Jennifer remembered how he used to crawl over to the radio, switch it on and gyrate with excitement the moment the music came on. But his memory didn't extend to the night of their mother's slaying, and he couldn't recall the murder. Jennifer often wondered whether it was by choice, or whether all the circuits inside his head that had to do with the incident had simply shut down, or whether the bullet that had skewered into his skull had destroyed that part of his brain.

Whatever the reason, the medical experts hadn't been able to answer those questions, and neither had she. But sometimes she thought that it was simply a case of Bobby being afraid to recall what had happened the night their mother was killed and their father vanished.

Any time she tried to bring up the subject, he'd turn away, or pretend not to hear, or simply want to be left alone. Not once did he ever open up and talk to her about the night that had destroyed both their lives. She knew it had hurt him greatly, scarred his soul as well as his body; but she also knew that until the day came when they could talk about it, neither of them could truly move on with their lives.

Now Bobby scrawled on the page with the ballpoint pen, then sat there, staring into space. He looked distracted. Jennifer picked up the pad. It read: '*Mom's grave.*'

'You wanted to visit the cemetery, is that it?'

Bobby nodded.

'Did you really, Bobby?'

Bobby nodded again. Jennifer realised he hadn't even mentioned that it was the anniversary and this was the reason he wanted to visit the grave; but that would have been too much for him. She put down the pad. 'You know it only gets you upset. But if you want, I'll call by tomorrow and drive you there.'

Bobby never liked seeing the grave. Whenever she had taken him he'd always got upset and he wouldn't be right for days afterwards. The last time she'd taken him he'd had a seizure, right after they left the graveyard. That was another legacy of the shooting; Bobby suffered from mild bouts of epilepsy. The doctors had told Jennifer it wasn't uncommon in those who had experienced head trauma.

But she guessed there was something else on Bobby's mind, apart from being upset about the anniversary, and that he was trying to get round to it, because that was his way. Sure enough, he held out his hand for Jennifer to give him back the pad. Sometimes he got frustrated because it took so long for him to communicate, and today was one of those days. His dark hair was damp on his forehead, and there were tiny beads of sweat on his face. His mouth tightened and his brow furrowed in concentration as he scribbled once more on the page. When he finished he tossed her the notepad almost angrily.

Jennifer read the pad. '*I want to get out of here. People are nice but they're not family.*' She looked back at Bobby. 'I think I know where this is leading.'

Bobby let out a deep breath and this time he signed his reply; she understood the meaning of his gestures as he pointed at himself, then directly at her, and crossed his fingers. When he finished signing a couple of seconds later, she knew exactly what he meant. '*I want us to be together. I want to go live with you. Permanently.*'

'Bobby, we've been through all this. You know I love you, you know I want you to be with me. You stay with me most weekends, but for the rest of the week my work takes up most of my day. Sometimes I don't get home until late. What if you need a nurse? What if you have a fall while I'm out and need help?'

She had tried it before, many times. The last time, the

Cauldwell had agreed that Bobby could come to live with her for two months on trial. She had hired a day-care nurse to look after him in her apartment. It was expensive, but the woman would make sure he ate, kept himself clean, and attend to his needs while Jennifer worked. Then one day she got a call from the nurse. There had been an accident and she and Bobby were at St Vincent's hospital.

It turned out the nurse had gone out to buy some groceries and Bobby had taken the elevator down to the ground floor all by himself. The nurse was standing in the checkout line, minding her own business, when she saw Bobby flash by the window in his chair, propelling himself with both hands. When she ran after him, Bobby sped up. Half a block away he ended up toppling over, falling out of the chair, barely missing the wheels of a delivery truck that swerved just in time, but he had cracked his head on the sidewalk.

He received fifteen stitches for that escapade. His excuse was that he was bored. Jennifer knew the real answer was simpler; her brother just wanted to taste freedom. Bobby promised not to do it again, but a month later he escaped from the apartment and vanished for four hours. The police found him in a park, just sitting there, happily watching some pretty girls his own age roller-blading.

The nurse resigned. She didn't want to be responsible if Bobby hurt himself or got run over or did himself an injury trying to flee the apartment. She said she also found Bobby 'difficult'.

'Then how do you think it must be for him?' Jennifer asked her. Some people saw only what was missing in Bobby, not what was there. She didn't particularly like the nurse, but she was sorry to see her go. She found a replacement, but there was another incident: Bobby got drunk on a half-pint of vodka he found in the apartment, tried to escape again and fell down the hall stairs. To make matters worse, he made a drunken pass at the nurse, a pretty young Mexican girl. The girl made it sound as if Bobby had assaulted her, which he hadn't. He just got frustrated with his immobility at times, but was far too gentle to do anything violent like that, and when Jennifer asked him why he had tried to squeeze the girl's breasts, he became crimson faced and wrote on his pad, '*I just wanted to know what they felt like.*'

Afterwards, it made Jennifer laugh, but it was easy to forget that her brother still had needs and desires, like every young man his age. But after that, the writing was on the wall. The nursing agency refused her any new help, and the Cauldwell suggested Bobby return. Now Jennifer watched as he grabbed the pad and wrote furiously, then handed it back.

'*Maybe it's time you got hitched.*' Jennifer read the words and wanted to laugh. 'You don't mean that.'

Bobby jerked his head and signed at the same time: a definite yes.

'You think that would solve our problems? You think I could then stay at home, raise a family, and help look after you?'

Another nod, and Bobby had a grin on his face, giving her the 'sure' sign with his thumb and finger.

Jennifer smiled back. 'I'll see what I can do. Not about getting hitched, about getting you another nurse. But right now the Cauldwell is the best place, OK?'

Bobby frowned and Jennifer said, 'It's not the best place?'

Bobby shook his head fiercely. Jennifer was aware that ever since she had allowed the Cauldwell to take Bobby back, their relationship had deteriorated. They argued with each other much more than they had in the past, and it seemed to Jennifer that Bobby was resentful, as if he felt she had betrayed him. He no longer made an effort to hug her, and he often seemed to avoid her attempts at affection. 'Why isn't it the best place?'

This time, Bobby looked angry as he wrote his reply in capital letters.

'*LONELY.*'

When Jennifer had read the word, she looked up and saw the hint of tears in the corners of her brother's eyes. It hurt, because there was nothing she could do to change things, not right now, and that made her pain all the more intense. She felt lonely too. Couldn't Bobby see that, although she seemed to have everything that he hadn't got, she was trapped in the same way that he was? And the only way both of them could escape their prison was to talk to each other about what had happened. But Bobby couldn't seem to do that.

She leaned over, tried to hug him, knowing he was frustrated in a hundred different ways, but Bobby deliberately pulled away, and that hurt her even more. Then she heard footsteps and looked round.

Leroy stood there. 'Sorry to disturb you, Jenny, but you've got a visitor.'

She was startled to see Mark Ryan waiting outside in the hallway. 'Hello, Jennifer.'

'This is a surprise.'

'I thought I'd take a drive up and see Bobby. Leroy told me you were here.'

'He'll be glad to see you. Is anything the matter?'

'With me? No, nothing.'

Jennifer noticed tension around Mark's eyes and mouth. 'Are you sure?'

He shrugged. 'Well, maybe two things.'

'Want to tell me?'

'It looks like the federal prosecutor will be pressing for a maximum sentence in the Nadia Fedov case.'

'She's just a kid, Mark. You really can't change their mind?'

'I tried. I'm sorry, Jennifer. I wish it were different, but it isn't.'

Jennifer suddenly felt angry. 'A young woman loses custody of her two-year-old daughter and gets locked away for the best years of her life. The people who made her commit the crime just lose five pounds of heroin, and walk away to do it again.'

'I don't write the rule books, Jennifer. I just do my job. How's Bobby?'

'I don't think this is one of his best days.'

'What's the matter?'

'I'm not sure, but sometimes I think we've lost whatever real closeness we had. But that's another story, Mark. I'll tell you some time, but not now.'

'Sure.' Mark looked away uneasily, as if there was something bothering him.

'You mentioned there were two things,' Jennifer reminded him. 'What?'

'You said there were two things on your mind.'

Mark was pale. A door led out to the sunny gardens and the pond, and he gestured towards it. 'How about we talk outside?'

They walked down to the pond. Mark was silent. When they sat on one of the benches, he said, 'Jennifer, I didn't just drive up here to see Bobby.'

'What do you mean?'

'It's you I really needed to see.' He took out an envelope, removed a sheet of paper from inside, and handed it across.

Jennifer saw that the page was a police report from Interpol. The body of an American male had been found in the Alps near the Italian–Swiss border, frozen in glacial ice.

And then she saw the name.

She sat in stunned silence, still holding the page, hardly believing what she had read. Dazed, she finally looked over at Mark. 'This . . . this is really true?'

Mark nodded. 'I've been trying to get hold of you all day but your cell phone was powered down. The office said you'd taken the afternoon off and didn't know where you'd gone. Then I figured maybe you'd driven over here.' He started to reach out to her, then stopped, as if wary of being rebuffed. 'You're upset.'

Jennifer had turned pale. 'Right this moment I . . . I'm too shocked to be upset. If my father's body has really been found . . .'

'He's been found, Jennifer. A climber discovered his passport near by.' Mark paused, then said quietly, 'Apparently, his corpse was well preserved in the ice and it's been there a long time.'

'How . . . how did he die?'

'I don't know, Jennifer. That wasn't in the report.'

'What was he doing in the Alps?'

'I don't know that either.'

Jennifer shivered. She looked away towards the pond, then back again. 'Who sent you to tell me?'

'A friend of mine with the Long Beach Police Department called me. He saw a copy of the report that Interpol sent to the detective unit. I offered to break the news. I thought it might be better coming from someone you knew. But I'll give you the number of someone with the detective unit and you can confirm it yourself.'

Jennifer felt confused, and anguished. Somehow, she had always hoped her father would still be alive. But now she finally knew the truth her mind was a welter of distress. 'Can I see the body?'

Mark nodded. 'I believe you'll have to identify it formally. I checked with Interpol and they told me that the region where the body was discovered is almost right on the Italian–Swiss border. The Carabinieri station that's running the investigation is in a town named Varzo, and a captain named Caruso is handling the case. It seems the best route for you to take is to fly to Switzerland and drive over the border to Italy. You could have the whole thing over and done within a couple of days.'

Jennifer sat back. Mark said, 'Are you OK?'

'There are a couple of questions that keep going round in my mind.'

'What questions?'

'How did my father's body end up in a glacier? What . . . what happened to him?'

Mark shook his head. 'It does seem pretty weird. But all I know is what I've already told you. Maybe this Caruso can tell you more.' He hesitated, looked at his watch. 'I've got to be getting back, but if it's OK with you, I'd like to see Bobby before I leave.'

'He's always glad to see you, Mark. But please, don't tell him about this. Not just yet. It might upset him.'

Mark nodded. 'Are you sure you'll be all right?'

'I'll be fine.'

Mark stood, looked down at her face, continued looking for a long time before he spoke. 'Can I tell you an old secret? Something I never told you before?'

'What?'

'When we were kids, I could see your bedroom from my window. I could see you sitting at your dressing table most nights before you went to bed. The lamp would be on and you'd be brushing your hair.' Mark half smiled. 'My old man, he used to do that for my mom, every night for over thirty years until he died. He used to say that there were two things a man could do to show a woman that he cared. One was to brush her hair, the other was to listen to her troubles. And after that night you came running to my parents' house and my dad found you on the veranda, I thought maybe, just maybe, you'd get to know me a little better and we could be even closer friends. That I could listen to your troubles, help you in whatever way I could . . .'

'You have helped me, Mark . . . You *are* a close friend.'

'Sure. But afterwards you withdrew into yourself, and we didn't see much of each other for a long time . . .'

'I didn't see anyone for a long time.'

Mark hesitated. 'I guess what I'm trying to tell you is that, just like the other night, maybe if you feel you just need a shoulder to lean on, or someone to listen, don't ever be afraid to call.'

When Jennifer returned to her apartment, her mind was still in turmoil. She called the detective unit at the Long Beach Police Department because she needed to hear the news again, just to be absolutely certain. Not that she doubted Mark; it was just that during the drive back to her apartment she was in such profound shock that she wondered whether she could have dreamt up their conversation.

The detective she spoke to confirmed everything Mark had told her and said she would be contacted formally. The next thing she did was find the photographs of her father. She kept them in an album in a big old cardboard box in her bedroom closet, and she stared at the photographs for a long time. The

69

image of Paul March was of a tall, smiling handsome man with raven-dark hair. There were snapshots of Jennifer with her father and mother and Bobby, others taken when she was on holiday in Europe with her parents: in Paris, London, Zurich. At the bottom of the cardboard box were the old postcards he had sent her as a child, neatly tied with string. She had always kept them as a memento, but she knew that to look at them now would only deepen her distress. She put the box away and fought back her tears.

Then she took down an atlas from the bookshelf and checked the mountainous area between Switzerland and Italy. She found Varzo, a tiny speck near the Italian border. It was incredible to think she was about to come face to face with the preserved corpse of her father after he had been missing for two solid years. She shivered as she thought again about telling Bobby the news, but decided against it. It might upset him too much, and she didn't want him upset. When it was all over, she'd explain everything as gently as she could.

She flicked through the Yellow Pages and phoned a local travel agent. Just as Mark had said, the agent advised flying to Zurich – there was no shortage of direct flights from JFK or Newark – and then take a train or hire a car to travel south to the Italian border, a few hours away. Next, she dialled Margaret Neil, the office administrator at the Federal Defender Division in Brooklyn.

'Jennifer, how are you, honey?'

'Margaret, I'm going to need some time off. I know it's short notice but something really urgent has come up. I've got to fly to Europe for a few days.' She resisted the temptation to explain why.

'Hey, some people have all the luck. I guess we're not too busy right now. But let me check. From when do you need?'

'Would the day after tomorrow be too soon? Let's say for five days.'

Margaret's voice came back on the line less than a minute later. 'Honey? The day after tomorrow sounds just fine.'

9

It was almost midnight when Mark Ryan finished his shift and drove home. It was pitch dark as he pulled into the driveway of his two-bedroom town house in Elmont. Some of the street lighting was out, but as he climbed the steps to his front door he glimpsed a dark-coloured Buick sedan parked fifty yards back on the far side of the street. He'd noticed the car as he drove past. There appeared to be two men inside, but because of the poor light Mark couldn't be certain, and he was really too tired to care as he let himself in the front door.

The house was comfortable, except it had the look of a bachelor pad. He had bought Ellen out after their divorce, and since she'd left him he'd found it difficult to keep the place tidy. But he lived for his job, it was what had kept him sane after the divorce, and he spent so many extra hours at the precinct he didn't have time for housework. Not that Ellen had ever kept their home tidy. Housekeeping wasn't one of her virtues, but then it wasn't one of his, either.

The place badly needed cleaning, newspapers were scattered on the dining-room table to serve as a makeshift tablecloth, and there were dishes piled high in the kitchen sink. For a guy who showered twice a day and was scrupulous about personal hygiene, it was ridiculous, and he reminded himself for the millionth time that he'd have to hire a maid to come in twice a week.

He went into the kitchen, boiled some water for Nescafé instant, opened the refrigerator door and looked inside. Some hard cheese, a couple of cans of beer and Coke, a tomato, half a carton of milk, and that was about it. As usual, his mind had been so preoccupied with work that he'd forgotten to visit the grocery store. He found a couple of slices of rye in the bread bin which were just about edible, so he made a cheese sandwich and went into the living room while he waited for the water to boil.

He didn't feel like watching TV, so he just sat there, hunched over the coffee table, eating the sandwich. *Some home life.* After his divorce, his parents had kept reminding him that he needed to find another wife. Mark told them one was enough for any man.

His old man would say, a grin on his face, 'You can't stay single and happy for ever, you know.'

'Relax,' Mark would say, smiling back. 'I'm still interviewing.'

But they were right. He was thirty-five next birthday and there was no one special in his life. He sometimes dated a couple of women he knew from the precinct, but they were casuals. Miss Right still hadn't come along. He had once believed it was Ellen, but Jesus, had he been wrong. A petite, fiery brunette with a terrific personality, she worked as a legal secretary for a firm of expensive Manhattan lawyers, and they had married within three months of their first date.

Big mistake.

Seven months into their marriage he came home early from night shift at about 1 a.m., feeling lousy with a flu bug, and found Ellen doing it on the couch with a guy – the same couch he'd bought her specially from Macy's, the one that cost him two weeks' pay, when Ellen had fawned over it.

When he saw them both pulling on their clothes, Mark had just stood there, enraged and trembling, tears in his eyes, resisting the urge to take out his Glock service pistol and shoot the guy, when he suddenly realised he knew his face. It was the slick, expensive lawyer they'd hired from Ellen's office to conveyance their house, the one who wore Armani suits and grinned a lot and said Ellen was a friend and he'd do all the legal paperwork as a favour. *Some favour.*

It turned out he was an old boyfriend, and she'd been seeing him again. That night, Mark hit him so hard he knocked out the lawyer's front tooth. After he'd thrown the son-of-a-bitch out of the house, kicked his ass down the pathway, he went back and confronted Ellen. She just sat there, crying, and confessed she'd been seeing Chad Tate for four months. 'You and me were a mistake, Mark. We're not working out and I want a divorce. Chad wants to marry me.'

Mark left the house that night, bought a quart of Scotch at a liquor store, drove out to a pier on Jamaica Bay and sat in his car and got drunk. When he couldn't cry any more he fell asleep. He woke to find a motorcycle cop knocking on the driver's window. The sun was up, the pier deserted except for a flock of seagulls, and when Mark rolled down the window the cop smelled the alcohol and asked to see his driver's licence. 'What exactly brings you here at this hour, sir?'

Mark handed across his licence and then for the first time in his life he just lost it and broke down. It was as if a dam had burst inside his head as he sobbed and told a complete stranger what had happened to his marriage.

'You poor son-of-a-bitch.' The cop handed back his licence. 'How about you do yourself a favour? Lock your car, go home and sleep it off, then go find yourself a good lawyer.'

But Mark didn't find himself a lawyer; he tried to make it work by patching things up, and the marriage limped on for another two months, but both of them hurled accusations and insults, and it was pointless. They were throwing bombs in a war that was over. Mark filed for divorce after Ellen left one fall weekend and didn't come back.

Forget Ellen, she's in the past. I shed too many tears over that woman and I'm not going to shed any more.

Except that some nights when he came home he just longed to hear a woman's voice, to have someone to talk to, to feel someone rubbing his back the way Ellen used to, right in there between the muscles where he got most of his tension, and tonight was one of them. It had been a lousy couple of days. The thought of the dead baby at Kennedy had upset him as much as it had Jennifer, only he didn't always wear his heart on his sleeve.

He liked Jennifer; she was the kind of woman he could go for. He could still remember her as a kid, but he was four years older than her and in those days he hadn't paid her much attention. They hadn't bumped into each other for years until he'd given a talk at Columbia three years ago and had spotted her in the audience and asked her for coffee. For a year, on and off, they'd met for dinner or lunch or drinks, and a friendship had developed. Nothing more to it than that, and it was exactly the way he wanted it because going through a bitter divorce was tearing his heart out and a new relationship was the last thing on his mind, but if he were honest, maybe in the long term he'd secretly hoped for more. But then the murder and attempted rape had messed up Jennifer's life.

He knew that she'd been totally devastated by her mother's death and her father's disappearance, and the frenzied assault she'd suffered. The night of the murder she'd come running to his parents' house and his father had heard the banging on the front door, and when he came down from his bed he'd found her unconscious on the veranda. His old man was dying of cancer even then, but he was a cop to his bones and sensed that something serious was up. He'd left Jennifer in the care of Mark's mother, grabbed his pistol and headed out across the lawns towards the March property. He'd found Jennifer's mother stabbed to death and young Bobby with gunshot wounds, but no one else in the house – whoever had committed the crime had fled.

Mark had heard about the crime the next day, but it was four more days before he was allowed to see Jennifer, and by then she didn't want to talk, not to anyone. Afterwards, she withdrew into herself, and it had stayed that way until she'd started to work at the Federal Defender Division. They'd resumed having dinner occasionally, and this time he'd tried to get closer physically, but it hadn't worked out in that department, though they'd remained good friends. Even allowing for the fact that it was bound to take her a long time to get over the trauma of the attempted rape, he guessed he just had to face it: either the timing was completely wrong or he obviously wasn't her type.

Mark heard the kettle boiling and he stood, leaving the unfinished sandwich on the coffee table.

Maybe it was his cop's mind, but he found himself still wondering about the Buick. He flicked off the lights in the living room, went to the window and peered out through the curtain. The Buick was still there. *Maybe it's a police stake-out?* Elmont was a respectable enough neighbourhood, but these days you couldn't be sure of anywhere.

He was about to let the curtain fall back into place when he saw a big black Pontiac pull up in front of his house. The driver's door opened and a man stepped out. In the wash of a street light Mark saw that he was maybe close to sixty, tall and tanned, very distinguished looking, with silver-grey hair.

And then two men got out of the Buick across the street. Well dressed, wearing suits, both looked in their early thirties. They walked over to join the silver-haired man from the Pontiac and all three came up the pathway. Mark frowned as he let the curtain fall. He wondered what the hell the men were doing at his house at a quarter after midnight. The doorbell rang. He'd left the porch light on and he crossed to the door and peered through the fish-eye security viewer. The three men were outside the door, the distinguished, silver-haired guy in the middle. They all looked respectable enough, but every cop made enemies in his work and he didn't intend taking any chances. He slid his Glock automatic from his hip holster as the doorbell rang again.

'Who is it?' he called out, holding the Glock at the ready and peering through the viewer again. The silver-haired man looked ballon faced through the lens.

'Mr Ryan? My name's Jack Kelso. I wonder if we might talk?'

Mark fingered his gun. 'Mr Kelso, it's past midnight, and I'm guessing it's a little late for you and your friends to want to share a Bible reading. So who in the hell are you, and what exactly do you want to talk about?'

'It's a little difficult talking to a door, Mr Ryan. May we come in?'

'I don't know you from Adam,' Mark answered. 'And you still haven't told me what you want.'

He peered through the lens, saw Silver-hair go for his inside pocket, and tensed. But Kelso didn't bring out a gun, just an ID, which he held up in front of the viewer. Mark whistled when he saw the ID, and lowered his gun.

'Mr Ryan. I'm with the CIA.'

Mark opened the door. The two younger guys wore neat two-piece suits and button-down shirts with ties, and he guessed they were CIA, like Kelso.

'I apologise for the lateness of the hour,' Kelso said. 'But there's something we need to talk about. And it's rather urgent.'

Kelso offered his ID again and Mark examined it. The blue Central Intelligence Agency logo was on one side of the badge, inset with the American eagle. On the other side was a photograph of Kelso that looked as if it had been taken a couple of years back when his hair was a little darker. He took a good shot – firm jaw, bright blue eyes, film-star looks. Kelso nodded to his companions. 'These two men are Agents Doug Grimes and Nick Fellows.'

The two men offered their CIA badges. Mark examined them and stepped back. 'I guess you had better come in.'

He closed the front door and led the way into the living room. Kelso had a limp, his left leg dragging slightly behind him. He saw the sandwich on the coffee table and said, 'I'm sorry if I disturbed your supper.'

'So am I. You want some coffee?'

Kelso shrugged, said politely, 'Coffee would be good. Thank you.'

'Take a seat.'

Mark made four mugs of Nescafé and brought them into the living room on a tray. Kelso sat in one of the easy chairs, the other two agents on the couch. Agent Grimes appeared to be the serious type; he was about thirty, with sleeked black hair and deep-set eyes. Agent Fellows looked as if he wasn't long out of college, baby faced, friendly looking, with soft hands and a boyish haircut. But Mark guessed he was able to handle himself. Both men had a look of quiet confidence that came with the comfort of a CIA badge in their pocket. Mark handed out the coffee and sat in the last free chair. 'So what's this about?'

'I'd like to talk to you about Jennifer March,' Kelso replied.

Mark frowned. 'Jennifer? Is it about the drugs bust at Kennedy?'

Kelso shook his head. 'No, it's not about any drugs bust.'

'Then what's it about?'

Kelso held the coffee on his lap, spooned in sugar and stirred. 'How long have you known Jennifer March, Mr Ryan?'

Mark half smiled. 'That's pretty personal.'

'I'd appreciate it if you'd just answer the question, please.'

'We grew up together in the same neighbourhood. I've known her since I was a teenager, going back fifteen years or more.'

'Would she consider you a close friend?'

'I think you could say that.'

'Does she trust you?'

'Sure.' Mark hesitated. 'Look, why all these questions?'

Kelso glanced at Grimes and Fellows, then back at Mark. 'I think you already know that her father's body has been found. If I'm not mistaken, you informed her of that fact. Am I correct?'

Mark frowned. 'Is *that* what this is about?'

'Yes, it is.'

Mark put down his cup. 'Sure, I told Jennifer. But I don't understand. What's that got to do with—'

Kelso put up a hand, set down his coffee untouched. 'Before we proceed any further with this conversation, Mr Ryan, I'd like to explain something. What we're going to talk about is *strictly* confidential. In fact, it's a highly secret and sensitive matter that pertains to national security. You break that secrecy and I'll bust your ass wide, and that's a solemn promise. Therefore, what I want from you is your word that you won't mention the conversation we are about to have, not to anyone. Do I have your word?'

Kelso's tone was faintly arrogant, and Mark took a dislike to the man. 'Look, what the hell's going on here?'

'I asked you a question, Ryan,' Kelso said firmly. 'And I apologise for my unseemly language. But I need to impress on you the gravity of the matter, and I'd like an honest answer. Do you agree to my request?'

Mark looked at Kelso, then at the other two agents. All three stared back at him. The CIA usually meant *serious business*. And these guys looked earnest, especially Kelso. Mark shrugged. 'OK. You've got my word. So what's all this about?'

Kelso cleared his throat. 'The CIA, and your country, needs your help.'

Mark almost laughed. 'Is this some kind of joke? Did Maguire in Homicide set me up for this?'

Kelso said grimly, 'This is no joke, Ryan. I can't even begin to convey how grave this is. Except that on a scale of one to ten, it would probably bust the scale. I emphasise, it's *really* serious.'

'Why *my* help?'

Kelso sat forward. 'Jennifer March intends to travel to Europe to identify her father's body.'

'So?'

'You know that her father vanished two years ago. And I take it, having known Jennifer for so long, you're aware of the other tragic circumstances of that time?'

Mark nodded. 'So?'

'At the time of his wife's murder and his own disappearance, Paul March was working on a highly secret assignment for the CIA.'

Mark frowned. 'Jennifer never said that.'

'Jennifer never knew.'

'The way I recall it, he was an investment banker.'

'That's true, but he was also working under cover for the CIA.'

'Let me get this straight. You're saying her father was a spy of some kind?'

Kelso shook his head. 'I think the less said, the better. All I *can* say is that he was involved in a covert international operation.

78

One that was both extremely important and highly dangerous. For reasons of security, I can't divulge what that operation was.'

'Are you implying that Jennifer's father didn't kill his wife?'

'To be perfectly honest, Ryan, I can't be one hundred per cent certain of that.'

Mark was confused. 'I don't follow.'

This time, Agent Grimes spoke up. 'You don't have to, Ryan. Just accept that lives may be in danger on account of Paul March's body turning up.'

'Whose lives? In danger from who?'

Grimes didn't reply. Mark looked at Kelso, who sighed. 'I can't give you those answers, Ryan. You'll just have to trust me when I say that what we're telling you is the honest truth. And I emphasise, this is a matter of grave importance.'

'So you keep saying, Kelso. But you're saying very little and asking me to trust you an awful lot.'

'You're right, I am. But if you care about Jennifer, then she'll need your help. And so will we.'

'What kind of help?'

'I want you to take some time off work. A week, maybe more if necessary. I want you to travel to Europe and follow Jennifer.'

'You mean tail her?'

'Exactly. It would be better if you could convince her to allow you to go with her as a companion, but if that isn't possible then we'd like you to tail her as inconspicuously as possible.'

'*Why?*'

'I'd like you to protect her. To be her guardian angel. You know Jennifer, and she trusts you. If she gets into trouble, you'll be there for her. You're a familiar face. And when people get in deep trouble, that's exactly what they like to see. A familiar face.'

'Get in trouble? Jennifer? What the hell for?'

'Because, Ryan, in all probability, someone is going to try to kill her.'

10

Mark sat there, shocked, letting the words sink in. *Someone is going to try to kill her.*

He stared at Kelso and asked the only two questions he could think of. 'Why? Who?'

Kelso shook his head. 'I can't tell you that. But believe me, Jennifer will be under dire threat. And that's a reality, not a speculation.'

Mark thought for a moment, then said, 'Who *exactly* are you, Kelso? What do you do for the CIA?'

'I'm an assistant director of special operations.'

'What kind of special operations?'

Kelso shook his head again. 'That's need-to-know, Ryan. And right now, you don't need to know.'

'You bet I do. Otherwise, you and your friends walk away right now.'

'Do you care about Jennifer?'

'You still haven't answered my questions.'

Kelso didn't flinch. '*Do* you care about her?'

Mark looked at Grimes and Fellows. They just sat there impassively, letting their boss do the talking. 'You're telling me nothing. This conversation is at an end. Goodnight, Mr Kelso.'

Kelso sighed and stood abruptly. 'Very well, as you wish.'

Mark thought: *He'll change his mind.*

Grimes and Fellows stood. Kelso said, 'As I mentioned, this conversation never happened. Please remember that.'

As Kelso and his men headed for the door, Mark knew he was wrong. Kelso was calling his bluff. He knew he cared about Jennifer, and that was the man's ace.

Mark said, 'We could continue if you told me a little more. You're telling me absolutely nothing except that Jennifer's life may be in danger. Tell me *something* concrete.'

Kelso looked back. 'I'm truly sorry, Ryan. But that's all I can honestly tell you. For the rest, you'd just have to trust me. Goodnight, and thank you for your time.'

He put his hand on the door, turned the handle.

'Wait a minute. Hold on.'

Kelso turned.

'This whole business, it's really *that* secret?'

'Yes, it is.'

Mark said, 'You know I care about her. But *how* you know, I can't figure out.'

Kelso didn't respond. He hesitated, then said, 'Will you help us? Will you help Jennifer?'

'On one condition. Just give me some clue, something that will make me feel like I'm not walking down a dark road. The way I see it, the CIA doesn't usually go out of its way to protect one of its citizens. Unless they're important people.'

Kelso glanced at Grimes and Fellows before he said, 'I'm compromising myself by even telling you this. But if it helps change your mind, then I will. Jennifer may be the key to helping us find a computer disk that vanished with her father. The disk contained information that is vitally important to a CIA investigation. That's why we've got to do our utmost to protect her.'

'Does Jennifer know about this disk?'

'I don't believe she does.'

'So how can she be the key to finding it?'

'That's speculation on my part,' Kelso answered. 'The disk vanished with her father. If she finds out what happened to him, how he ended up dead in a glacier in the Alps, it may offer a clue as to where we can locate the disk. But other people will also want it, and they're the ones who will almost certainly want to kill her.'

'Which still tells me nothing. What's on the disk?'

Kelso sighed and shrugged. 'I'm sorry, Ryan. My hands are tied.'

81

'Then where might it be?'

'We don't know. A young American climber named Chuck McCaul who found the body also located a rucksack near by. I'm hoping its contents may point to the disk's whereabouts, or there may be some clue on the body. But we'll just have to keep our fingers crossed and wait and see.'

'It sounds to me like you're using Jennifer to get what you're after.'

'You're entitled to your opinion, but I wouldn't entirely agree.' Kelso's eyes betrayed nothing, but there was a sudden, pleading look on his face that almost made Mark feel sorry for the man. 'Can you help us, Ryan? Even if only for Jennifer's sake?'

'I think you misunderstand my relationship with Jennifer. We're close friends, sure, but it doesn't extend any deeper. Besides, there's something else I don't understand. Why can't you use your own men to tail her? Why me?'

'I don't want Jennifer to get the slightest feeling that the CIA are watching her. And the people who may try to harm her, they'll certainly smell any CIA involvement a mile off. Which would jeopardise both Jennifer *and* my men. You, on the other hand, are just a cop. I don't mean that disparagingly. I mean you're a legitimate friend, maybe the closest one she's got, and someone who's concerned about her safety. But you're also a highly trained police officer whose talents I can use. You can stay close enough to protect her and observe her movements. At the same time I can have my men safely in the background, far enough away not to arouse suspicion but close enough to call on quickly, should you need their help.'

'You mean I could get hurt?'

A faint smile flickered on Kelso's face. 'We'll do our utmost to make sure you're not. Besides, I hear you're a good detective, and I'm confident you can handle yourself. Otherwise, I wouldn't have involved you.'

'Which still tells me nothing, and doesn't answer the question.'

Kelso cleared his throat. 'I have to be honest and say there could certainly be an element of risk for you.'

82

'Then it might help if I knew what I was up against.'

'Let's just say that the people you may be in danger from if you go are probably more ruthless than you'll ever have to deal with in your career. And that's truly all I can say on the matter.'

Mark hesitated. Kelso said, 'I'll ask the question one last time. Can you help me, Ryan?'

'I don't know. Maybe. But I've got cases I'm working on. I'm not sure if my captain—'

'Tell him you need leave. Tell him you're ill. Tell him anything you have to. If you've really got trouble getting time off, you tell me, and I'll see what background strings I can pull discreetly. But naturally you don't tell your captain *anything* about my request, about the CIA's involvement, or what you'll be doing. You don't tell your colleagues, either, not even your dog.'

'I don't have a dog.'

Kelso said knowingly, 'But your neighbour has, a Labrador named Douglas. And you don't even mention it to him. Not even to the cockroaches on the walls or the mice under the floorboards.'

'I've got mice?'

Kelso smiled faintly. 'I'm afraid so. And I truly hate to make threats, Ryan, and detest even more having to repeat them. But if you do talk to anyone about this, I'll personally see to it you're writing parking tickets in shitty side streets for the rest of your life. And that's if you're lucky.'

'You already made your point.'

Kelso looked directly at Mark. 'So?'

'I'll see what I can do.'

Kelso exhaled. 'That's not the affirmative answer I was expecting, Ryan.'

'I told you, I've got some important cases I'm working on. The station is understaffed. It's going to take me a few days to sort things out.'

'But you'll do it?'

'I'll do it because of Jennifer.'

Kelso sighed with relief. 'Thank you, Ryan. I deeply appreciate your help.'

'You're not lying to me about her being in that much danger?'

'I'm not lying, Ryan,' Kelso said resolutely. 'I can't impress that on you firmly enough.'

'Would I carry a firearm?'

'Of course.'

'You said it would be better if I could convince Jennifer to let me accompany her. Do you mean you want me to just ask her directly?'

Kelso nodded. 'But do it tactfully, and don't push the issue. I don't want you making her suspicious and I don't want you telling her the real reasons. Just bring up the subject casually. Tell her you think maybe she might need moral or emotional support when she goes to identify the body, and you'd like to offer to travel with her, as a friend. If she says no, you tail her anyway. Which shouldn't be a problem, since you've worked under cover before, right?'

'Sure.'

'Which means it shouldn't be too difficult for you to keep your face out of sight. The simplest disguise often can work wonders, as I'm sure you know.'

'What if Jennifer spots me? It's going to look pretty suspicious me turning up in Europe.'

'We'll cross that bridge if we come to it. But probably the best course of action would be to come clean and tell her you were worried about her. That you had some time off work and decided to take the trip and be with her at this difficult time. You tell her anything you have to, except the truth. Make her believe you're a caring and concerned friend who wants to help. But just make sure you can stay with her after that, if it happens.'

'You really think she'd believe me?'

'At that point it probably wouldn't matter. You'd be out in the open and free to watch and protect her. And let me make this clear: the only reason for you being there is to protect her.'

'It might be a lot simpler all round if you just explained to Jennifer that she may be in danger.'

Kelso shook his head. 'Not possible, Ryan. The point is, neither

Jennifer nor anybody else must get an inkling that the CIA is involved. If they did, we'd probably put Jennifer in worse jeopardy and ruin any hope we have of finding the disk.'

'So what exactly do you want me to do?'

Kelso reached inside his pocket, removed an envelope, handed it to Mark.

'What's this?'

'Airline tickets, in your name. They're open, business class.'

'You must have been pretty damned sure I'd agree?'

'No, just prepared in case you did,' Kelso said. 'My cell phone number's inside the envelope. Call me after you've talked to Jennifer. And do try to convince her to let you accompany her, because it would make things simpler all round. There are also some expenses, five thousand dollars in cash, to be precise. And a Visa credit card in your name. Just sign the back and don't worry about any amounts you charge. The card will be valid anywhere you choose to use it, and for any amount. But naturally, I'd appreciate receipts for any costs you incur, so we can keep Uncle Sam happy.'

Mark looked at the envelope. 'It seems you've got everything planned down to the last detail.'

'Have you ever been to Switzerland, Ryan?'

'In my dreams.'

'You'll love it.'

Switzerland, 5 p.m.

Chuck McCaul stood on the viewing promontory at the Furka pass and thought: *Awesome!*

The mountains looked terrific at this time of evening. Ahead of him, beyond the granite promontory wall, jagged lines of snow-capped crags filled the horizon, tinted by the dying light of the afternoon sun, the sky on fire with pink and purple colours. Down below, he saw the Audi strain up the steep winding road from the pass.

His own hired Renault was parked near by, and near the

promontory there was a souvenir store for the tourists who came up here in season, but its shutters were down and locked, the place deserted, and McCaul was alone. The Furka glacier was behind the store, a vast oasis of blue ice. Holes were burrowed deep into the glacier for the tourists, and you could venture inside for a few francs and have your photograph taken with a couple of idiots dressed as penguins. Which was pretty dumb really, McCaul considered, when the only place you saw penguins in Switzerland was in the fucking public zoo.

There was a terrible feeling of desolation, a bone-chilling coldness, but he enjoyed the feeling, taking deep breaths. Three kilometres back down the winding road stood the Furka Pass Hotel, a massive old granite building that looked like a barracks. It had been built in the last century when it was popular to build sanatorium hotels in places like this with lots of clean, dry air, but this time of year the hotel was deserted, with not a tourist bus or another car in sight, except the Audi.

It finally made it up the last tortuous, rocky bend and came to a halt beside the Renault. A man wearing a green padded wind-cheater stepped out, a Nikon camera slung over his shoulder, and he smiled as he came over, offering his hand. 'Mr McCaul? I'm Emil Hartz, a freelance reporter with the *Zurich Express*. A cold evening indeed. I'm sorry now we didn't meet somewhere varmer.'

Hartz spoke excellent English, but he pronounced his W's like V's. McCaul shrugged. 'Well, you said you wanted some shots near a crevasse.'

'So I did, and I thought this place might be perfect, but it is rather chilly.'

'You ought to come up here in midwinter,' McCaul suggested. 'It's cold enough to freeze the balls off a polar bear.'

The man grinned. He was tall, wore glasses and had thick black hair, which on closer scrutiny looked like a pretty lousy-fitting wig. McCaul said, 'So what exactly do you want to do?'

Hartz smiled. 'Seeing as the glacier is out of bounds, I had thought some shots of you there, out on the ice, would be just as good. The readers should not know the difference.'

86

He pointed over to where the glacier ended. A white fountain of frozen ice toppled over the edge of a truly frightening precipice. There was a sheer drop, down to the deep Furka valley, almost a thousand feet below.

'With respect, sir, it's pretty fucking dangerous out there. And I didn't bring any safety gear.'

Hartz smiled. 'Don't worry, I'll make sure you're not in any danger. But I'd like a dramatic shot for the readers, you know the sort of thing, I'm sure: "American climber Chuck McCaul, who discovered the body in a glacier." The shot will be perfect with the ice in the background.'

McCaul thought for a moment and shrugged again. 'OK. When you phoned me at the hotel you mentioned you'd pay a fee. How much had you got in mind?'

Hartz smiled and took out a notebook. 'That can be discussed later. So, tell me, did you notice anything unusual about this man you found?'

'He was dead.'

Hartz smiled thinly. 'I meant did you notice anything unusual about the corpse.'

'I didn't see. It was still in the ice.'

'Did the police find anything on the body? Papers, documents?'

'I really can't say. All I know is that his name was Paul March. I think they had to wait until the guy had thawed out so they could check his pockets and clothes. But I found a rucksack in the crevasse, right next to him.'

Hartz was definitely interested. 'Go on.'

'There was a document folder and a pistol inside.'

'Really?' Hartz frowned and scribbled away. 'What was in the folder?'

'A passport in the guy's name, Paul March.'

'That's all there was?'

'Some clothes, I think, but the cop in charge, Captain Caruso, can tell you more.'

'Did you notice anything else about the body?'

'No, I couldn't see it clearly through the ice.'

'Just for the record, Mr McCaul, what's your age?'

'Twenty-one.'

'Your home town?'

'New York.'

'And your address in America, so I can send you a copy of the article.'

McCaul told him. Hartz smiled and said, 'I've been to New York many times. Great city. You live there with your family?'

'Just my old man.'

'Is he a climber, too?'

'No, he's a private investigator.'

'Really? How interesting.' Hartz finished jotting, put away his notebook. 'Right, now let's get some pictures.'

McCaul followed him to the crevasse, near the edge of the precipice. Hartz started to check his Nikon for the light. The sun was fading fast, its pink light washing over the mountains, as if a million distant fires were merging on the horizon. McCaul didn't like standing so near the edge of the precipice. Not since his accident. To tell the truth, it had scared him shitless and left him just a little frightened of mountaineering. Fifteen feet out on the ice the frozen glacial water fell away, a sheer drop to the bottom of the pass. *Pretty dangerous, man.* You slipped over there and you were fucked, big time. He thought he had gone far enough. 'Is this OK?'

'Excellent. Just point towards the crevasse.' Hartz shot a couple of frames. 'Now step back, just a little, Mr McCaul. And do try to smile just a tiny bit, please. Not a vide grin, but try to look slightly amused.'

Slightly amused? How the fuck could you look slightly amused with the edge of a precipice and a thousand-foot drop only a few steps away? McCaul glanced down towards the Furka pass and said nervously, 'I think I'm fucking close enough, sir.'

'Fine, fine. Now, no pointing this time, just look at the camera. Keep it like that, don't move.'

McCaul remained still. It was the first time he'd have his photograph in a newspaper. He'd told his old man about it on the phone that morning and he was pretty fazed.

Hartz clicked a couple more shots, then came over and said, 'That's it. I think I have everything I need. Your information has been most helpful.'

'What about the fee you talked about?'

Before Hartz replied, he directed a long, thoughtful look towards the deserted valley, then looked back up and smiled. 'Oh, I'm afraid there won't be one.'

McCaul was puzzled. 'I . . . I don't understand.'

'I'm sure you don't, it's all rather complex. And you're a pretty dumb young man to agree to meet a complete stranger in a desolate place like this, wouldn't you say?'

McCaul noticed that Hartz no longer pronounced his W's like V's. Now his accent was kinda neutral. And he noticed something else, a sudden, chilling stare in Hartz's eyes. Something was clicking in McCaul's brain as he said nervously, 'You're . . . you're not a reporter, are you?'

'Most definitely not.'

McCaul turned ashen. 'Hey, what the fuck's going down here, man?'

Hartz's hand came up quickly. It took just the slightest push for McCaul to lose his balance. He fell back, slid over the ice towards the precipice, his cry echoing around the mountains as he went over the edge and dropped away like a stone, vainly grabbing for handfuls of air.

Hartz smiled. 'I'm afraid you are.'

11

It was almost noon when Jennifer pulled up outside Mark's house. She saw his car parked in the driveway, went up the path and rang the doorbell. When Mark opened the door his hair was wet and he had only a towel around his waist, as if he had just stepped out of the shower. He looked faintly embarrassed, but glad to see her.

'You're a little early. Come on in.' He led her into the living room and Jennifer saw that the place was in disarray. Mark smiled when he noticed her looking at the mess. 'I promise you it isn't always like this.'

'No?'

'Sometimes it's worse.'

Jennifer laughed and Mark said, 'You want some coffee?'

'I'm still wondering why you phoned last night and wanted to see me.'

'Why don't you make the coffee while I get dressed, and then we can talk?'

'Done.' She watched Mark as he left the room and heard him go up the stairs. He was of average height, had a good body, masculine and well proportioned, with muscular legs and broad shoulders. His looks stirred something in her that she refused to acknowledge. She knew very little about his marriage break-up because he wasn't really the type to talk about his personal life, but she knew he'd thrown himself into his work since the divorce. He had phoned that morning and asked her to call by, that he wanted to discuss something.

She was still wondering what it might be as she looked around the living room. There were lots of books on the shelves, mostly to do with police work, and a Sony hi-fi was tucked in a corner, along with stacks of tapes and CDs. Classical and opera mostly, and she remembered he'd once told her that his father had loved that kind of music.

The kitchen was clean enough but there were dishes stacked in the sink and a fern plant on the window looked as if it was dying of dehydration. She cleaned away some of the dishes, watered the plant, and had finished making the coffee when Mark came in wearing jeans, a white T-shirt and sneakers. 'Why don't we go into the living room, Jenny?'

She sat on the couch, and Mark in the easy chair opposite. She sipped her coffee and put down her cup. 'I'm glad I got the chance to see you before I left because I've got a favour to ask.'

He seemed surprised. 'Really?'

'While I'm gone I'd like to leave your number with the Cauldwell in case there's any problem with Bobby. I'll have my cell phone with me so you can call me in Europe at any time, if you need.'

She saw Mark go noticeably red. He hesitated a moment. 'Sure . . .'

'You're certain it's not a problem?'

'No . . . I could handle it.'

'You still haven't told me why you called.'

'Did you make your travel arrangements?'

'I fly to Zurich tomorrow, from Newark. I've rented a car and I'm going to drive down to Varzo. Why?'

'That's what I wanted to see you about, Jenny. I've been think-ing, how would you like some company?'

'You mean you'd want to come to Europe with me?'

'Sure.'

'But why on earth would you do that?'

Mark shrugged. 'Identifying your father's body is going to be traumatic, so I thought maybe you might need a shoulder to lean on and some emotional support. I figured that I could arrange some time off and book a ticket this afternoon. What do you say?'

Jennifer sat back, surprised. 'That's very kind of you, and I really appreciate the offer. But I think I'd appreciate it even more if you were there for Bobby while I'm away. Can you understand that, Mark? Besides, I really don't want to drag you all the way to Europe.'

'I could have someone fill in for me if Bobby needs help.'

'Who?'

Mark shrugged. 'Friends, colleagues. It wouldn't be a problem.'

'But it might be a problem for Bobby. He's not happy around people he doesn't know.'

'Think about it, Jennifer,' Mark persisted. He always used her full name when he wanted to emphasise something. 'You're going to be in a distant country and it's not going to be an easy time. The last thing you need is to be alone.'

She studied his face. 'Why do I get the sudden feeling that you're afraid for me?'

'Afraid?' Mark shook his head and almost laughed, but something in his tone made Jennifer suspect that he was uneasy. 'Not afraid, just concerned. I happen to think you could do with a friend by your side. I've seen it a lot on the job. Before you even step into the morgue, you're going to be distressed and you're going to be sensitive. All the memories you have of your father are going to come flooding back. It may be difficult to cope with.'

'Maybe you're right, but I'll be fine on my own, believe me.'

'You're sure you don't want me to go along?'

'I just think it's something I need to do alone.'

Mark sighed. 'I guess I really can't make you reconsider.'

Jennifer studied him. Mark toyed with his coffee spoon, but when he met her gaze he quickly looked away. She said, 'Is there something else on your mind?'

'Nothing's on my mind apart from wanting to help you.'

'You're sure?'

'Sure. And I meant it about going with you. Just say the word, Jenny, and I'll organise everything. It won't be any trouble.'

Jennifer declined. 'It's too much to ask. And thanks for offering, but I really want to do this myself.' She stood. 'And now I'd better be going. I've still got to pick up my tickets and pack.'

Mark looked disappointed as he led her to the door. 'How long are you going to be away?'

'I'm not sure. Three or four days, but I left my ticket open. I'll probably have to make arrangements to have my father's body flown home.'

'What time does your flight leave tomorrow?'

'Nine-fifteen p.m. I get into Zurich before noon the next day. You could come with me to the airport if you like.'

Mark blushed. 'I just remembered, I've got something on. Can I ask you a question, Jenny?'

'What?'

'Have you any idea what your father might have been doing in that part of Switzerland? If he had business dealings to take care of there, or maybe something private to attend to?'

'No, I don't. Why?'

'No reason. I've just been thinking about it a lot.' Mark shook his head and spoke as delicately as he could. 'But there has to be a reason why he was there. It all just seems so weird, his body ending up in a glacier, of all places.'

'Nobody's more confused by it than me. You ought to know that, Mark. You're *sure* everything's OK?'

'Positive.' He kissed her on the cheek. 'Good luck.'

'Thanks again for the offer. The Cauldwell will be in touch if there's any problem.'

Jennifer went down the path. When she climbed into her car Mark was standing in the porch. He waved to her but still had a troubled look on his face. As she drove away, Jennifer glanced back at him with the uneasy feeling that he was keeping something from her, but she couldn't imagine what.

It was after lunch when she drove to Long Beach. Instead of heading back to her apartment, she decided to drive to Cove End. It had been three months since she had last checked on the house and she was due a visit.

She parked in the side driveway but had no desire to enter the house – she always found that too upsetting – so she strolled round the side, past the kitchen, and walked along the garden path towards the jetty. When she came to the boathouse she looked back at the house. The lawns needed a trim, and a stretch of guttering had come loose, but apart from that the property was in pretty good shape. Now that she knew that her father wasn't coming back, she realised she had to make a decision soon about whether to sell the house. *There are too many ghosts here,* she thought.

The sea was calm. She stepped over to the boathouse and rattled the lock, making sure the door was securely fastened. The window was smudged with dirt and spider's webs, but when she peered inside she saw her father's blue-and-cream-painted motorboat languishing there, along with a couple of rusting oil drums and shelves of tools and spare parts. She felt a stab of pain as she turned away and went to sit on the wooden jetty. *See that star, Jennifer? That's Sirius. And that one over there – that's Capella.* For some reason she remembered the hollow sound of her father's footsteps on the boardwalk, and she closed her eyes and bit her lip. She had to accept the certainty that her father was never coming back. *Never.* There was such a finality to it all. But God, she still missed him.

She realised too that moving on with her life meant telling Bobby about their father's death and making him bring it all out in the open. Difficult as that was, she knew she had to do it, but it could wait until after she identified her father's body. She opened her eyes and shivered. As she stood up from the jetty she finally made up her mind, there and then. Just as soon as she returned from Europe, she'd put Cove End on the market and finally try to move on with her life.

Lou Garuda was pretty tanked up after five Jamesons and three Buds, and looked as if maybe he needed an ambulance to take him home, and not a cab.

Garuda was of medium height, part Hispanic, darkly handsome, his sleek brown hair worn halfway down his back like that of a rock star. He was a cop with a reputation as a ladies' man, the joke among his colleagues at the Long Beach Police Department being that Garuda had a Velcro fly because he had to have sex at least half a dozen times a day.

94

The beachside tavern had a happy hour between five and seven, all drinks half price, which was enough in itself to keep Garuda blissful, but what put the cherry on the cake were the three strippers dancing on the bar to a medley of rock numbers. A dusky Puerto Rican beauty and two blonde girls were strutting their velvet-smooth skins for the early evening drinkers, mostly young and middle-aged guys who wanted more than just a cheap beer, and were prepared to slip a couple of dollars into the girls' garter belts for the privilege.

Right now, Garuda was pretty much flying after eight drinks, and the Puerto Rican girl was dancing right above him, smiling down every now and then, jiggling her ass and big brown titties, trying to catch his eye and get him to part with his bucks. There were little bowls on the edge of the bar with nuts and munchie stuff, and Garuda grabbed another handful of free eats and popped some into his mouth.

At thirty-eight, he'd been hitting the liquor hard for the last couple of years, which partly explained why he was no longer a detective but back behind a desk as a community officer with the Long Beach Police Department, pushing papers, which bored him out of his tree. He didn't see Ryan come up behind him, but he felt the gentle pat on the back. 'Hello, Lou. It's been a while. How's it hanging?'

He turned, saw Ryan standing there, a pleasant smile on his face. They knew each other from way back, when Garuda had served with the NYPD and they'd been patrol partners for a year. They weren't exactly close friends, more like acquaintances, but Ryan was a good guy, and he'd been a diligent and reliable partner, the kind you could count on. 'No longer than usual,' Garuda grinned. 'At least ten inches when the mood's right. So, you found the joint.'

'Sure, I found it.' Ryan leaned over, picked up Garuda's glass and sniffed. 'I'll take a guess and say Jameson?'

'There's a guy knows his liquor.'

'Only because it killed my old man, and cancer of the liver ain't a nice way to go.' Ryan put the glass down. 'You want to take it easy, Lou. You worry me.'

'Don't hit me with the stern lectures crap, my man. I got anti-bodies, I'm immune.' Garuda looked around the bar. The girls were dancing to the Stones' 'Satisfaction', the music a little too loud, and the Puerto Rican girl had moved her big brown eyes on to Ryan, hoping for a score, but Garuda knew the guy wasn't a sucker.

'You want a booth or a table? Or you want to stay here and watch the girls show us the beaver for a few bucks? I'm easy, whichever.'

Ryan laughed. 'The music's too loud. Let's take a booth.'

Ryan led the way to an empty booth at the back. Garuda said, 'How about a beer?'

'Not for me, I'm driving.'

'So am I, but what the fuck.'

'Lou, I catch you climbing into a car like that I'll arrest you myself.'

'Only kidding. I've had my bellyful. After this I'm taking a cab.'

'Good man.'

'Your father used to say that.'

'Say what?'

'*Good man.* Only he sounded more Irish. A fucking accent I could hardly understand.'

'From County Cork.'

'Wherever. I miss the guy. Best and biggest man I ever saw in an assistant commissioner's uniform.' Garuda smiled. 'Six foot six, which makes me wonder, how come his only son's a runt?'

Ryan didn't take offence, just smiled back. 'I'm average height, so don't go hurting my feelings.'

'You seeing any women since that divorce of yours?'

'Not really.'

'No one you like?'

'Sure.'

'Then why the frig hasn't it worked out?'

Ryan shrugged. 'Lots of reasons.'

'You reckon?'

'For sure. But what's a guy supposed to do?'

'Make yourself indispensable. Women like that in a guy. And try to listen. That always wins them over. In fact, do lots of listening. Most guys think their most important organ is the one between their legs, but it ain't, it's their ear. All good lovers are good listeners. That's a sure fact.'

'Lou, I'll try and remember that sterling advice.'

The waitress came and Ryan ordered a Coke. Lou told the girl he'd have a double Jameson for the road. Ryan said to her firmly, 'Make his a single,' and looked back at Garuda before he could object. 'The March case. Two years ago. You remember it?'

'I remember all my cases, drunk or sober. And what's with the single?'

'You'll thank me in the morning.'

Garuda rubbed his eyes, gave a drunken sigh, feeling pretty steamed already. 'Maybe you're right. You're talking about Jennifer March who lived across your street, the one whose father vanished. Her mother was murdered and her kid brother ended up in a chair. That's the one you wanted to see me about?'

'That's the one.'

'What do you want to know?'

'Everything you can remember. Especially the important stuff.'

'Hey, I thought you already sniffed that case inside out. Far as I recall, you never stopped asking questions about it at the time. Drove my partners up the frigging wall.'

'Sure, because I knew Jennifer, and the murder happened right across the street from my folks' place. But it wasn't my case, Lou, and those partners of yours in Homicide didn't like the idea of an outsider from NYPD sticking his nose in. They kept things close to their chest, so I'm pretty sure I didn't hear everything. But you worked the case.'

'For a couple of months, until I got my ass reassigned to desk duty.'

'No matter, I'd like to hear it again from the horse's mouth. Unless you've got a problem with that?'

'No, I ain't got a problem. The case is as cold as a hooker's kiss. It's history, man.'

The waitress came back with their drinks. Garuda took a mouthful of whiskey and looked over at Ryan, who was sipping his Coke. 'OK, from the top. Detectives arrived at the scene about fifteen minutes after the local cops got there, right after the call from your old man. It must have been about one a.m. We found the wife's body in the main bedroom, her and the teenage son. She'd been stabbed twice in the chest and once in the throat. The boy had been shot through the back, only the angle the bullet travelled, it came out the back of his skull as well as shattering part of his spine. His mother was dead, but by some miracle the kid was still breathing. The daughter was over in your pop's place, traumatised as hell.'

'That I already know. Go on.'

'When we checked the house, there was no sign of a break-in. Whoever did the dirty deed, maybe they already had a key to the home, or else they were damned good, real professional. The girl said she'd noticed an upstairs window open, but we found no prints or evidence of a forced entry. 'Course, it could have been left open deliberately. Apart from that, the girl was pretty certain it was a guy who attacked her. And you know we never found her old man. He just vanished off the face of the earth.'

'Your partners figured it might be the father who set it up?'

'Maybe.'

'Why maybe?'

Garuda picked up a handful of nuts from the table bowl, palmed them into his mouth. 'I thought you knew the facts as well as I do? The guy travelled to Switzerland on a company business trip, flying American Airlines. We checked with the airline, and Paul March was checked aboard the flight, sure, but after the plane landed in Zurich, he disappeared. We had the fucking Swiss gendarmes buzzing around, completely blue-assed, checking every hotel in Zurich. They got this thing in Europe where you got to register in hotels, show your passport and stuff, fill in a visitor's card. It's mandatory, every guest's got to do it. The Swiss cops checked every damned one of those cards and couldn't find March. We were left with a likely "what if". What if March arranged to have his family murdered and then did a runner?'

'What about motive?'

Garuda shrugged and swallowed some more whiskey. 'Now there you got me. That was our big problem. There wasn't any money involved, or a skirt he'd kept hidden on the side, at least as far as we could tell. The insurance policy on March's wife wasn't a bundle. And whatever there was, it went to the kids. Besides, the guy was supposed to have been a doting father and loved his wife, all that crap.'

'So you're saying no one came up with a motive?'

'Right. The only thing we figured was, maybe his wife or kids knew something about him, like maybe a dark secret. Something that might have jeopardised or compromised him in some way. Maybe he meant to change his identity and start a new life some-place else, without his family, but wanted to cover up something important before he left. Either way, it could have meant March wanting to have his wife and kids bumped off. The only trouble was, we never found a motive after two months of working the case. That doesn't mean he hadn't got one, only that we couldn't find it. But there were damned few leads, and the few we had led absolutely nowhere.'

'There were no other suspects apart from March?'

Garuda shook his head. 'Not one that we could find. No strangers seen in the vicinity before the murder, or right after it happened. No prints around the house, except those of the family. And there's another important factor. There was a pretty bad storm the night of the murder. The airport closed down for four hours, and all flights in and out of New York were delayed. March would even have had time to check in, drive back to his house and do the business, then drive back to the airport. It wasn't outside the bounds of possibility.'

'You really think March would have attempted to rape and kill his own daughter?'

'Hey, you're a cop, Mark. You know as well as I do, there's a lot of weird fucks out there, and it's a sick fucking world. Husbands kill their wives and kids, and moms murder their children for all kinds of warped reasons. And not just because of insanity. They do it for money, an insurance pay-out maybe. They do it out of jealousy, or to mask another crime, or just to cover their tracks before they vanish and start a new life. But you lived across the street from the guy. You tell me.'

Ryan shrugged. 'I hardly knew him. When I was growing up he seemed to be away a lot. He'd say hello once in a while, and seemed a pretty normal family man, but that was about it.'

'OK, look at it this way. The attempted rape would have helped disguise the crime, if you follow what I mean. Most people wouldn't be inclined to think that a father would sexually assault his own daughter in the course of a crime. The suspicion would fall on some psycho who broke into the house, or a burglar with a history of sexual assault at the scene. My own gut feeling was that maybe he paid someone to kill his family. Maybe he really meant to go to Zurich before the event, then come back and play the innocent. But the airport delay fucked up his schedule, he got scared, and he vanished in Europe and stayed hidden, with a new identity.'

'That's a lot of speculation.'

'And I'm telling you, that's all we had, speculation. Mainly because there was something pretty weird about March. What I said about a dark secret in his past that maybe he wanted to cover up. We didn't just pluck that out of thin air.'

Ryan frowned. 'What do you mean?'

'You never heard when you were sniffing around the case?'

'Heard what?'

'For one, March had no past. Certainly none that we could find. No family background, no brothers or sisters, no relatives we could locate. We tried the Feds, the missing persons bureaus, Interpol, you name it. No one had anything on him. He was a mystery man who appeared out of nowhere, and then just disappeared. When someone goes AWOL, you know as well as I do we'll usually do three things. We check his past, we check his friends and enemies, and we check his bank accounts. Now here's the weird thing. March had no close friends, or even enemies, at least as far as we could discover. He had money in a couple of accounts we found, sure, but nothing majorly significant, and none of it had been withdrawn. And get this, his past only went back to about a year before he met his wife. An address in some small hick town in Arizona that turned out to have been a room in a cheap motel. That was where the trail started and the mystery of Paul March began. Like he was a fucking alien who just arrived from outer space. Jennifer claimed that when she was a kid she'd once found a photograph of a man wearing a prison uniform who resembled her father. She found the snapshot in the attic and the name on the photograph said Joseph Delgado. But we checked into the name and searched the prisoner database of every US prison. None of the names we turned up had any connection to Paul March.'

Ryan frowned, shook his head. 'I never knew all that.'

'Believe me, there were a lot of weird things about that guy that didn't make sense. Like I said, no family, no relatives, no past.'

'What about his employer?'

'Prime International Securities is a small Manhattan investment bank, very discreet and ultra-respectable. March had been employed by them for sixteen years, and he was made a vice-president a year before he disappeared. But all that Prime really had on him was his employee history, which told us nothing we didn't know already. We did some snooping around his office and questioned his colleagues. But there wasn't a shred of evidence that he had ever committed any financial irregularities or tried to embezzle from the company or been anything other than an upstanding employee. There was absolutely nothing we could find that told us any more about the man, or why he vanished. And most of the people who worked with him knew pretty much nothing about the guy, except that he was ambitious, a workaholic who kept to himself.' Garuda sat back. 'And that's about all I can tell you.'

He took a long drink while Mark stared down at his own glass.

Finally he said, 'I need to ask another favour. Is that pal of yours still with the CIA?'

Garuda nodded. 'He was more a buddy of my old man's, but sure, I think he's still at Langley. Why?'

'You still keep in touch?'

'Now and then, but it's been a few years.'

'I need to get the rundown on someone. His name's Jack Kelso. But I need it to be discreet. Very discreet. Can you see what you can do for me?'

'Who is he?'

'Some kind of assistant director of special operations, whatever that is. I don't know what section or department.'

'How soon do you need to know about this guy?'

'Like yesterday.'

Garuda shrugged. 'OK, I'll make a call when I get home and see what I can come up with.'

Ryan smiled. 'You sure you'll be sober enough?'

'Listen, I've been a lot worse and still found my way to the can.'

'Thanks, Lou.' Ryan finished his drink. 'You want a ride home?'

Garuda shook his head. 'You mind me asking why you wanted to talk about the March case?'

'One of your old buddies in the detective unit told me they got word that his body had been found.'

'Whose?'

'Paul March's.'

Garuda put down his glass, stunned. '*Where?*'

'In Europe. The Swiss–Italian Alps. He's been dead a long time. Frozen into a glacier.'

'You mean like an *ice* glacier, on a fucking mountain?'

Mark nodded.

'You're not shitting me, man?'

'No, Lou, I'm not.'

Garuda gave a low whistle. '*Jeez,* I guess now I heard it all.'

12

It was just after eleven that evening when Mark arrived home. Ten minutes later he was packing his suitcase for the trip when he heard the doorbell ring. He went downstairs, looked through the peep-hole and opened the door. Kelso was standing alone in the porch, carrying a briefcase. 'Good evening, Ryan. Mind if I come in?'

'Why not, you're almost one of the family.'

Kelso didn't react to the wisecrack. Mark let him in and closed the door.

'I'm sorry I couldn't meet sooner, but it's been a hectic day,' Kelso said.

'Like I told you on the phone, I tried convincing Jennifer but it didn't work.'

'A pity, it would have made things a lot simpler. However, I've taken the liberty of confirming your seat on the American Airlines flight to Zurich tomorrow evening. You'll be picked up from here at fifteen hundred hours by Agents Grimes and Fellows and taken to JFK. The three of you will leave on the same flight, over three hours before Jennifer's departure out of Newark on Swiss Airlines. That means you'll get into Zurich airport well ahead of her, so it should give you enough time to get yourself organised.'

'What happens after I get to Zurich?'

'Jennifer's travel agent booked her a car hire at the airport. Her intention seems to be to drive over the border to Varzo and identify her father's body. Naturally, there'll also be a hired vehicle reserved in your own name, but at the Avis desk.'

'She told me she didn't know how long exactly she'd be away. That she left her airline ticket open.'

'And her car hire, so we'll just have to play the cards as they fall.' Kelso patted his briefcase. 'And now, if you don't mind, there are some important items I need to go over with you.'

Mark led the way to the coffee table and Kelso flicked open the briefcase. Nestled in the soft grey foam inside was a mobile phone, a charging unit and a couple of spare batteries. There was a Sony transceiver, and what appeared to be some kind of small hand-held electronic device the size of a TV remote control, but with a tiny retractable aerial. Mark also noticed a pair of powerful miniature Zeiss binoculars, and several road maps in a plastic pouch.

'You'll probably be familiar with most of this surveillance equipment,' Kelso said. 'And by the way, here's a photograph of Jennifer's actual hire vehicle. Take note of the licence plate. I don't want you following the wrong one.'

Kelso handed Mark a snapshot of a white Toyota four-wheel-drive, its Swiss registration plate clearly visible. 'How come you know that this is the actual vehicle she'll be driving?'

Kelso picked up the hand-held device with the tiny aerial. 'It's better not to ask. But there'll be a bug planted in the jeep, a simple electronic transmitter, and this is the receiver. It gives a magnetic heading that will help you keep track of the Toyota. Should you lose it at any point just follow the direction of the pointer. And if you're following Jennifer in darkness, remember that the Zeiss binoculars have a night-vision attachment.'

'It seems that once again you've thought of everything.'

'I try to.' Kelso picked up the map pouch. 'Road maps of Switzerland and northern Italy. The most likely routes Jennifer will take to Varzo have been marked, so study them thoroughly, seeing as you'll be on unfamiliar terrain. There's also a map of Zurich's Kloten airport.' Kelso unfolded the airport map. 'You'll notice that a slip road next to a gas station has been highlighted. It's about a quarter of a mile from the Avis pick-up area, and Jennifer has to pass that point on her way out. It's the only exit, so I suggest that once you've organised yourself at the airport, you proceed there and wait.'

Kelso placed the Sony transceiver in his palm. 'One of my

men will call you up on this and give you advance notice when Jennifer's about to drive out of the airport. You'll wait until she's driven past, then follow her Toyota at a safe distance. Questions?'

'What happens if the equipment goes bust or I lose her?'

'The equipment is reliable, Ryan, so that shouldn't happen. But if it does, or you lose Jennifer, then call me or my men immediately. My number's pre-programmed into the first memory location in the cell phone, so all you've got to do is hit the button. I'll have my guys a safe and discreet distance behind you in the event that you need help.' Kelso raised an eyebrow. 'Have you got all that?'

'I think so.'

Kelso was irritated. 'Either you have or you haven't. If there's anything you want me to go over again, I'd be happy to. But I don't want "think so's", and above all I don't want mistakes. Not when Jennifer's life may be at stake.'

There was a hard, aggressive edge to Kelso's voice, but Mark let it pass. 'I've got it.'

Kelso replaced everything in the briefcase. 'I'd strongly advise that you use only the cell phone I've provided and not to bring your own phone with you on the trip. It might get in the way of things, and besides, you've got more than enough communications equipment without adding to the list.'

'If you say so.'

'Something else you should know. I don't anticipate Jennifer being in any real danger until after she identifies her father's body.'

'Why do you say that?'

'Let's just call it instinct,' Kelso replied enigmatically, and snapped shut the briefcase. 'So I'd caution you to be especially careful from then on.'

'You said I'd have a weapon.'

'An envelope in the name of Charles Vincent Jones will be left for you at the information desk at Zurich airport,' Kelso explained. 'Inside, you'll find a luggage chit and a key. Take the chit to the left-luggage desk where you'll be given a locked holdall in return. Inside, you'll find a Glock automatic and three clips of ammunition.'

'You really think I'll need the gun?'

'I told you, this isn't some game we're playing, Ryan. Any questions?'

'Lots, but I know you're not going to answer them. But maybe you can answer one. What happens if I have to use the Glock and get arrested?'

'I'm hoping either won't be the case. But trust me, the CIA is not going to leave you high and dry. It's not in our interests.'

'You wouldn't care to give me that in writing?'

Kelso saw something humorous in the request and offered a thin smile. 'Nothing in writing, Ryan.'

'What about back-up?'

'Grimes and Fellows will accompany you on the flight, and will be in your vicinity every minute of the day or night. After you arrive in Zurich, you won't see either of them unless you need to, in which case you call them up on the radio. They're good men, trustworthy and reliable in the extreme. Me, I'll be a phone call away, either by using the cell phone or by getting in touch with Grimes or Fellows. If things get difficult, I'll be there within minutes rather than hours.'

'How?'

Kelso placed the briefcase on the coffee table. 'Let's just say I'll be close behind and leave it at that. And don't worry about carrying the case through Customs. No one's going to bother you.'

'I'll have to take your word.'

'I presume you've packed and got yourself organised?'

'Just about.'

'Have you any more questions?'

'None that I can think of right now.'

'Then I imagine the next time we'll meet will be in Europe. Again, I want you to know how grateful I am for your help.'

'I'm only doing this for Jennifer,' Mark answered. 'But you know what the funny thing is? I still don't know exactly what I'm letting myself in for, and that bothers me, big time.'

Kelso didn't answer, simply offered his hand. 'Goodnight, Ryan. Get some rest. I've a feeling you're going to need it. And have a pleasant flight tomorrow.'

13

Mark was drifting off to sleep when the phone rang. He flicked on the bedside lamp, picked up the receiver and heard Lou Garuda's voice. 'Mark? You awake?'

'I am now. What is it, Lou?'

'It's about that guy, Kelso. I checked him out like you asked. Made a call tonight to that pal of my old man's down in Virginia. He's retired from the CIA, it turns out, but we chewed the cud for a time, then I dropped in a casual mention about this guy from the Agency I'd heard about in passing, name of Kelso.'

'Tell me.'

'My man's been out to pasture a couple of years but he'd heard of Kelso in the past. It seems he's one of their senior honchos, and definitely not the type to fuck around with, unless you want your balls chewed for grapes.'

'What else?'

'The way my friend told it, Kelso's a highly respected guy. Works only the big cases, stuff of national importance, that kind of shit.'

'Did you try to find out which section Kelso belongs to?'

'That's when the shutters came down, and I didn't press it in case it sounded like I was getting too interested. All my friend could tell me was that Kelso was transferred to something called special projects some years back. He didn't tell me what special projects meant.' Garuda gave a tinny laugh. 'Hey, I guess it could mean anything. Like maybe Kelso even kills people and funny CIA stuff like that.'

'Yeah, right. Anything else?'

'What more do you want? The name of the guy who sold him life insurance? That's all I've got.'

'Thanks, Lou. Listen, I need to ask another favour.'

'Ask away.'

'Jennifer March's kid brother, Bobby, he's in the Cauldwell home. I need someone to call by in the next couple of days and keep an eye on him for me, make sure he's OK, check whether he needs anything. Could you do that?'

'Sure. You mind me asking why?'

'I promised Jennifer I'd keep an eye on him while she's out of town, but it turns out I'm going to be away.'

'Where?'

'I can't say.'

'How do I get in touch?'

'You can't. But I'll call you.' Mark decided not to giver Garuda his cell phone number in case his calls were monitored.

There was a silence, then Garuda said quietly, 'Mark?'

'What?'

'I don't know what the fuck you're up to, but take some advice. Whatever it is you're doing, especially if it concerns the CIA, you keep one eye firmly on your ass, old buddy, OK? Those guys are fucking dangerous. They're a law unto themselves, can do pretty much anything they want.'

'Sure.'

'I mean it, Mark. There's nothing those guys from Langley can't do. Tap your phone, check your bank statements, even listen through your fucking walls if they want to. Shit, I mean, who knows half the stuff that goes on in Langley? My old man's buddy once told me about some of the dirty deeds they get up to, and it would curl your fucking hair. So you watch yourself, you hear?'

'I'll try and remember that.'

'Sweet dreams, amigo.'

Lou Garuda and Angelina were lying in bed, naked. Angelina was a pretty, dusky young woman ten years younger than the cop, and she had a liking for older men. She was half American, half Colombian, and they had met a few months earlier. Usually for Angelina the sex was sensational, but tonight Garuda was having a problem.

'This isn't like you, baby. What's the matter?' she asked softly. 'You want me to play with you some more, get you hard?'

His mind was far away. 'No. I've already got a boner.'

'I don't see it,' she teased.

'It's in my mind, Angelina. I've got a boner for a case. Something pretty weird that's going down.'

'Want to tell me about it?'

'Two years ago I bust my balls on a case that went nowhere. A guy vanishes into thin air. The same night an intruder breaks into his house, his wife is murdered, his teenage son's badly wounded, and someone tries to rape and kill his adult daughter. There's no motive for the murder and the guy who vanishes is never seen again. Now I hear his body turns up frozen into a glacier in the Alps. I checked the Interpol report and by the sound of it he's been dead a long time.'

'That *is* weird.'

'You said it, baby.' Garuda lit a cigarette, took an angry drag.

'Who was the guy?'

'He worked for a firm called Prime International Securities. It's a small investment bank in Manhattan, a pretty respectable outfit.'

'What did the guy do?'

'He was one of their vice-presidents. I'm tempted to go see his daughter, the chick the intruder tried to rape, and talk to her off the record, but I'm guessing she won't want to talk unless it's official. My instincts tell me maybe it's worth following up.'

'Whatever you say.' Angelina gripped him and started to stroke. 'But meantime, sweetie, how about you put out that cigarette and set *me* alight . . . ?'

PART TWO

14

Zurich, Switzerland

Jennifer approached a clerk behind the car-hire desk at Zurich's Kloten airport.

The man looked up and smiled. '*Guten Tag. Kann ich ihnen helfen?*'

'*Guten Tag.* I have a reservation.'

'Of course. Your name?'

'Jennifer March.'

The clerk checked through some papers and smiled. 'Do you intend staying long in Switzerland, Frau March? It's just you didn't specify how long you needed the vehicle.'

'I'm not sure yet. Three or four days, perhaps longer. I'm travelling on to Italy.'

'But of course, as you wish. I'm afraid we're rather short of cars today, but I've specially arranged a four-wheel-drive at the same rate. It's not one of our usual vehicles, but I think you'll find that it's excellent transport. Will that be suitable?'

'I guess so. I need to get to Varzo, just over the Italian border, and also the Wasenhorn mountain. How long will it take to get there?' Jennifer had already made up her mind that she wanted to see where her father's body had been found.

The clerk produced a map and showed her the route. 'It's not very far. Switzerland is a relatively small country. It shouldn't take more than three or four hours from the airport. You may keep the map.'

The man filled in the documents, accepted her credit card, and had her sign for the Toyota. When he had finished explaining all the details he handed her a set of keys. 'Enjoy your stay in Switzerland, Frau March. *Guten Tag.*'

As Jennifer walked away she didn't see the clerk observe her leave, then pick up the telephone.

Mark had landed in Zurich just before 8 a.m. He'd managed to sleep only a couple of hours on the plane and he felt exhausted after the eight-hour transatlantic flight. Once he'd reclaimed his luggage, he went through Customs, but no one stopped him and he eventually found the information desk on the arrivals floor.

He'd seen Fellows and Grimes on the flight but neither man had approached him, and once the flight had landed both of them had quickly disappeared. The envelope in the name of Charles Vincent Jones was waiting for him at the information desk. The ticket and the key were inside and he went over to the left-luggage desk. When he handed in the ticket he was given a small canvas holdall with a sturdy metal lock.

He found the men's restroom and locked himself in one of the cubicles. Inside the holdall he found a Glock 9mm automatic and three ammo clips, just as Kelso had promised. When he came out of the restroom he checked the arrivals board and saw that it was only 8.45. Jennifer's flight wasn't due to arrive until 10.55, and by the time she cleared Customs and finished her business at the car-hire desk it was going to be early noon. He had packed several changes of clothes to help disguise himself, but he figured he needed a hat.

He walked into one of the airport tourist stores and tried on an olive-green Swiss Loden hat. It looked faintly absurd when he checked in a mirror, but the slouched rim partly covered his face. He had a knee-length reversible raincoat he had bought in New York, and when he tried it on with the hat he couldn't help but smile. If Jennifer could have seen him now she'd laugh. He went up to the cash desk. 'How much for the hat?'

'*Wieviel? Ein hundert fünfzig Franc.* One hundred and fifty francs.'

Mark did a quick calculation. 'Over a hundred dollars for a hat?' he said.

The prissy shopkeeper shrugged. 'This *is* Switzerland, *mein Herr*. The garment is excellent quality.'

Mark thought: *What the hell, it's Uncle Sam's money.* He handed over the credit card. 'I'll take it.'

Two minutes later he walked into the terminal wearing the hat and raincoat and caught a glimpse of himself in a shop window. He felt kind of ridiculous but he looked like a different man. He checked his watch: 9.15 a.m. He had plenty of time to buy himself breakfast before he found the Avis desk.

A black Opel Omega was booked in his name and he handed over the credit card and filled in the forms, then found the pick-up point. The Opel was a rugged-looking sedan with dark-tinted windows, and he stashed his luggage in the back. It was raining as he drove out of the terminal, taking the main avenue that led towards the Zurich ring road. He had the map on the seat and minutes later he saw the slip road just beyond the gas station and pulled in. He had been to Europe twice before, on vacation. His first experience had been a six-week hitch-hiking expedition around Germany and France when he was eighteen, staying in youth hostels and flea-ridden hotels, but he'd enjoyed every minute of it. The second was a five-day luxury trip to Paris, his honeymoon with Ellen, which had cost them a small fortune. But this trip was something else entirely.

He took the Sony transceiver and the tracking monitor from the briefcase, switched both on, and placed them on the seat beside him. The tracking monitor gave him a heading back towards the airport and the indicator read-out told him he had a strong signal level. It also told him that the transmitter bug on the vehicle wasn't moving. Mark reckoned Jennifer's jeep was still parked in the car-hire lot, waiting to be picked up, and he switched off the monitor. He was still sitting there, going over the route almost two hours later, when the transceiver squawked. 'Ryan, are you there?'

Mark almost jumped. He couldn't tell whose voice it was, Grimes or Fellows. 'I'm here. Receiving you loud and clear.'

'Good. This is Grimes. Are you all set?'

'I guess so.'

'Then get ready, the target's on the way. Good luck.'

'Thanks.' Mark switched on the tracking monitor and saw the heading indicator change. Jennifer's vehicle was moving. His heart thumped when five minutes later he saw a white Toyota drive past, Jennifer in the driver's seat, looking straight ahead, her eyes on the road. It felt weird seeing her flash past him like that, unaware that he was watching her, and he felt a wave of guilt wash over him, but it passed when he told himself he was there to help protect her.

The only trouble is, I don't know from who. Mark started the Opel and pulled out after the Toyota.

Jennifer loved Switzerland; it was one of the most beautiful countries in the world. She had visited Zurich once with her parents as a child and she had marvelled at the incredible scenery, the snowcapped Alpine mountains, the deep aquamarine lakes and steep glacial valleys. She was tired after the flight but she didn't want to waste time overnighting in Zurich, and she was anxious to reach the Italian border before darkness fell.

She consulted the map again before she drove on to the airport highway and headed south. An hour later she had reached the pretty lakeside city of Lucerne, then she took the E2 east along the lake, before heading south on the E35 and beginning the steep climb into the Alps, through deep pine valleys and past nameless wooden villages and sleepy hamlets, the hillsides dotted with pretty chalets and grazing cows, tiny bells jangling around their necks.

And then suddenly she was climbing up through the tortuous, winding roads of the mountainous Furka pass. This high up, there was ice and snow all around, and the views took her breath away. When she descended out of the Furka, she reached Brig. The centuries-old skiing town was the ancient Swiss gateway into Italy, and was dominated by the beautiful Stockalper Castle Palace, with its onion-dome tower. She skirted the centre of Brig and drove farther south towards the Simplon pass and the Italian border.

★

The whole drive was mentally exhausting. Some of the mountain roads had no side barriers, the edges dropping away thousands of feet below, and not being familiar with the route Jennifer had to drive carefully. She finally decided to stop at an Alpine café for lunch. There was a viewing balcony for tourists, and she bought a cup of steaming black coffee and a thick cheese roll and went out on to the balcony. It was incredibly cold, and as she stood looking out at the stunning scenery, a ring of white mountains all around her, she saw the Italian border lying far below in the long valley of the Simplon pass.

An elderly Swiss hiker with a feathered Alpine hat came out on to the balcony to admire the view. He smiled over at her. *'Sehr schön, nicht war? Sind sie Ausländer?'*

Jennifer spoke only a few words of French and German, just enough to get by. *'Ja. Aus Amerika.'*

'America, really?' The man beamed.

Jennifer looked out at the mountains all around her. 'Could you tell me which is the Wasenhorn?'

'Natürlich.' The man pointed to a ragged, towering crag far off to the left, a mist of cloud swirling around its icy top. 'That's the Wasenhorn over there. Are you going to climb it, young lady?'

'I don't think so.'

'Very wise. Only the other day I heard they found a body up on the glacier. The poor *schwein* had been frozen in the ice for years.'

Mark found it difficult to concentrate. His adrenalin level was high but the Swiss mountain roads were difficult and he was still exhausted after the flight. To make matters worse, the high altitude made him feel sick. It was the cold which kept him awake: he left the driver's window rolled down – the freezing air that blasted into the car was bone chilling, but at least it kept him alert.

He had to keep his eyes on the road every moment, yet still try to watch Jennifer's Toyota at the same time. The white jeep became almost a blur after two hours, but so far he had managed to keep a safe distance behind her. The traffic was pretty light and he hadn't noticed another vehicle following behind him. Grimes and Fellows were damned good, he'd give them that. Suddenly, up ahead, he saw Jennifer pull in at a roadside café and he turned off the road, a hundred metres behind her. Fifteen minutes later she came out again, climbed into the Toyota and pulled out. Mark started the Opel again and followed her.

The sun had come out as Jennifer drove into the tiny Italian border village of Iselle. She passed through the border post without any fuss, the green-uniformed Italian Customs police barely scrutinising her passport, and reached Varzo ten minutes later. It was a small, sleepy town, typically Italian, and she found the local Carabinieri station with no difficulty.

It faced on to a tiny cobbled square, a solid-looking three-storey old villa with mustard-coloured walls. Stone steps led up to a first-floor veranda, the patio decorated with lots of earthenware potted plants. The place had a casual air, more like a home than a police station, and Jennifer was reminded that she was in Italy, and not the neat, ordered formality of Switzerland. She noticed an intercom box on the wall outside. She parked the Toyota across the square, walked over and pushed the button.

Up on the veranda a couple of sleepy-looking men appeared. They stared down, rubbing their eyes, dressed only in their vests and underwear, one of them attempting to drag on his uniform trousers as he hopped around the patio on one leg, and Jennifer was tempted to laugh. It wasn't long after lunch, and she guessed she had woken the men from their siesta. A young corporal came down the steps, hastily dressing himself, sticking his shirt inside his pants.

'*Signorina. Cos'e caduto?*'

Jennifer didn't speak Italian, and she tried to explain why she was there, but with no success. Finally, the corporal called out in rapid Italian, and a burly man in his late forties with a thick moustache appeared on the veranda. He came down the steps, wearing a holstered pistol and red-striped trousers, and buttoning his tunic. '*Signorina*.'

'Do you speak English?'

'*Si*, a little. My name is Sergeant Barti. How can I help you?'

Jennifer explained.

'Please follow me, *signorina*.'

The sergeant led her up the steps and into a cluttered office. He offered her a seat and went to sit behind a desk. 'An officer named Captain Caruso is in charge of the case. You will need to speak with him.'

Barti hesitated, as if unsure of his English, and Jennifer said, 'May I see him?'

'His office is at Turin headquarters, but unfortunately he is in Switzerland on police business. He returns tomorrow afternoon. I am sorry I cannot help you more, *signorina*.'

'Where's my father's body?'

'In Turin.'

'I'd like to see it.'

Barti shrugged. 'I'm afraid that's not possible. Captain Caruso will need to be present for the identification.'

Jennifer was becoming frustrated. 'Then I'd like to see where my father was found.'

'Really, it would be better to speak with the captain about that. The place is far from here, and dangerous, and it would be dark before I could get you there and back.'

The sergeant wasn't exactly being very helpful, but Jennifer guessed his hands were tied and she really needed to see Caruso. 'Very well, I'll wait to speak with the captain tomorrow. What time would be best?'

'In the afternoon, I think. Say two. I will telephone his office and explain that you will be arriving in Turin.'

As Barti rose from behind his desk, Jennifer said, 'May I ask if you saw my father's body?'

'*Si*.'

'Can you tell me how he died?'

The sergeant made to speak, then seemed to change his mind. 'It would be better if you waited to see the captain. He will explain everything.'

Jennifer sighed in defeat. The man was telling her nothing. 'Is there a hotel around here where I can stay the night?'

'There are two small hotels in the town, and several just over the Swiss border. The Berghof Hotel in Simplon is very popular with visitors.'

'Thanks.' All she had got out of the man was a hotel recommendation. As she was about to go, she said, 'I believe an American found the corpse?'

'*Si*. A young man named Chuck McCaul.'

'Could I meet him?'

'*Scusi*, that's impossible.'

'Why?'

'I'm afraid he's dead.'

Fifteen minutes later, Jennifer drove back over the border into Switzerland. She decided to stay in Simplon for the night because Varzo seemed ill equipped for tourists, and besides, she was determined to see the glacier where her father's body had been found. The sergeant had seemed reluctant to offer an explanation about the climber's death, except to tell her that the young man had had an accident at the Furka pass, and that the Swiss police were investigating the matter. The young man's death struck Jennifer as odd, but perhaps Captain Caruso could tell her more?

Ahead of her the road forked left into the tiny, quaint village of Simplon. It hardly looked up to much, just a couple of long, narrow cobbled streets, with an onion-domed, whitewashed church at one end, and several hotels and cosy inns.

As she checked her rear-view mirror to turn left into the village, she noticed a dark-coloured Opel fifty metres behind her. She was certain it had been behind her all the way along the winding mountain road from Varzo. She couldn't see who was inside because the vehicle had dark-tinted windows, but she had the strangest feeling that it was following her.

She pulled up in a parking lot outside a hotel. The sign outside said: *Berghof Hotel*. As she stepped out of the jeep, the Opel drove past. There was something menacing about its dark windows, but she put the thought from her mind as the Opel drove down the cobbled street to the far end of the village, before it turned on to the main Simplon road and disappeared.

Mark was confused. He had followed Jennifer after seeing her leave the Carabinieri station in Varzo. He thought she might have driven on to Turin, but instead she had doubled back over the border to Simplon. That had puzzled him and he wondered what the hell was going on. After all, Paul March's body was in the police morgue in Turin. Looking at the map, Mark saw the Wasenhorn clearly marked, looking slightly closer to Simplon than to Varzo. He could only guess that Jennifer intended to see the place where her father's body had been found. Maybe she was going to try to find a local hotel. It was the only explanation he could think of for why she'd driven back across the border.

Suddenly his radio squawked. It was Grimes. 'Are you there, Ryan?'

'Yeah, I'm here.'

'We're about five hundred yards behind you. What the hell's she up to?'

'It looks like she's heading back towards Simplon.'

'What in the hell for?'

'I'd take a guess that maybe she wants to see where her father's body was found. Except it's getting a little late and she's probably going to have to stay overnight.'

'It figures. You want us to take over the tail for a while?'

'No, I'll be fine.'

'OK, but if she checks into a hotel you'd better find another one near by where you can keep a close eye on her. We'll try and do the same. Over and out.'

Mark put down the radio and saw Jennifer drive into the village and pull up outside a hotel called the Berghof. Below the sign it said: *Zimmer Frei*. He knew from his hitch-hiking days that the German for room was *Zimmer*, and *Frei* meant there were rooms available, but definitely not for free. There were several hotels and inns either side of the cobbled street, but he didn't realise until it was too late that he was in a one-way street. There were cars parked on both sides and nowhere he could pull in. There was another car behind him, and it honked for him to move on.

Damn.

It would mean he would have to drive straight past Jennifer.

The tinted windows gave him cover, but as he passed ten metres from Jennifer he saw her stare at the Opel. Mark was sweating as he drove out of the village. He pulled into the side of the road and flicked on the tracking monitor. It showed a constant heading and the indicator wasn't moving, which meant the Toyota was still stationary. Damn again. It was a pity Jennifer had noticed the Opel. He'd have to be more careful in future.

He checked the time. Almost four. He'd wait an hour and drive back into the village, see whether he could find a hotel near to Jennifer's, and just hope she didn't spot him.

The Berghof Hotel was no more than a cosy inn, with oak beams overhead and white-painted walls. When Jennifer went up to the reception desk a young, cheerful woman was chatting on the telephone. She finished her call and looked up. '*Ja?*'

'Do you have a single room for tonight, please?'

'I have as many as you want.' The woman smiled, her English perfect. 'It's the end of the season and the hotel is almost deserted.'

She had Jennifer fill in a registration card and then led her up to a rather large, oak-beamed room overlooking the Simplon valley. The view from the window was exquisite. 'I could ask the chef to cook you something if you're hungry, Frau March?'

Jennifer wasn't; the thought of having to identify her father's body the next day filled her with trepidation, but she realised she had better eat something. 'Thank you, I'd appreciate it.'

'*Sehr gut.* You may eat in the dining room or the bar down-stairs, but the bar's probably better, there's a bit more life.'

Jennifer showered, changed into jeans and a sweater, went down to the bar and sat in a pine booth. A log fire blazed and half a dozen men stood at the far end of the bar, chatting among them-selves. They appeared to be mostly local farmers, and a couple of them looked over at her as if she were from another planet, but she knew she was a stranger in a small town and invited curiosity. The woman reappeared and handed her a menu, then brought her the food she ordered, a steaming bowl of *Jägerspiel* soup, a cold plate of Swiss cheeses and various meats, a tossed salad and a glass of frothy beer. When she finished her meal she noticed the men at the bar staring at her. Finally, one came over and placed a glass of white liquid on her table. 'With my compliments,' he said in fluent English. 'The local schnapps. It's the nearest thing to rocket fuel we have in these parts. But actually it's not that bad so long as you drink it down quickly. You're an American, I believe?'

He was of medium height, in his late twenties and pleasant looking, and he had a scraggy beard and wore a brightly coloured roll-neck sweater and jeans. Jennifer was certain he was trying to pick her up. She pushed the glass away and said as politely as she could, 'Yes, I'm an American. And thank you for the offer of a drink, but I'd really prefer to be alone, if you don't mind . . .'

The man smiled and offered his hand. 'Of course, but seeing as you're my guest, I thought I'd say hello. Anton Weber. I run the hotel.'

Jennifer flushed. 'I . . . I'm sorry.'

'No need to apologise. Are you a tourist, Frau March?'

'Is it that obvious?'

The man laughed. 'I'm afraid so. Will you be staying long in Simplon?'

'No, just one night. I'm passing through.'

'A shame, really. The area is quite beautiful.'

'So I've seen. But I understand that a body was discovered near by recently.'

Weber sat down, frowning. 'You heard? A rather strange discovery, to say the least. I'm told it was perfectly preserved in the ice.' He raised his eyebrows. 'You're not a journalist by any chance?'

Jennifer didn't feel like opening up her heart to a stranger and confiding the truth. 'No. Just curious. The story seemed intriguing.'

'A young American climber found the body in the Wasenhorn glacier. In fact, he was a guest here at the hotel, but I'm afraid he died three days ago. Fell into the Furka pass, his body smashed to pieces. I understand from the local sergeant that they're still not through investigating the matter, and it's uncertain whether his death was an accident.'

Jennifer stiffened. 'You mean he might have been murdered?'

Anton Weber shrugged. 'I really can't say. But a couple of detectives came by yesterday to search his room and take away his things. It all seemed most strange.'

Jennifer felt a shiver go through her. 'Could I see the glacier where the body was found?'

'Of course, but you'll need a guide to get to the Wasenhorn. It isn't safe this time of year with the snow melting. May I ask why you wish to see it?'

'Just curious. And I'm sure the glacier's quite a beautiful sight. Where could I find a guide?'

Weber laughed. 'Actually, you're looking at one. Before I managed this hotel that's how I made a living. I know the Wasenhorn glacier very well.'

'Could you take me?'

'Why not? There's no climbing involved really, just a rather tough hike.'

'I'll gladly pay for your time.'

Weber smiled. 'Nonsense, there's no need. For you, I'd consider it a pleasure. Do you have any gear with you?'

'Gear?'

'Mountain gear, boots and so on.'

'I'm afraid not.'

Weber shrugged. 'No matter. My sister Greta is an expert climber and I'm sure she'll loan you anything you need. She's the young woman who checked you in, and I'd say she's about your size. I'll meet you down here at six thirty in the morning. After breakfast, we can drive up the Wasenhorn as far as we can go, then continue the rest of the way on foot, which shouldn't take more than a couple of hours. Wear warm clothes, it gets quite cold up there.'

Jennifer lifted her glass. 'Thank you.' She sipped the

schnapps. It felt like liquid fire in her throat and she winced. 'Oh my God!'

Weber laughed. 'Don't say I didn't warn you.' He stood and again offered his hand. 'And now, I'd better see to my customers. It's been a pleasure meeting you, Frau March.'

Mark drove back into the village. He passed Jennifer's hotel and he noted that her Toyota was still there. Directly across the street was another hotel, Die Seefelder. It looked like the most expensive place in town, with hand-painted Alpine hunting scenes on the pastel-coloured external walls, but best of all there was a car park at the back which would be perfect for keeping the Opel out of sight. The trouble was, he didn't know whether Jennifer intended staying the night at the Berghof. He could only make a guess, but it was a risk he'd have to take. He drove round the back of the hotel, parked and went into the reception. 'I'd like a single room.'

The receptionist looked up and spoke in English. 'Of course, sir. For how many nights?'

'Probably just one,' Mark replied. 'And I'd like a room facing the street.'

The man frowned. 'The best views are at the back, looking out on to the Alps. Wouldn't you prefer one of those?'

Mark handed over his credit card. 'I'm sure the views are terrific, but I'd like a room at the front. And you'd better take my card imprint, just in case I have to leave early.'

Jennifer lay awake in her darkened bedroom. Outside, a church clock struck twelve. After all this time, the day had finally come when she was going to see her father's face again. She suddenly felt alone and afraid, and at that moment she wished she had accepted Mark's offer to join her. She could have done with his support to help her through the coming day. Seeing her father's body and confirming him dead would be a closure of some sort, but she was conscious that it might raise more questions than it answered, and that prospect made her feel scared and uncertain.

As she lay there trying to sleep, she thought again about the young climber named McCaul. The fact that his death might be suspicious sent a cold shiver down her spine, but she would have to wait until she met Caruso to learn more.

Something else bothered her: the Opel that had followed her, but she tried to convince herself it was only her imagination running wild.

Beyond the window she heard the rumblings of a storm. Thunder and lightning crackled and echoed around the Alpine valleys, building to a deafening crescendo, and then the rain came in a drenching downpour, hammering on the roof. She always found it difficult to sleep during a storm, and tonight was no different, as her mind dredged up the same disturbing images: finding the blood-spattered bodies of her mother and Bobby; plunging the blade into the masked man's neck; her frantic race across the lawns as he pursued her.

She tried to tell herself that she had nothing to fear, but no matter how many times she reassured herself, the nightmares still came, and it was another hour before she finally drifted off to sleep, completely exhausted.

Mark sat in his darkened bedroom, the curtains open, the Zeiss binoculars in his hands. It was pitch dark outside and he had slipped on the night-viewer attachment. Everything looked green through the night-viewer, but he could clearly see Jennifer's car and hotel. The town was deathly quiet, apart from the storm that had kicked up, which thundered around the mountains. He had been scanning the Berghof windows an hour ago when he saw Jennifer closing the curtains. Now the lights had gone out in her room.

Mark relaxed and put down the binoculars. He hadn't heard any more from Grimes or Fellows, and he assumed they had checked into one of the other hotels in the village. If Jennifer intended driving up to the glacier the next morning, then all kinds of problems faced him. It wouldn't be easy to tail her, because the mountain roads would have little traffic. He didn't even know what time she intended to leave the hotel. Eight seemed reasonable, but he decided to set the travel clock alarm for seven just in case. He'd left out a change of clothes and his single luggage bag was ready to go. He closed the curtains and flicked on a bedside light.

His room was pretty luxurious, with a four-poster bed, chintz curtains and expensive antique furniture. There was also a mini-bar in the corner. He hadn't eaten very much since the flight that morning and he hadn't wanted to risk ordering room service in case it interrupted him watching Jennifer's hotel. The long drive had drained him, he was hungry and thirsty, and he still felt groggy from the high altitude.

He unlocked the mini-bar. There was the usual beer and liquor, soft drinks and peanuts and various snacks and chocolate, but this being Switzerland there were miniature Toblerone bars and neat, hand-made chocolate liqueurs. There were a couple of miniature Jack Daniel's and he took one, then his cop's instinct made him look at the price list. It worked out at twelve dollars. Even a pack of nuts cost five dollars; six for the Toblerones, ten for the chocolate liqueurs.

There ought to be a law against this kind of thing.

To hell with it, he told himself – I'm on expenses. He poured a beer and a Jack Daniel's, dropped in some ice, then ate a couple of packs of peanuts and a Toblerone bar, saving the chocolate liqueurs for last. He was about to pour another Jack Daniel's when his cell phone buzzed. It was Kelso. 'Have you settled in, Ryan?'

'Sure, it's just like home, except for the mini-bar. Where the hell are you?'

'Close enough.' Kelso didn't elaborate. 'What's happening with Jennifer?'

'She's staying in the Berghof, right across the street. Where are your men?'

'In a hotel at the far end of the village. Did the equipment work OK?'

'It's fine.'

'Good. We may have a busy day tomorrow, so I'd suggest you

get some sleep. And remember, you call Fellows and Grimes if you need help.'

'Don't worry, I haven't forgotten.'

'Goodnight, Ryan.'

Mark flicked off the cell phone and finished his Jack Daniel's. Then he checked his equipment again. It all seemed to be in perfect order. The whole business of tailing Jennifer seemed like an absurd dream and he was finding it hard to adjust. He just wondered how she'd react when she finally came face to face with her father's body. And for the thousandth time he asked himself the same question: *how could Paul March have ended up in an icy Alpine grave?*

He opened the window, undressed and climbed into bed, feeling exhausted. The stormy mountain air that blew in through the window was like a sleeping draught, and he was asleep almost as soon as his head hit the pillow.

The man drove into the village and halted outside the Berghof. It was pouring with rain as he switched off the engine. He rolled down the window and stared at the darkened hotel for several minutes, the building illuminated by the flickering light of the storm.

It was 3 a.m., and when he was certain the street was deserted he stepped out of the car and into the drenching downpour. He walked over to the white Toyota jeep, took the tools from under his wet raincoat and set to work. When he finished five minutes later, he climbed back into his car and drove out of the village the way he had come.

16

New York

Lou Garuda spent all Monday going back through his old notes on the March case, but when he finished he was none the wiser. He wondered what Mark was up to that he couldn't leave him a number in case he needed to talk. In frustration, he telephoned an acquaintance who was a desk sergeant at Jamaica Precinct. 'Woody, it's Lou Garuda.'

'My Latin drinking buddy, the stud with the ten-inch dick. What can I do for you, Lou?'

'Mark Ryan, I hear he's on leave right now. You know where he went?'

'Mark? Naw.'

'Any idea how I could get in touch with him?'

'Naw.'

'You know how long he's gonna be away?'

'Fucked if I know.'

'Thanks a bunch, Woody. You sure are a mine of information.'

'Hey, any time.'

Garuda put down the phone. Ryan had lived on the same street as Jennifer March. Maybe his family knew where he was? Garuda drove his fifteen-year-old silver Porsche 944 over to Long Beach. The Porsche had over 180,000 on the clock, but the engine still ran sweetly, and Garuda loved the damned thing.

The March house backed on to the water, had its own small private jetty with a boardwalk and still looked much the same as he remembered: two-storey, colonial style, with clapboarded windows, a large lot and a tidy, well-kept garden. As he drove past he wondered whether Jennifer March had sold the place. He parked the Porsche by the kerb and walked back.

The house opposite the March property was smaller, and not as prosperous looking. Garuda went up on the veranda and rang the doorbell. When there was no reply, he walked round the back. The side gate to the garden was locked. In frustration, Garuda walked over to the house next door and rang the doorbell.

An elderly woman appeared behind the glass-fronted porch. She was overweight and unattractive, had pink curlers in, and clutched a hideous floral dressing gown to her chest. Garuda thought: *Jeez, if I ever had to share a bed with a dame like that, I'd shoot myself.* The woman was wary. 'Yes?'

Garuda flashed his ID. 'Sorry for bothering you, ma'am, but I'm trying to locate a buddy of mine, Detective Ryan. His family lives next door.'

The woman studied the ID, then relaxed and said pleasantly, 'You mean Mark?'

'That's right, ma'am. His precinct said he was on leave. You didn't happen to see any of his family around, did you? It's pretty important I talk with him.'

'I'm afraid Mark doesn't live here any more, and hasn't for years, only his mom. But she's staying in Phoenix with his sister and she'll be away at least another month.'

'You know where I could find Mark?'

'No, I don't. But Wilbur's got his address, only he isn't here right now.'

'Wilbur?'

'My husband. I can give him a call.'

Garuda smiled, all charm. 'I'd sure appreciate it, ma'am. Thanks a lot.'

Garuda drove back to his Brooklyn apartment. Angelina wasn't there, but the flimsy panties and bra she'd worn last night were still scattered on the bed and the musky smell of sex was still in the air. Garuda felt a boner coming on, but quickly put the thought of Angelina from his mind: he had work to do. He'd driven over to Mark's address in Elmont only to discover from the guy's next-door neighbour that he'd left town the previous day, and the neighbour didn't know where he'd gone. Garuda wondered about that – Ryan and Jennifer March both leaving town the same day – and then he had a weird idea. He called a number at JFK. A woman's voice answered sexily, 'Debbie Kootzmeyer, Customer Relations, how may I help you?'

'Debbie, it's Lou Garuda. I need a favour.'

'Lou, I told you before, next time my husband catches me screwing on the side, he's gonna fucking divorce me.'

'Not that kind of favour, babe. You still got access to passenger flight manifests, don't you?'

'Why?'

'I need to know if someone travelled on a flight yesterday. Maybe out of JFK, maybe out of La Guardia. A guy named Mark Ryan.'

'Lou, you know I can't give you that kind of information—'

'It's really important, Debbie. Just one name. Mark Ryan. Next time I see you, I'll make it up to you, any way you want.'

Debbie protested. 'Jesus, Lou, have you got *any* idea how many people travel through JFK and La Guardia every day? Ain't you got a flight number or something?'

'It's just a hunch, but try flights to Switzerland first. Some time yesterday evening might be a good bet. The guy's got an address in Elmont, Long Island. Maybe that might help.'

Debbie sighed. 'I'll have to call you back.'

Fifteen minutes later, she rang back. 'A passenger named Mark Ryan travelled on an American Airlines flight to Zurich last night. He's got an Elmont address.'

Garuda smiled. 'Debbie, you're a sweetheart. You sitting in front of your computer?'

'I'm never away from the fucking thing.'

'Then just check one more booking. There should have been a woman on the same flight. Her name's Jennifer March.'

Garuda heard keys tapping, and then Debbie said, 'No one by that name travelled on the same flight.'

'You're sure?'

'I'm staring at the fucking list on my screen, Lou.'

'Can you tell me *when* she travelled?'

'Lou, you're really pushing it.'

'Next time you feel like us getting together, I'll do that thing you like, with the ice cubes in my mouth.'

'You're tempting me, Lou. Don't do that.'

Garuda grinned. 'And then guess where I'm gonna put my tongue?'

'You're a fucking major-league tease, you know that?' Debbie sighed, tapped away at her keyboard. 'What you doing next Tuesday?'

'Why?'

'There's a possibility my husband's out of town.'

Garuda grinned again. 'You're a slut, Debbie.'

'Yeah, but you love it.'

Garuda put down the phone, walked to the window and stared out at the towering skyline of New York in the distance. He was puzzled. Mark Ryan had also travelled to Switzerland. But why had he chosen an earlier flight? It wasn't as if he couldn't have booked the *same* flight as Jennifer March: when Debbie checked, she'd said there had been plenty of seats available on *both* flights to Zurich. So why had Ryan and the girl travelled separately, with different airlines? It didn't make any fucking sense. Something a little *weird* was going on here, Garuda sensed, and it was beginning to tickle his detective's instinct.

Still, he had a problem. Ryan wasn't around to talk to and he needed information. But he had another angle he could try. He stepped away from the window and picked up the telephone again.

17

Switzerland

Jennifer woke just before six. When she drew back the curtains and opened the windows the sun was almost up and it was a beautiful spring morning outside. The cobbled village streets were still covered in rain puddles after the storm, and across the street she noticed the Seefelder, a picturesque, expensive-looking hotel which had a stunning view of the snow-dusted Alps.

After she had showered and dressed, she went down to the dining room. A couple of places were already set at one of the tables and Greta appeared a few moments later, carrying a thermos of hot coffee. She looked lively despite the hour. 'I hope you slept well?'

'Apart from the thunder waking me a couple of times,' Jennifer confessed. 'It got pretty noisy during the storm.'

Greta smiled. 'Whenever we get thunder and lightning in the Alps it sounds like the world's coming to an end. Anton should be with you shortly. He stayed up late, drinking with some of the locals. He tells me he's taking you up on the glacier. I'll leave some of my hiking gear and a sturdy pair of boots outside your room. I hope they fit.'

'Thank you, you're very kind, Greta.'

'My pleasure. I just wish I had time to go with you. The mountains can be quite beautiful once the clouds clear away after a storm. Enjoy your breakfast.'

Anton appeared ten minutes later, just as Jennifer finished breakfast. He wore a thick woollen sweater and high socks, knee breeches and heavy boots, and he carried a small backpack and a pair of powerful binoculars. 'Frau March, *guten Morgen*.'

'*Morgen*, Anton. And please, call me Jennifer.'

He rubbed his eyes. 'Jennifer it is, then. I'm afraid I slept rather badly. The weather woke me a couple of times.'

'That makes two of us.'

Anton poured himself a cup of steaming black coffee and drank most of it in one gulp. 'That's better. Did Greta mention that she had some clothes and boots for you?'

'Yes.'

'Good. Then whenever you're ready we'll get under way. It looks like an excellent morning for a hike. You have transport, I presume?'

'A four-wheel-drive.'

'Perfect. We'll take that, if you don't mind, it's better able to handle the mountain tracks. They can be rather muddy and treacherous after a storm, you know.'

The views really were incredibly clear. The clouds had completely vanished and the air was perfectly still. As Jennifer drove up towards the Wasenhorn, Anton pointed out some impressive-looking mountains in the distance.

'Over there's the Matterhorn, and beyond it the Eiger. Have you ever been to Switzerland before, Jennifer?'

'My parents took me on holiday once when I was a child, but that was a long time ago.'

'Do your parents live in America?'

Jennifer considered the question a moment, but decided it was better not to tell Anton the real reason why she wanted to see the glacier. He seemed just a little too inquisitive, but she reminded herself that he might just be making conversation. She was a stranger in a small village, and that was bound to invite curiosity. 'I'm afraid they're dead.'

Anton looked repentant for having asked. 'I'm sorry. I didn't mean to pry . . .'

Jennifer changed the subject. 'Have you any idea what the man might have been doing in the area where they found his body?'

She thought: *It feels odd saying the man, instead of my father.*

Anton shrugged. 'There's a long history of people using some of the more remote mountain tracks in this area as a route over the frontier, if they want to avoid the border and passport checks. Fugitives and criminals mostly. And it's well known that smugglers have used some of the tracks to cross in and out of Switzerland over the centuries.'

'Smugglers?'

Anton smiled. 'Switzerland is all about banks and secret money, but I'm sure you know that. Cash, diamonds, precious metals, and anything valuable you care to name, have been carried over these borders.'

'You mean illegally?'

Anton smiled again. 'Of course. Smuggling has always been a way of life in these mountains, and has gone on for genera-tions. In fact, one or two of the locals you saw in the bar last night made an excellent living out of it for years, and probably still do. There's not much work in these remote mountain areas, so it's wise to have some way to earn money.'

'There's obviously a lot more to Switzerland than I thought.'

Anton laughed. 'Obviously.'

The steep mountain track was treacherous and muddy. It was only wide enough for one vehicle, and was cut into the side of the mountain along a sheer precipice. On the inside of the track was the solid rock of the mountain, and on the outside a drop of hundreds of feet to jagged rocks below. The wheels skidded a little in the soft mud as Jennifer drove.

'Easy does it,' Anton said. 'But it's coming down when we really have to watch. You go too fast or skid and we might be in trouble.'

Jennifer looked up as they came round a bend and a magnif-icent sight met them. The Wasenhorn rose majestically out of the clouds like some enormous ancient fossil, and then suddenly they were at the end of the track. As Jennifer jerked on the hand-brake, Anton climbed out, slinging the small haversack on his back and grabbing his binoculars. 'Right, the rest of the way's on foot, I'm afraid. But I really think you're going to enjoy it.'

18

Mark heard a sound like car wheels rattling on cobble and turned over in bed. He felt groggy as he came awake. The sound of traffic came from outside his window, muted voices talking in sing-song Swiss-German, and it sounded as if the village was a riot of noise. His head felt lousy. And then he realised why: alcohol and high altitude didn't mix. The drinks he'd had last night had knocked him out. He lay there, one eye open and focused on the alarm clock: 8.05.

Shit.

He'd slept late.

He climbed out of bed frantically. He remembered the alarm clock going off, but he must have been so exhausted he'd reached over and turned it off. He stumbled to the window and looked towards the Berghof's parking lot. Jennifer's Toyota was gone.

Jennifer had never had such a feeling of raw, rugged power all around her. The air was chilled and hurt her lungs, but when she and Anton reached the glacier she marvelled at the breathtaking sight. A sea of solid ice stretched before them, duck-egg blue and cracked in places by crevasses. The glacier was very wide but its length was impossible to determine, for it seemed to stretch either side of them like an endless, wide frozen river.

'Careful now. The ice is solid enough, but stick behind me and follow in my footsteps.' Anton led the way and pointed to a crack in the glacier about a hundred metres from the far side. 'That's the crevasse where they found the body. It's just over the Italian side of the border.'

Jennifer's heart pounded as they walked closer to the spot

Anton had pointed out. Her mind was beset by a storm of feelings, and the terrible anguish of knowing that the father she had loved had died here, in such a remote, God-forsaken place. *If only I knew why?* When they came nearer the crevasse, Anton said, 'Don't step too close, Jennifer. It's really quite dangerous.'

She peered down and saw that the crevasse got darker the deeper it went. 'Do you have a rope and a torch?'

'Yes, in my backpack. Why?'

'Could you let me down?'

'*What?*'

'I'd like to see where the body was found.'

'Jennifer. . . . don't be foolish.'

She was determined. 'It's got me curious. Have you ever abseiled down a crevasse before?'

'Of course, many times, but—'

'Then we ought to be safe enough. Besides, if the police went down there, it can't be all that difficult.'

Anton sighed. '*Gott im Himmel.* And I thought you were just a quiet, unassuming American tourist.' He unslung his backpack, uncoiled a nylon rope and began to hammer some stays into the snow to secure the rope. 'Very well, but I'd better go down with you. I'm sure the last thing the police want is another corpse on their hands.'

The first thing Mark did was switch on the tracking monitor. The aural signal sounded weak and the pointer showed a heading due north. The signal read-out indicated five kilometres and steady, which meant the Toyota was stationary. He consulted the map and estimated that Jennifer was somewhere near the Wasenhorn.

She had probably driven up to the mountain and halted. He thought of using the radio to find out where the hell Grimes and Fellows were, but decided not to waste any more time; he would call them on the way. He dressed quickly, grabbed his bag and went down to reception. There was a young female receptionist on duty. 'How do I get to the Wasenhorn?' he asked urgently.

The girl shrugged. 'You will see the signposts when you take the road north out of the village, or if you drive back towards Brig.'

Mark didn't even thank the girl. He ran out to the parking lot, stashed his bag in the Opel and started the engine.

The crevasse was incredibly cold, like being in a deep freeze. The chamber walls were solid blue, smooth as glass in places, jagged in others, and as Anton played the torchlight around the crevasse, it seemed an eerie place. Jennifer saw the deep hole in the glacier where her father's body had been cut out and she shuddered, her sense of grief overwhelming.

Anton said, 'You look quite pale. Are you OK?'

'I'm . . . I'm fine.' Suddenly she noticed a smaller hole cut into the bottom of the crevasse around which ice chips lay scattered. 'What's that?'

Anton shrugged. 'I heard from our local police that McCaul discovered a rucksack near the body. Perhaps that is where they found it.'

Jennifer frowned. 'What was in the rucksack?'

'God knows.'

'What else do you know about McCaul's accident?'

'Nothing. Why?'

'It's just that his sudden death seems kind of . . . well, strange.'

'He was a good climber, apparently. But even the good ones make mistakes, and he was young, in his early twenties, too young to be that experienced. After all, he fell into the crevasse in the first place.'

'What exactly was he doing up here?'

Anton shrugged again. 'He was just a tourist. He booked into the hotel for a week, seemed a pleasant enough sort, but he was out most of the time and I hardly ever spoke with him. You know, you're really a very curious girl, Jennifer.'

'You think so?'

Anton gestured around the crevasse and said suspiciously, 'Wanting to come up to the glacier, for one. Then wanting to see exactly where the body was found. And now you're asking about McCaul. You're sure you're not a journalist of some sort?'

'Certain.'

She looked up at the mouth of the crevasse high above them, light pouring through the narrow gash from the clear blue sky, then took a long, lingering look around the frozen chamber.

'Have you seen enough?' Anton asked finally.

Jennifer shuddered. 'I think so.'

They sat resting in the snow and Anton took a thermos from his backpack and poured them each a cup of steaming hot coffee. 'That ought to keep out the chill. There's no brandy to go with it, I'm afraid. Alcohol and high altitude really don't mix.'

'Thanks, Anton.' Jennifer looked out at the view. It was stunning: Italy lay far below them, and it seemed as if they were sitting on top of the world, the sun beating down, dazzling white snow all around. 'Which direction do you think the man might have been headed?'

'God knows.'

'Where's the nearest town or village?'

Anton pointed down into the valley to the Italian side. 'Over there. A village called San Domenico, near Varzo. It's part of the Alpe Veglia, an Alpine nature reserve.'

'How far away is it?'

'About five kilometres. It's where McCaul was headed when he found the body. It's the normal route for anyone crossing the glacier from the Swiss side.'

'And there's nothing in between?'

'Nothing except a mountain hut. It's called a *Berghut*, and it's a resting lodge for climbers and hikers. These trails have been used for centuries and the Alps are dotted with rest huts for a very good reason.'

'Why?'

'If the mountain weather suddenly turns bad, having proper shelter can often mean the difference between life and death. There's a hut just over the Italian side of the border. It's not far, only a short walk.'

'Could I see it?'

Anton checked his watch. He seemed reluctant, but said, 'OK, why not?'

Jennifer stood, brushed snow from her trousers, touched his arm. 'You're being very patient, Anton. Afterwards, I promise to buy you a beer.'

'I'll hold you to that.'

It didn't take them long to reach the hut. It was built of stone and wood with a slate roof, was large and solid looking, and stood on a ridge overlooking the valley. Anton opened the creaking door and they stepped inside. It seemed the place had been deserted for a long time, and it had an eerie feeling.

'The hut hasn't been used much all winter,' Anton explained. 'There's a caretaker who looks after it from late spring until early winter, but for the rest of the year it's nearly always deserted.'

He showed Jennifer around. Thick oak beams ran overhead and there were a couple of bedrooms with bunk beds, and a kitchen that was quite basic. Winter wood fuel was stored against a couple of the stone walls and a pair of deer antlers were mounted above a huge fireplace. Visitors had carved their initials and left dates and graffiti on some of the wooden beams.

'That's it, I'm afraid. It's nothing much,' Anton commented, and he closed the door after them as they stepped outside.

Jennifer noticed what looked like a small village some distance away, far down in the valley. 'Where's that?'

'The village of San Domenico that I told you about.'

'Could I borrow your binoculars?'

'Of course.'

Jennifer focused on a collection of Alpine-style houses, more Swiss-looking than Italian. Then, farther down on a rocky hillside, she noticed a solitary, striking collection of walled buildings with pan-tiled roofs, a fortified structure built dramatically on solid rock and overhanging a sharp precipice, with a cliff face below. She pointed out the walled buildings to Anton. 'What's that?'

'The old monastery of the Crown of Thorns. It's been there at least a couple of hundred years.'

'It looks so striking, perched on the hillside.'

'The Alpine region has a long tradition of monasteries and convents. This area alone has dozens of them. It's the remoteness, you know. It seems to appeal to solitary religious minds.'

'The monastery's still in use?'

Anton nodded. 'It belongs to an order of Catholic monks, but there aren't that many of them left and the place is neglected. A pity – I hear the cloister's quite beautiful, and it used to be famous as a sanctuary. Climbers have been known to use it as a refuge when the weather turns really bad.'

'How do I get to see the monastery?'

'Once you cross the border, it's well signposted from the main road. But why would you want to do that?'

'No reason, except that I was just thinking how incredibly dramatic and isolated it looked.'

Jennifer studied the monastery. For some reason she felt a chill run through her that she didn't understand. A moment later, she noticed Anton checking his watch. 'And now I really think it's time we were getting back. Greta will be expecting me at the hotel.'

As they drove back down the track, Anton said, 'Better to arrive safely than not at all, so remember to take it easy. This part of the track is pretty treacherous.'

Jennifer drove slowly, but suddenly the track dipped down sharply and she pressed on the brake.

Nothing happened.

She felt a cold chill go through her. She pumped the brakes again, harder this time, but the pedal was soft. She was filled with terror as the jeep picked up speed on the downward slope.

'*Jesus.*'

Anton said, 'What's wrong? You're going too fast. The brakes, Jennifer. *Use the brakes.*'

'I am. They're not working.'

'*Scheisse!* Try them again.'

Jennifer tried again, pumping the pedal with all her strength, but still nothing happened. She shifted down a gear and the jeep slowed for a few seconds but then kept coasting faster and faster. It was becoming difficult to control the vehicle, and she had to work hard to keep from skidding and going over the edge. Her heart pounded as the jeep kept picking up more and more speed, gaining momentum with each passing second, and she was afraid to take her eyes off the road.

'Pull the handbrake!' she shouted at Anton.

Anton reached over and jerked on the handbrake, but it had absolutely no effect. Jennifer shifted down to first gear and the Toyota jerked violently and slowed, but suddenly she saw a sharp bend up ahead, curving over the edge of a rocky cliff that dropped away hundreds of feet below.

Her heart hammered. 'Oh God!'

Anton must have seen what lay up ahead too because he covered his eyes with his arms and screamed, '*Mein Gott!*'

Jennifer yanked the steering wheel to the right and the jeep went out of control and skidded towards the edge of the cliff.

19

Jennifer saw the cliff up ahead and knew with certainty she was doomed. At almost the last moment Anton managed to overcome his shock, frantically yanked the wheel from her hands and tried to steer them out of the skid, but it was useless, and the jeep kept careening across the track towards the edge. *I'm going to die*, Jennifer thought.

They were only seconds from the cliff when suddenly a blue Nissan four-wheel-drive came out of nowhere, moving slowly around the blind uphill curve of the road. There was a deafening crash of metal as the two vehicles collided and the Toyota came to a grinding halt a couple of metres from the cliff edge. Jennifer was wearing her seat belt but the force of the crash lifted her bodily and her head struck the roof.

As the jeep settled, Anton let out a sigh of relief. '*Gott im Himmel!*'

He looked white with shock but seemed uninjured. Jennifer sat there for several moments, too traumatised to speak or move, before she unbuckled her belt and climbed shakily out of the Toyota. When she looked towards the cliff she saw a frightening drop to a rocky valley below, and she felt light headed. They had been only a couple of metres from the edge and the accident had saved them. She suddenly felt dizzy, and when she turned back she saw the driver step out of the Nissan, steam rising from its mangled hood. 'Are you OK?'

The man's accent sounded American. He was good looking, ruggedly built, and appeared to be in his fifties. He wore an open parka, a white T-shirt, jeans and suede desert boots. He came over to her. 'I asked are you OK?'

Jennifer blinked. When she tried to answer the words wouldn't come. She realised she was still in shock. The bang on her head must have done more damage than she thought because suddenly the man's face went out of focus, everything became foggy and she fainted.

When she came to Anton was gone and the man was kneeling over her, dabbing her forehead with a damp handkerchief and gently slapping her face. 'Wake up. How do you feel?'

Jennifer blinked and felt a throbbing headache in the top of her skull. 'I . . . I don't know.'

'Let me have a look.' The man held her face in his hand, lifted her eyelids and looked into her eyes before he felt her pulse. He held up his fingers. 'How many fingers do you see?'

'Three.'

'Good. Just lie still and don't move.' He walked over and examined the Toyota, then his own vehicle. The Nissan's fender had buckled and a wheel arch was crushed in against one of the front wheels. 'Mine's bad enough, but yours is a damned mess.'

'Where's . . . where's Anton?'

'Your friend? Gone down the track on foot to phone for a doctor. He seemed pretty concerned, but I think you're going to be OK. You've just got some mild concussion and a bump on your head the size of a camel's hump.'

'What . . . what happened?'

The man nodded towards the cliff edge. 'I crashed into you, that's what happened. And lucky for you I did, by the looks of it. Your friend said you're an American, is that right?'

'Yes.'

'You came down that track like you had the Fifth Cavalry after you. What in the hell were the two of you trying to do – kill yourselves?'

'My brakes failed.'

'Your friend didn't mention that.' The man frowned, went over to the Toyota and pumped the brake pedal a couple of times before sliding under the chassis. He reappeared a few minutes later, wiping his hands. 'If you ask me, those brakes have been tampered with.'

Jennifer sat up. Her head throbbed. 'What do you mean?'

'The hydraulic hoses have been loosened. The brake fluid slowly leaked away every time you put your foot on the pedal.'

'I . . . I don't understand.'

'It's almost impossible for those hoses to loosen. If the vehicle was old, then sure, maybe it could have happened. But that jeep's pretty new. It looks to me as if it was done deliberately.'

Jennifer let the words sink in, and still couldn't believe what she had heard.

'But . . . but why?'

'I'm damned if I know, but you can worry about that later. Are you feeling any better?'

'Yes.'

'Where do you think your friend has gone?'

'I don't know. Maybe back to Simplon. I'm staying there, at the Berghof Hotel.'

The man frowned, looking surprised. 'I was headed there later myself. I think maybe we'd better try and get you to the hotel and not waste time waiting for your friend to return. With a little luck, maybe I can get this baby going.'

He went round to the back of his Nissan and came back with a sturdy metal wheel brace. He jammed the brace under the wheel arch, put his foot against the tyre and pulled hard on the brace. He was in good physical shape, but Jennifer could see the muscles in his arms bulge with the effort. The damaged arch didn't seem to want to move, but the man kept pulling hard until finally he managed to free the tyre from the twisted metal.

'OK, let's try it.' He climbed in and the Nissan started first time. He shifted into gear and very carefully reversed away from the cliff, then jerked on the handbrake and climbed out. 'Looks like we're in business. We'll catch up with your friend Anton on the way down. You think you can stand?'

'I think so.'

He helped her to her feet and made her take a couple of steps. 'Nothing seems to be broken.'

'I'll be fine.' Jennifer's head still throbbed but the dizziness had gone. She suddenly realised that she had never even asked the man his name, or thanked him. It seemed absurd, but the accident had saved her life.

'I . . . I . . . never thanked you. If you hadn't driven up the track when you did Anton and I could have been killed.' She offered her hand. 'I'm Jennifer March.'

The man's eyes narrowed the instant he heard her name, and he didn't shake her hand. He looked angry as he picked up the wheel brace and tossed it into the cab. 'I know who you are. You're Paul March's daughter. Now let's get you out of here, and then I think we need to talk.'

Jennifer was totally confused. 'Who . . . who are you?'

'My name's Frank McCaul. Chuck McCaul was my son.'

It took a moment for the name to register with Jennifer. 'The . . . the climber who died at the Furka pass?'

'My son didn't just *die*. He was murdered.'

20

'*Still, bitte.*'

Jennifer winced. Her skull felt painfully sore. She sat on the bed in her hotel room as the local doctor finished putting a dressing and sticking plaster on her head while Greta looked on. The doctor said something in rapid German, and Greta translated. 'He says you really should have an X-ray. You don't need any stitches, but it's quite a nasty bump.'

Jennifer started to shake her head and the doctor said again, '*Still, bitte!*' She told Greta to tell the doctor she was fine. Her headache was still there, but the light-headed feeling was gone. As soon as she had arrived at the hotel, Greta had taken her up to the bedroom while Anton phoned the local surgery. Now the doctor spoke again, and Greta said to her, 'He says if you start to see double again or the headache gets any worse, you're to call him at once.' Greta shook her head. 'Poor Anton still hasn't got over it. But you're both still alive and that's all that matters. I think you should rest here for a little while. It would be better, *ja?*'

Jennifer agreed, but ten minutes later, when Greta and the doctor had gone, she was bored lying on the bed. She got up and put on her sweater. She still felt a little shaken up as she went down to the bar. The place appeared empty, Anton and Greta were nowhere to be seen, but then she saw McCaul sitting alone at the end of the bar, a bottle of Scotch in front of him. He looked over. 'Feeling any better?'

'A little.' Beyond the panoramic windows Jennifer saw that a shroud of heavy fog had rolled in over the mountains. 'Where's Anton?'

'He seemed pretty concerned when I told him about your

brakes, so he went to see the local police sergeant. I guess he'll probably want to question you later.' McCaul picked up his Scotch. 'You want a drink? You look like you could do with one.'

'Thanks.'

McCaul went to fetch another glass from behind the bar. He dropped in some ice then came back and poured her drink. Jennifer said, 'I'm really sorry about your son.'

It was all she could think of saying. She saw McCaul's face tighten with grief. 'It hasn't been easy. Chuck was my only child.'

'I'm . . . I'm sorry,' Jennifer repeated, but she knew her words would be of little comfort. 'Can I ask how you knew about me?'

McCaul sounded suddenly harsh. 'Because I made it my business to know.'

When he didn't elaborate, Jennifer asked, 'Why are you so certain your son was murdered?'

McCaul put his glass down. 'The evening before he died, Chuck phoned me in New York. He said a reporter named Emil Hartz from the *Zurich Express* wanted to interview him up at the Furka pass about finding the body. When I got the call from the Swiss police to tell me my son had died up at the Furka, I phoned the newspaper in Zurich and asked to speak with the reporter. Guess what? No one named Emil Hartz works for them, or with any of the other Zurich newspapers I contacted. That's when I got the first flight over here.'

'Maybe your son made a mistake about the reporter's name?'

McCaul shook his head. 'I made sure to ask if any of their other reporters might have made the call. None of them did. Besides, this guy Hartz had promised Chuck a fee for the inter-view. The newspaper said they would never have done that kind of thing.'

Jennifer paled. 'Did you tell the Swiss police all this?'

'Sure. Not that it helped much. In fact, when we crashed I was on my way up to the glacier to see where Chuck had found the body. I intend to investigate his death for myself.'

'Why would you want to do that?'

'Because it's what I do. I'm a private detective. And there are factors that don't exactly inspire me with confidence that the Swiss can even begin to solve Chuck's death.'

'Like what?'

'For one, they didn't find a single clue, not one piece of evidence, so they can't say for sure whether he was murdered. You push someone off a mountain with no witnesses around and that's pretty much the perfect crime. The police admit they can't even be sure this guy Hartz really exists, and all they've got is my word. But I took Chuck's phone call and I'm certain Hartz exists, whoever he is. The question is, why did he kill my son? Me, I figure it may have something to do with Chuck finding your father's body.'

'I don't understand.'

McCaul stared across at her. 'Neither do I. But let's just say my intuition tells me there's something weird about all this. And I figured maybe you could tell me more.'

Jennifer blushed. 'Are you trying to suggest that *I* might be involved?'

'Not until I know any better. But finding that corpse up on the mountain is about the only reason I can think of why Chuck was murdered.'

Angrily Jennifer put her glass down. 'Now you're beginning to make me feel like I'm a suspect. I'm sorry about what happened to your son, I really am. But I don't know any more about this than you do. And now, if you don't mind, I have to see about my jeep.'

As she turned to go, McCaul gripped her arm. 'I've been a private investigator for ten years, and before that I was a cop. You get to know when things smell bad. And if you ask me, this whole business smells worse than a cow shed. First your father's body is found, then Chuck dies. And now maybe someone's trying to kill you. Is there anything you're not telling me?'

Jennifer flushed. 'Let go of my arm, please, you're hurting. I've told you everything I know. And if you're looking for an alibi, I was in New York when your son died.'

McCaul let go, his tone suddenly more conciliatory. 'Then how about I ask you a favour?'

'What?'

'I checked with the Carabinieri. They say you've made arrangements to see your father's body.'

'What about it?'

'I'd like to go along. I'd like to see exactly what Chuck found up on that glacier.'

'I'm sorry, but this is a personal matter.'

McCaul continued to stare at her, and a more dangerous look she had never seen before in her life. 'It's personal for me too.'

'Then you'd better ask the Italian police yourself. Good day, Mr McCaul.'

Mark was hopelessly lost. He had driven up three different mountain tracks and found himself in dead ends. He tried calling Grimes on the radio but all he got was heavy static. The cell phone didn't work either: when he tried to contact Kelso the service was completely dead. To make matters worse, a fog had begun to descend, and it had started to drizzle rain. Halfway up another rocky track, as he came round a bend, he suddenly saw Jennifer's white Toyota.

He pulled over, switched off the engine and climbed out, his heart thumping. The Toyota was perilously close to the edge of a cliff but there was no sign of Jennifer. It looked as if there had been an accident; the jeep's chassis had been badly damaged, and there were gashes of blue paint on the white bodywork. He tried the doors but they were locked. *What the hell's happened? Where's Jennifer gone?*

As he examined the damage, he noticed a pool of brown liquid under the right front wheel. He slid under the jeep and saw that a hydraulic hose line had worked loose, and brake fluid had seeped round the screw thread. He figured the leak had probably been caused by the crash. He stood as he heard a car coming up the track, then a police Volkswagen came round the bend and halted. A burly Swiss officer stepped out. He looked over at Mark's Opel and raised his eyes. '*Wer sind sie?*'

'Sorry, but I don't speak German.'

'Are you English?'

'American.'

'I'm Sergeant Klausen. What are you doing here?'

'I saw the jeep abandoned and thought there'd been an accident and stopped to see if I could help. Do you know what's happened?'

The sergeant scratched his head. 'There's been an accident, all right. An American lady had a narrow escape. A vehicle crashed into her, and lucky for her it did or she would have gone over the edge. Her jeep looks *kaput*.'

Mark tried not to appear overly concerned. 'Is she OK?'

The sergeant shrugged. 'The other driver took her back to Simplon. She had a few bruises, but I believe she's fine. Are you a tourist?'

'Yes.' Mark felt relieved that Jennifer was safe.

'If I were you I'd forget about driving up to the mountain. These roads are too dangerous after a storm. And this rain and fog may get worse.'

'Thanks, I'll take your advice.'

As Mark walked back to the Opel, he saw the sergeant kneel down and examine under the jeep. The first thing a cop usually did at the scene of an accident was examine the damage and take measurements. But the sergeant seemed more interested in looking *under* the Toyota. Mark was curious and went back. 'You need a hand? I happen to know something about cars.'

The sergeant looked up. 'You Americans always know some-thing about everything.'

'I'm just trying to help.' Mark pointed to the pool of brake fluid. 'You'd want to watch yourself there. Some hydraulic fluid's leaked out.'

The sergeant grimaced. 'Are you a mechanic?'

'No, but I know about engines. The reason for the leak is because the brake line has worked loose.'

The sergeant thought for a moment. 'I'll have to ask the local mechanic to take a look, but tell me, in your opinion, do you think that the brake line has been interfered with?'

'Interfered with?'

'Apparently, the man who crashed into the American lady thought the brake line had perhaps been loosened deliberately.'

Mark frowned, then slid under the chassis again and examined the hose. He stood up and dusted his hands. 'I really couldn't say for certain. I think you'll have to ask an expert.' He was telling the truth; the screw thread could have loosened over time, except the jeep looked fairly new. But the mountain track was bumpy, strewn with jagged lumps of shale. The hose could have worked itself loose with excessive vibration or from the crash, but the sergeant's suggestion that it could have been deliberate almost made him panic. He looked at the flakes of dark blue paint embedded in Jennifer's white Toyota. 'What kind of car was the guy driving?'

'It was a Nissan jeep. Why?'

Mark shrugged. 'No reason.'

The sergeant looked at him suspiciously and he decided it was time to leave. Before the policeman could say another word, he walked back to the Opel, climbed in and drove back down the track.

Jennifer stood at her bedroom window, watching a curtain of fog and drizzling rain descend over the Alps. What McCaul had said about her brakes being tampered with disturbed her. *Who would have done such a thing? And why?* She shivered, and for some odd reason she remembered the dark-windowed Opel that had followed her into the village, and the feeling she had got that she was being watched by whoever was inside. Maybe McCaul was right. Maybe someone *had* tried to kill her. But *why?* It didn't make any kind of sense.

She thought again about McCaul. She knew he must be going through terrible grief, having lost his son. She remembered what it had been like when her mother had died. First disbelief, then anger, and then a livid need for revenge. She still felt irritated by the way McCaul had treated her like a suspect, but she understood his emotions. Suddenly her remorse got the better of her. 'Damn you, McCaul.'

She went back downstairs to the bar and found him standing at a window, staring out at the mountains, smoking a cigarette. When he turned round his eyes looked wet. 'What the hell do you want?'

She said softly, 'Are you OK?'

McCaul nodded, his tone softening. 'Maybe I was a little too harsh. I'm sorry, but I'm just impatient to find answers. And I guess I'm simply too accustomed to applying the first rule of investigation.'

'What's that?'

'Suspect everyone.'

'You looked miles away.'

'I was thinking about Chuck, and how he lived for climbing. He worked for a computer firm in New York, but ever since he was a kid he loved the outdoors. We used to hike and climb together back home, but he always loved coming to Switzerland. He said it was every climber's dream.'

'I'm truly sorry.' Jennifer went over to join him. 'May I have a cigarette? I don't smoke, but after this morning I'm thinking of taking it up.'

'It scared you that bad?'

'I think I'm still shaking.'

He gave her a cigarette, lit it for her.

'Thank you, Mr McCaul.'

'Call me Frank. It's bad enough the Swiss being so formal.'

'Will you tell me how you knew about me?'

'Easy. When I had no luck with the Swiss, I called a detective friend of mine at Carabinieri headquarters in Rome. He filled me in on the investigation, or as much of it as he could, and happened to mention you'd be formally identifying your father's body.'

'Were you really serious about someone tampering with the brakes?'

'From what I saw, I'd say it's a possibility, but it might be difficult to prove. With all that bumping over rough terrain, it might appear that the brake hose worked itself loose.'

Jennifer felt the cold chill go through her again. 'I just don't understand it.'

'Then I guess we've both got a lot of questions that need answering.'

'Maybe I'm beginning to feel paranoid, but I was sure a car followed me here yesterday.' She explained about the Opel.

'Did you see the licence number?'

'It didn't occur to me to notice.'

McCaul shrugged. 'Maybe it's nothing. But if you see it again, it might do no harm to get the licence number and tell the cops.'

Jennifer hesitated. 'If you still want, and for what it's worth, you can come with me when I identify my father's body.'

'Why the change of heart?'

'I think I owe it to you after what happened this morning. I doubt the Italians will object. Do you think your jeep could make it to Turin?'

'Let me worry about that.'

'I'll call the detective in charge of the case and try to explain. Then I'd better phone my car-hire firm and tell them about our accident.'

As Jennifer turned to go, McCaul said, 'You mind me asking what your father was doing up on the Wasenhorn when he died?'

'I honestly don't know.'

'My detective friend suggested that he'd been dead quite a while.'

'My father disappeared two years ago. I've never seen or heard from him since.'

'I guess that must have been tough on you?'

'Getting over the grief wasn't easy, though at least now I'll have some kind of closure.' Jennifer stubbed out her cigarette. 'But I'm really not looking forward to the identification.'

Mark pulled up outside the Berghof Hotel. There was no sign of a blue Nissan in the parking lot and he tried to figure out what to do next. He was tired of the deception of tailing Jennifer, and after seeing the accident scene he wondered whether it was time to put an end to the whole charade. What if someone had tried to kill her and her life was in danger, just as Kelso had said?

But where the hell were Kelso and his men? He'd tried the radio again and got nothing but static, and the cell phone service provider was still down. He decided to tell Jennifer the truth and worry about the consequences afterwards. He stormed into the hotel and saw a woman behind the reception desk. 'I'm looking for Jennifer March. She's a guest here.'

'Frau March left half an hour ago.' The woman frowned. 'Your accent sounds American. Are you a friend of hers?'

'Yes. Left for where?'

'Turin, I believe.'

'But the police told me she had an accident . . .'

'You heard?' The woman shook her head. 'Such a terrible thing, but she's lucky to be alive. She left with Herr McCaul.'

'*Who?*'

'An American, like yourself. In fact, he saved her life when he crashed into her jeep. My brother Anton was her passenger when the accident happened.'

McCaul, Mark wondered where he'd heard the name before. 'If you don't mind me asking, who's McCaul?'

'His son died up on the Furka pass. A terrible tragedy. He was a guest here at the hotel. It was quite odd, really, a strange twist of fate.'

'What do you mean?'

'The young man discovered a body up on the Wasenhorn just a few days before he died.'

Mark remembered the name. *Chuck McCaul.* The climber who had found Paul March's body. But now the woman was telling him that Chuck McCaul was dead. He was totally confused, wanted to ask the woman more, but there wasn't time. 'You say they left half an hour ago?'

'At least that.'

Turin

The Carabinieri headquarters turned out to be a large, modern grey-brick building, four storeys high, with an underground car park. McCaul parked the Nissan across the street and they went up the steps to the reception hall. Jennifer asked for Caruso. A few minutes later a small, overweight man appeared. He had a bushy moustache and penetrating grey eyes. He shook Jennifer's hand and said in excellent English, 'I'm Captain Caruso, signorina. We spoke earlier on the telephone.'

His gaze shifted to McCaul as Jennifer introduced him. 'Captain, this is Frank McCaul.'

Caruso shook McCaul's hand and said sympathetically, 'I was sorry to hear about your son's death. The Swiss police told me you had arrived to identify his body.' He was puzzled as he turned to Jennifer. 'But forgive me, I was confused after we spoke on the telephone. Do you both *know* each other?'

'I can explain, Captain. Is there somewhere we can talk?'

'Of course, upstairs in my office.'

It was on the second floor, overlooking a neat courtyard with a bubbling fountain. A red file was open on the desk and there was a photograph in a silver frame of Caruso and a handsome, dark-haired woman who could have been his wife. He listened as Jennifer told him that she had met McCaul that morning. 'Now I understand.'

'You said you spoke with the Swiss police about Chuck's death.'

Caruso looked at McCaul. '*Si*, yesterday.'

'What did they tell you?'

'That they believe his fall was an accident.'

McCaul said angrily, 'That's horse shit. It was murder.'

Caruso raised his eyebrows. 'And what makes you say that?'

McCaul tossed his business card on the desk. 'I'm a private detective, and there are a couple of things about Chuck's death that just don't add up.'

Caruso studied the card, then said with a hint of resentment, 'Are you suggesting that the police are not doing their job? If this is your opinion, then perhaps you would explain, because so far the Swiss have no evidence to suggest murder. This reporter he was supposed to have met at the Furka pass . . .'

'Emil Hartz.'

'The Swiss say there is no reporter of that name working for any Zurich newspaper.'

'I know, I checked too.'

'You're quite sure your son didn't make up the story? Or that he was mistaken about the name? Also, he was a young man and perhaps not a very experienced climber. Isn't it possible he had another accident?'

McCaul sounded irritated. 'Chuck was a pretty good climber and I'm certain he didn't fall. And I'm pretty sure about the name, Emil Hartz.'

'Are you saying that this man Hartz, if he really exists, murdered your son?'

'If he didn't, then maybe he knows who did.'

'And what would have been the motive?'

'You tell me, Caruso, you're the cop,' McCaul replied angrily. 'All I know is that Chuck discovered the body, and now he's dead. You're the one who's paid to find motives. But so far all I see is a fat man sitting on his ass who's not even bothering to find answers.'

Caruso flushed. 'I can understand your anger. But I can only repeat that the Swiss examined the scene of his death, and they are usually very thorough.'

'What about footprints?'

'They found none, apart from your son's. They also examined his hired car and found nothing to suggest that he might have gone to the Furka pass with the intention of meeting someone. No notes in the car, on his body or in his hotel room.'

'Footprints in the snow are easy to get rid of. You brush them away and no one knows the difference.'

'I repeat, Signore McCaul, no signs were found that would suggest murder. The Furka pass is popular with tourists, but it's also quite dangerous. There have been many accidents over the years when tourists have fallen to their deaths. Is it not possible your son had an unfortunate accident?'

'I told you, Chuck didn't have an accident. If anything, he would have been more careful after his fall. And there's something else you should know. Someone may have tried to kill Jennifer.'

'Is this true, signorina?'

'The brakes on my jeep may have been tampered with.'

Jennifer told him what had happened that morning and Caruso frowned at McCaul. 'You're certain about the brakes?'

'I checked them myself. The hydraulic hose had been worked loose.'

Caruso looked perplexed as he scribbled in a notebook. 'Most strange. Can you think of anyone who might want to harm you, Signorina March?'

'No, I can't.'

Caruso shook his head. 'I'm afraid whatever happens on Swiss soil is outside my authority. However, I will ask that these matters are investigated more thoroughly. But for now, there is nothing more I can do.'

McCaul was about to speak again but Caruso raised his hand. 'We are forgetting the real reason for this meeting. Signorina March, you are here to identify your father's body.'

Jennifer felt a flutter in her stomach and saw Caruso pick up the red file on his desk. He hesitated, as if something bothered him. 'Just one more thing, signorina.' He opened the file and Jennifer saw a passport which Caruso opened on the photograph page. 'Is this your father's passport?'

Jennifer swallowed. Her father looked just as she remembered him: dark hair, blue eyes, a smiling, handsome face. 'Yes.'

Caruso replaced the passport in the file and stood. 'Thank you. And now, if you would come this way, we are expected at the morgue.'

A white sheet was draped over a human form on a stainless-steel table in the centre of the autopsy room. Jennifer had to force herself to look. She knew her father's body lay under the sheet and she felt weak.

A small, cheerful man with a white goatee beard and metal-rimmed glasses was scrubbing his hands at a washbasin when they entered. He dried himself, came over, and Caruso introduced them. 'This is Vito Rima, our forensic pathologist. He speaks excellent English.'

'A pleasure to meet you.' Rima shook their hands and said to Jennifer, 'I'm sure this is a difficult time, but there are some things I must explain. The body has been carefully thawed and is in remarkably good condition. So well preserved, in fact, that your father may look just as you remember him, which may be something of a shock.'

'How . . . how did my father die?'

'In my opinion, he probably froze to death,' Rima answered. 'There were bruises on his chest, arms and legs, which may have been caused when he fell into the crevasse. But the autopsy will tell us more, and I'll begin immediately after the identification. However, there is something you should be aware of. Many of the tests that determine time of death will depend on body and organ temperatures. In the case of your father, obviously that's impossible because his corpse has been frozen for so long. But the belongings we found should help prove that he died almost exactly two years ago. Will you explain, captain?'

'The body was fully clothed,' Caruso told Jennifer. 'And we found personal belongings in the pockets, and also in a rucksack near by.' He hesitated, as if there were something else he wanted to say. 'But I will explain later, after our business here is done.'

Rima slipped on a pair of rubber surgical gloves. 'If you feel ill, signorina, there's a plastic bucket in the corner.'

Jennifer felt ill already. On a metal trolley in the corner was a selection of surgeon's implements lying on a white rubber sheet, ready for the autopsy: a set of surgical scalpels, an electric saw and a drill among them. The thought of her father's body being mutilated by such instruments of death sent a cold shiver down her spine.

'Are you ready, signorina?'

'Y . . . yes.'

Rima led them to the steel table. He gripped the edge of the white sheet, his eyes asking Jennifer whether she was prepared. She took a deep breath and nodded.

As Rima started to pull back the sheet Jennifer closed her eyes, suddenly unable to watch. She was filled with a terrible dread and her heart pounded. In her mind she saw her father as she remembered him, saw him come up the garden path with open arms, saw his smiling face and felt his strong arms around her. *This is all too much to bear.*

She felt McCaul's hand gently grip her waist. 'Take your time, Jennifer. It's OK, I'm right beside you.'

She forced herself to open her eyes, and when she saw the naked torso, she gasped. Dark, ugly bruises covered his chest and arms. She looked closely at his face. His features were distorted, his skin the palest white, and his blue eyes were open and stared blankly up at the ceiling. Jennifer's stomach churned. Overcome, she looked away.

Caruso said quietly, 'Jennifer March, I must ask you formally to identify the body you see before you. Is this your father, Paul March?'

This time Jennifer took a long hard look at his face and felt her legs weaken.

'Signorina, is this man your father?' Caruso repeated.

She was struck dumb. Caruso said, 'Are you all right? Do you feel ill?'

Jennifer trembled, stared down at the corpse, the words spilling out in a torrent. 'I . . . I've never seen that man before in my life.'

22

'How are you feeling?'

Jennifer looked across at Caruso as they sat in his office. 'Shaken, but I'll be OK.'

Caruso handed steaming cups of coffee to her and McCaul but Jennifer ignored hers. *If the stranger in the morgue wasn't my father, then what if he's still alive?* She felt feverish at such a thought, and said to Caruso, 'What was the man doing with my father's passport?'

The detective shook his head. 'For now, that is a mystery, signorina.'

'Where exactly did you find it?'

'In the rucksack, among the clothes. There was also an automatic pistol.'

'You said you found belongings in the victim's pockets.'

'*Si.*'

'Could I see what you found?'

'Of course.' Caruso punched in a number on his phone, spoke for several moments and replaced the receiver. 'The evidence will be here shortly.'

'What about the guy's clothes?' McCaul asked.

'You will see those too.' Caruso studied Jennifer's face. 'Of course, the real question is, who is the man lying in the morgue? You're certain you never saw him before?'

'Never.'

'There is something else I should mention. Because he suffered frostbite to his feet and hands, we found it impossible to get a good set of fingerprints. Of course, we still have DNA evidence, and with luck we may identify him that way.'

There was a knock on the door and a female lab technician in a white coat carried a large cardboard box into the room and laid it on the desk. Caruso thanked the technician and she left.

'Let me show you the evidence we found,' Caruso said to Jennifer. 'And I have to tell you, signorina, some of it has me puzzled.'

The white Fiat telecommunications van pulled up a hundred metres from the Carabinieri headquarters. Two men wearing blue work overalls sat in the front seats. The passenger's cell phone rang, and he took the call. The conversation lasted less than ten seconds, then he switched off the phone, stepped out of the Fiat and went round the back to unlock the rear door. Inside were racks of engineer's supplies, cables and stacked plastic containers of parts and several boxes of tools. The man stepped into the van and closed the door. He lifted a false bottom in the floor. Stored underneath were fifty kilos of Semtex high explosive, enough to destroy an entire apartment building.

He made sure the explosives were securely packed, carefully checked that the remotely controlled detonator was in position, then replaced the cover over the floor. From one of the toolboxes he took a remote control device and slipped it into his overalls, then climbed back out of the van and went to join the driver. The driver started the van and drove directly across the square to the mouth of the HQ's underground car park, where a corporal was on duty beside the barrier.

The driver produced a company ID and a work sheet, handed them over as he smiled and said in Italian, 'We've got some phone lines to check. It shouldn't take too long.'

The corporal examined the ID and the work sheet. 'Who requested this work?'

The technician shrugged. 'God knows. Some bastard of a captain, no doubt.'

The corporal smiled, handed back the ID and lifted the barrier.

Caruso slipped on a pair of rubber surgical gloves and removed the contents of the evidence box. Each item was individually wrapped in a clear plastic bag: a heavy grey parka, a white woollen scarf, a green sweater, thick woollen trousers, climbing boots, and a vest and underpants. There was also a canvas rucksack, and in two other plastic bags were more clothes and an automatic pistol. Caruso opened the one containing the clothes: a white silk shirt and striped tie, a pair of black, patent-leather shoes, a pale blue suit.

'We found these in the rucksack. They are the kind of clothes a businessman might wear, and it seems this man had expensive tastes. The suit is American, and the shoes are Italian and hand made. The shirt is English, and made of silk. What's wrong, Signorina March?'

Jennifer stared at the clothes, resisting the urge to touch them. 'I . . . I think these belonged to my father.'

'You're sure?'

'I'm almost certain. They look like his things.'

'What about the other belongings? Do you recognise any of those as your father's?'

'No, only the clothes from the rucksack.'

Caruso frowned. 'I would like you to look again at your father's passport. Do you have any doubts it's him in the photograph?'

He opened the red file, placed the passport on the desk, and Jennifer studied the photograph again. 'No, it's definitely him.'

'Your father and the dead man have the same hair colour and face shape, and would appear to be about the same age, but I could not be sure they were not the same man until you identified the body. I will have our lab in Rome examine the passport to see if it is a forgery, but I have to say, it looks in order.'

Caruso opened several of the smaller plastic bags and laid their contents on the desk. A slip of torn paper, and two ticket stubs. He handed Jennifer and McCaul each a pair of surgical gloves. 'Please put these on before you touch the evidence.' He picked up the slip of torn paper. 'Take a look at this. It's one of the more interesting things we found, and the most puzzling. But unfortunately, it has been damaged and a part of the paper is missing.'

Jennifer studied the piece of paper. It was faded, and at the bottom of the ragged page was a series of numbers. Some more numbers appeared to have been completely dissolved, perhaps by melting ice, but the rest of the note was clearly distinguishable.

H. Vogel
Berg Edelweiss
705

'What does it mean?' Jennifer asked.

Caruso shrugged. 'H. Vogel looks like it may be a name, perhaps. And Berg means mountain in German. However, there is no Edleweiss mountain in Switzerland. As for the numbers, some of them appear to be missing, but they could be anything. Part of an account number, or a phone number, perhaps. Who's to say?'

Jennifer handed the paper to McCaul as Caruso showed them the ticket stubs. 'These were in the man's trouser pocket along with the slip of paper. Two one-way railway tickets from Zurich to Brig, second class, dated fifteenth April, two years ago. The tickets have been clipped, which suggests they were used. Two tickets for the same train journey could mean that, whoever the victim was, he travelled to Brig with a companion before he made his way up to the glacier. But whether his death happened the same day or not is impossible to know. I had the Swiss police check the hotels in the area, but none had any record of a Paul March as a guest.'

Jennifer examined the ticket stubs. 'What else did you find?'

'This.' Caruso opened one of the smaller evidence bags and held out a small silver key. 'It was found in a pocket of your father's clothes. Did you ever see the key before?'

Jennifer's heart skipped as a memory jolted her. 'Yes, I think so. I've just remembered.'

'Explain.'

'A month before my father vanished, I remember he was really anxious about something. One day I went to see him in his study and noticed a yellow legal pad open on his desk. Across the top of the pad he'd written the word "Spiderweb". It was all I had time to notice, because he realised that I'd seen the pad and got really angry. He said I shouldn't have been reading his papers, that it was his private business. Then he locked away the notepad in a security box, along with a computer floppy disk.'

Caruso frowned. 'What do you think spiderweb meant?'

'I've no idea. But the box was one of those metal fireproof ones that they sell in business supply stores, and I remembered it had a silver key. I'd never seen the box before.'

'Where's the box now?'

'I searched my father's study after he vanished and couldn't find it.'

Caruso pursed his lips. 'Strange.'

Jennifer indicated the evidence box. 'Is that everything you found?'

'*Si.*'

'The man had no wallet?'

'No. But if he had one, it could still be somewhere in the glacier. We searched as much as we could, but it would be danger-ous to cut away too much ice in the crevasse – it might collapse.'

'You mean there could be more evidence that you haven't recovered?'

'Of course it's possible. But I have to think of the safety of my men. A crevasse is a very dangerous place to work, especially at this time of year when the snow starts to melt and the ice plates shift. It can suddenly close up, or crack open wider, and a man could easily lose his life. We were lucky to find what we did.'

Jennifer handed the tickets to McCaul and said to Caruso, 'It doesn't make sense. Why would someone use a route that's obviously dangerous? Unless they were trying to cross the border illegally and in a hurry?'

'True.' Caruso shrugged. 'There is, however, another possibility to consider.'

'What?' Jennifer asked.

'Your father played some part in this man's death.' Caruso

hesitated. 'I learned through Interpol of the terrible crime that happened before he vanished. It occurred to me that your father may have been running from the law. That he may have fled Switzerland for that reason and may have killed the man on the glacier and left behind his own passport and a rucksack full of clothes. Hoping perhaps that if the body was ever found, it would appear to be that of Paul March.'

Jennifer flushed and her eyes met Caruso's stare. 'Captain, I knew my father. He would never have committed murder. I'm certain of that.'

A moment later there was a knock on the door and Rima entered. 'The autopsy is almost complete. Perhaps you'd like to know what I've found so far?'

Caruso nodded. 'You'd better tell us.'

'There were no internal injuries of any kind, and the bruises look like they were caused by the fall into the crevasse. It seems the victim simply froze to death. There are some further tests to be done on the internal organs, and that will take time. But from what I've already seen, don't expect any surprises.'

'Thanks, Vito. That will be all for now.'

The pathologist shook hands with Jennifer and McCaul and left. 'You see, there's no evidence of murder,' Jennifer said.

'It seems not,' Caruso admitted. 'But the mystery remains. Where are you both staying?'

'At the Berghof Hotel in Simplon.'

Caruso closed the red file and gathered the evidence bags and replaced them in the box, as if their meeting had come to an end. He took a card from his breast pocket and wrote on the back. 'My home number, in case you can't reach me here. If you have any more accidents like the one you had this morning, I would appreciate it if you called me at once.'

'Thank you,' Jennifer said.

'And now, I must say good afternoon.' Caruso took his jacket from the back of his chair, gestured to the photograph on his desk and smiled faintly. 'When an Italian wife cooks dinner, it is wise not to be late.' He turned to McCaul. 'I again offer my sympathy, and I assure you I will speak once more with the Swiss and ask them to look into your son's case more closely. But may I make a suggestion? It would be better if you left the investigation to the proper authorities.'

'As a private citizen, I can investigate all I want.' McCaul's voice flared angrily. 'Just so long as I don't break the law or obstruct any official investigation.'

Caruso nodded. 'True, that is your right.'

'Then understand that I mean to find whoever killed my son. And no one's going to tell me to keep my nose out of this, including you, captain. This is my business as much as anyone's.'

Caruso took the outburst calmly. 'I can imagine how you must feel. You have suffered a terrible loss. But I would ask you to try not to get in the way of the police if you insist on a personal investigation.' He stuffed the red file in his briefcase. 'I will study my case notes on the evidence tonight. Perhaps there may be some small clue I've missed. If there is, I promise I will contact you at once.'

In the underground car park the two men worked quickly. They reversed the van towards a thick metal fuel pipe that ran from a massive external storage tank which supplied the building's heating fuel. Next to a stairwell, they noticed the black-lettered sign with the outline of a finger, pointing up: *Mortuaria*.

One of the men armed the remote-controlled detonator in the Semtex while the other watched the car park and anxiously clutched a silenced Beretta pistol concealed in his pocket. Five minutes later, their work finished, both men removed their overalls. They wore business suits underneath. They locked the van and crossed the car park to the stairs that led up to the ground floor. No one challenged their exit, and two minutes later they stepped out of the front entrance.

Caruso went down to the underground car park and squeezed into his white Lancia. He was already late for dinner and his wife wouldn't be pleased. But the Lancia had a portable blue strobe light and a siren for emergencies, and Caruso intended to use both to get clear of the traffic.

It was against regulations, but he'd rather face his superior's reprimand than his wife's temper. He started the engine and drove up to the mouth of the basement car park. As he checked for traffic, he caught sight of two men climbing into a black BMW parked across the square.

Both wore dark business suits; one was thin and blond, and the other short and stocky, his head shaved close to the skull. Caruso frowned. For a moment he thought he had passed the same two men in the car park stairwell. Perhaps he was mistaken? He thought no more about it as he swung left, out on to the square. Fifteen minutes later he was already halfway home, his Lancia doing 120 kilometres per hour on the autostrada.

Mark pulled up outside the HQ building and saw a blue Nissan across the square. He felt a surge of relief and took out his note-book. Before leaving the Berghof Hotel he'd asked the woman for McCaul's licence number, which she got from his guest registration card. *Bingo*: the numbers matched. He figured Jennifer was still inside the building, identifying her father's body. As he slipped his notebook back in his pocket, he noticed a trattoria across the square which had a good view of the HQ building. He decided to have a coffee and wait there.

As he locked the Opel, he suddenly saw Jennifer come down the HQ's steps in the company of a tall, rugged man. They were no more than thirty yards away when, to Mark's horror, Jennifer suddenly glanced in his direction.

He averted his face and walked away. Sixty yards up the street, he mustered the courage to glance back. To his relief he saw that Jennifer and the man had crossed the square and entered the trattoria.

The trattoria was almost deserted. Jennifer and McCaul each ordered paninis and a glass of red wine. 'You look shaken.'

'Do you believe in the theory that everyone has a double?'

'I don't follow.'

Jennifer felt totally confused as she stared out of the window. 'I just saw a man as we came out of the building and he looked the absolute double of someone I know. I could have *sworn* it was Mark.'

'Who?'

'A friend of mine. I'd almost convinced myself it was *really* him, but that's crazy. He's back in New York.'

'What happened in the morgue probably upset you more than you realise. A shock can do that, set your mind running wild.' McCaul left his food untouched as he excused himself to make a phone call. 'If you don't mind, I've got to make arrangements to have Chuck's body flown home.'

Jennifer saw the distress etched in his face. 'Is there anything I can do to help?'

McCaul was grim. 'Thanks, but I guess not.'

Jennifer watched him walk towards the telephone at the back of the restaurant. He looked tired, as if the burden of his grief was wearing him down. She looked out on to the street. She could have *sworn* the man she saw was really Mark. But that was absurd: he was five thousand miles away. She scoured the street for any sign of his double, but the man was nowhere to be seen. Maybe McCaul was right, and what had happened in the morgue had addled her mind. Then a moment later she noticed a black Opel parked some distance across the square, near the front of the headquarters building. The car looked to her to have dark-tinted windows. Could it be the same Opel that had followed her in Simplon?

Or am I becoming paranoid? Earlier she thought that she had seen Mark, which was absurd, and now she had almost convinced herself that she was seeing the same Opel again. She suddenly felt that she was being ridiculous, and tried to push her thoughts from her mind.

She felt worn down by her own frustration, plagued by the puzzles she couldn't find answers to: *What has become of my father? How did his passport and belongings end up in the dead man's rucksack? Where did he vanish to? What if he's still alive?* The very thought of that possibility was driving her to distraction. Her head throbbed, racked by confusion.

McCaul came back. 'It's done. They're going to fly Chuck's body home just as soon as the Swiss authorities sign the release.'

He looked broken hearted and Jennifer touched his hand. 'Maybe you shouldn't be so angry with Caruso. I really think he means well.'

'Maybe he does. But last night I had to identify Chuck's body at a morgue in Brig. I guess I still can't get it out of my mind that he's really dead. And having to ship my son home in a coffin cuts my heart out.' There was sudden rage in McCaul's voice. 'Right this minute I want to find the son-of-a-bitch who was responsible and tear them apart, limb from limb.'

Jennifer held his hand. 'Are you OK?'

'I guess I'm just about holding up. What about you?'

'I don't know what to think. I came here believing I was finally going to see my father, and instead I saw a stranger. But why did he have my father's passport and belongings? A moment ago I was even convinced I saw the black Opel again.'

'What are you talking about – *Jesus!*'

A tremendous explosion erupted across the street and the sheet-glass windows in the trattoria shattered. A violent draught of air swept through the room with the force of a hurricane, and McCaul pushed Jennifer to the floor. 'Get down!'

He flung himself down beside her as a thick cloud of dust rolled in from across the square, and then they heard a crashing sound like a heavy clap of thunder.

Mark was back sitting in the Opel, observing the restaurant and wondering whether Jennifer had really spotted him, when something weird happened. One minute he was looking at Jennifer and McCaul engaged in conversation, and feeling a pang of jealousy, when suddenly there was burst of brilliant white light and an incredible sound like thunder exploded in his ears.

The Opel rose several feet off the ground as if suspended in midair, then Mark felt the full force of a powerful blast and his car was turned violently on its side. As it rolled over, his skull cracked off the roof. Seconds later there was another explosion and his gas tank ignited.

When the noise died, Jennifer struggled to her feet. The entire HQ building was demolished, collapsed like a house of cards. Fires raged in the debris, a vast cloud of dust rose above the building, and several cars parked across the square were in flames. Jennifer put a hand to her mouth. '*Oh my God!* What . . . what happened?'

'It sounded like a bomb went off.' McCaul was ashen.

People streamed out of nearby buildings, dazed and confused, some of them screaming, others trying to help the injured. It seemed like seconds but it must have been minutes later when the sound of sirens filled the air and a couple of fire tenders and ambulances suddenly appeared.

McCaul grabbed her hand. 'Come on, there's nothing we can do. Let's get the hell out of here.'

23

They took the autostrada that led north out of the city, and as McCaul drove they heard the wail of sirens and saw a convoy of ambulances and fire engines speeding towards Turin.

Ten minutes later they drove off the highway and into a village. The sign said it was called Miasino, and it looked to be no more than a collection of narrow cobbled streets, a church and a dingy-looking bar with a couple of shiny aluminium tables out front. McCaul halted at the kerb. 'Are you OK?'

'I . . . I think so.' Jennifer was shaking and had hardly spoken, too numbed by the explosion.

McCaul nodded towards the bar. 'I reckon we both need a stiff drink.'

A young man stood behind the bar, lazily polishing some glasses. McCaul ordered two whiskies, took the glasses and led Jennifer to a window seat that was out of hearing of the bartender. Her hands shook as she swallowed the whiskey. 'How can you be so sure that the blast was caused by a bomb?'

McCaul ignored his drink. 'Let's just say that intuition tells me it wasn't an accident. Whatever it was that ripped apart that building, it sounded like a pretty powerful explosive, and from the look of the damage it did whoever was inside didn't stand a chance. Besides, if it was deliberate that would make some kind of sense.'

'What do you mean?'

'Think about it. First Chuck is killed, then your jeep is tampered with. A little while ago you thought you were being followed, and now this. All the paperwork on the case was probably stored in the building, as well as the body, the most importance evidence of all. Getting rid of both would make it almost impossible for Caruso to carry on with the investigation. If you ask me, someone doesn't want this case to go any farther.'

'But why? Who'd do such a thing?'

But suddenly McCaul wasn't listening. 'Give me Caruso's card.'

'What for?'

'Maybe now he'll believe there's something weird about this whole business.' He stood and walked towards a wall phone by the bar.

McCaul dialled several times without getting through, then put the phone down in frustration. He asked the bartender for a phone directory, searched through the pages and jotted something down, then spoke with the bartender again and came back. 'There's no reply from Caruso's number.'

'He's probably still on his way home.'

'We need to talk to him.' McCaul waved the slip of paper he'd written on. 'He's listed in the book and I've got an address from the phone number. He lives in some place called Osoria. The bartender speaks a little English. According to him, it's a village maybe half an hour from here.'

It took them almost thirty minutes to reach Osoria. The tiny mountain village was no more than a dozen streets, a jumble of stucco and cut-stone houses set below rolling hills of thickly forested slopes. Darkness was falling, but McCaul found the street they were looking for, at the end of the village. It was high up on a winding, hilly road lined with modern detached villas. They counted off the house numbers until they found Caruso's address. A gravel driveway led up to a two-storey villa with a steep garden of pear and olive trees. A garage was off to the right, the doors closed, a white Lancia parked in the front driveway.

'Let's see if anyone's home.' McCaul climbed out of the jeep and Jennifer followed him up to the front door. He rang the doorbell half a dozen times, but when no one appeared he tried the handle. The door was unlocked and he pushed it open. 'Anybody there?'

When there was no reply they stepped into a narrow hallway. It was empty. McCaul opened a door to the left. They found themselves in a large, deserted front living room with a panoramic view of the village.

McCaul said, 'We'll try the other rooms.' They moved back out into the hallway and opened another door. As they stepped into a kitchen, Jennifer froze. The room was in disarray, chairs overturned, broken crockery scattered around the floor. A body lay face up in a pool of blood. It was the dark-haired, middle-aged woman she had seen in the photograph on Caruso's desk. She had been shot through the head, her eyes bulged open in death, and a crimson pool had spread obscenely around the back of her skull. Jennifer watched in horror as McCaul knelt and felt the woman's wrist. 'Is . . . is she dead?'

McCaul stood and nodded. 'But not long. The body's still warm. You look pale. You'd better sit down.'

Jennifer was in shock as McCaul put his arm round her and led her into the front room. He sat her down on the couch, crossed to a drinks cabinet near the window and found a bottle of brandy. He poured a glass and forced it into her hands. 'Drink this.'

Jennifer tried, but she couldn't swallow the raw spirit. 'Will someone please tell me what's going on? I feel like I'm going out of my mind.' She stared up at McCaul, but he had no answers, neither of them had, and she knew it. She put her glass down. 'What . . . what about Caruso?'

McCaul stepped towards the door. 'Stay here. And don't move or touch anything.'

Jennifer stood shakily. 'No, please, I'd rather go with you.'

They searched upstairs but there was no sign of Caruso. The bedrooms were undisturbed, the closets unopened and no drawers ransacked. McCaul had found a pair of household rubber gloves in the bathroom, slipped them on, and warned Jennifer again not to touch anything. 'The police will dust the house for fingerprints. You wouldn't be doing yourself any favours by leaving your prints all over the place.'

One of the bedrooms at the back of the villa was used as a study. Lying on top of a writing bureau was Caruso's briefcase. McCaul flipped it open and examined the contents. 'Remember the case file that Caruso took home? It's gone.'

'What do you mean?'

'Either Caruso left it someplace else or somebody took it. Here, see for yourself.'

McCaul held open the briefcase and Jennifer saw some papers, but there was no sign of Caruso's red file.

'So where the hell's Caruso?' McCaul said aloud as he put the briefcase down and searched through the bureau's drawers. Except for a couple of fresh writing pads, some domestic bills and receipts, there was nothing else inside. The last drawer was locked. McCaul found a metal letter opener in one of the other drawers and forced the lock. A pistol lay inside. It was a small .32 Beretta automatic, the kind of weapon someone might use for target practice. He checked that the pistol's seven-round magazine was fully loaded and stuffed it in his pocket.

'What are you doing?'

Sweat beaded McCaul's face. 'What do you think? I'd like to be prepared, Jennifer. What happened here wasn't some kind of domestic argument gone wrong. Now how about we check downstairs again.'

They went back down to the kitchen and McCaul opened the back door. When they stepped outside on to the back patio they saw another door leading to the garage. McCaul opened it carefully. It was pitch dark inside and he fumbled until he found a light switch and flicked it on. A neon light came on overhead. A small red Fiat was parked in the centre of the garage and Jennifer guessed it had probably belonged to Caruso's wife.

She noticed a darkened figure in the driver's seat and recognised the face at once. Slumped across the seat, shot through the mouth and with half the back of his skull blown away, was Caruso.

Jennifer tried to control herself. Her body shook and bile rose in her throat. The sight of Caruso and his wife so brutally slain was almost too much to take in, and she could barely watch as McCaul opened the passenger's door and felt Caruso's wrist. Blood had partly congealed on his mouth and throat and the rivulets of crimson had spread down his shirt front and on to the car seat. 'He hasn't been dead for longer than half an hour.'

Jennifer turned away, unable to look at the grisly scene. She tried not to break down, and then she felt McCaul's hand on her shoulder and turned into his arms. 'Take it easy, Jennifer.'

'I'm OK. I'll be fine.' She steeled herself to look at Caruso again. Clutched in his right hand was an automatic pistol. His thumb was still caught in the trigger guard, the gun lying on his lap, as if he had put the weapon into his own mouth and the force of the gun discharging had propelled it away.

'If you ask me, someone did a pretty neat job,' McCaul said.

'What . . . what do you mean?'

'Think about it. What I said about the scene in the kitchen not being a domestic argument gone wrong. But maybe somebody meant it to look that way. Fixed it so it appeared that Caruso killed his wife and then shot himself. Whoever did it, they're experts, that's for sure. I'd guess that when the cops dust this place for prints they're not going to find a single one belonging to whoever committed the murders.'

A terrifying thought occurred to Jennifer: whoever had executed Caruso and his wife might be the same people who had killed her mother. Old sorrows came rushing in, stabbed at her heart, and she felt like breaking down, but McCaul took a firm hold of her arm. 'I think we've seen enough. Let's get out of here.'

★

As they stepped into the living room again, McCaul suddenly pointed towards the window. 'We're about to have company.'

Jennifer saw a police car, approaching fast from the village. The flashing blue light disappeared behind some trees, then reappeared again as the car sped up towards the villa.

'Either someone alerted the cops or else they're on their way to tell Caruso about the blast.' McCaul took a handkerchief from his pocket and quickly wiped the brandy bottle and glasses and replaced them in the cabinet. 'Just in case anybody gets the wrong idea. OK, let's move.'

'Shouldn't we wait for the police?'

'Are you crazy? That's the last thing we want to do. They might be tempted to suspect *us*. And after seeing what happened to Caruso I'd say nobody's safe around here, not even the cops. I think it's better we paddle this boat on our own until we can figure out what's going on.'

Jennifer thought she saw what looked like raw fear in McCaul's eyes. Before she could protest he led her out to his jeep. He started the engine and shifted into gear, but left the headlights off until they had sped down the driveway and were heading in the opposite direction to the village. 'Where are we going?'

'I wish the hell I knew.'

The two men sat in the black BMW, parked in one of the narrow village streets above Caruso's villa. The blond passenger had a pair of powerful infrared binoculars in his hands. He watched as the blue-and-white police Fiat strained up the hill, its strobe light flashing, then he eagerly shifted his view back to McCaul's Nissan as it sped away from the villa. He put down the binoculars and nodded to his driver. 'Follow the jeep.'

PART THREE

24

New York

Lou Garuda approached the reception desk at the Cauldwell home. A Puerto Rican nurse looked up. 'Can I help you?'

Garuda smiled. The Puerto Rican woman had terrific tits. 'I sure hope so. Robert March. He's a resident here. You know him?'

'Sure, I know Bobby. How can I help?'

'His sister Jennifer left for Europe yesterday. I was asked to stop by and keep an eye on him.' Garuda held up a brown paper bag. 'So I thought I'd say hello. Brought him some candy, thought he might like that.'

'Are you a relative?'

'No.' Garuda showed his badge. 'I'm a cop. Why, is there a problem with Bobby?'

'Not at all. Just wait here, I'll have someone take you to him.'

The big black man with Leroy on his name badge frowned at Garuda as they walked towards the gardens. 'How come I ain't seen you here before?'

'I'm a friend of Mark's. He and Jennifer are travelling and Mark asked me to call by.'

'Well, there's the man.'

Garuda thought: *Jesus, some people have got it tough.* The kid was in a wheelchair, his head lolled to one side. 'Hi. I'm Lou. Mark asked me to call by and say hello.'

Leroy left them but the kid said nothing. Garuda sat beside him and handed over the bag of candy. He saw that Bobby had a notepad and pen stuffed down the side of his chair. 'I brought you a present. Can you understand me, kid?'

Bobby looked up with a vacant stare, slow to respond, as if he was unused to strangers coming to visit him. Garuda sighed and thought: *The poor kid, this is going to be a waste of fucking time.* 'I'm a cop, just like Mark, and I'd like to ask you some questions, Bobby. Maybe you can help me. I guess you heard they found your father's body?'

This time the kid's eyes opened wide. Garuda took out his own notebook and said, 'I was kind of wondering if Jennifer told you anything about that?'

Silence. But now the kid had a wild stare. 'Can you understand me? Just nod if you can.'

Garuda thought: *I'm talking to my fucking self. The kid's a vegetable.* 'Bobby, nod if you understand me.'

The kid sort of nodded, but still had that funny stare. Garuda decided to tell him everything he knew. When he finished, the kid started to cry. Garuda stood, alarmed. *I've put my fucking foot in it.* Nobody could have told him. 'Hey . . . steady on, kid.'

Bobby's crying got worse, and then his limbs began to shake, and a gurgling sound came from his throat. Leroy came out into the garden. 'What's going on, man? Bobby's all upset . . .'

'Beats me.' Garuda put away his notebook. 'Well, I gotta go.'

What a waste of fucking time, Garuda thought as he drove the Porsche back to the Long Beach Police Department on Westchester Street. He'd hoped the kid might have been able to help him, but he'd been wrong. He'd already had Debbie Kootzmeyer over at JFK check the passenger lists and she confirmed that Jennifer March had taken the Swiss Airlines 9.15 p.m. flight from Newark to Zurich the previous night. When he got to his desk, he took out his old notes on the March case. He went through them again but came up with nothing.

Across the hall sat Janice H. Fortensky, one of the department's civilian secretarial staff. She was terrific at trawling the Net for information. Garuda hated computers, but that was where the information was these days. Janice seemed to know how to find any information she needed on the Net, and fast, whereas it took him fucking *hours*.

He strolled across to her desk. She wasn't much to look at. Unmarried, thick glasses and a figure that was about fifty pounds overweight in all the wrong places. Besides that, she had body odour. He put a hand on her shoulder. 'Janice, honey, I need a favour.'

She barely looked up from her computer console. 'So do I, and badly. But you know how difficult it is to find a man in New York?'

Garuda smiled. 'Help me on this one and I promise you a favour in return. A company called Prime International Securities, ever heard of it?'

'Nope.'

'Well, it folded a year ago, but I need to find out everything I can about them. Newspaper reports, anything about their business and top personnel, that kind of thing.'

'Gee, I'm pretty busy right now. Got two reports to finish.'

Garuda smiled, stroked her hair. *Jesus, it felt like she hadn't washed it in months. No wonder she had trouble finding guys to bang her.* 'I'll buy you dinner. How's that?'

She blinked up at him through thick lenses. 'Will you fuck me afterwards?'

Garuda sighed. 'Never mind, I'll do it myself.'

Four hours later Garuda had as much information as he could find on the Net. Prime was no longer in business, sure, but one of the former company vice-presidents was listed as a Frederick Kammer. Except there wasn't much on Kammer's personal details and the information on the company was pretty minimal, corporate bullshit mainly. He read through the material again, then looked back over his reports, the ones he'd written at the time when the March case made the papers. As he reread one of the reports, something struck him. He blinked at the words on the page in front of him, read them again, and felt strangely excited.

When he got home that evening, Angelina was asleep. He undressed and climbed in beside her in the darkness. He fumbled under the duvet, slid his hands expertly over her taut body, and worked away until his fingers were down between her legs. Angelina started to squirm. He took her hand, guided it down to his hardness. 'Feel what I've got for you, baby.'

'*Jesus*, you're like a fucking rock.'

Garuda grinned in the darkness. 'The case I told you about. I think I've got a lead.'

'That's some fucking lead. Last time I thought you'd only got the hard-on in your head?'

Garuda climbed on top, eased himself into her, heard Angelina moan. 'Not this time, baby.'

25

Italy

Half an hour after leaving Osoria, Jennifer and McCaul had reached the outskirts of a village named Biella. Dusk was falling and dark rain clouds were gathering overhead. A few hundred metres outside the village McCaul drove into a lay-by. A wooden gate led to a forest clearing, where a picnic rest stop was dotted with rough wooden tables and benches, surrounded by thick pine trees. He halted and took a tourist map and a Maglite pencil torch from the glove compartment.

'Shouldn't we keep going?'

'To where, Jennifer? We can't just drive aimlessly. We need to find out where in God's name we are.'

Jennifer was still shaking, but she forced herself to climb out of the jeep and join McCaul as he sat and opened the map out on one of the benches. 'I've worked some weird cases in my time, but this thing takes the prize.'

'Why . . . why would anyone have wanted to kill Caruso?'

McCaul looked at her. 'For the only reason I can think of. To stop this investigation dead in its tracks. First the corpse is destroyed. Now the paperwork has disappeared and the detective in charge of the case is murdered. It seems to me like someone's desperate to stop this inquiry from going any farther, even if it means wholesale slaughter.'

Jennifer knew that McCaul's suspicions made sense. There was no other logical reason she could think of, but she couldn't even begin to imagine *who* would want to obstruct the investigation. 'What would be the point?'

'You've got me there. But I reckon the answer's got to be in your father's past. No matter which way you look at it, it all goes back to him. Murder doesn't just *happen*. There's always motive of some kind. There's got to be something in his past, or even your mother's, that points us in the right direction.'

'What do you want to know?'

'Everything, Jennifer. Everything you can remember.'

She told McCaul about the night the masked intruder broke into her home, and about her life before and afterwards. When she finished, he put a hand on hers. 'It sounds like you had a pretty rough time of it.'

'Seeing Caruso and his wife brought everything back to me.'

'What do you know about your father's firm?'

'Almost nothing, apart from the fact that it was involved in private investment. He never really talked that much about his work. The police questioned his colleagues, but they were mystified as to why he vanished. And the police said they found nothing to suggest he was in any trouble at the office that might have caused him to disappear.'

'Did he ever travel to Switzerland or Italy on business?'

'Often. He travelled a lot.'

'How long did he work for Prime?'

'Seventeen years.'

'It's still in business?'

'No, the company folded last year.'

'Why?'

'There's no reason that I know of.'

McCaul thought for a moment, then said quietly, 'The stuff you found in the attic that had to do with this guy, Joseph Delgado. What do you think happened to it?'

'I honestly don't know.'

'Could your father have hidden the papers someplace?'

'I never gave it much thought. There were too many other things happening in my life that seemed more important, and after my mother's death I was preoccupied with Bobby.'

'What about the security box you saw in his study? Is there

somewhere special your father might have kept it hidden? Maybe a bank where he or your mother had a safety deposit box?'

Jennifer shook her head. 'You think the attic stuff or the box might have something to do with my father's disappearance, don't you?'

'I don't know, Jennifer. Maybe I'm clutching at straws here, but I'm looking for anything that might open the door of this mystery just the smallest crack. So try and think. Please.'

Jennifer thought hard. 'I can't think of anywhere special my father might have used as a hiding place. And if there was, he probably would never have told me.'

McCaul was frustrated. 'We're getting absolutely nowhere with this, aren't we? OK, let's think about what we *do* know. Someone using your father's passport made their way up to the glacier. Whether it was to cross the border illegally or not we don't know, but that's the only likely reason. But there's a snowstorm and the guy winds up either falling into the glacier or else, as Caruso suggested, he's deliberately pushed by an accomplice who planted the passport on the body. Caruso was probably right about one thing. If your father was on the run from the authorities, the last thing he'd want found in his possession was a document that betrayed his identity.'

Jennifer flushed at the accusation. 'My father wouldn't have killed anyone. He wasn't a murderer.'

'Don't get defensive, I'm not saying he did. But let's face the fact that it would have been a pretty neat deception. If ever the body's discovered, it's going to look like the guy in the crevasse is Paul March, wanted on suspicion of murder. But what gets me is what were the two people doing up there in the first place? Did they know each other? Were they friends, acquaintances or what? And where the hell were they headed?'

McCaul broke off and massaged his temples, as if his own barrage of questions was too much to take in. 'It's going to be dark soon. We can't hang around here all night. We'll need to find a hotel.' He studied the map using the Maglite. 'There's another town not far from here, maybe ten miles.'

'I stopped to look at a small *Berghaus* when I was on the Wasenhorn with Anton.'

McCaul looked up, confused. 'A *what?*'

'A mountain hut. It's a rest stop for climbers.' Jennifer pointed to the area on the map. 'Close by, on the Italian side of the border, I saw an old Catholic monastery, the Crown of Thorns. Anton said it's been there for centuries and is often used by mountaineers when the weather turns bad.'

'So?'

'When he mentioned that, it made me think. Whoever tried to cross the Wasenhorn that night had to be heading in the general direction of Varzo, and the monastery's the first place they would have reached.'

'What are you suggesting?'

'I know it's a long shot, but someone there might remember if anyone came looking for shelter on the night of the storm. We could be at the monastery in less than an hour and then try to find somewhere to stay in Varzo.'

Suddenly they saw a white Fiat with blue Carabinieri markings streak past on the road. McCaul waited until it was out of sight and got to his feet, just as a crack of thunder exploded and rain started to drizzle down.

'OK, we'll give it a try. I guess the monastery's all we've got, apart from a big bunch of questions. And here's the one that really stumps me. Why the hell is somebody so scared that they're prepared to commit murder to halt a police investigation?' McCaul folded away the map, slipped the torch in his pocket, stared back at Jennifer. 'If you ask me, it can only mean somebody, somewhere, has a damned big secret to hide.'

26

Turin

Mark came awake to the sound of a female voice and opened his eyes. He was in a hospital bed, apparently in a private room. A pretty young nurse leaned over him as she adjusted his pillow. *'Come sta?'*

He looked up, groggy and confused. Beside her an elderly, white-coated man with a cheerful face said something in rapid Italian, but Mark didn't understand a word.

'He wants to know if you speak Italian, Ryan.'

Mark suddenly noticed Kelso standing by the door and said, 'What – what happened . . . ?'

Kelso came over. 'I'll explain later. Right now, the doctor wants to examine you. He doesn't speak English, so I'll translate. By the way, the nurse asked how you felt.'

'Apart from a pounding headache and ringing in my ears, pretty confused.'

Kelso translated for the doctor, who shone a small torch into Mark's eyes, then held up a couple of fingers and asked a question. 'He wants to know how many fingers you see,' Kelso said.

'Two.'

The doctor checked Mark's ears with another instrument, then went to work with his stethoscope, before checking his pulse.

'I need an explanation, Kelso.'

'Don't you remember?'

'There was an explosion. My car caught fire . . .'

'You were pulled free. The doctor tells me you suffered some cuts, bruises and mild concussion, but your X-rays show no obvious damage.'

Mark's head throbbed. He put a hand to his brow and felt a

strip of sticking plaster across his forehead where he'd cracked his skull against the car's roof. 'How long have I been here?'

'Several hours.'

He had completely lost track of time. He recalled the terrible *crack* of the explosion and the intensity of the aftershock. He vaguely remembered being dragged from his car and hearing the endless bleat of ambulance sirens, but then he'd passed out and everything afterwards was a blur.

The doctor finished his examination, gave him a friendly pat and spoke again in Italian.

'He says you're to rest,' Kelso explained. 'Those are his firm orders. He wants to make certain you suffered no permanent damage. *Grazie, dottore.*'

'*Prego.*'

Kelso pulled up a chair after the nurse and doctor had left. 'You sure look like shit.'

'Spare me the concern, Kelso, and just give me the low down.'

'The Carabinieri headquarters is rubble. I heard they counted six dead, five of them cops, and dozens more are seriously injured.'

'What caused the explosion?'

Kelso shook his head. 'I don't know. But a local radio report suggested there was a fuel storage tank near the basement that may have ignited.'

'You don't sound very convinced.'

'Until the forensics teams have sifted through the pieces, there's no telling with any certainty what caused the blast. Personally, I suspect it may have been a bomb.'

'A *bomb*?'

Kelso sighed, spreading his hands in a helpless gesture. 'Look, Ryan, I'm going to be frank here. The blast seems too much of a coincidence. Sure, accidents happen all the time, but if it was deliberate and someone didn't want this case to go any farther, then they sure went about it the right way. I went to see the damage for myself, not half an hour ago. The basement morgue was completely destroyed and probably the corpse and any evidence along with it. Which pretty much puts paid to any swift progress being made on the case. Am I making myself clear?'

'But why? Who'd want to obstruct the investigation?'

Kelso's face showed his concern. 'Let's just ignore that question for now and worry about Jennifer.'

'The last time I saw her was in a restaurant across the square, seconds before the explosion.'

'You'd better tell me exactly what you saw, Ryan.'

Mark told him and Kelso jotted in a notepad. 'Did you get the vehicle's number?'

'It's in a notebook in my jacket pocket, wherever the hell my clothes are.'

Kelso noticed a locker beside the bed and found Mark's clothes inside. He rummaged through the jacket pockets and handed the notebook to Mark, who read off the licence number. Kelso wrote it down. 'You say this guy McCaul was at the hotel?'

'He's the father of the kid who found the body on the glacier.'

'Who says so?'

'It's what I was told at the inn.' Mark explained about his visit to Jennifer's hotel, and about her accident. 'Someone may have tampered with the brake hose on her jeep.'

'You're *sure* about that?'

'That's what the sergeant confirmed. Something else I learned. The kid who found the body is dead.'

Kelso was sombre. 'So I heard. The Swiss police claim he had another accident at the Furka pass, but it seemed suspicious to me, so I'm having it looked into.'

'The innkeeper said McCaul was here to identify his son's body.'

Kelso looked doubtful. 'It still doesn't explain what he's doing with Jennifer. I'd better have his background checked out. If he isn't who he says he is, Jennifer could be in grave danger.'

Mark sat up. 'What makes you think that?'

'Nothing, but right now I wouldn't discount *anything*.' Kelso put away his notebook. 'We tried calling her cell phone as a last resort. If she answered, we could at least have figured out where she was by having the signal triangulated. Except her phone was switched off and until she turns it on again we haven't a hope of locating her, but we'll keep trying.'

Mark felt exasperated, and struggled to get out of bed, but Kelso said angrily, 'What the fuck do you think you're doing?'

'I'm going to try to find Jennifer.'

Kelso put a hand on his arm. 'Talk sense, Ryan. The fact is, maybe I overstepped my mark. This whole business of using you was probably a big mistake.'

'Why?'

'You could have been killed. And by staying on the case, you could put yourself in even more danger. I don't want that on my conscience. So how about you do us both a big favour and as soon as you're discharged you take the first flight home?'

'Like hell I will.' Mark pushed Kelso's hand away and struggled to get out of the bed, but he felt dizzy the moment his feet touched the floor.

Kelso caught him as he collapsed back on to the bed. 'Take it easy, Ryan. You need to rest.'

'You've *got* to find Jennifer. You've got the CIA behind you, Kelso. Call in the Carabinieri. Call in more men. *Find her.*'

'I can't just put out an all-points bulletin. Remember that this is a covert operation. Involving the Italians might cause questions to be asked, and I can't afford that. But trust me to do everything in my power to find her.'

'What's that supposed to mean?'

'I'll hire a couple of piloted choppers at the nearest airport. With the description of the vehicle you've given, and the licence number, I'll have them scour the main roads to search for the damaged Nissan.'

'And what? Hope you get lucky?' Mark was frantic. 'It's not good enough, Kelso.'

'Look, Ryan, I've been working this case since long before Paul March vanished. It's taken four goddamned years out of my life and right now I'm two months away from retirement . . .'

'What's that got to do with it?'

'I want the damned lid closed on this thing before I say goodbye to my career. Which means I'll do whatever I have to in order to get to the bottom of it. And right now, the best thing you can do to help me is try to recover.' Kelso went to turn towards the door. 'I'll be in touch if I have any news about Jennifer. If you need anything, you can call me on my cell phone. Now, if you don't mind, I've got work to do.'

'*Wait.* You have to know who's behind this. *Who?* Who'd want to kill Jennifer and why?'

Kelso limped towards the door and turned round. 'I guess that blast probably didn't do your ears much good. How many times do I have to spell it out, Ryan? That's highly classified info and it's worth way more than my job to tell you. There are serious security issues at stake here. Grave ones.'

Mark was exasperated. 'I thought your two buddies, Fellows and Grimes, were supposed to stay on my tail this morning.'

Kelso looked embarrassed. 'Their vehicle broke down.'

'You've got to be kidding me.'

'They tried to contact you on the radio, but got no response. Maybe you didn't know it, but mountain terrain can play havoc with radio reception, and that's exactly what happened. By the time they got their vehicle going again they'd lost you. Then they found out at the inn where you'd gone and arrived at the head-quarters building moments after the explosion. And in case you're wondering who pulled you from your car before your car went up in flames, it was Fellows and Grimes. So maybe fate played a hand, otherwise you might be in the morgue right now, crisper than a Frito. But that's neither here nor there. What's important is that Jennifer's gone missing with a stranger we don't know from shit, and we don't know where the hell she is.'

'Look, Kelso, how about you telling me what's going on here?'

'I told you, it's not within my authority to tell you anything. So cut the questions, Ryan. Meanwhile, I'd better try to find out if this guy McCaul is who he says he is.'

'Kelso, wait!'

But the door closed and Kelso was gone.

27

Darkness had fallen and the rain was still pouring down. Jennifer tried to relax as McCaul drove. The truth was, she felt secure in his company, even though he was a total stranger. There was a strength about him that was reassuring, and if she were to be honest, it felt comforting to have the protection of a fatherly figure.

'Tell me about your son.' The words were out before she even realised the hurt her question might cause. She saw the pain in McCaul's face, but for the next few miles he opened up to her. Chuck was his only child whose mother had left them when the boy was five, moved to LA and never came back.

'To tell the truth, it wasn't much of a marriage to begin with. But Chuck and I were always close. He was a great kid, even if he was a little headstrong at times. I wasn't crazy about the idea of him coming to Switzerland alone. But there was no talking to him. I just wish he'd listened to me.'

Jennifer saw the grief etched on McCaul's face, so intense it threatened to overwhelm him. After that, he talked mainly about himself, and how he had quit the NYPD to work for a private investigation firm. 'A couple of years back I started out on my own, handling crappy matrimonial cases mostly.'

Jennifer noticed he wore no wedding ring. She was tempted to ask whether he'd ever remarried but thought it might seem intrusive.

'It looks like we're here,' McCaul announced suddenly.

They had reached Varzo. The narrow streets of pan-tiled houses looked deserted in the heavy rain. McCaul drove past a broad plaza and headed towards the railway station. 'You said the monastery was outside the village?'

'That's what Anton told me.'

A few minutes later, beyond the edge of the village, they saw a narrow road that rose up steeply, and a sign that said: '*Monastero*'.

'I'll take a guess that's it.' McCaul turned on to the road and drove up a hill for a kilometre until they came to a tiny cobbled square, drenched by rain and completely in darkness.

He halted the Nissan and rolled down his window to get a better look. In the wash of the headlights they saw a stone-built cloister surrounded by mustard-coloured walls, a pair of solid-looking wrought-iron gates set in the middle, a metal crucifix on top. A small plaster statue of the Madonna was set in a recess in the wall, and there was an ancient bell-pull by the gate. The gardens beyond were in darkness, but Jennifer glimpsed a courtyard with shadowy archways. McCaul said, 'You speak any Italian?'

'No. Do you?'

'The kindergarten variety, a couple of words here and there, just enough to know what to order in an Italian restaurant, and even then I've made a few mistakes.' He jerked on the hand-brake, took the pencil torch from his pocket and nodded to the crucifix above the gate. 'Better pray there's someone here who speaks English.'

They stepped out into the pouring rain, McCaul illuminating their way with the torch. He yanked the bell-pull and a tinkle echoed somewhere deep inside the darkened archways. When no one appeared, McCaul pulled again, several times, until they heard footsteps. A figure came scurrying out of the monastery towards the gates, holding an umbrella. It was a young monk wearing a brown habit and carrying an electric torch. '*Si?*'

'You speak English? *Parla inglese?*'

'*Non. Non parla inglese. Auto kaput?*' The monk shone the torch over at the jeep, then back at McCaul and Jennifer, puzzled by the presence of his visitors. Jennifer said in frustration, 'No, our auto's not kaput. Look, we need to talk with someone who speaks English. The abbot, maybe, or one of the monks. *Capisce?*'

The young man shook his head. McCaul tried to explain again, slowly this time, but it was a waste of time. '*Momento*,' the young man said, and darted back into the monastery. He returned a few moments later, still carrying the umbrella and torch, but in the company of an older, bearded monk. He wore a plain brown habit with a knotted cord at his waist from which hung a large crucifix. His face was full of strength, firm and aesthetic. 'Do you speak English?' McCaul asked.

'Yes, I speak English. I'm Father Angelo Konrad. What do you want here?'

'We need to speak with whoever's in charge. The abbot, I guess.'

'For what reason?'

'It's a little complicated, Father. But we promise not to take up much of your time. Ten minutes, no more, and we can explain everything.'

'The abbot is away on Church business. Are you Americans?'

'Yes.'

'I thought so from your accent.' The monk glanced at the Nissan parked outside the gate. 'Are you lost, or have you a problem with your jeep?'

'No, but maybe we could explain inside?' McCaul suggested.

'I'm very sorry, but it's late.' The monk sounded impatient. 'We have just finished vespers, and we retire early at the Crown of Thorns. If you come back tomorrow . . .'

'Look, fella . . .'

'Please, I ask you to respect my wishes.'

The monk made to go, but Jennifer persisted. 'Father, believe us, this is important. It may even be a matter of life or death.'

The monk turned back, frowning. 'This is all very strange, signorina. Whose life or death?'

'Ours.'

Standing there in the downpour, the monk seemed to take pity on his visitors, or perhaps his curiosity got the better of him, Jennifer couldn't tell which. Then he sighed, took a bunch of keys from under his habit, slid one into the lock and opened the gate to admit them.

28

Father Angelo Konrad led Jennifer and McCaul across the rain-soaked courtyard. They ducked under the shelter of a darkened archway until they came to a solid wooden door at the end. Flashes of lightning exploded in the darkness and they were all drenched as they stepped inside. Konrad shook rain from his habit, then held up the storm lamp to illuminate the room. 'A terrible night, not helped by the fact that our electricity and telephone were knocked out by lightning. Sit down, please.'

The room was a tiny office, with a floor of worn terracotta slabs. The monk placed the lamp on a desk as he addressed Jennifer. 'You said this was a matter of life and death.'

'Five days ago a body was discovered on the Wasenhorn glacier. Perhaps you heard about it, Father?'

The monk shook his head. 'I know nothing of this. What happens beyond these walls is of little concern to me. A body, you say?'

'Of a man. The Carabinieri believe it had been in the ice for two years.'

The monk shrugged. 'It's not unusual to hear of such stories in these parts. The glaciers are treacherous places. I have heard of people who went missing in the mountains and were never found again until their bodies were exposed by melting ice decades later.' He regarded his visitors with a frown. 'But may I ask who you both are?'

McCaul made the introductions, offered his card, and Konrad studied it. 'I don't understand. Why should an American investigator be involved in this matter?'

'We can talk about that later. The fact is, the man who died may have had an accomplice when he tried to cross the glacier. We think the accomplice could have headed here, for the monastery.'

The monk frowned. 'And why would you think that?'

'There was a blizzard that night,' Jennifer explained. 'And I'm told that it's not unusual for climbers to look for shelter in the monastery in bad weather.'

Father Konrad nodded. 'True, but I'm not sure I follow.'

Jennifer explained about the train tickets found on the body. 'The victim's companion may have survived the storm and made it here to safety.'

The monk let out a sigh. 'Two years ago? Anything is possible, signorina. It's true our monastery is well known as a sanctuary, but we have had many visitors who come here to pray and reflect, as well as those who seek shelter.'

'Do you keep a record of visitors?'

'*Si*, the abbot keeps a record in his journal. But if you're talking about two years ago, the journal for that period is probably stored in the cellar archives among the abbot's private papers. However, I can tell you now it is unlikely that every single visitor has been recorded.' Father Konrad looked impatient with their questioning. 'And now may I ask where all this is leading?'

'Would it be possible for you to check your records for us, Father?'

'*Now?*'

'Yes, now.'

Konrad sounded exasperated. 'Signorina, I'm not sure what all this is going to achieve, and why the urgency? Is there some explanation you can offer?'

'The man could have been murdered.'

Konrad raised his eyes. 'This is all very intriguing, signorina. But it explains little. Murdered by whom? For what reason?'

'That's what we're trying to find out. If we could trouble you to let us see your visitor records, it may help . . .'

Father Konrad firmly shook his head. 'Signorina, it's late, and believe me, on a night like this, I'm in no mood to go searching in the cellars. You could be wasting my time.'

'Father, I wasn't misleading you when I said it was a matter of life and death. People have already died because of this.'

Father Konrad was totally baffled. 'Because of what?'

'I can't explain why exactly, but I can tell you this. If I told the police you may have information that's important to their investigation, they'd be swarming all over the monastery, keeping you up all night.'

'This is preposterous,' the monk spluttered. 'We are simple men of the cloth here. We have done no wrong. For what reason would they do that?'

Jennifer grabbed the storm lamp from the table, determined to have her way. 'It's complicated, Father. And you're probably going to think we're crazy if we tell you. But if you help us I'll forget about contacting the police for tonight. Then I'll do my best to try and explain exactly what brought us here in the first place.'

Jennifer and McCaul descended a winding granite stairway to the monastery cellars, Father Konrad leading the way. He was preceded by the young monk who had met them at the gate, who carried a couple of lanterns on a pole. Konrad was sullen, and Jennifer tried to soften his mood. 'Tell me about the monastery, Father.'

Konrad shrugged. 'What is there to tell? Except there aren't many of us left at the Crown of Thorns. Only four, including the abbot. Brother Paulo here is our youngest recruit. Too few friars for such a big old place. But many years ago this was a busy sanctuary, and our little church was quite famous.'

'Why?'

'Mostly because of these very same cellars. They run directly under the church.'

'What's so special about them?' Jennifer asked.

'You'll see.'

They came to the bottom of the stairs and an ancient oak door with a sturdy, rusted lock. Konrad took down a big key from a nail on the wall, inserted it in the lock, pushed hard, and the heavy door creaked open. Steps led down to a chamber with stone archways on either side, in almost total darkness.

'The Crown of Thorns has an interesting history,' Konrad said. 'This part of the building is especially fascinating, but I warn you, like many of our visitors you may be shocked by what you are about to see. Show them, Brother Paulo.'

The young monk raised the lanterns and Jennifer saw that the cellars were part of a crypt, with the bones of the dead everywhere: ribs, hands, feet, femurs and tibulas were cemented into the archways and walls, skulls piled high in corners. The most horrifying thing was the bodies, some lying down, some seated, others hanging from metal hooks in the cement. All were skeletons, but some retained skin and hair and teeth, and the tattered remnants of clothing.

'What in the hell's all this?' McCaul asked, horrified.

'These people are monks belonging to the Crown of Thorns,' Father Konrad told him, his mood thawing as he warmed to his subject. 'And wealthy landowners and aristocrats and their families who down the ages chose to be entombed here. You will find much the same thing in the catacombs of churches in Sicily and Rome. The monastery's founding abbot came from Palermo and made it his business to carry on the tradition.'

The remains of a young girl in a tattered lace dress hung from a wall hook near by, and Jennifer shuddered. The darkness of the catacombs seemed hostile, filled with eerie death. They passed an ancient throne in faded white marble. It protruded from the wall of the crypt at an odd angle, as if mounted on hinges. A decayed figure dressed in an ancient Cistercian robe was ensconced on the throne, hollow eye sockets peering out from beneath the hood.

Father Konrad said, 'Padre Boniface, our prior at the beginning of the eighteenth century. A saintly and pious man. And also the keeper of a long-forgotten secret.'

'What do you mean?' Jennifer asked.

'Look behind the throne,' Konrad said, and the young monk brought the lanterns closer. McCaul and Jennifer saw that the angled marble was attached to the wall by a pair of massive, ancient hinges, so heavily rusted they had long ago seized up. A two-foot-wide gap between the wall and the back of the throne revealed a dark passageway with tunnels leading off.

'The tunnels date from Napoleon's time, when the French invaded the region,' Konrad explained. 'An escape route if the monastery was ever attacked, or so rumour has it.' He turned away from the throne. 'But I didn't bring you down here to offer a lecture.'

They paused outside a heavy oak door, blackened with age, and Konrad unlocked it. The room they stepped into was large, with high stone walls and vaulted ceilings. A lectern stood in the centre, and around the walls were thick wooden shelves, sagging under the weight of old ledgers and journals, and bundles of parchment documents with wax seals. Father Konrad directed the young monk to move the lanterns over the shelves. 'Padre Leopold is our abbot. His old journals are stored here, in the library vaults.'

He climbed on to a stool, searched among the shelves until he found a handful of bound journals, and took them over to the lectern. He removed a pair of reading glasses from under his robe and slipped them on. 'Two years ago, you say. Which month?'

'April. The week of the fifteenth.'

'I tell you again, this will probably be a complete waste of time,' Konrad said irritably, then opened one of the journals and started to flick through the pages.

29

Mark came awake with a start and sat up in bed. His headache had gone, but he felt groggy. Thunder cracked beyond the window, and he guessed the storm had woken him. He was covered in perspiration, his hospital gown damp with patches of sweat.

And then he realised why. After Kelso had gone the nurse had given him a sedative. It had taken effect and he'd drifted in and out of an uneasy sleep. He wiped the perspiration from his face and fumbled for his watch in the bedside locker: 7.30 p.m. He'd slept for over two hours.

He climbed shakily out of bed and removed his clothes from the locker. He felt he had to do something to find Jennifer because the uncertainty was torturing him. He dragged on his trousers; slipped on his shoes, and was about to put on his shirt when Kelso opened the door. 'Thinking of going somewhere, Ryan?'

'What's it to you?'

'I'm glad to see you're feeling better.'

'I've had it, Kelso. I'm getting out of here.'

'And going where?'

'I'll think about that later.' Mark pulled on his shirt. 'Have you found Jennifer yet?'

Kelso sighed and closed the door. 'Sit down, Ryan. We need to talk.'

'I don't think we've got anything to talk about, unless you've found Jennifer.'

'No, but I've got some interesting news about our friend McCaul.'

Mark stopped buttoning his shirt. 'I'm waiting.'

'The kid who died at the Furka pass, it turns out his father's name is definitely Frank McCaul. He arrived in Switzerland on Tuesday to identify his son's body, and it seems he is who he says he is. In fact, he was once a detective with the NYPD.'

'I've never heard of him.'

'I had a photo e-mailed from New York that I'd like you to take a look at.' Kelso sat down, took an envelope from his pocket and opened it. 'Was this the guy you saw with Jennifer?'

Mark looked at the grainy colour shot made by a computer printer. McCaul's face stared out at him. Handsome, with high cheekbones, he looked the rugged type most women would be attracted to. *Would Jennifer be attracted to a man like this?* Probably. He felt a pang of jealousy. 'It looks like him.'

Kelso slipped the photograph back in the envelope. 'At least we've established that Jennifer's not in any immediate danger.'

'How can you be sure?'

'If I'm to accept what I've been told, this guy McCaul can look after himself. He's definitely a private investigator. And if the NYPD are to be believed, a very capable one at that. I thought at first he might be a complication we could do without, but on second thoughts I feel a little more secure that Jennifer's with a guy who might at least be able to help protect her.'

'Whatever you say,' Mark said flatly.

A hint of a smile curled the edges of Kelso's mouth. 'Do I detect a note of jealousy?'

Mark ignored the question and began to button his shirt again. 'It's been nice knowing you, Kelso.'

'Where do you think you're going?'

'I told you before, if you can't at least give me an idea of what this thing is about, I'm out of here.'

'And what about Jennifer?'

'I'll find her myself.'

'If *I* can't find her, then what hope have *you* got?'

'And why can't you?'

Kelso gestured to the rain squalls gusting against the window. 'In case you hadn't noticed, it's a bitch of a night out there. We've managed to charter two helicopters to help search for McCaul's jeep, but the pilots refuse to go up until the weather clears, which could be some time in the early hours of the morning if we can believe the forecasts.'

'Terrific. So we still haven't a hope in hell of finding her?'

'I wouldn't say that. We're still keeping tabs on her cell phone in case she switches it on, but there's nothing I can do about the weather. Meantime, I've sent Fellows to Jennifer's hotel in Simplon, in case she turns up there.'

'And what if she doesn't?'

'Cut me some slack here, Ryan. I'm doing the best I can.'

Mark grabbed his jacket and moved towards the door. 'Maybe if I told the newspapers her story and got her face splashed on the front pages it might get some results.'

Kelso's face darkened. 'I told you before. This is a sensitive, covert operation. You can't do that. I won't allow it.'

'Try and stop me.'

Kelso sighed in defeat and suddenly collapsed in the chair. 'OK, Ryan, you win.'

'You're finally going to tell me what this is about?'

'It looks like I don't have much choice. Besides, I spoke with my superiors and they agreed I could give you a limited amount of information, but only *in extremis*. I guess this is *extremis* enough.' Kelso shook his head. 'You're a very persistent man, Ryan.'

'How limited?'

'Enough for you to know what we're dealing with here. But I'm giving you a warning, you don't repeat a word of what I say to anyone. And I mean *anyone*.'

'I can live with that.'

Kelso grimaced, and indicated the bed. 'You'd better sit down.'

'I'm fine standing.'

'I'd suggest you sit, Ryan. Because there's a good chance that what I've got to say is going to blow your mind.'

30

It didn't take long for Father Konrad to find the correct journal. The entries on the lined pages were written neatly in black ink, but unfortunately in a language neither Jennifer nor McCaul could understand. They watched the monk thumb the pages until he came to one that began *Aprile 15*. 'See. I told you. Nothing.'

Jennifer's heart sank. There was no entry for that date, the line beneath it blank. 'What about the next day, April sixteenth?'

'Signorina . . .'

'Father, this is important.'

Konrad sighed in protest and studied the pages. Finally he shook his head. 'There is nothing of importance. The entries are just about the normal day-to-day happenings in the monastery.'

'Like what?'

Konrad shrugged. 'Work carried out by the monks. A request from a couple in San Domenico to be married in the monastery church. Now are you satisfied?'

'You're certain no other visitors are mentioned, even in the following pages?'

Konrad was irritated as he flicked over the page. 'Just one, five days after, on the twentieth.'

'Who?' McCaul asked.

Konrad impatiently scanned the lines again and pointed to another entry, then frowned and fell silent. 'What's wrong?' Jennifer asked.

Konrad scratched his jaw. 'I recall it now.'

'What?'

'A man arrived here. The entry was written by Padre Leopold and reads: "*A visitor arrived last evening. He claimed he had got lost while hiking, and he needed medical attention.*'" Konrad looked up. 'I remember now. He had suffered minor frostbite to his face and feet.'

Jennifer felt a shiver go through her. 'What else do you remember?'

'That he was hungry and in some distress. I believe he stayed for several days, and that we wanted to call a local doctor for him, but he refused.'

'Why?'

'God knows. But the frostbite wasn't life threatening and the abbot tended to his injuries with temporary dressings and suggested he visit a hospital.'

'Who was the man?'

'A complete stranger. I never saw him before, or since.'

'What age was he?'

'Middle aged.'

'Did he give a name?'

'If he did, none is mentioned, and I don't recall it.'

'Was he Swiss? Italian?'

'No. Foreign. He spoke English, I believe.'

Jennifer opened her bag. Her hands were shaking as she showed Konrad her father's photograph. 'Was . . . was this the man?'

Konrad studied the snapshot. 'It is difficult to say. We are talking about two years ago . . .'

'Please, take your time.'

Konrad looked at the photo again, then shrugged as he handed it back. 'Perhaps it was the same man, but I really cannot be certain.'

'Do you have *any* idea who he might have been?'

Konrad was losing his patience. 'Obviously someone who got into difficulty in bad weather, as his condition would imply. But this was five days after the date you suggest, so the man could have been anyone. Now, are we finished?'

'Does it say anything else about him?'

'Signorina. My patience is at an end.' Konrad started to close the book.

'This one last thing, Father. *Please.*'

With a heavy sigh, his face flushed with anger, Konrad indicated some lines on the page. 'There is only one other mention. The man left us two days later, on April twenty-second. The abbot mentions that he took him to the local railway station.'

'Where did he travel to?'

'I really have no idea.' The priest snapped the journal shut. 'You promised me an explanation.'

'The dead man's passport said he was Paul March. That was my father's name and he disappeared two years ago. The passport belonged to him, but the body wasn't my father's.'

'Then whose was it?'

'I don't know. I'd never seen the man before in my life.'

Konrad looked puzzled. He removed his glasses, his mood softening. 'All very strange. But your father's disappearance must have been a terrible loss, my child.'

Jennifer thought: *You've no idea.*

Konrad gathered up the journals. 'Now that we are finished here, let me take you back upstairs.'

They left the crypts and moved back up the granite stairway, the young monk leading the way, carrying the lamps on the pole. They came to the entrance hallway and Konrad opened one of the doors. The storm was still raging outside, a maelstrom of rain, wind and thunder. 'Where are you staying tonight?'

'We thought we'd find somewhere in Varzo,' McCaul replied.

'There are not many hotels in the village.' Konrad looked out at the rain hammering the courtyard, as lightning lit up the hallway. 'It's no night for man or beast. Perhaps it would be wiser if you remained here. Our guest rooms are basic, but comfortable. You are welcome to stay, if you wish.'

'That's very kind of you, Father.'

Konrad shut the door. 'Brother Paulo will show you to your rooms.'

'Is there anything else you remember about the man, Father? Anything at all?'

'I'm afraid not. Apart from the fact that he seemed anxious to leave here as soon as he was well enough.'

'One more thing. Do you know of a mountain in the area called the Edelweiss?' Jennifer unfolded the slip of paper on which she'd written *H. Vogel. Berg Edelweiss 705.*

Konrad studied the paper. 'What is this?'

'A similar note was found on the body. We don't know what the words and figures mean, apart from the fact that *Berg* means mountain in German. The paper had partly dissolved and some of the numbers may be missing.'

Konrad scratched his chin. 'I think you'll find that Vogel is a common enough name on the Swiss side of the Wasenhorn, especially around Brig. But I've never heard of a mountain of that name in these parts.' He handed back the paper. 'And now, I will say goodnight.'

He left them, taking one of the lamps from the pole. With the other, the young monk guided Jennifer and McCaul along a stone-flagged corridor, lined with oak doors. He showed them two tiny rooms, side by side, with plain wooden crucifixes on the whitewashed stone walls. Each room had a tiny window set high up, a single wooden chair, a night stand, a fold-up metal cot with a thin mattress, and a simple bathroom. '*Momento. Prego.*'

The monk crossed to another of the rooms near by and came back with an armful of coarse grey blankets, fresh white sheets, soap bars, and a couple of thick beeswax candles, which he lit from the lamp. He handed one candle each to Jennifer and McCaul. '*Buona notte, signorina, signore.*'

'Goodnight. *Grazie.*'

'*Prego, signorina,*' and then the monk turned and left them, his footsteps fading down the corridor.

31

McCaul waited until they were alone, then gestured to the rooms. 'You want to pick which one you want?'

'Does it matter?'

'I guess not. We're not exactly talking five-star here, but any port in a storm.' McCaul picked the room on the right. 'I'll take this one. I'll let you get settled in, then I'll help you with the fold-up bed.'

Jennifer stepped into her room. The old stone walls of the monk's cell were smoothed by time. She placed the candle on the bedside locker as a lightning flash lit up the window above her head. Pulling over the chair, she stood on it and looked out. She could make out another courtyard, drenched by rain, and what looked like a tiny private garden, with neat flower beds and a stone bird fountain.

Perhaps it was the same man, but I really cannot be certain.

She recalled Father Konrad's words, and questions tumbled around her mind. What if the man who arrived at the monastery was her father? There was a knock on her door. 'Mind if I come in?'

She turned to see McCaul standing in the doorway. 'I don't know about you, but it seems a little early to be turning in. It's not even eight thirty, for God's sake.'

Jennifer stepped down off the chair and was tempted to smile. 'I guess that means you don't find monastery life appealing?'

'Not a chance in hell.' McCaul came into the room. 'You mind me asking what's outside?'

'It looks like a courtyard. The storm's not letting up.'

'Then I guess we're in for a lousy night. Here, let me help

you with your bed.' McCaul opened out the fold-up and helped Jennifer fix up the sheets and blankets. 'So, what do you think?'

'About what?'

'The stuff Konrad told us.'

'I . . . I don't know. It's confusing.'

'I know what you're thinking, Jennifer, but you heard what he said. This place often gets unexpected visitors: climbers, skiers, hill-walkers. The guy who showed up could have been anyone. Besides, he arrived five days after the date on the train tickets. The person we're looking for couldn't have survived on the mountain in freezing cold for five days.'

'What about the mountain hut? He could have found shelter there and then made his way up here?'

'Why wait five days?'

'Maybe the mountain was impassable. Or he couldn't move because of his injuries until the weather improved.'

McCaul nodded. 'Fair enough, but we're still into speculation. And it isn't exactly one part fitting into another like a good Swiss watch. Sure, what Konrad said about the name Vogel may be a help, and we can drive to Brig first thing tomorrow and check it out. But there's not much we can do about anything tonight, not when we're stuck in the middle of nowhere and in a place that looks like it's still in the Dark Ages.'

A gust of wind rattled the window and McCaul got to his feet. 'I can't say it hasn't been an interesting evening, but I think you could do with some rest. You sure you'll be OK in here?'

Jennifer glanced around the room. 'I think so. And thanks for helping me, Frank.'

'What's there to thank? We're in this together.' He put a hand on her shoulder. 'You'd better get some sleep. You need me, just call, OK?' Then he went out, closing the door behind him.

Jennifer sat on the bed. She had sensed something like a small electric shock down her spine when McCaul had touched her. It was the first time in a long while a man had had that effect on her. She had definitely felt a charge of sexual electricity between them, and it felt strange, but for some reason it didn't worry her. She found McCaul attractive.

She could acknowledge that there was a spark of attraction between herself and Mark, but she found it difficult to deal with that situation. For some reason she could deal with her attraction to McCaul. It didn't feel awkward; it felt like something she could act on. Maybe because he was older, and because she trusted him. And there was something else: he made her feel safe in a way that so reminded her of her father.

For now, she put such thoughts from her mind. She felt dishevelled and needed to wash. Her luggage was still back at the hotel in Simplon, as was McCaul's, and all she had was her tote bag with some underwear and a T-shirt and a pair of jeans. She undressed and scrubbed herself at the enamel basin, then slipped on a fresh T-shirt and panties and climbed into bed. The mattress was hard and the bed creaked, but on a night like tonight she was just grateful for somewhere to rest.

Her tote bag was on the floor beside her and she plucked out her cell phone and powered it on. She was tempted to phone Mark and check on Bobby but her battery was almost down and she had no way of recharging it until the monastery's electricity supply was working again. She switched it off again; she would call Mark tomorrow.

She was exhausted, but she knew she couldn't sleep yet. Everything that had happened in the last twenty-four hours was torturing her with questions that she could find no answers to. She understood none of it, and it frightened her. Finally, she blew out the candle, lay back in the darkness and tried to sleep.

The two men in the black BMW drove into the deserted streets of Varzo. The rain was pelting down, and when the driver came to the far end of the village he halted, but kept the engine running. In the wash of the headlights he could make out the hill leading up and the sign that said '*Monastero*'.

The blond passenger nodded to the driver, who turned the BMW up towards the Crown of Thorns.

32

Turin

'What's the biggest long-term threat to the national security of the United States, Ryan?'

The hospital room was quiet. Mark sat on a chair facing Kelso and said, 'You tell me.'

'Terrorism? Some rogue state with a nuclear weapons programme and a grudge against America?' Kelso shook his head. 'It's organised crime. Or let me be more specific. Russian organised crime. The Red Mafia.'

'I don't get it.'

'You want to know why? Because they're into every kind of crime imaginable, and the list is as long as an elephant's dick. International drug trafficking, extortion, prostitution, bank fraud, smuggling, contract murder – you name it, they're involved. In the last five years the CIA estimates that the Red Mafia has had a worldwide turnover in the region of fifty *billion* dollars, but that's just a conservative estimate. Global crime, that's what we're talking about here, and these guys are so well organised and brutal in their criminal conspiracy, they make the Italian Mafia look like a bunch of boy scouts.'

Kelso went over to the window, pulled back the curtain. 'It might interest you to know that there's a school not far from here, just inside the Swiss border. The most expensive private school in the world. Charges a hundred thousand bucks a year for every student. Guess what? A quarter of the students are the children of Russian mobsters.'

'I appreciate the lecture, Kelso. But what's it all got to do with Paul March?'

Kelso let the curtain fall back into place. 'I'm coming to it.

With laundered money the Red Mafia have purchased real estate, company stocks and shares, and legitimate businesses. They gain control over these businesses for one primary reason. To launder their illegal profits, because a legitimate business is the perfect laundromat. I'm not exaggerating when I say that the biggest threat facing the West today is the billions of dollars that the Red Mafia have generated. Because guess where they invest most of it? In the United States. In our companies, our stock market, our real estate, our banks, and by the criminal takeover of legitimate companies.'

'I get the picture. So what about March?'

'You're aware that he worked for a company called Prime International Securities?'

'Sure.'

'The company was wound down a year ago, all done quietly, no big fuss. But before that, and to all outward appearances, it was a perfectly legitimate investment bank. Except that it was owned by the Red Mafia. And for one good reason. It laundered vast sums of dirty cash for the shell company it was controlled by in the Cayman Islands. It was all part of a slick international operation, one that's still ongoing, and that's much bigger than Pablo Escobar's business ever was, but run by a bunch of criminals you probably never heard of, the Moscaya clan.'

'I haven't. Who are they?'

'The nastiest rats in the shithouse, and not the kind you'd ever want to get on the wrong side of.' Kelso snapped his fingers. 'They'd have your life snuffed out just like that. If you had a wife and kids, they'd kill them too, no hesitation.'

'How come I never heard of them?'

'The Moscaya clan operates from behind offshore banks and companies and always kept itself well insulated with an intricate bureaucracy. They made it a policy never to get their hands dirty: that only happens to the little guys who work for them, people way down the chain. Four days ago you investigated an incident at JFK. An infant's dead body was used to smuggle drugs from Moscow.'

'How'd you know about that?'

'By then I'd already had my men watching Jennifer for her own safety. It's hard to believe that anyone could do something so depraved as happened at the airport. But that's just the kind of despicable crime the Moscaya clan commits. In fact, their organisation was probably responsible. They don't care what heinous crime they have to commit or who they have to kill to make a profit.'

'Why did they close down Prime?'

'Because we were getting too close to them. Our Crime and Narcotics Division had been keeping an eye on their overseas operations for years, along with the FBI and DEA. The Moscaya clan runs businesses like Prime through the shell companies they control in Switzerland and the Caymans.'

'What's all this got to do with Jennifer's father?'

'My team spent four years trying to get a strong case together on the Moscayas. We called it Operation Spiderweb. Part of that operation involved tracking their illegal accounts, tapping their phones, tailing their top mobsters, all the usual stuff, but the Red Mafia operates in extreme secrecy and we got absolutely nowhere. So we decided we needed someone on the inside of one of the Moscaya companies to help us get the evidence. Paul March was one of Prime's top executives, the ideal guy, and we reckoned that with his help we could get access to some of the company's secret files that they kept in their New York offices.'

'You're saying he knew what Prime was up to?'

'I was never quite sure if he'd had his suspicions, and he claimed he didn't, but he sure knew once we put him wise and made him the kind of offer he couldn't refuse.'

'What do you mean?'

'Outwardly, March was a fine, upstanding citizen. But we did background checks on Prime's top employees. When we turned up nothing on March's early life, we dug deeper, and bingo. Back in his past he had served time in prison for serious criminal offences that Jennifer is not aware of.'

Mark reeled. He couldn't believe what he was hearing. What would Jennifer think if she learned that the father she idolised was a convicted criminal? She'd be devastated. 'What kind of crimes are you talking about?'

'Manslaughter, for one. His real name was Joseph Delgado and he was an orphan from the age of ten, a kid on a fast track to nowhere who'd spend most of his early life in foster care, with a couple of spells in juvenile prison for theft. When he was nineteen he got himself in a shitload of trouble with his first employer and was charged with embezzlement. He got a year in prison, but as soon as he was released he killed a guy in a knife fight outside a bar in Phoenix. March claimed that the fight was provoked and managed to get off on a manslaughter charge with four years in jail. But he put his time in prison to good use, stayed on the straight and narrow, and after his release he legally changed his name, got himself a college diploma, and moved to New York. He had brains and ambition, too, because he turned his life around, and soon he was climbing the career ladder. A few years later he joined Prime. Then four years ago, it was bought by a shell company owned by the Moscayas, right after March was appointed as the company's financial controller. He retained that position even after Prime was bought.'

Mark was still struggling to take in the revelations about Paul March, and he felt so angry that Jennifer's image of her father might be shattered that he took his anger out on Kelso. 'What did you do? Offer March witness protection? Promise you'd keep his past a secret if he played ball?'

Kelso responded firmly. 'I was prepared to use any means at my disposal to nail these murdering sons-of-bitches. March was promised half a million dollars and witness protection for his family if he helped us nail the Moscaya clan's US and Caribbean operation. He readily accepted and made only one demand which he insisted I agree to.'

'What was that?'

'He wanted all public evidence of his past life as Joseph Delgado destroyed. His prison records, the records of his court case, and every single shred of evidence that pointed to his previous existence. That was the deal.'

'*Why?*'

'He claimed that his past haunted him, that his wife knew about it but that he'd always lived in fear that one day the truth was going to be uncovered and that his children would find out. And the proof of that was that the CIA had discovered his secret. I could only guess that he had some kind of deep psychological need to wipe the slate clean. But whatever the reasons, my people agreed to March's demand. His prison records, his court case files, and everything else about his life as Joseph Delgado was permanently erased from public record.'

Mark thought: *So that's why Garuda couldn't find any trace of the man's past.* 'What precisely did the CIA want March to do?'

'Let's just say we came up with a scheme to finally put the Moscaya's top mobsters behind bars, with March's help. Except it didn't work out the way we intended.'

'Why?'

'Because, Ryan, something weird happened and it all went crazy.'

33

Kelso took a deep breath, as if he were about to wade into deeper water. 'Once or twice a year, March would take a business trip to Switzerland where Prime had several accounts. His job was a simple one; to make sure the books were in order and report back.'

'Go on.'

'A week before March flew to Zurich, we got a tip-off that the Moscayas were arranging a big deal with an Italian trafficker, which required them to pay fifty million dollars for a number of major drug consignments. Forty million was to be in gilt-edged bonds, and the rest would be in diamonds and cash. One of the Moscaya's top henchman, a dangerous gangster named Karl Lazar, was going to pay over the fifty million in Zurich. Then we learned from March that he'd been instructed to withdraw the cash, bonds and diamonds from safety deposit boxes in a certain Zurich bank used by Prime, and hand them over to Lazar. We figured if we could catch Lazar red handed we might be able to trace the fifty million back to his bosses. So I had my team set up in Zurich. We'd tail Lazar every step of the way until it came time to grab him.'

Mark nodded. 'I'm listening.'

'Everything goes dandy at first. March lands in Zurich and straight away meets Lazar, visits the bank and makes the withdrawals. With the fifty mill in bonds, cash and diamonds stuffed into four large briefcases, he and Lazar walk to their hotel, three minutes away, to check in. Then it all took a weird turn.'

'What do you mean?'

Kelso sighed, and massaged his forehead. 'One minute they

were being tailed as they walked to their hotel, and the next minute they'd vanished into a maze of side streets. And I do mean vanished, Ryan. We scoured every street for five blocks, but they'd both disappeared. We checked March's hotel, and he'd never checked in, nor had Lazar. We had the airports watched, but that turned up nothing, either. Paul March and Karl Lazar had disappeared without a trace, and the fifty million had vanished with them.'

Mark frowned. 'What happened?'

'There can only be a limited number of possibilities.'

'Like what?'

'One or both men colluded to steal the fifty million.'

'Why?'

'Greed, pure and simple.'

'You really think March would have risked stealing fifty million from dangerous international gangsters?'

'Put it this way. Karl Lazar was a criminal to begin with, so I wouldn't have put it past him to steal from his own organisation. But I can't ignore March's prior criminal record. Fifty million dollars is a big temptation, maybe too big a temptation to let pass. March would have been hiding for the rest of his life under our witness protection, but with fifty million he may have figured he could afford to hide in a lot more comfort.'

'You're suggesting it was March who did it?'

'Look, all I know for certain is that he and Lazar went AWOL, never to be heard from again, so any damned thing's possible. It had to be one or the other, or both.'

'I still haven't figured out how the body ended up in a glacier.'

'We discovered that one of the ways the Red Mafia moved dirty money into Switzerland is using "mules". The same way that poor girl at JFK was used as a mule. But in this case it's dirty cash being smuggled, not drugs. The Moscayas would hire someone trustworthy for the job. They'd be kitted out as a hiker and given a rucksack stuffed with, say, five million, and then make their way illegally over the Alps. Once they handed over the cash to the bagmen on the other side, the money would be deposited in a bank, laundered and moved on to the US or the Caymans. Multiply five million by hundreds of trips a year and you see the kind of figures we're getting into.'

'I get the picture. But how did the body end up in the glacier?'

'Whoever took the fifty million knew that their chances of getting out of the country legally with that kind of stash would have been nil. So I reckon they would have already decided to use an illegal route over the mountains, maybe one of the safe routes used by the Moscaya's mules. I'd say that was the plan, but then a storm blew up, and one of them fell into a crevasse and froze to death.'

'You mean March.'

Kelso sighed. 'I told you this was going to blow your mind, Ryan, and here's the ditsy part. The body on the mountain wasn't Jennifer's father.'

'*What?*'

'It wasn't Paul March up on that mountain.'

'But the missing person's report—'

'Said the victim had a passport in the name of Paul March. But I had Interpol send me a photograph of the victim in the glacier. The photograph was compared electronically to the one in March's passport and it didn't match. The corpse wasn't her father's. Which is also why I wanted you to be here for Jennifer. I knew it was going to be a shock for her when she found out.'

'Then who *did* the body belong to?'

'There's a good chance it was Karl Lazar's. But we can't be certain unless the Italians manage to scrape DNA evidence out of the ruins.'

The door opened suddenly and Grimes came in, carrying a map. 'What is it?' Kelso snapped.

'Can I speak with you a moment, sir?'

Kelso stepped over to the door and both men held a whispered conversation over the map, until Kelso said urgently, 'Go get the car. I'll be right with you.'

Grimes left and Mark said, 'What's up?'

'Maybe we've got a lead, maybe not. Jennifer switched on her cell phone five minutes ago.'

'Where is she?'

'We don't know for sure. The phone was switched on only briefly and the triangulation was pretty rough, but it suggested somewhere near Varzo, which isn't a great help. However, Fellows has just called the Berghof Hotel. There was no sign of Jennifer but he spoke with the manager, some guy named Anton. He didn't know where she'd gone but he mentioned that when he took her up to the Wasenhorn she seemed very interested to know about a monastery called the Crown of Thorns, outside Varzo.'

'Why?'

'Who the hell knows? Grimes showed me the place on the map. It's about forty minutes away by car, and right now it's about all we've got. Fellows is already on his way to the monastery, and Grimes and I will meet him there.'

'I'm going with you, Kelso.'

Kelso grabbed Mark's arm. 'I thought you were told to rest . . .'

Mark pulled himself free and reached for his jacket. He found it difficult to keep his voice steady. 'Forget it. I'm not staying here. And there's a lot more you need to tell me. Such as why Jennifer's life is in danger. And if it wasn't Paul March's body, then where the hell did he disappear to?'

34

The two men in the black BMW halted outside the Crown of Thorns. They spotted McCaul's Nissan parked near the monastery gates and the driver doused his headlights and reversed the BMW under a clump of trees. Both men wore leather gloves, dark rainproof coats and black ski masks. They climbed out of their car in the drenching rain, approached the jeep and, when they found it deserted, moved towards the monastery gates.

One of the men produced an electric torch and directed it on the lock while his accomplice took a leather tool pouch from under his coat. He had the lock open in less than a minute and both men moved inside. They crossed the rain-soaked courtyard and slipped under the cover of the darkened archway until they came to the oak entrance door.

The man with the tool pouch went to work again, fumbling at the ancient lock until the tumblers clicked and the big wooden door sprang open. He nodded to his accomplice, and both intruders unbuttoned their raincoats to reveal Skorpion machine pistols slung around their necks. They readied their weapons and moved into the monastery.

Father Angelo Konrad came awake in the darkness of his sparse cell. He thought he was having a nightmare and he couldn't breathe. His eyes snapped open and he got a terrible shock. Two black-masked intruders had invaded his cell. One of them had a hand over Konrad's mouth while the other flashed an electric torch into his face. As the startled monk struggled for breath, he felt the steel tip of a knife press into his throat.

'Don't move or talk unless I tell you to,' the intruder whispered.

Konrad, totally confused by the strangers' presence, saw the flash of a needle-thin stiletto in the man's hand. 'Otherwise you die, understand?'

Konrad nodded, terrified, and the hand came away from his mouth. 'You will answer my questions. Lie to me and I'll cut your heart out.'

The threat in the hoarse voice was truly frightening, and Konrad nodded again.

'Where are your two visitors?'

Konrad was silent. Anguish welled up inside him, and he feared the worst.

The intruder pressed the knife tip into his throat and Konrad grimaced in pain. '*Answer*. Or I kill you.'

Konrad told him everything and the intruder said, 'How many others are in the monastery?'

'Two . . . two others.'

'Where, precisely?'

'Bro . . . Brother Paulo is three doors away. Brother Franco is in the first cell past the next corridor.'

The intruder grinned behind his mask. 'Thank you for your cooperation.' His hand came up to cover Konrad's mouth and he slid the knife across the priest's throat.

Jennifer woke with a start in the darkness. Her breath came in ragged bursts and her heart beat wildly. It could have been hours or even minutes after she'd fallen asleep, but she wasn't sure. The storm was still raging, splashing ghostly electric shadows on the walls, and she was bathed in perspiration. Her nightmares had come back again and she shuddered at the memory as she sat up in bed. The tiny cell was freezing and in the inky darkness she could barely make out the walls.

A second later, she heard the noise.

A faint sound.

From somewhere outside in the corridor.

Then she heard it again. Footsteps, the soft slap of leather on stone. The noise faded. She listened again, but heard nothing.

A chill shot through her. Had the storm caused the noise or was it just her imagination? She fumbled for the candle on the night stand, almost knocking it over in the process. Then she realised it was useless. The monk had left her no matches. From the tiny window in the wall above, she heard the ebb and flow of the tempest, the wind gusting in bursts, sending rain flailing against the glass. For a couple of seconds the wind faded. And then . . . She heard the footsteps in the corridor again.

Jennifer's heart raced as she forced herself up off the bed. The flagstoned floor felt like ice beneath her feet. She started towards the door in the pitch darkness. She was surprised at how scared she was, her legs shaking, her mind racked with fear.

She put her ear to the door. Silence. The footsteps had disappeared. She let out a sigh and her fear relaxed. But a moment later she heard another noise, this time a faint rattle. To her horror, she realised what the noise was.

Someone's outside the door.

The handle was turning.

Jennifer staggered back, terrified. '*Who . . . who's there?*'

And then suddenly the door burst open. As she tried to scream, a hand went over her mouth.

35

As Jennifer was forced back into the room a man's voice whispered, 'Don't make a sound.'

Panic seized her and she struggled. The voice hissed in her ear, 'For Christ sakes, Jennifer, do as I say!'

McCaul's hand came away from her mouth and his Maglite torch flashed on. Jennifer saw that he had dressed hastily and was in his stockinged feet, his shoes hanging around his neck by the laces. He put a finger to his lips for her to be silent, then closed the door. She saw Caruso's pistol in his hand. 'What . . . what are you doing?'

'Keep your voice down,' McCaul hissed. 'Just get your clothes on and come with me, quick as you can. We're leaving.'

'*Why?*'

'Because we've got company, that's why.' McCaul gripped her arm. 'Just do as I say, Jennifer, and right away. But do it quietly. And leave your shoes off. Carry them, don't wear them.'

Jennifer got her belongings together as McCaul went to listen by the door. When she finished dressing she grabbed her bag and went to join him, carrying her shoes. 'Will you please tell me what's happening?'

'I couldn't sleep with the storm and heard a noise in the corridor. But as soon as I went to see if you were all right I saw two guys wearing black ski masks come out of one of the cells. It was Father Konrad's. He's dead, Jennifer. His throat's been cut.'

Jennifer was seized by an icy terror and couldn't speak or move. She was barely listening as McCaul continued.

'The second I saw them I ducked back inside my room and grabbed the gun. When I looked again, they'd disappeared down one of the corridors. That's when I checked Konrad's cell.'

'They . . . they didn't see you?'

'I've got a feeling if they had I'd be dead.' McCaul faltered, as if he dreaded what he had to say next. 'A little down the hall I found another monk dead in his cell. Same thing. His throat had been cut. The third one's probably dead too, or soon will be, if what I've seen is anything to go by.'

Jennifer felt light headed, as if the room was about to start spinning. 'We . . . we have to call the police.'

'It wouldn't help. How long is it going to take the cops to get here?' Sweat beaded McCaul's brow, and for the first time Jennifer saw real fear in his face. 'Those guys had machine pistols, Jennifer. They looked like professional killers, ready to deal with just about anything. And that includes us. Are you *listening* to me, Jennifer?'

Jennifer was in a daze. 'Y . . . yes.'

'It's time we got out of here.'

A corridor away, Brother Paulo didn't hear the intruders invade his darkened cell. But he felt their rough hands rousing him from his sleep and then he felt the gag being tied over his mouth.

This isn't happening, Paulo told himself. *I'm having a nightmare.*

He tried to struggle but the intruders dragged him from his bed. One of them had slipped something around his neck. His eyes bulged in terror when he saw that it was a noose and the end of the rope was tied to the bars of his cell window.

They're going to hang me, Paulo thought. *Please God, tell me I'm dreaming!* But it wasn't a dream. The intruders forced him to stand on his bedside chair, and the chair was kicked from under him. Paulo tried desperately to scream behind the gag but the rope bit into his neck and strangled him.

When his body fell limp one of the intruders stepped on to the chair and removed the gag. The other one picked up the bloodied stiletto he'd left on the floor and tossed it on the bed. Then he nodded to his accomplice and they moved out into the corridor.

'Stay right behind me and don't make a sound.'

'Where . . . where are we going?'

'To see if there's another way out of here.' McCaul raised the gun and flicked off the torch before he opened the door. He listened, then stepped out, Jennifer behind him. The corridor was empty, candlelight casting flickering shadows on the stone walls. They had gone twenty yards when they came to the winding stairway that led down to the cellars. They heard a noise and looked round.

Twin torch beams cut like knives through the darkness as two men suddenly rounded the end of the corridor. Both wore menacing black ski masks and long raincoats. Jennifer saw their machine pistols and was panic stricken. There was a split second of recognition as the men reacted and raised their weapons.

'*Run, Jennifer!*' McCaul pushed her down the staircase towards the vaults.

36

The stairway was in total darkness and McCaul flicked on the torch as they hurried barefoot down the stairs. They heard racing footsteps in the corridor above as the two men came after them.

Jennifer reached the bottom of the stairs and saw the oak door, the key hanging from the hook in the wall. She inserted it frantically in the rusted lock and turned the handle, but the door wouldn't budge.

'Let me try.' McCaul stepped in, turned the handle and slammed his shoulder hard against the wood. The door opened with a creak of protest and he shoved Jennifer into the darkness and moved in after her. As he locked the door from the inside the footsteps grew louder on the stairwell.

McCaul was desperate. 'The lock mightn't hold. We need a wedge. Try and find something. *Anything.*'

Jennifer shone the torch over the stone archways and saw the bones of the dead cemented into the walls. The feeling of death was all around her and her heart beat so rapidly it was difficult to move or breathe.

'*Jennifer, for Christ sakes!*'

'I'm . . . I'm looking.' She spotted a ceremonial staff clutched in the bony hands of an ancient nobleman, his emaciated skeleton dangling from a hook. She stood on tiptoes, tried to grab the staff, but her fingers came inches short.

'I can't reach . . .'

McCaul pushed past her like a bull and yanked the staff from the skeleton's clutches, but the wooden stem crumbled in his hand. '*Damn it!*'

The footsteps on the staircase halted. The men were outside the door.

'Forget it. Keep moving,' said McCaul, and pushed Jennifer farther into the crypt.

The intruders reached the bottom of the stairs. One of them turned the handle and slammed his shoulder against the door. The heavy oak didn't budge and he examined the rusted lock: the cast iron was far too solid to attempt to shoot open. In frustration, the man stepped back and he and his accomplice started to kick savagely at the door.

McCaul flashed the torchlight on the walls. As they moved deeper into the crypt, the pounding on the door became more violent. It sounded as if the men were trying to kick their way in.

'This way.' McCaul pointed along the passageway and they pressed on. The chamber was smothered in darkness and Jennifer found it difficult to see, the light from the torch becoming weaker, but there was no mistaking the macabre sight of death everywhere. She shuddered as they passed the skeletal remains of the young girl in a tattered lace dress, and the enthroned figure of Padre Boniface. The eerie chamber seemed hostile, filled with invisible enemies. They came to another oak door, its frame covered with a veil of spider's webs. McCaul tried the rusted handle but it wouldn't give. 'What's wrong?' Jennifer asked.

'The mechanism's probably rusted, or else the door's locked or wedged from the inside. See if there's a key somewhere . . .'

They desperately scoured the door frame with the torchlight, but found no key. McCaul swore in frustration.

Behind her, Jennifer heard the men renew their pounding on the door. There was a sound of wood splintering, then the pounding got louder. In desperation, McCaul turned the handle again, slamming his weight against the wood. When nothing happened, he tried kicking in the door, but after half a dozen attempts he finally gave up. 'It's no good. It won't budge. We're wasting our time. Let's go back the way we came. Hurry, Jennifer.'

They raced back along the chamber and reached the marble throne. McCaul shone the torch into the narrow gap and they saw the tunnel beyond. 'It's our only chance.'

The tunnel looked dark and forbidding, the entrance covered in cobwebs, and Jennifer heard what sounded like a scurrying rat. 'I . . . I don't think I can go in there.'

'You want to stay here and die? Those guys aren't breaking down the door for the hell of it, Jennifer.' He held up Caruso's pistol, sweat glistening on his face. 'How long do you think I can hold them off with this? It's not worth a shit against a couple of machine pistols.'

Behind them came an almighty crash of splintering wood. McCaul grabbed Jennifer's hand, forced her into the narrow gap, and squeezed in after her.

At the bottom of the stairs, the two intruders had splintered the oak door, but it still hung stubbornly on its rusted hinges. One of the men raised his Skorpion machine pistol, aimed at the top hinge and squeezed the trigger. The silenced weapon stuttered and the rusted metal was turned to shreds in a hail of gunfire. The man lowered the pistol and fired another volley at the second hinge. It shattered, he gave a final kick, and the door burst in.

The tunnel was cold and stank of mildew. They had barely gone a dozen yards when the light from the torch weakened to a glimmer.

'The batteries are almost gone.' McCaul handed the torch to Jennifer and fumbled for his cigarette lighter. He flicked it on and the cavern lit up with the burst of flame. Jennifer saw rough-hewn walls, glistening with trickles of water. She realised to her horror that they were in another charnel house: stacked against the base of the walls were more human bones. Death was behind her in the form of two killers with machine guns, and now it lay ahead of her. She was too terrified to speak.

'It looks like an overflow from the crypt.' McCaul pushed on until the tunnel became two low passageways, barely high enough to stand up in. He stepped towards the passageway on the left and held up the lighter flame. A weak draught of wind made the flame quiver.

'There's air coming from somewhere. *Damn!*' McCaul shook his hand as the heat from the lighter scorched his fingers. He doused the flame and tried flicking on the torch, but it was useless, and he had to use the lighter again. In despair, he pointed to the second passageway. 'We'll try this way.'

'What if we're wrong?' Jennifer said.

'Don't even think about it.'

It took the intruders less than a minute to search the crypt. When they couldn't find their quarry they started again, methodically retracing their footsteps, exploring every archway, their torch beams flicking over the macabre walls. As they passed the marble throne, one of them shone his torch around the plinth. He saw the gap and beckoned to his companion.

As Jennifer and McCaul felt their way deeper into the passageway, the torch beam became a faint glimmer and every few seconds McCaul had to flick on his lighter. They came to dead end: a mound of rocks piled high against the passageway wall. 'Looks like maybe we picked the wrong way,' McCaul said bitterly.

It seemed hopeless, and McCaul grabbed at the larger rocks, tossing them aside, his despair turning to blind rage. When he had cleared away a good part of the mound he waved the lighter flame over the remaining rocks and a weak stream of air made the flame dance. 'Give me a hand here, quickly. We could be on to something.'

Jennifer helped him clear away the debris until a hole appeared, followed by a rush of cold air and the sound of heavy rainfall. 'It looks like Konrad wasn't spinning us a yarn.'

McCaul crawled through the hole first, then pulled Jennifer after him. They were out in the open air, on a ridge of high ground that ran along the monastery walls. The earth fell away steeply, covered in loose stones and wild brush, a dark ravine below. The thunder and lightning had stopped but the rain was still constant. 'Get your shoes on, the ground looks pretty rough.'

Voices echoed behind them and they looked back through the opening in the rocks. A moment later a powerful beam of torch-light shone from the darkness. McCaul aimed the Beretta into the passageway, fired off a volley of shots, and they scrambled down the incline.

They scrabbled over loose stones, feeling their way through thickets of coarse brush. When they reached the bottom of the ravine McCaul dragged Jennifer by the hand and they ran head-long until they came to a narrow track with forest on either side. They were drenched and breathless, and Jennifer felt totally lost. 'Where are we?'

'At a guess, somewhere to the north of the monastery.'

They kept to the track and minutes later they found them-selves back at the monastery gates, where the Nissan was still parked. 'Wait here,' McCaul whispered. 'I'd better see if those guys left us company.'

He gripped the Beretta in both hands and crouched over to the jeep and looked in. Then he opened the driver's door, checked inside, and came back. 'We're in the clear. Let's go.'

They raced to the jeep and McCaul slipped the key in the ignition. He was completely drenched and at that moment he looked as fearful as Jennifer.

'What in the hell was all that about? Who the frig *are* those guys?'

'I don't think we should wait to find out.'

'Damn right.' McCaul started the engine, swung the jeep round and accelerated down the hill with a burst of speed.

37

Five minutes later, McCaul sped into the village of Varzo. Jennifer checked behind her but saw no sign of anyone following. McCaul skidded on to the rain-swept main plaza, hung a sharp left into a narrow cobbled lane and halted. 'Why are we stopping?'

'We need to decide what we're going to do.'

Jennifer was on edge. 'Shouldn't we be trying to find the police?'

'Get it into your head, Jennifer, we're on our own. Even if the cops believe our story, which I doubt, they'd lock us up for our own protection. You think that's going to keep us alive? Whoever those guys are working for, they murdered Caruso and his wife. You think some two-roomed local cop shop is going to stop them from killing us?'

'How could they have known we were at the monastery?'

'They had to be following us, that's for sure, except I didn't see anyone on our tail. My guess is, they used electronic surveillance. It's simple, no big deal. All they've got to do is plant an electronic bug on the jeep and they know where we're headed. It could be anywhere. We could be looking for the damned thing for hours.'

'You mean they know where we are *this minute*?'

'That's exactly what I mean. And if we stay in the jeep we're sitting ducks.'

Carlo Perini was bored out of his tree. It was a shitty night to be stuck on the late shift, with the rain pissing down. He wished he were back in his flat getting his nuts off with his girlfriend, but instead he was stuck behind the ticket booth at Varzo railway station, which had to be the crappiest gig in town.

A handful of miserable-looking passengers waited on the

platform; most of the trains were delayed because of the storm. Carlo looked up as a couple approached the booth. They were both like drowned rats, but the woman was a looker, and had a good figure. '*Si?*'

'*Parla inglese?*' the guy said.

Carlo almost laughed. If he spoke English, he wouldn't have a lousy job selling tickets in a lousy train station in the middle of Shitsville. Still, he remembered a few schoolboy phrases, crappy useless lines like: *The cat is on the mat. Would you like a glass of red wine with dinner?*

He shrugged, held up two fingers, a very tiny gap between the tips.

'*Putino* . . . a little.'

'We need two tickets on the next train out of here. It doesn't matter where.'

'*Prego?*'

The guy spoke again, more slowly. Carlo still didn't get it. He didn't get it the third time either, or the fourth. It took a few more frustrating minutes, the help of a pen and paper and some sign language for the guy to get his message across, and the way Carlo saw it, he and the good-looking chick wanted to get out of Varzo *fast*, on whatever train was leaving town. A very wise decision, Carlo thought.

'The train . . . that comes soon . . .' Carlo said, searching for the right words, feeling like a twelve-year-old again, '. . . go to Brig, in Svizzera, via the *galleria* Simplon.'

The couple seemed to grasp that, Carlo thought. The next train was going to Brig, Switzerland, via the Simplon tunnel.

'*When?*' The guy was agitated, pointing to his watch. Carlo thought: *These two sure are in a fucking hurry.* The train was half an hour late because of flooding on the line, but it was due in the next five minutes. Carlo held up five fingers. '*Cinque minuti.*'

The guy slapped a fistful of banknotes on the counter.

Five minutes later, the train for Brig pulled up beside the rain-sodden platform with a squeal of brakes. Carlo watched from the ticket booth and saw the couple climb into one of the carriages with the other passengers. The train pulled out. Carlo wondered what had made the pair act so strangely; they looked so worried, ill at ease. But what Carlo didn't see was the powerful black BMW that drew up outside the station and the two hard-faced men who climbed out.

Dressed in raincoats, no longer wearing ski masks, they were just in time to see the train disappear down the tracks. They dashed up to the ticket booth and one of them said urgently in Italian, 'Excuse me, but I think we missed our train. The one that just left, where was it headed?'

Carlo looked at the guy. Blond, maybe forty, tough looking, with a scar above his right eye. His companion was stocky and had a shaven head and dark, menacing eyes. 'Brig. But you're out of luck if you want to get there by train tonight, mister. The next one isn't due until the morning.'

'Does the train that left stop anywhere?'

'Sure. It stops at Iselle in about twelve minutes. But with the way the storm's been, it will probably take longer. There are hold-ups all along the line.'

The blond smiled. 'Thank you so much.'

38

Mark and Kelso were speeding towards Varzo. The rain had stopped but Kelso kept his eyes firmly on the wet road.

'You still haven't answered all my questions, Kelso. Who exactly is Jennifer in danger from and why would they want to kill her?'

Mark was in the passenger seat, Grimes in the back. The evening traffic was thick out of Turin and Kelso reacted as a tiny Fiat suddenly overtook their Opel, rocketing past at over a hundred kilometres an hour. 'This has got to be the most insane country in the world to drive in. That dumb asshole's going to kill himself.'

'Answer me, Kelso.'

'All I've got is a theory, but I'll give it to you for what it's worth.'

'I'm listening.'

'Whoever stole the fifty million, they would have laid low for a time, maybe got themselves plastic surgery and started a new life.'

'Go on.'

'But the body turning up on the mountain suddenly presents a big problem.'

'Why?'

'Because now the cops will be sniffing around, and maybe the Moscaya clan will be doing the same, hoping to get a bead on what happened to the fifty million. So whoever the culprit is, he's going to want to stop the bloodhounds from picking up his trail.'

'You think that's why Jennifer's life is in danger?'

'I reckon that's part of it. There's something else you ought to know. The detective investigating the case was a man named Caruso. He and his wife were found shot dead this afternoon.

The information I got was that the crime scene looked as if Caruso shot his wife and committed suicide. But I figure that's total bullshit and they were murdered.'

Mark was stunned. 'Who killed them?'

'Someone who's desperate enough to want this case closed, *permanently*, and on their terms. Either Paul March or the Moscaya's henchmen.'

'Why them?'

'I told you there was a computer disk. On our instructions, March was able to make a copy disk of a bunch of Prime's Swiss account numbers. Once we had the disk we'd be able to link them to the Moscayas and have them by the balls.'

'So?'

'March refused to hand over the disk until after he'd been paid the half-million and he and his family were safely in witness protection. But the disk vanished with him.'

'Where does all this leave Jennifer?'

'A bunch of personal items were found in a rucksack near the body, and may just offer a clue about what happened to March and the disk. I've got a gut feeling the Moscayas will think the same. That's why they'll want to get their hands on Jennifer, and once they do, they'll find out all they can and kill her.'

Mark said angrily, 'You're just using Jennifer as bait, Kelso.'

Kelso exploded. 'Look, Ryan, I've spent years on this case, so I damned well want to get to the bottom of it. But Jennifer chose to come to Europe of her own free will. Me, I'm here to protect her, or can't you get that into your head? OK, so I told you that I never believed Paul March murdered his wife, shot his son and tried to rape his own daughter just to cover his tracks. But if I got it wrong, then Jennifer needs to be protected, not only from the Russian mafia, but maybe from her own father.'

Before Mark could reply, Kelso's cell phone rang and he flicked it on. 'Kelso. What is it?'

Mark couldn't hear the caller, but he saw Kelso stiffen. 'You're sure they're not there? OK, don't touch a thing without being extra careful, you hear me? Not a damned thing. Call me if you've got anything. We'll be there in half an hour.' Kelso flicked off his phone, his face mournful.

'What's up?'

'That was Fellows. He's at the monastery. You're not going to believe this . . .'

39

McCaul had picked a carriage near the middle of the train. Each of the carriages had separate compartments, and they had found an empty one all to themselves. Jennifer did her best to clean her muddied clothes but she was on edge. To make things worse, the storm showed no sign of letting up, and five minutes after leaving Varzo the train still hadn't picked up much speed. McCaul peered out of the rain-lashed window. 'The weather's probably slowing things up, but I figure we ought to be entering the Simplon tunnel pretty soon.'

Jennifer had heard of the tunnel. One of the longest in the world, it was in fact a series of connecting tunnels that burrowed for twenty kilometres through the Simplon pass, between Switzerland and Italy. She stood up anxiously, slid open the compartment door and checked the corridor. The train was half full and the passengers looked a mixed bunch: office workers and a group of schoolkids with rucksacks, accompanied by a couple of their teachers. The kids looked drenched, as if their school outing in the mountains had been ruined by the storm. Jennifer reassured herself that the two men were not lurking in the corridor and slid the door shut.

'You're on edge,' McCaul said flatly.

'Of course I'm on edge. Why the hell shouldn't I be?' Jennifer felt ill at the thought of the carnage in the monastery. She sat down again, buried her face in her hands. 'It's all a complete nightmare.'

McCaul came over and put an arm around her shoulder. 'There was nothing we could do, Jennifer. Nothing. If we hadn't escaped we'd be dead too.'

'Why would *anyone* want to slaughter Father Konrad and the others? Why would they butcher *everyone* if they were only after us?'

McCaul shook his head, his voice strained. 'I don't know. This whole thing gets crazier by the minute.'

Jennifer got to her feet and paced the compartment, racking her brains for a motive. 'There has to be a reason.'

'Like what?'

'The only thing I can think of . . . You said yourself that someone's desperate to destroy every shred of evidence. What if that's the reason Konrad and the others were killed? They *saw* the man who survived the storm. They were witnesses and the journal entry was evidence of that.'

'Maybe you've got something there.'

'The man mentioned in the journal *has* to be the one we're looking for, so why don't we just go to the police right now?'

'I told you, Jennifer, we could be putting ourselves in danger.'

The train slowed, the pitch of the engine changed and they plunged into a tunnel. Seconds later they came out the other end. Jennifer felt a stab of fear as McCaul moved towards the door. 'Where are you going, Frank?'

'To find a washroom and clean up. Unless you want to go first?'

Jennifer declined. McCaul had fared the worst as he'd led their scramble down the embankment, and his clothes were muddied and ripped. But Jennifer still felt uneasy being left alone. He seemed to sense it, and touched her face. 'Don't worry, we're safe for now. I'll be back soon and we'll talk some more. But just keep the door shut, OK?'

As Jennifer sat alone in the carriage, her imagination was unable to suppress the images of slaughter at the monastery, and her stomach churned. For some reason she had a desperate urge to phone Mark and make certain that Bobby was all right. She searched in her tote bag but couldn't find her cell phone. *Damn.* She must have dropped it during the scramble out of the monastery. Now she'd have to wait until she reached Brig to phone Mark. She just hoped he had kept to his word to look after Bobby, but the more she thought about his behaviour before she left for Europe, the more it puzzled her. It was almost as if he'd had a premonition about her safety, which seemed strange . . .

The train slowed, interrupting her thoughts, and she looked out of the window as the lights of a station came into view.

The BMW screeched into the Iselle station's car park. The driver slammed on the brakes and the two men clambered out just as the train pulled alongside the platform. The driver locked the doors and the two men raced towards the station, where a weary-looking clerk sat behind the ticket counter. '*Si, signore?*'

'Two tickets,' the blond said in Italian, and handed him a couple of banknotes.

'Where to, mister?'

'Brig.'

'You made it just in time. That's the last train to Brig tonight.'

The blond grinned. 'Then it seems we're in luck.'

40

McCaul came back five minutes later, looking fresher, just as the train started to pull out of the station. He shut the compartment door and went over to join Jennifer. 'You want the bad news or the good?'

'Does it matter?'

'The nearest washroom's three carriages down and there's no hot water. But the storm seems to be easing up, and about time. Maybe there's a dining car where I can get us coffee. You want some?'

Jennifer flushed. Still preoccupied with the gruesome images her mind had conjured of Father Konrad and the others with their throats cut, she felt bile rise in her throat and got to her feet.

'What's wrong?' McCaul asked. 'You don't look too good.'

'I need to use the washroom.'

The washroom door was unlocked and she stepped inside. The train lurched from side to side as it picked up speed again and Jennifer felt a wave of nausea overcome her. *I'm going to throw up.*

She turned to the washbasin, threw water on her face, and then ran the cold tap over her wrists . . .

The two men advanced quickly through the corridors. They scanned the face of every passenger they passed, and when they came to the end of the carriage, they moved into the next . . .

Jennifer took deep breaths. As the ice-cold water cooled her wrists, her nausea subsided. She examined her face in the mirror above the basin. Her features were drawn and her hair unkempt.

I look a mess. She tidied herself as best she could, then dabbed her wet clothes with water to clean away the traces of mud and grime.

There was a knock on the door. Before Jennifer could even reply, the handle turned and the door burst open. She started as an impatient young woman almost barged in on top of her. '*Scusi, signorina. Finito?*'

'Pardon?'

The woman babbled something in rapid Italian, indicating that she wanted to use the washroom. Jennifer turned off the taps, dried her hands with a clutch of paper towels, and left her to it.

As she made her way back to her carriage, her fear hadn't gone away. She felt tense and her head throbbed. The thoughts that had preoccupied her since the monastery returned. *Who are those two men and why do they want to kill me?* Her nausea came back, her chest felt tight, and she had a desperate need for air.

She was at the end of the corridor and there was a glass vent near the top of the carriage window. Jennifer yanked it open and a cool draught washed her face. The engine changed pitch again as it entered a series of connecting tunnels and she guessed they had started their journey through the Simplon pass. Moments later she heard the rush of air as the train burst out the other end of a tunnel. The storm had eased, and as she stood there taking deep gulps of air, she heard the door slide open at the end of the carriage.

A man stepped in. He was blond, with a thin scar over one eye, and he wore a pale raincoat. Another raincoated man stepped in behind him; he was bald and stocky, with sinister eyes, and Jennifer immediately felt uncomfortable. Both men had cold, impassive faces, and unlike the other passengers she'd seen there was something infinitely dangerous about these two, as if they were no strangers to violence.

Jennifer was filled with terror. She knew instinctively that they were the men from the monastery. *But how? How have they found me again?* She felt small and defenceless, her mind numb with fear. And in an instant, with chilling certainty, she knew she was going to be murdered.

The men lunged towards her.

Jennifer screamed and ran back along the carriage.

41

Jennifer raced to the end of the corridor and glanced back. The two men were gaining ground. She felt light headed, her legs shaking. The men's hostile faces only confirmed what she already knew: *they're going to kill me*. She grabbed at the door leading to the next carriage, yanked it open and darted through. She was panic stricken as she stumbled into a crowd of the schoolchildren who had boarded at Varzo. They blocked the corridor, jostling and chatting among themselves. Jennifer didn't even think of trying to explain what was happening to her, and feared that if she got caught among these students she might put their lives at risk. She was certain the men would spare no one in their urge to kill her, even some innocent teenager who got in their way.

'*Scusi! Scusi!* Let me through! Please get out of the way!' As she pushed forward, the bemused students looked at her as if she were crazy, but she stared fixedly ahead, her eyes locked on her compartment, twenty yards away. She knew her only hope of staying alive now was to reach McCaul. *He has the gun. He can protect us.* Breathless with fear, she looked back. The men were ten yards behind, pushing their way through the throng of students. Jennifer reached her compartment door and yanked it open. '*Frank! For God's sake help me!*'

But McCaul was gone.

In that stark moment of terror, Jennifer knew she was dead. Petrified, she stared at the empty compartment. *Where is McCaul? Have they murdered him?*

For a split second she was rooted to the spot. Fear swamped her body and every instinct told her she was doomed. She was close to tears. She knew it would be a waste of time locking the door: the men would simply break it down.

It seemed absurd, but in her panic she felt a sudden anger that

244

electrified her. *No*, she told herself fiercely. *You're not going to die. You're going to fight. They're going to have to work to kill you.*

She dashed out into the corridor again. Less than fifteen feet away, the men had almost pushed their way through the crowd of students. There was a chilling determination in their faces that terrified Jennifer. As they broke through the crowd and lunged towards her, she ran.

She was in a frenzy. Her only thought was to get as far away from the men as she could, and when she reached the next carriage she tore open the door. In her panic she'd barely noticed the compartments she'd passed, but now she realised she was in an empty section of the train, with not a single passenger in sight.

No one can help me. I'm alone.

Her mind began to race, searching for some kind of escape. She noticed two exit doors, left and right. A window was open in one of them. A blast of noise from the train's wheels funnelled in through the window, roaring in her ears, and an ice-cold stream of air clawed at her face. She thought of jumping from the train. But it was speeding along at over sixty miles an hour and she knew she faced a stark choice of terrors. She was trapped between a solid mountain wall rushing past on one side of the train and a deadly drop into dark space on the other.

I have to keep moving.

As she started to yank open the carriage door she heard a rush of feet behind her and the bald assailant appeared, carrying a machine pistol in one hand. He lunged forward and Jennifer staggered back against the train door. She tried to fend him off but he slapped her, a stinging blow across the face, and then his hand went around her throat. She struggled but in vain. The man pushed her head back through the open window, his grip so powerful she could hardly breathe. *I'm going to die*, Jennifer thought.

She felt the blood draining from her head and she started to black out . . .

42

A razor-sharp blast of icy air slashed at Jennifer's face. Her head and shoulders were half out of the window, the freezing air all that kept her conscious as her attacker's hand tightened around her throat. She fought to keep her eyes open, fought to breathe, but it was a vain fight, and her brain refused to function. It was as if all the circuits inside her head were already closing down, preparing for the darkness of death.

If I'm going to die, please God, let it happen quickly.

The man was enjoying her terror, a cruel sneer spreading across his face which incited her to summon her last reserves of energy. *No, you're not going to die like this. You're going to fight back.*

And then she knew what her mind was trying to tell her. *Use any weapon you can get hold of.* She fumbled blindly in her bag with her free hand. She found something long and hard, recognised the feel and shape of a ballpoint pen. She got a firm grip on the end and with all her remaining strength she plunged the pen into the man's cheek.

He screamed and staggered back, dropping his weapon, clapping a hand to his bloodied face, the pen embedded below his left eye.

Jennifer could barely breathe as she pulled herself in from the open window. The man lay writhing in agony on the floor, blocking her path. She was hemmed in, had no way of escape, and she watched in horror as her attacker wrenched the pen from his wound.

In her panic she yanked open the exit door and a powerful

rush of air almost knocked her off her feet. She knew her only hope was to jump from the train, but as she tried to muster the courage the man reached out blindly and grabbed her leg.

Jennifer saw the machine pistol on the floor. She reached for the weapon and twisted her leg free just as the man pulled himself up and came at her like an angry bear.

Jennifer brought up the machine pistol and squeezed the trigger. The Skorpion stuttered, a round hitting the man in the shoulder. He grunted and a cloud of crimson spread across his coat. As he staggered back he almost fell out through the open door, but at the last moment he managed to grab hold of the door frame and cling on defiantly, his coat flapping in the train's slipstream. Wild fear lit up his eyes as the roar of the engine suddenly changed in pitch and the train sped into a tunnel.

Jennifer saw terror in the man's face as his fingers lost their grip. He fell away with a scream. A split second later his body slammed into the tunnel arch and disappeared into darkness.

Jennifer turned away in horror as the carriage door behind her burst open and McCaul rushed in, clutching the Beretta. She was in a daze, the Skorpion still in her hand, and McCaul took it from her and guided her back into the carriage. 'You're OK, you're safe,' he reassured her, breathless. 'What in the hell happened?'

She opened her mouth to speak but no words came. *I've just killed a man.* She wanted to throw up. A body lay in the corridor and Jennifer saw it was her attacker's blond accomplice. 'Is . . . is he dead?'

McCaul held up the Beretta. 'No, but I had to hit him a couple of times with this before I knocked him out cold.' He knelt and took the machine pistol from underneath the man's raincoat, removed the magazine and emptied the round of ammunition from the breech, then did the same with the second Skorpion, before he tossed both weapons from the train's window. 'Those guys meant business. A thing like that could cut you in two with a single burst.'

Jennifer noticed that McCaul's face was badly scratched, his jacket ripped at the shoulder, and there was a nasty gash across his right eye. 'Where . . . where did you go?'

'To see if I could get us some coffee.' McCaul stood. 'When I came back I saw a commotion down the hall. That's when I had the punch-up with our friend here. Are you hurt? Do you need a doctor? What went on back there?'

'I . . . I killed a man . . .' And then suddenly she was in McCaul's arms, fighting back tears as she told him what had happened.

'Calm down, Jennifer. You had to protect yourself.'

'I'm sure they were the two men from the monastery. How could they have found us again?'

McCaul had no answer, and shook his head. 'Whoever they are they don't give up easily.' He rummaged in the man's pockets, found a cell phone and wallet, and examined the wallet's contents.

'What are you doing?'

'I'd like to know who just tried to stiff us.'

'Who is he?'

McCaul stuffed the wallet and cell phone in his pocket. 'We'll talk about that later. Our buddy here may have company on board. It's time we got off the train.'

McCaul found the emergency stop lever in the next carriage. Jennifer saw that the train had left the Simplon tunnel and was speeding along a flat run of track towards Brig.

'Better brace yourself and pray the passengers don't get hurt.'

McCaul pulled the lever. For a couple of seconds nothing happened, and then Jennifer heard a ferocious squeal of metal as the brakes bit the tracks. The train shuddered violently, throwing them off balance, and the carriages ground to a halt. McCaul yanked open the exit door and jumped. An incline led down from the tracks to a darkened roadway lit by a few desultory street lamps. 'Get out, Jennifer.'

Jennifer saw no sign of life in the surrounding darkness. 'Where are we going?'

'We'll try to make our way to Brig, then figure out what to do. Move, Jennifer. Get down from the damned train.'

She was still in shock. Dazed and confused passengers were coming out into the corridors to stare from the carriage windows. McCaul held out his hand. 'Jennifer, for God's sake jump!'

She grabbed his hand and leaped off the train. He led her, stumbling, down the incline.

PART FOUR

43

Switzerland

The farm was remote, more than three kilometres from the nearest village. The man lived there alone, except for his two ferocious black Dobermans, which gambolled about his feet that foggy evening as he finished milking the cows in one of the barns. As he carried the two metal pails back to the farmhouse, the dogs started to bark and leap with excitement. '*Sitz*, Hans! *Sitz*, Ferdie!'

The Dobermans obeyed his instruction instantly, whimpering as they came to heel. The man set down the milk pails in the kitchen and wiped his hands on his jacket. He was sturdily built and wore green rubber farm boots and a stained work jacket. His shock of dark hair was patched with grey and his weather-beaten face bore the ravages of frostbite. The plastic surgeon had done his best, but despite his efforts a chunk of flesh was missing from the tip of the man's nose, and to make matters worse he'd lost the tips of three fingers on his left hand.

He nervously licked his lips as he went to peer through the curtains, then he turned back towards the table. A clutch of news-papers lay there, and a pair of rubber-encased Zeiss binoculars. He picked up the powerful binoculars and pointed them towards the main road, half a kilometre away from the craggy western slopes of the Wasenhorn. There was no sign of the car or the men, but they were out there, somewhere, watching him, he was certain of it. He had lived in fear ever since he'd heard of the discovery of the glacier corpse. Lived in fear for the last three days since he'd started seeing the car with two men, watching his property. He put down the binoculars and for reassurance dug his hand into his jacket pocket and took out a Sig Sauer automatic pistol. He checked that the magazine was fully loaded with fifteen 9mm rounds before he slammed the magazine home again. The weapon was his insurance, just in case.

'*Hans! Ferdie! Kommt, meine Liebchen!*'

The dogs bounded over and he patted their heads. The Dobermans would kill instantly on his instruction: their savage jaws could rip a human throat to bloody shreds in seconds. '*Ferdie! Hans! Draussen! Wartet draussen!*'

The dogs rushed towards the door and went to sit in the front porch. The man diverted his attention to a corner of the kitchen. A TV/video security screen was linked to two cameras which monitored the front and back of the farmhouse. He had installed the cameras for his own protection. That evening the screen showed nothing unusual: an unchanging shot of the front of the house, the gravel driveway and the road leading up to the farm. He flicked a switch on the monitor and the image altered to a view of the barn and the garage. Nothing there either.

Satisfied, he tucked the pistol back in his pocket. He was still fearful that somehow his secret had been compromised by the corpse's discovery. But he was prepared to deal with any unwelcome visitors. And if they came, he would kill them if he had to.

44

Lou Garuda drove his Porsche into mid-town Manhattan. Prime International Securities had once had its offices in one of the most imposing pieces of real estate on Fifth Avenue. It was a stunning display of architecture, all shimmering mirrored glass and solid burnished metal, a building that oozed wealth and power. As he drove past Garuda thought: *These guys sure had money.*

He'd found too little information on Prime and reckoned that a personal visit to one of its former vice-presidents might help. Frederick Kammer, he had discovered, now worked for another Manhattan investment corporation called Cavendish-Deloy Securities, and Garuda found it farther along Fifth Avenue. He went in through revolving doors and found himself in a private lobby, decorated with Italian marble and expensive murals. A middle-aged woman sat behind the reception desk. Garuda strolled over. 'Cavendish-Deloy, please.'

'Whom do you wish to see?'

Garuda flashed a smile. 'One of the head honchos. Mr Kammer.'

'All Mr Kammer's calls must go through his secretary, but I can call her. Who shall I say wants to see him?'

'Officer Lou Garuda.' He showed his badge. 'I'm with the Long Beach Police Department. And listen, lady, it's personal, so I want to speak with Kammer himself, not his secretary.'

The woman frowned and punched in an extension number on her phone. She spoke to the person on the other end, and then she said, 'Yes, I'll put him on.' She handed Garuda the receiver. 'Mr Kammer will speak to you.'

255

Garuda took the phone. 'Hello?'

A man's impatient voice came on the line. 'Yes? This is Frederick Kammer.'

'Hello, Mr Kammer.'

'Who is this?'

'My name's Lou Garuda. I have some information that might interest you, sir. It's about Paul March.'

'*Who?*'

'Paul March. He was a former colleague of yours when you worked for Prime Securities.'

There was a moment's silence and then the man said, 'Who *exactly* are you, Mr Garuda?'

'I'm a goddamned cop,' Garuda answered back. 'And I'd really appreciate it if you talked to me, and pretty damned soon.'

There was total silence at the other end of the line, then the voice said, 'Where are you calling from, Mr Garuda?'

'Downstairs in the lobby.'

'I can see you in five minutes. My office is on the sixteenth floor.'

Garuda took the elevator up to the sixteenth floor and stepped out into a plush suite of offices. There was a reception area with half a dozen office doors leading off. A woman came out of one of them. Her hair was tied back and she had a dour look of authority. 'Mr Garuda?'

'Guilty.'

'I'm Mr Kammer's secretary. Please follow me.' She led him down a hallway, knocked on a door, opened it and said, 'Go right in. Mr Kammer is waiting.'

Garuda stepped into the office and the door closed behind him. A thin, middle-aged man sat behind a glass-and-metal desk, a laptop computer in front of him. He wore a crisp white shirt, silk tie and braces, and his deep-set eyes narrowed as they took in Garuda. He didn't stand or offer his hand. 'Sit down.'

Garuda took a seat and thought: *Asshole.* He glanced at a couple of contemporary prints, splashes of colour, that hung on the walls. They looked good, but made absolutely no fucking sense to him. 'Pretty jazzy set of offices you got here, Mr Kammer. Very state-of-the-art.'

'Thank you, Mr Garuda. But let's get down to business. You say you're with the police?'

Garuda handed over his ID and Kammer studied it. 'You're a little off course from Long Beach. Is this an official visit?'

'Not exactly. You could say I'm here in a private capacity.'

'Then what do you have to say to me that's so important?'

'Paul March was a former employee of Prime Securities, and a colleague of yours. Two years ago he vanished on the same night his wife was murdered and the police had reason to believe he might have been the culprit. I covered the case at the time. It was a pretty gory homicide. March's son was crippled and his daughter viciously assaulted in the same attack.'

'Yes, it was very tragic. March was a fine employee and much respected. However, I had only been with the company a year and hardly knew the man, so what has this matter got to do with me?'

Garuda took out his notebook and pen. 'We'll come to that in a minute. First, how about you tell me about Prime?'

'It was a private firm involved in financial investment, Mr Garuda. But surely you know that already?'

'Exactly what areas of financial investment?'

'Too many to mention, or you'd be here all day.'

'I've got the time.'

'I'm sure you have, Mr Garuda. However, I no longer work for that company so I'm not going to go into details that may have been confidential between that firm and its clients. My contract with Prime would have stipulated that. Now, I believe you said you had some information?'

'Why did Prime fold?'

'I've got no idea. Business seemed to be good, so you'll have to ask the registered owners. But I'm sure they had their reasons.'

'Who are they?'

'A shell company in the Caymans.'

'I'm not with you.'

'The company was owned by another company, which in turn may even have been owned by another. That kind of convoluted corporate ownership structure can be for tax-efficiency reasons or for reasons of anonymity, frequently both.'

'You're saying a guy might not be able to find out who actually owned Prime?'

'Precisely.'

Garuda thought for a moment, let the information sink in. 'Do you know if Paul March was involved in any projects that might have put him in any kind of danger?'

Kammer was exasperated. 'Mr Garuda, as I already said, I hardly knew the man. Now, about this important information you claim to have.'

'OK, here's my news. Paul March was found dead five days ago, frozen into a glacier on a mountain near the Swiss–Italian border.'

Kammer looked surprised. 'I . . . I'd no idea.'

'March turning up dead like that after two years, it's kind of weird, don't you think? There were a lot of unanswered questions when he vanished. No motives for why he disappeared. Which is why I'm thinking of getting back on the case. Maybe you could help by answering some of the questions I've asked?'

'I'm sorry, but I think I've helped you all I can.'

Garuda slapped shut his notebook and sighed. *I'm being given the run-around.* 'You sure are a mine of information, Mr Kammer. Why don't you just tell me to go fuck myself?'

Kammer came round from behind his desk, indicating that the discussion was over. 'I already told you, I knew virtually nothing about March. Now, I must insist you leave. I have a one o'clock appointment.'

Garuda gave it one more try. 'Listen, if you could just—'

Kammer held open his office door, indicated the hall. 'Whatever it is, no, I can't. Good day, Mr Garuda.'

45

Varzo

'I counted three bodies, two with their throats cut, and the third looks like he hanged himself.'

'Who were they?'

'Monks.'

'*What?*'

'Catholic monks.' Fellows shone the electric torch ahead of them as he addressed Kelso and led them hurriedly in through the monastery gates. 'When I got here I found the entrance gate unlocked and let myself in. The place is deserted.'

'You're positive there was no sign of Jennifer or McCaul?'

'No, I searched. Two of the cells look like they were occupied, but now they're empty. There's a stairwell that leads down to a crypt, but you don't want to go down there, it's a charnel house. One of the doors was kicked in and had its hinges shot off.'

'Did you touch anything, leave any prints?'

'No, I was careful, just like you said.'

'Show me the stiffs, and let's be quick about it,' Kelso said grimly. 'And remember, nobody touches a thing.'

Mark followed Kelso and his men as they raced across the courtyard to a darkened archway. Their footsteps echoed on the wet cobble, the monastery eerily deserted as Fellows led them in through a pair of oak doors and along a corridor into one of the monk's cells. To his horror, Mark saw the lifeless body of a young man, dressed in nightclothes. He hung by his neck from a rope that was tied to the bars on the window. The chair beneath his feet was toppled, his eyes bulged in death, and a bloodied stiletto knife lay tossed on the bed. '*Jesus.*'

'Like I said, it looks like the guy hanged himself.'

'And the others?'

'It gets worse,' Fellows told Mark as he escorted them into two other rooms down the hall. When Mark saw the two bodies with their throats cut, he wanted to throw up. 'What went on here?'

'The way it looks,' Fellows suggested, 'is that maybe the young one went crazy, killed the other two, then decided to top himself.'

'Or that's the way it's *meant* to look.' Kelso studied the blood-ied corpse of one of the victims, closely examining the slash across his neck. 'The stiletto we saw in the other cell isn't the kind of weapon a man of the cloth is likely to carry, now, is it?'

'*But why?* Why were they killed?'

'I'm damned if I know.'

Mark took out his cell phone and punched in a number.

'What are you doing?' Kelso asked.

'Trying Jennifer's cell phone.'

'Forget it, her phone's off. I have my people trying her number every single minute. Either she's powered her phone off again or her battery's dead.'

Mark couldn't hear a dial tone, just a garbled message repeated in Italian from the line's service provider. He flicked off his phone in frustration as Kelso took a final look at the dead victim and turned towards the corridor. 'I suggest we get out of here fast, before the local cops discover they've got three dead monks on their hands. Fellows, you go with Grimes. Ryan will stick with me. We'll scour the town and see if we can get a bead on Jennifer.'

Half an hour later they found the blue Nissan parked on Varzo's deserted main piazza, and Mark immediately recognised the licence number. It was Grimes who had spotted the jeep first, and when they pulled up he was probing the chassis with a torch. Kelso went over to talk to him, then beckoned Mark. 'Grimes thinks it's been abandoned. The keys are still in the ignition.'

'Where did Jennifer and McCaul disappear to?'

'Grimes has an idea. Tell him.'

'We took a good look around the town,' Grimes explained. 'There isn't a single hotel in Varzo that they could have booked into. So I decided to check the railway station, in case they'd left town. A scheduled train stopped here en route to Switzerland over an hour ago. I think they were on it.'

'What makes you think that?'

'The guy on the ticket desk remembered a couple resembling McCaul and Jennifer who bought tickets for Brig.'

'Did he see them board the train?'

'He says he did. Except it turns out there was some trouble on board.'

'What kind of trouble?'

'Someone hit the emergency stop, about a mile outside of Brig. The ticket clerk didn't know any more, except that a couple were seen leaving the train.'

Kelso reached for a map and torch in the Opel's glove compartment. 'I don't believe in coincidences. Get moving, Grimes, we'll follow you. Ryan, come with me. If we can believe that Brig is where they were originally headed, there's always a chance it's still their destination.'

Kelso climbed into the Opel and Mark slid into the passenger seat. 'It doesn't make sense. Why would they abandon the jeep and take a train?'

Kelso tossed the map over to Mark and shot him a meaningful look. 'There's something Grimes didn't mention.'

'What?'

'We had our suspicions McCaul might have been followed as soon as he met up with Jennifer, so Grimes checked it out and found a bug planted under the Nissan's chassis.'

'You mean someone's been tailing them besides us?'

'That's exactly what I mean. And judging by the blood bath we just saw, they probably followed them to the monastery. But what happened after that only Jennifer or McCaul can tell us, assuming they're still alive.'

'What the frig's happening, Kelso? For Christ's sake, tell me if you know.'

Kelso started the engine. 'I've got a hunch about the monastery deaths.'

'What kind of hunch?'

Kelso swung out of the piazza with a squeal of tyres. 'Those monks weren't killed just for the hell of it, Ryan. There's a pattern here. Like Caruso's, their deaths were made to appear like a tragic act of violence. Why did they have to die? Because they knew something, or were part of the evidence, and someone wanted to cover up that fact. I'm damned well convinced of that.'

'Who's the someone?'

'That's the fifty-million-dollar question.'

46

New York

Lou Garuda was driving home when halfway there his conscience got the better of him and he turned the car round and drove out to the Cauldwell. When he went up to the reception desk a nurse was busy on the phone. She finished her call and looked up. 'Can I help you, sir?'

'I've come to visit Bobby March. He's a resident here. My name's Lou Garuda.'

The nurse studied him suspiciously. 'You called to see Bobby the other day, didn't you, Mr Garuda?'

Garuda looked sheepish. 'Yeah, that's right.'

The nurse frowned and came out from behind her desk. 'Will you wait here, please.'

'Why, is there a problem?'

'Just wait here and I'll be right back.'

Leroy led Garuda down a hall. 'Bobby's withdrawn, won't communicate with anyone, like he's in a trance, man.'

'What's up?'

'He had a mild seizure, right after you left. The seizures happen sometimes, and they ain't major, something medication can take care of. But since then he's been distressed. Never saw him so upset before. He won't even eat, or listen to his music. That ain't like Bobby. All he wants to do is see Jenny, but it seems like her cell phone's permanently switched off and we can't get in touch with her. What the hell did you say to him, man?'

Leroy stopped outside a private room and cracked open the door. Garuda saw Bobby sitting in his wheelchair, his head lolled to one side as he stared blankly out of the window. 'Listen, Leroy, I got a confession to make. I've been an asshole.'

'How come?'

'I told the kid about his old man's body being discovered.'

'*What?*'

'You didn't hear?'

'I didn't hear nothing, man.'

Garuda explained. 'Seems like I opened my big mouth and told Bobby something I shouldn't have. Jennifer obviously didn't want to upset him.'

'Jeez, that's way out, man. I mean about his old man's body.'

'You said it.'

'Seems to me somebody ought to tell Jennifer about Bobby's state. Can't you even get in touch with her buddy, Mark?'

'He's out of the country right now, and I ain't got a number for him. But I'm hoping he's going to call me. You mind if go see Bobby?'

'Naw, but this time I keep you company. And if he starts to get upset, you better back peddle your ass out the door, pronto, OK?'

'You're the boss.'

'How you doing, Bobby?'

Bobby didn't even look up, just sat there vacantly, his mouth pursed, saliva running down his chin. Leroy leaned over and wiped his mouth with a tissue. 'That friend of Mark's is here to see you, Bobby. Are you OK, man? You need anything? You don't want to see this guy again, just tell me, and he'll go.'

Bobby didn't reply. Leroy said to Garuda, 'See what I mean.'

Garuda sat on the bed next to Bobby's wheelchair. 'I thought I'd call by again, make sure you were OK. Are you OK, Bobby?'

The kid said nothing, but Garuda saw a notepad and pen on the table by the wheelchair. He leaned over, gently lifted the pad. 'Is this yours, Bobby?'

No reply. 'You like to draw?'

No response, not even a blink. Garuda studied the notepad, open on a page that was a mass of incomprehensible squiggles.

Or at least it looked that way at first. Then he started to notice some shapes in among the abstract scrawl, kind of saw-tooth forms, like mountains maybe, but he couldn't be sure. 'Hey, listen, Leroy here tells me I might have upset you the other day. If I did, I'm truly sorry, OK? I didn't know Jennifer didn't tell you about . . . well, you know . . .'

This time Garuda saw a distressed gaze, and a hint of tears. 'Bobby, you heard what I said, didn't you? You want to write down something on your pad? Let me know what's wrong?'

Bobby's hands started to move, slow and painstaking hand and finger gestures, and Garuda said to Leroy, 'What is that? Some kind of sign language?'

'Sure is. Bobby wants to know what else you know about his father.'

'Nothing,' Garuda answered. 'I told you everything I know, Bobby. That's all I got, I swear.'

Bobby turned his head away, continued to stare out of the window.

'Listen, Bobby,' Garuda pressed on, 'have you got anything you want to say to me? Anything at all?'

Bobby didn't even look round, but the gesture he made at Garuda by raising the middle finger of his right hand was unmistakable.

Leroy almost smiled. 'Ain't no mistaking *that* particular piece of sign language. Guess the man wants to be left alone.'

They stepped away a couple of feet and Garuda whispered, 'What happens now?'

'Dr Reed's going to see him this afternoon. She's one of our best counsellors. I'll tell her everything you said.'

'Thanks. Maybe she'll have more success.' Garuda looked down at the saw-tooth shapes on the open notepad on the table, then tore off a slip of blank paper from the pad, wrote a number, and handed it to Leroy. 'Maybe you'd let me know what the doctor has to say?'

'You'll speak to Mark?'

'Sure, soon as he calls.'

47

Brig, Switzerland

The taxi carrying Jennifer and McCaul slid to a halt on Brig's main street. Jennifer noticed that the town was a mix of casinos, banks and skiing shops, the cobblestoned streets dotted with cosy Alpine hotels. They found one called the Ambassador, on the Bahnhofstrasse. It was all dark panelled wood and antique furnishings, and when McCaul punched a brass desk bell a slim, effeminate-looking man with manicured hands and wearing a black suit and silk tie appeared at reception. '*Guten Abend, meine Dame und mein Herr.*'

'We'd like two rooms for tonight. Adjoining singles if you've got them.'

'Have you reservations, sir?' The receptionist spoke in immaculate English and studied them with mild suspicion. Jennifer wasn't surprised: it was well after midnight, they were dishevelled and had no luggage except for her tote bag. They had trekked from the railway line towards Brig's outskirts, then hailed a cab to take them the short distance into the centre of the town.

McCaul produced his credit card to soothe the clerk's fears, and said by way of explanation, 'Our car broke down outside of town and we got caught in the rain. We don't have a reservation. Is that a problem?'

The receptionist pursed his lips, suggesting it might be. 'There's a bankers' conference in town and the hotel is quite full, but perhaps we can still help you, *mein Herr.*' He tapped on a computer, then looked up. 'We have no adjoining single rooms available, I'm afraid. But we do have two single rooms on the third floor, three rooms apart. The rate is two hundred francs per room. Would these be suitable?'

'They'll have to do.'

When they had filled in the registration cards, the receptionist asked to see their passports. He checked the details, then finished on his computer and took an imprint of McCaul's credit card before returning it with a smile as plastic as the two door cards he offered them. 'Your rooms are 306 and 309, and the elevator is across the lobby. If there's anything I can do to make your stay in Brig more enjoyable, don't hesitate to ask.'

Room 306 was the closer as they stepped out of the elevator, and McCaul opened the door with the key card. The room overlooked Brig's magnificent Stockalper Castle Palace, and McCaul studied the view for a moment before he closed the curtains. 'Are you OK?'

'No. I'm tired and confused. And I keep thinking about the man I killed.'

Jennifer had a sensation of nausea in the pit of her stomach and it refused to go away.

'There's a remedy for that.' McCaul unlocked the mini-bar and selected a couple of miniature Scotches. He splashed them into two glasses, added soda, and handed one to Jennifer. 'Here, you look like you could do with it.'

As she swallowed the Scotch, McCaul took out the items he'd removed from the assassin's pocket and tossed them on the bed. He emptied the wallet. 'Let's see what we've got here.'

Jennifer saw a handful of Swiss and euro banknotes, what looked like a couple of crumpled receipts, and two credit cards: an American Express and a MasterCard. McCaul said, 'The cards are in two names. Tom Bauer and David Wayne. But I'd take a guess they're both aliases.'

'What else?'

McCaul studied the two receipts. 'One's a bill for breakfast at a restaurant at Zurich airport, dated for just after nine a.m., two days ago. The other's a bill for two rooms and dinner for last night at an inn in Simplon called the Rasthof, which is down the street from the Berghof. I saw it as I drove into the village.

It's pretty obvious these guys have been tailing you since you arrived in Zurich. They were already waiting at the airport before you landed. Whoever they are, I'd lay my last cent that they're the professionals who killed Caruso and his wife. Except now there's one fewer of the bastards to worry about.'

McCaul picked up the two cell phones and tossed one of them across. 'One's a regular cell phone, but the other one's something else entirely. Take a look.'

Jennifer examined the device. It resembled a cell phone, with a keypad and a miniature screen, and had a stubby, rubber-encased aerial that protruded from the top. 'What is it?'

'A radio-frequency tracking monitor. They used it to locate us. All they had to do was follow the signal and it led them straight to us, every time. I've used the same kind of thing on a couple of cases I worked.'

Jennifer handed the monitor back to McCaul. He switched it on. The miniature screen lit up and he punched some buttons on the keypad. 'It's telling me the target signal's out of range, which probably means the bug's still on the car and not planted on either of us. They can't track us any more, so we can relax, at least for tonight.'

'Could they do that? Plant a bug on your body?'

'Sure, it's no big deal. They could stitch one into the lining of your clothes, or hide a miniature transmitter in your bag, and you'd never know the difference. It could be made to look like a pen, or a make-up compact, or even a credit card. You'd better check your bag and your clothes, just in case. I've already checked mine.'

Jennifer examined her clothes, feeling the material of her sweater, jeans and jacket, then McCaul helped her search her tote bag and examine her belongings. 'It's OK, you're clean,' he declared.

'How did they know we boarded the train?'

'At a guess, simple deduction. They probably found the jeep, realised that we'd fled town, and the train station was as good a bet as any.' McCaul switched on the cell phone and punched some buttons. 'Just our luck. The keypad's locked out. It needs a password.'

'Can you unscramble it?'

'Not a hope. It's a pity because it might have told us who the hell those two guys were in touch with, and who's pulling their strings.'

'Is there any way to crack the password?'

'Sure, if you've got the know-how and the right equipment. I know an ex-con in the Bronx who'd do it for fifty bucks, but we're a long way from New York.' McCaul swallowed his Scotch, replaced the contents of the wallet and slipped it into his pocket, along with the cell phone and monitor. 'I'd better let you get some rest. You'll be fine here on your own, but don't leave your room for any reason, unless you need me. Remember, I'm only three doors away. I'll call you at seven, OK? After breakfast we'll see about buying ourselves some fresh clothes and hiring another car.'

McCaul made to leave, but Jennifer didn't want him to go. She trembled as she remembered the terror she had felt on the train when she ran to her compartment and thought McCaul had been killed, and suddenly she was frightened again. There was a frantic need in her for company, and it had nothing to do with sex. It was a need for someone to hold her, to reassure her, to let her know she wasn't alone, and that she was safe. 'Please don't go.'

McCaul seemed to sense her fear, stopped and turned. 'What's wrong, Jennifer?'

'I don't understand why all this is happening to me. I don't understand how I've become a person who could kill a man. Do you see? I don't want to be alone right now.'

McCaul came over and gently touched her face. 'I understand. But I don't know the answers, Jennifer. I think we've just got to try to work out what it is you might know or have that someone wants. I'd like you to keep thinking about the past, about what it might be that they're after. If we can work out what the men want, we'll be ahead of the game.'

Jennifer held on to McCaul's hand, as if desperately seeking reassurance, or just a simple connection to someone. 'You really think so?'

'For sure.' McCaul nodded, slowly let his hand fall away. 'You'll be fine. I'm convinced they're not going to find us tonight. So just try and get some sleep. We'll try and see what we can turn up on the name Vogel in the morning, even if it means scouring every street in Brig.'

Five minutes later, Jennifer stood by her window, staring out at the lights of the town. She was exhausted, her body drained of energy, but her mind was so troubled she found it impossible to sleep. She still felt frightened and confused, but as she stood there an idea came to her.

McCaul had warned her not to leave her room, but what she intended to do wouldn't take long. She took her key card from the night stand and quietly let herself out.

48

'What's the plan, Kelso? Do we have one?'

'Try and grab a few hours' rest. Then we'll check every hotel in town if we have to.' Kelso had halted on Brig's market square and jerked on the handbrake. The town was in darkness, the streets deserted.

'Why can't we do it right now?'

'Use your head, Ryan. It's one thirty a.m. If we start prowling around town questioning hotel clerks this late at night, and one of them gets suspicious and calls the police, that's trouble we can do without. We'll find somewhere to bed down for a few hours. My guess is that McCaul and Jennifer can't be doing much else at this hour, that's if they're not in any immediate danger.'

'And how are we supposed to find them? They could be anywhere. Some cheap dive of a pension or a bed and breakfast out in the sticks, or maybe even a public park.'

'We'll discuss that later.' Kelso flashed his headlights as a Volkswagen pulled up in front. Grimes stepped out and walked back. 'Sir?'

'I want you to try and find us a hotel where we can all put our heads down for a couple of hours, then I'll tell you what we're going to do.'

The hotel was in an alleyway near Brig's railway station. The Altdorf wasn't up to much, a touch shabby and right next door to a beer hall. A couple of scrawny cats wandered around the alley, and when they pulled up outside, Kelso surveyed the hotel with disgust. 'Christ, is this the best you could find, Grimes?'

'We're lucky to get it. There's a bankers' conference in town and the two others I tried were full. It's either here or we bed down in the cars.'

The sight of four Americans with only overnight bags didn't seem to unsettle the night porter, a barrel-chested Swiss who looked used to questionable guests calling at odd hours of the morning. He had them fill in the guest registration cards before marching them upstairs to four single rooms on the second floor. 'Breakfast is from six thirty until nine, *meinen Herren. Ich wunsche ihnen guten Nacht.*'

'Wait a minute, I'd like a word.' Kelso collared the man as he marched back downstairs, spoke to him for a few moments on the landing, then handed him a generous tip and came back. 'Leave your bags in your rooms and meet me in mine in two minutes. You too, Ryan. Then I'll tell you how we're going to find Jennifer.'

Mark unlocked his door. The quilt cover and the curtains on his single bed were a hideous floral design and looked as if they should have been replaced years ago, but at least the room had a telephone. He knew he ought to call Lou Garuda and check up on Bobby, and he estimated the time difference was six hours, which meant it was a little after 7.30 p.m. in New York. Knowing Garuda, he'd stop off in a bar on the way home, so he decided to make the call straight after Kelso's meeting. He left his overnight bag on the bed, slipped out into the hallway and knocked on Kelso's door. Grimes and Fellows were already seated at either end of the single bed. Kelso beckoned him inside the cramped room.

'I figure they'll need transport,' Kelso began. 'So they'll probably try and hire a car or take a train or a bus first thing in the morning. There's only four of us, so we'll have to cover what we can. According to the night porter there's just one major car-hire office in town, and it's a Hertz, so we'll stake it out before it opens. Ryan, that'll be your job. Fellows will watch the bus depot, and I'll take the train station. While we're doing that, Grimes will phone around the hotels and try to find out if Jennifer or McCaul have checked in anywhere. The porter says the town has about a dozen hotels, big and small, along with a few dozen more on the outskirts, and he'll give us the list.'

'Fine, but that doesn't answer my question. What if they've picked a pension or a bed and breakfast?'

'We may still be able to locate them. But we'll start with the hotels first and work our way down the list to the smaller establishments. As soon as we're done here I'll call Langley and have them hack into the databases of every major hotel chain and car-hire firm within fifty miles of here and check their booking records. I'll also have their names flagged for credit card transactions. If they use any charge cards in their names, we'll know about it, even if it's in some crummy pension. With a little luck, we may even have news of their whereabouts before morning.'

'You're sure you can do all that?'

'I told you, Ryan, I've got the entire assets of the CIA at our disposal. Any questions? Good. I suggest we all get some sleep. I've told the porter to call us at six a.m. That gives us only four hours in the sack.'

Mark got undressed. His head still ached and he hadn't slept in the hospital the previous evening. He looked at himself in the bathroom mirror. With the sticking plaster on his forehead and his singed hair, he looked a mess. He filled the washbasin and scrubbed himself, then went to sit on the bed and dialled Garuda's home number. His answering machine kicked in after a couple of rings, and he left his hotel and room numbers, along with a message to call him back urgently.

He was exhausted as he went to peer out the curtains at the lights of Brig. If Kelso was right, Jennifer was out there somewhere with McCaul. They had looked pretty close as they strolled to the restaurant in Turin, and he wondered just how close they'd got. He felt another pang of jealousy and knew he was torturing himself. He wanted to go out into the streets right now and start checking the hotels, but Kelso was right; walking into a lobby at 2 a.m. and making enquiries could invite suspicion.

With that thought, he lay down on the bed, closed his eyes and tossed restlessly as he tried to sleep.

49

New York

Lou Garuda entered the lobby of the Trump Hotel and headed straight for the cocktail bar. *Jesus, it's a fucking skirt fest.*

The Trump was a great place to pick up chicks, and the bar was packed with some ace-looking women, but Garuda had to remind himself that he was there on business. He found an empty table, ordered a dry martini and saw Madeline Fulton enter the bar like a whirlwind.

Madeline was in her middle fifties, but dressed younger: a low-cut top and a black slit skirt under her open Armani coat. She wrote a tough-talking business column for the New York *Post*, went to every business bash in town, and knew every corporate player the Big Apple had to offer. Garuda had banged her on and off for a couple of years in his younger days.

Madeline got a few looks from the hawks at the bar as she sashayed over and sat herself down at Garuda's table with a flourish. 'This better be fucking important, Lou. I've got a cab and a photographer waiting outside and the meter's running.'

Garuda was all charm as he took her hand and kissed it. 'Good to see you, Madeline. What'll you have?'

'Skip it, I'm late for a Fortune Five Hundred function. Tell me why I'm here.'

That was Madeline, thought Garuda: feisty, and always in a fucking hurry, skipping from one glitzy business reception to the next. He'd phoned her that afternoon and asked whether she could spare him five minutes some time, someplace, that evening. They settled on the Trump at seven. 'Prime International Securities. Ever heard of it?'

'Should I?'

'They folded about a year ago. Used to have their offices on Fifth. A very low-key outfit.'

Madeline lit a slim menthol cigarette with a gold lighter, ignoring the fact that this particular area of the cocktail lounge was non-smoking. But no one in their right mind would argue with Madeline Fulton, not unless they had balls made of titanium. She blew out a puff of smoke, tapped her ash on to the carpet, and furrowed her brow. 'Sure, I seem to remember the firm. What about it?'

'It was owned offshore by a Cayman shell company.'

Madeline looked at Garuda and blinked. 'Like I should *give* a fuck?' She stubbed out her cigarette in the nut bowl on the table. 'The meter's running, Lou, and I've really got to go. I thought you said this was fucking important.'

'It is important. Real important, Madeline. I need to find out who was behind Prime. You've got corporate friends in high places. I'm pretty sure some of those contacts may have ways of finding out where the offshore trail leads.'

'Unless you've moved into corporate crime, you mind telling me why you want to know?'

'I worked a case a couple of years back. Bust my balls but it went nowhere. Let's just say that it's fresh again and I'm fishing for information about Prime, hoping to get a lead. And I need the information like yesterday.'

'You still screwing that Angelina chick?'

'Regular as clockwork.'

Madeline gave him a lecherous look and flicked a razor-sharp nail along Garuda's inside leg until she reached his crotch. 'How about you put a piece by for me for old times' sake?'

Garuda patted her hand. 'You do this for me, Maddy, and who knows?'

Madeline grinned, withdrew her hand and stood. 'I'll make a few calls. Talk to some corporate honchos I know. And there's a business reporter in the Caymans that the newspaper uses who's pretty good at turning over stones. How about I call you if I've come up with anything?'

'Do your best for me, baby.'

50

Brig, Switzerland

The telephone buzzed in Mark's bedroom. He came awake and fumbled for the receiver. It was Garuda. 'The hell's going on, Mark? I got your message. What the frig are you doing in Switzerland?'

Mark tried to marshal his thoughts as he reached for his watch on the night stand: 5.30 a.m. He was barely awake. 'It's too long a story to go into right now, Lou, so just listen up. I wanted to ask after Bobby, and I've also got something I need you to do for me. You know Danny Flynn in the NYPD Organised Crime Division?'

'Sure, I know Danny. Why?'

When Mark explained what he wanted Garuda to do there was a noticeable silence at the other end of the phone. '*Jesus*, first it's the CIA, now you're talking about the Red Mafia. What the frig's going on here, Mark? And what are you doing in fucking Switzerland? You're sniffing around the March case, aren't you? I bet that's it.'

'Lou, please, let's skip the explanations for now and I'll owe you one, OK?'

Mark had one last request, this time a personal one. 'There's something else I need you to do.' He explained and heard another brief silence down the line.

'Has this got anything to do with that CIA gorilla, Kelso, you had me check up on?'

'Lou, please, I can't go into it right now. I've got my reasons.'

'This thing gets more weird by the fucking minute . . .'

'I'd be on the line for hours if I even tried to explain.'

'Yeah, but maybe it's about time you did. I need some answers, man.'

'Lou, I can't, not just yet.'

'Then when?'

'I'll let you know.'

'You know what I was thinking? It's time I got out from behind a fucking desk and went back to being a detective. And maybe this is my big chance. Maybe we can work on this together, solve this case once and for all. What do you say?'

'I'll think about it.'

'Is that a fucking yes or a no?'

'It's a maybe. I said I'd think about it, Lou.'

Garuda sighed. 'How do I get in touch? You want I should call the same number?'

Mark thought again about giving Garuda the number of the cell phone Kelso had given him, but scotched the idea. 'No, I may be on the move, so that's a problem. How about I call you? You can give me your cell phone number.'

'Yeah, well, you got yourself another problem, old buddy. I called over to the Cauldwell to see Bobby just like you asked, and you're not going to like this . . .'

Jennifer woke at seven. She had slept soundly, exhausted by the events of the previous evening, but pleased with her discovery. Before she had turned in she'd gone down to the reception desk and asked to borrow a local phone directory.

The clerk had handed her one for the Canton of Valais, of which Brig was a part, and back in her room she had searched the directory. At least a dozen people named Vogel were listed for the Brig area, but her heart sank when none of them had the initial H. Then a thought occurred to her and she made a single phone call that lasted almost five minutes before she climbed into bed and fell into a deep sleep.

She showered and dressed, then went along the corridor and knocked on McCaul's door. He opened it dressed in a hotel bathrobe, his hair still wet from the shower. 'Sleep OK?'

'As soon as my head hit the pillow. But I did some checking last night on the name Vogel. I think I may have turned up something.'

McCaul frowned and stopped towelling his hair. 'Tell me more.'

Jennifer was excited. 'Get dressed and we'll go down to breakfast and I'll tell you what I found.'

51

New York

Garuda was having sex with Angelina later that morning when his cell phone vibrated with a text message. He rolled off her, reached for the phone and flicked it on.

'Jesus, Lou, can't you leave that fucking thing switched off?'

'Sorry, baby. I'm expecting an important call.'

'What's more important than screwing me, for Christ's sake? I was just about to come, Lou!'

Garuda read the message. *Meet 9 a.m. Marriott, Broadway. Important. Maddy.*

'Who's it from?'

'It's work, Angelina. Real important work and it can't wait.' Garuda consulted his watch. If he hurried, he could grab a cab and meet Madeline by nine. He climbed out of bed, threw on his shirt and slapped Angelina's bare buttocks. 'Keep it warm for me, baby. I'll be back in an hour.'

'Screw you.'

Garuda walked into the Marriott Hotel on Broadway. Madeline was already there, sitting in a booth in the breakfast dock, drinking coffee and wearing dark glasses as she nursed a hangover. 'I've got five minutes, Lou, then I've got to head to fucking La Guardia, but the word is that the way Prime had the Cayman's shell configured, it's unlikely you'll ever really get to the bottom of who owns it.'

'*Shit.*'

'However, sweetie, my reporter friend down in Grand Cayman kicked over some stones. Turns out that one of the nominal shell directors was a banker who has a reputation as someone who isn't averse to doing business with major-league criminals. The word is, you put your ear too close to the ground to try to find out who was behind Prime and you're liable to get run over.'

'How come?'

'Do I have to spell it out, Lou? It may be dirty money behind it. That's the intimation I was given. What is it you're after?'

'Like I told you, I'll explain some other time. How dirty?'

'Big-time filthy, from eastern Europe, so don't go there unless you got a US state agency behind you, and even then I'd wish you lots of luck.'

Garuda whistled, then grinned. 'It all kind of figures.'

'What does?'

'Nothing.' He blew her a kiss as she grabbed her bag and got to her feet.

'I've got to go, Lou, got a flight to catch. That's all I've got.'

'I owe you one, baby.'

'And just don't you forget it.'

Brig

The hotel restaurant was crowded. A waiter led them to a corner table. Jennifer was ravenous. They helped themselves to a breakfast of fresh *Brötchen* rolls, cheese, ham and steaming coffee.

'I called the telephone operator and told her I was a visiting American tourist looking for a Swiss relative living near Brig who I couldn't find in the phone directory. She found two unlisted people named Vogel with the initial H.' Jennifer consulted her notebook. 'There's one who lives in a place called Murnau, a village about five kilometres from here. And there's another near the same town.'

'Did she give you their addresses and phone numbers?'

'No, she couldn't. She said that was against the law if they're unlisted. But she suggested we try the town hall in Murnau.'

'Why?'

'They have the addresses and telephone numbers of everyone in the locality on their register.'

McCaul finished his coffee eagerly. 'Let's go hire a car and find Murnau.'

Mark went down to the lobby at 6.15. Grimes and Fellows were already there, settling the hotel bill. When Kelso came down the stairs he looked haggard. 'What's the matter, have a bad night?'

Kelso sounded brittle. 'I spent most of it on the phone. My people are still checking the hotel databases.'

'And?'

'Zilch, but they'll call me the moment anything turns up. Grimes is going to trawl the hotels, so you'd better head over to stake out the Hertz office. Everyone stay on their toes.'

Fellows finished settling the bill and beckoned Kelso aside for a private word. As they spoke, Mark saw Fellows shoot him an accusing glance. When Kelso came back, he gripped Mark's arm. 'Fellows tells me you made a call to New York last night that's itemised on your bill. Would you care to explain, Ryan?'

'I phoned a police colleague. Why, what's the big problem?'

Kelso looked enraged. 'What did you call this colleague to discuss?'

'That's none of your business.'

'It is if you discussed anything to do with this case. Did you, Ryan?'

Kelso gave him a menacing stare that sent a chill through Mark. But he figured that if his call had been monitored Kelso would have known about it before Fellows spoke to him, so he decided to lie: the last thing he wanted was to get Lou in any kind of trouble. 'Why would I do that? The call had to do with a case I'm working on. I had some checking up to do.'

'You're sure about that?'

'The guy I called is with the NYPD. You can check the number if you don't believe me. What more do you want? Now let go.'

Mark wasn't sure whether he'd convinced Kelso but the CIA man suddenly released his grip. 'My apologies, Ryan, but try to understand. This business of losing Jennifer has got me on edge, and one loose word and a four-year investigation could go down the can.' He turned to his men. 'Let's get moving. As agreed, I'll take the railway station and Fellows, you cover the bus depot. If anyone spots them, get in touch right away.'

52

With Swiss precision, most of the stores in Brig opened their doors promptly at 7.30. By 8 a.m., Jennifer had managed to purchase a couple of sweaters, jeans, fresh underwear, and a Tauber waxed hunting jacket. McCaul bought two pairs of jeans, some T-shirts, a new carry bag, and a jacket in a green Loden material. They changed into their new clothes back at the hotel and then checked out. 'We need to hire a car,' Jennifer told the desk clerk as they settled the bill.

'Of course,' the woman answered politely. 'There's a car-hire firm I can recommend. Let me give you directions to their office.'

Fifteen minutes later the young man behind the desk in the car rental office completed their details and handed Jennifer the keys to a dark blue Volkswagen Golf. 'I think everything is in order. *Ja?*'

'We need to visit the town hall in Murnau. How do we get there?'

He offered them a map and marked the route in blue pen. 'It's quite easy, really. Take the main road out of town and you'll see Murnau signposted after about a kilometre. You shouldn't have any trouble finding the town hall. In German it's called the *Rathaus.*'

Mark watched the Hertz office from across the street. He wore his raincoat and the feathered Alpine hat that he'd bought at the airport. He still felt absurd wearing the hat but he had to disguise himself in case Jennifer spotted him on the street.

He also felt uneasy. Kelso's reaction to the phone call had been extreme, and Mark couldn't understand the man's paranoia. And something else troubled him: Lou's information about

Bobby. But he was five thousand miles away, and what the hell could he do about the problem?

He observed a couple walk into the Hertz office. They were middle aged and neither of them resembled Jennifer or McCaul: the man was short and thin, and the woman overweight. They were only the second customers he'd spotted in the last half-hour. How much longer would he have to wait?

What if Jennifer didn't show up? What if she weren't even in Brig, for Christ sakes? He was sure that trying to find Jennifer and McCaul in a large town with only four men was pretty hopeless. Jennifer had a right to know that she was in danger. He felt the whole charade had to end soon, and he made up his mind there and then that if he spotted her he'd confront her and tell her what was going on, and to hell with Kelso.

His cell phone buzzed. It was Kelso, his voice urgent. 'Ryan?'

'Nada. They haven't shown up.'

'Forget it, we found them! Stay right where you are, I'll pick you up in two minutes.'

The Opel screeched to a halt at the kerb. Kelso was agitated. 'Get in.'

Mark jumped into the passenger seat. 'Where are they?'

Kelso gunned the engine and did a U-turn on Brig's main street. Half a dozen irate Swiss drivers honked their horns in fury, but Kelso ignored the protest. 'The database trawl turned up two guests in their names who checked into a hotel last night at one fifteen a.m.'

'*Where?*'

'Right here in Brig. A hotel called the Ambassador.'

53

Grimes was pacing the sidewalk and he ran to join them as they pulled up in front of the Ambassador. 'The hotel desk clerk said that right after they checked out half an hour ago, they went to hire a car.'

'They couldn't have,' Kelso told him. 'Ryan had the Hertz office covered.'

'It wasn't Hertz. It was a small local operator the hotel likes to recommend.'

'*Shit.*'

'The office is only a short walk away. Fellows called round and the guy there said they left in a dark blue Volkswagen Golf less than fifteen minutes ago. Fellows got the licence number. They asked for directions to the town hall in a place called Murnau, about three kilometres from here.'

'You're sure of that?' Mark asked.

'That's what Fellows said. He had the guy show him Murnau on a map.'

'Did they say *why* they wanted to visit the town hall?'

'No, and the clerk didn't ask.'

'Where's Fellows now?'

'On his way back.'

Kelso said in a panic, 'Get in your car, we'll pick him up on the way.'

Jennifer took the main road out of Brig. A signpost pointed to Murnau and they followed a tortuous road through stunning countryside, complete with grazing cows and snowcapped mountains.

Ten minutes later they reached Murnau, a pretty village with dozens of small inns and ski lodges. The town hall was a centuries-old limestone building with a modernised annexe built of steel and glass. They parked the car and entered the building through a pair of glass doors. They found a counter manned by a middle-aged Swiss. He spoke little English, and fetched one of the other clerks. '*Grüss Gott*. How may I help you?' the young woman said pleasantly.

Jennifer explained what they were looking for. 'Do you have the addresses on your register?'

'*Ein moment.*' The woman went off to tap on a desk computer, scribbled down some notes, and came back. 'Herr Hubert Vogel lives in Bauer Strasse, near the old market square, which isn't far from here. He's a retired policeman. The second man, Herr Heinrich Vogel, lives at a farm property three kilometres from Murnau. His occupation is given as mountain guide and climbing instructor. Would one of these be the person you're looking for?'

'Maybe. Do you have their phone numbers?'

'*Ja.* I believe so.'

The woman went back to her computer. She wrote out the numbers, and when she came back Jennifer felt a jolt of excitement run through her when she saw that the figures 705 were the last three digits of Heinrich Vogel's phone number. 'How do we get to Heinrich Vogel's address?'

The woman consulted her notes. 'The property is not far, about a ten-minute drive. However, it's quite remote, near the northern slopes of the Wasenhorn. But if I give you directions you should find it easily enough. The farm is called the Berg Edelweiss.'

54

Heinrich Vogel scraped mud from his boots with a kitchen knife and flung the clumps in the fire. The soggy earth hissed in the flames as he went to study the TV security monitor. It was blank, nothing but an empty picture of the front of the house. He picked up the binoculars and moved to the window. A thin veil of fog covered the lower ground and swirled around the meadows where cows grazed, but he could see the majestic Alpine peaks in the near distance, the Wasenhorn dominating his view. He scanned the road but there was no sign of the car or the men. But they were out there; he felt it in his bones. He put down the binoculars and poured himself a glass of schnapps to calm his nerves.

Always.

He had always known that he was playing with fire when he got involved in the whole sorry business; had always known that it could bring him only trouble. Greed had been his downfall. But he had kept his secret for two years now, and if he had his way he intended keeping it for ever. He took a sip of schnapps and felt the liquid burn his throat, then he slapped the glass on the kitchen table and wiped his mouth with the back of his hand.

He looked towards the porch, where his two massive black Dobermans sat, watchful and waiting. There was no sign of any strangers yet, but they would come, it was only a matter of time.

Let them come.

He had the pistol in his pocket, ready for use if need be. The Dobermans suddenly whimpered and Vogel tensed. The dogs had incredibly sharp senses, could detect an intruder up to a quarter of a kilometre away, long before they were caught on camera. Had they sensed something?

'*Ferdie! Hans! Sitzen sie da!*'

The dogs obeyed, sat rock still. Vogel heard the sound of a car engine and moved to the window.

Jennifer drove from Murnau through stunning Alpine scenery, and after two kilometres they came to a narrow track that branched off from the main road.

McCaul consulted the directions they'd been given. 'Hang a left.'

Jennifer turned on to the track, her anxiety growing. A kilometre farther on they arrived at a pair of open wooden gates with a metal mail box off to one side. An inscription on the box said: *Berg Edelweiss.* A big, traditional Swiss farmhouse with a collection of outbuildings loomed in the distance, a thin shroud of early morning fog swirling around the property. Jennifer tensed and halted the Volkswagen. 'What happens now?'

'You've got a few words of German, so I'll let you do the talking.' McCaul slipped out the Beretta and examined the magazine. 'But go easy, OK? This whole thing may turn out to be a wild goose chase.'

'What if it isn't?'

McCaul tucked the pistol back in his pocket. 'We've only two rounds of ammo left, so keep your fingers crossed we're not walking into any kind of trouble.'

55

Jennifer halted the Volkswagen on the gravel driveway. She saw a barn and a double garage at the back of the farmhouse. The garage doors were open, revealing an old brown Mercedes and an ancient red tractor, the chassis dented and muddied. A pair of massive black dogs sat outside the farmhouse front door and their attention was riveted on the two visitors. They didn't move or make a sound, just stared menacingly.

McCaul said, 'The dogs are Dobermans, and savage as hell. If they make a move towards you, don't even blink. They're liable to rip your throat out.'

'Thanks for that comforting thought, Frank.' Jennifer felt a tremble in her voice.

McCaul stepped out of the car. 'Stay beside me and walk slowly.'

They took a couple of paces and the dogs growled, baring their fangs. Jennifer halted and McCaul gripped her arm. 'Just stand still a minute.' The Dobermans looked truly frightening, but they didn't budge, as if some unseen force was riveting them to the spot. McCaul started to take another step, but the dogs snarled and rose off their haunches, as if to attack.

'*Sitz, Ferdie! Sitz, Hans!*'

A man appeared in the doorway and the dogs obeyed his command instantly. He looked to be in his fifties, with a shock of greying hair, and wore a frayed work jacket, his left hand tucked inside the front pocket. Jennifer saw that a chunk of flesh was missing from the tip of his nose, which gave him an unsettling appearance. '*Sprechen Sie* Englisch?' Jennifer asked.

The man looked hostile, but she put it down to the fact that two complete strangers were trespassing on his property. His stare settled on McCaul, then shifted back to her. 'Yes, I speak English,' he said at last.

'We're looking for Heinrich Vogel.'

The dogs growled and the man grunted an order in German. Both animals immediately fell silent. 'I'm Heinrich Vogel. What do you want?'

'Herr Vogel, I'd feel a lot more comfortable if you called off your dogs.'

Vogel's accent was definitely German, but his English was flawless. 'You are both trespassing on my farm. What is it you want?'

'If we could talk inside, Herr Vogel, we'll try not to take up much of your time. But it's important.'

'Who are you?'

'My name is Jennifer March and this is Frank McCaul. We're both Americans.'

'If you wish to hire a mountain guide to take you up to the Wasenhorn, I suggest you look elsewhere. I'm busy right now.'

'We don't need to hire a guide. But we do need to talk.'

Vogel frowned. 'About what?'

'Please, Herr Vogel, I'd really appreciate it if we could talk inside and you'd call off your dogs.'

Vogel continued to stare, as if he was trying to estimate the risk in allowing two strangers to enter his home, then he pursed his lips and uttered a high-pitched whistle. The Dobermans bounded into the house and their master jerked his head towards the open door. 'Come, follow me.'

They moved into the kitchen. Vogel allowed them to enter the room first. As soon as they were inside the Dobermans appeared again and Jennifer felt uneasy. The dogs took up position silently in front of the door, as if blocking any retreat.

The kitchen was typically Swiss, with a big pine dresser and an open wood stove blazing in a corner. A pine table dominated the centre, and a pile of scattered newspapers and a pair of powerful binoculars lay on top. Mounted on a wall near the dresser was a video monitor that displayed a picture of the front yard. Jennifer wasn't surprised by the security; Vogel seemed the cautious type.

She noticed several framed photographs on the dresser. One was of a group of four men, all wearing mountain gear, standing on a rocky ledge as they posed for the camera. One of the climbers was Heinrich Vogel. Beside him stood a dark-haired man with a thin face, a slash for a mouth and thick black eyebrows. He wore a blue parka. Jennifer thought his face looked familiar.

Vogel gestured for them to join him at the table. 'What is this about?' he demanded.

Jennifer began by explaining about the Wasenhorn corpse. 'Perhaps you heard about it, Herr Vogel? The Carabinieri believe that the dead man had lain in the glacier for two years.'

Vogel glanced towards the video monitor before he shifted his gaze back to his visitors. '*Ja,* I heard talk about it in the village. But what has this got to do with me?'

'The police found something on the body that might interest you,' McCaul suggested. 'You mind if we show it to you, Herr Vogel?'

'Why should I?'

Jennifer removed the note from her bag. Vogel's left hand remained stubbornly in his jacket pocket. He took the offered notepaper with his right, carefully studied it and frowned.

'You can see that the name H. Vogel is clearly written,' Jennifer explained. 'Underneath are the words Berg Edelweiss, along with three numbers. The same numbers as the last three digits of your telephone number.'

Vogel was suddenly more wary. 'So it appears.'

'We thought you might be able to help explain why the dead man had this note in his possession, Herr Vogel.'

'I have no idea.' He studied them cautiously. 'Are you police?'

'No, I'm a private investigator,' McCaul replied.

Vogel looked confused. 'And why should you be interested in this matter?'

'We can get to that later. Is there no reason you can think of why the victim had your name and address?'

Vogel glanced at the video monitor again, then towards the window, and anxiously licked his lips. 'I am a climbing instructor and mountain guide, and often take people up to the Wasenhorn. Perhaps this man once used me as a guide. What was his name?'

'The police didn't identify the body,' McCaul answered. 'And they probably never will. The morgue in Turin where it was being kept was destroyed yesterday by an explosion.'

Vogel shifted slightly in his chair. '*Ja*, I read about the explosion this morning.' He pointed to the front page of a Swiss newspaper lying on the table and said, 'See. Five dead, it says. The newspaper suggests it may be the work of terrorists.'

Jennifer recognised a photograph of the smouldering ruins of the Turin headquarters, with a brief report in German underneath. 'What else does the newspaper say?'

'Very little. Just that the police are still investigating the matter. But this is most strange. I really don't understand why this man should have my name and address.'

Jennifer had the feeling that Vogel was playing them for fools. 'Do you run a legitimate business here, Herr Vogel?'

'*Legitimate?* What do you mean?'

'Your guide business. Is it legal and registered?'

'Yes, of course. Swiss law is very strict about such things.'

'Then I imagine that the law requires you to keep a record of the people who hire you as a guide?'

'Well . . . yes . . .'

'Which means you keep their names?'

'Well, of course . . .'

'Perhaps you could take a look at your engagements for around April fifteenth, two years ago.'

'Why?'

'The police think that the victim died around that date.'

'Are you suggesting that *I* guided him up to the mountain?'

'No, I'm not. But if there's a chance the victim once hired your services, as you suggest, then your records may help prove his identity.'

Vogel didn't reply, and McCaul said, 'Herr Vogel, the police no doubt will want to ask you the same questions. What harm can it do if you help us?'

Vogel remained silent. He was on edge, and seemed to have difficulty making up his mind. Reluctantly, he got to his feet, and removed his hand from his pocket. Jennifer saw that the tips of three of his fingers were missing.

'Frostbite,' Vogel explained, noticing her stare. 'Surgery helped, of course, but it came too late to save all my fingers.'

'I'm sorry.'

'*Nein*, it is me who should apologise, for being so cautious when you arrived. But you see I live alone, and one has to be careful these days. Now, if you will excuse me, I will see if I can find my records.'

Vogel suddenly seemed to be making an effort to be more pleasant. He left the room, his footsteps fading down the hall as the Dobermans continued to stare at their visitors.

McCaul took the Beretta from his pocket and flicked off the safety catch. 'When he comes back, let me do the talking.'

Jennifer stared at the gun. 'What's the idea?'

McCaul grabbed the binoculars from the table. 'Look at these. It's as if Vogel's expecting someone at any second. There's something weird about all this, Jennifer. You saw the way he kept watching the security monitor. The guy's on edge. And I've got a gut instinct he knows a lot more than he's telling. Maybe it's time to play hardball.'

'How?'

'If need be, try a little gentle persuasion. I don't intend to harm the guy, but those dogs look like they'd tear me to pieces if I said the wrong word to Vogel, so I'd like to be prepared.' He replaced the gun in his pocket.

Jennifer stood up and the Dobermans stared at her, but made no attempt to move.

'What the hell are you doing?' McCaul asked.

She put a finger to her mouth for him to be silent and crossed the room, the dogs watching her movement. She stopped by the photograph of the group of men.

'You mind telling me what's the matter?'

Jennifer pointed at the photograph. The dark-haired man with a thin face and thick eyebrows still drew her attention. 'Take a look.'

McCaul joined her. 'What is it?'

'There's something familiar about him. Look at his eyes, Frank. And his mouth. I know I've seen . . . *Oh my God.*'

'What's the matter?'

'The man in the ice. It's *him*. Can't you see it?'

McCaul studied the photograph. They heard the dogs snarl. When they turned Vogel was standing in the doorway, a pistol clutched in his hand. McCaul made to reach for the Beretta but the dogs bristled, ready to attack.

'Take your hand out of your pocket,' Vogel ordered McCaul, and waved his pistol at Jennifer. 'Reach over very slowly and remove his weapon.'

Jennifer obeyed, her hand shaking as she prised the Beretta from McCaul's pocket.

'Place the gun on the table.'

She laid the Beretta down and Vogel reached across and slipped it into his pocket.

'Why . . .' Jennifer whispered. 'Why are you threatening us?'

'I think you know why.' Vogel waved the pistol, indicating the chairs. 'Sit, and keep your hands on the table. Attempt to move and I will kill you both.'

56

Kelso was sweating as he jammed on the brakes in front of Murnau's town hall. The centuries-old building had a modern annexe of steel and glass, and Mark saw streets of pretty Alpine houses and stores, busy with pedestrians. Kelso gestured for Fellows and Grimes to remain in their car then jabbed a finger at Mark. 'You come with me.'

He charged in through the doors of the town hall and Mark followed.

Silence engulfed the kitchen. Perspiration beaded Vogel's brow and every now and then he glanced towards the video monitor.

Jennifer broke the silence. 'Herr Vogel, why are you threatening us? We didn't come here to harm you, only to look for information.'

'Don't lie. You had a gun.'

'The gun was for our own protection. If you'd only listen we can explain—'

'*Still!* Be quiet. No more questions.'

Jennifer rose from her chair. The dogs snarled and bared their fangs, but she disregarded the danger. She was determined to find out what Vogel knew about her father's disappearance. 'No, I want you to listen to what I have to say.'

McCaul tugged at her arm. 'For Christ's sake, Jennifer, don't push it or there's no telling how this might end.'

She ignored McCaul's appeal as she pointed at the photograph on the dresser. 'One of those men in the photograph is the Wasenhorn victim, isn't he, Herr Vogel? And you know his identity. But he wasn't alone on the glacier when he died. My father may have been with him. Or maybe you know that, too?'

'Your father? What are you talking about?'

'My father went missing two years ago. The police found his passport near the body and that's the only reason why we're here. I have his photograph in my bag. If I could show you . . .'

Vogel's eyes flickered with suspicion. 'No, hand the bag here. Do it slowly.'

Jennifer laid her tote bag on the table and Vogel rummaged with his free hand until he found the photograph.

'My father's name is Paul March. Have you ever seen him before, Herr Vogel?'

Vogel turned ashen as he studied the snapshot. He didn't lower the gun, but suddenly his expression changed from suspicion to curiosity as he looked back at Jennifer. 'Tell me *exactly* why you came here.'

Kelso and Mark approached a counter manned by a young female clerk. She was busy dealing with an elderly Swiss, but Kelso pushed past him and spoke directly to the woman. 'Do you speak English, Fraulein?'

'Yes, but you must wait your turn.'

'I'm afraid this is an emergency. Have you ever seen this young woman?'

Kelso slapped a photograph of Jennifer on the counter.

The clerk studied it. '*Ja*. I spoke with her this morning. She called in here looking for information. Why?'

Kelso adopted a grave look as he slipped the photograph back in his pocket. 'I'm her father, and I'm afraid there's been a terrible automobile accident. A family member has been seriously injured and I need to find my daughter *urgently*.'

'I . . . I'm sorry. She was here half an hour ago, with a man, looking for the addresses of two locals. I searched the town register to give her the information.'

'*Which* two locals exactly?' Mark asked.

'To tell the truth, she seemed only interested in one of the men, Heinrich Vogel. So I gave her directions to his property.'

Kelso almost sighed with relief. 'How do we get to this guy Vogel's address?'

When Jennifer finished talking, the only sound in the kitchen was the ticking of the clock. Vogel's face was white and his hands trembled.

'You know the man who died on the Wasenhorn, don't you?' Jennifer said.

'*Ja*, I know.'

'Who was he?'

'My brother, Peter,' Vogel admitted hoarsely. He looked badly shaken, as if he was having difficulty holding himself together.

'What was he doing up on the mountain?'

'You don't know, do you? You really don't know anything.'

'Know what? Did you kill him? Is that why you're afraid, Herr Vogel?'

'Kill him?' Vogel spluttered. 'Why would I have done that?'

'What happened to your brother on the glacier?'

'The night before he died, Peter drove here with two men he had picked up from Brig railway station. One of them was a fellow named Karl Lazar, and the other was this one . . .' Vogel tapped the photograph. 'The man you say was your father. I'd never met him before, but I knew Karl Lazar. For many years he visited Murnau to ski, and that's how he became acquainted with my brother and me.'

'Why did they come here?'

'Lazar asked me and my brother to guide them. . . . no, *told* us to guide them across the glacier into Italy. It was obvious they were very anxious. Especially your father. He looked the most worried of the two. But it was only later that I learned they were trying to flee from their Russian mafia friends.'

Jennifer was stunned. 'I don't understand.'

'I thought you had come here to kill me. I thought you were

one of them. That's why I was so cautious. But the photograph, it explains why you're *really* here. I've been a fool.'

'One of *whom*? What does the photograph explain?' Jennifer hadn't the faintest idea what Vogel was jabbering about, and she shot a look at McCaul, who looked equally bewildered.

'Herr Vogel, you need to tell us exactly who Karl Lazar was and what my father was doing with him.'

'I told you, they were trying to escape over the border. Lazar worked for the Russian mafia.'

'But *why* was my father with him?'

Vogel was suddenly alarmed. He got to his feet and studied the security monitor. 'There isn't time to explain. They will be here soon, I'm certain of it. I understand now why they were watching the house. *You* were the reason. And when they come, they will kill us all. You have to leave right now.'

'What are you talking about? *Who* will come? Who will kill us?'

Clutching the pistol, Vogel moved to the window. In an instant McCaul jumped to his feet and upturned the table. It lifted off the floor with a crash, knocked Vogel flying and sent Jennifer reeling back, but McCaul didn't stop there. Pushing the table before him, he charged like a bull towards the dogs as they moved to attack, and it slammed into both animals and sent them tumbling out of the door. He rammed it up against the door frame and turned back.

Vogel was still holding the gun as he desperately tried to raise himself off the floor, but McCaul lunged and wrenched the weapon from his hand. He fired two shots into the ceiling, but the deafening noise didn't silence the Dobermans; they clawed at the wood, snarling viciously as they tried to leap over the table. 'Call them off!' McCaul shouted. 'Call them off or so help me I'll shoot them!'

'*Sitz, Ferdie! Sitz, Hans!*' Vogel ordered.

The dogs growled defiantly, then sat still.

'Tell them to move outside. Tell them!'

'*Draussen! Draussen sofort!*'

The dogs scampered into the hallway. McCaul managed to slam the door shut, wedging the table hard against the frame again, but as he did so Vogel fumbled in his pocket for the Beretta.

'Frank!' Jennifer screamed as a single shot exploded, slamming into McCaul's arm, punching him back. Jennifer flung herself at Vogel and tried to prise the pistol from his grasp. Eventually McCaul managed to stagger over and wrench the gun from his hand.

'Please . . . please . . . don't shoot me,' Vogel begged. 'I didn't mean to harm you.'

'You've got a funny way of showing it, buddy.'

'I meant only to protect myself. I swear it . . .'

McCaul clapped a hand on his arm. 'See if you can find something to stop the bleeding.'

Jennifer found a kitchen towel and tied it tightly around McCaul's arm until the bleeding subsided. 'Are you OK? Let me see.' She examined the wound and found two holes where the bullet had drilled through his jacket and passed through his upper arm.

McCaul said to Vogel, 'I think we need to have another talk, buddy.'

They heard the sound of a car and Vogel became alarmed. 'You . . . you're too late. They are already here. I told you they would come.'

Jennifer moved to the window and saw a powerful black BMW speed in through the gates and roar up the driveway. Her heart pounded as the vehicle came closer and she saw the outlines of the passengers. 'He's right, Frank. Somebody's coming.'

'Who?'

'Two men.'

57

Jennifer watched as the BMW halted on the gravel in front of the house. McCaul joined her at the window, dragging Vogel after him, just in time to see the car doors swing open and two men climb out.

One was the blond from the train. He had a sticking plaster across his forehead and he spoke into a cell phone. This time his accomplice was a fit-looking man in his thirties who was carrying a machine pistol. McCaul said to Vogel, 'Who are those guys?'

'I . . . I don't know.'

'You don't *know*?' McCaul exploded.

'They could be the same men who have been watching the house for three days now, ever since reports of the body were in the newspapers. Sometimes they follow me in different cars when I travel to and from the village, and they always keep their distance. But they must be fools if they think I don't see them.'

'Who do you *think* they are?'

'Russian mafia. The same people Lazar worked for.'

'Why were they watching the house?'

Vogel fell silent, and McCaul said angrily, 'You've got a lot more explaining to do, buddy.'

Jennifer saw the blond man finish talking on his cell phone. He took out a pistol, nodded to his companion, and they started to move forward. 'Frank, they're coming closer.'

McCaul stepped away from the window. 'Listen to me, Vogel. One of those guys tried to kill us twice already. Now he's here to finish the job. You need to tell us what the hell's going on here.'

Sweat beaded Vogel's face, but he remained obstinately silent.

'What are they after?' Jennifer persisted. 'What did my father have to do with the Russian mafia?'

Before Vogel could answer, McCaul said urgently, 'Leave it, Jennifer, there isn't time. You'd better have a back way out of here.'

'That . . . that way.' Vogel pointed nervously to a door at the rear of the kitchen.

'Where does it lead?'

'Down to the basement and out the back, to the barn and garage.'

McCaul opened the door. A short hallway lay beyond, smothered in darkness. He flicked a light switch and a bulb flashed on below, revealing steps leading down to a basement room which was obviously used as a fuel store. Thick wooden logs were piled high against the walls. 'Is the Mercedes in the garage working?'

'Yes.'

'Where are the keys?'

'Where I always leave them, in the ignition.'

'What about a back road out of here?' Jennifer asked.

'There's only a rough forest track. It runs behind the barn and leads on to the main road after half a kilometre.'

McCaul was sweating. 'We'll have to take our chances. You're coming with us.'

Vogel was suddenly fearful. 'Please . . . don't harm me.'

McCaul hissed, 'That's pretty rich, considering you just put a bullet in me. But I'll tell you this for nothing. You'll stand a better chance of remaining alive if you stick with us.'

'My . . . my dogs. I need to call them—'

McCaul cocked the Beretta and gestured towards the basement steps.

'There's no time. Get moving.'

The two men halted at the farmhouse door. The blond snapped his fingers and his accomplice immediately took up a position by the door. As he reached for the handle, a whimpering sound emerged from inside the hall. For guidance, he flicked a look at the blond who cocked his pistol and nodded for him to proceed.

He turned the handle.

McCaul locked the basement door behind them, and as they hurried down the stairs Jennifer said to Vogel, 'What happened the night you took my father up to the mountain?'

'I warned Lazar it would be crazy to cross the glacier at night, that they were risking death, but he wouldn't listen. He had a gun and said he'd shoot me and Peter if we didn't guide them over the border. Lazar wanted climbing gear for him and your father, and three big rucksacks. Once they had properly dressed for the journey I saw him stuff some briefcases into two of the rucksacks, and put his and your father's belongings into the third rucksack. Then we all set off before midnight, with electric torches.'

'Go on.'

'We reached the glacier two hours later, just as the weather suddenly turned ugly. It became a terrible blizzard and the snow and wind made it impossible to see more than a couple of metres in front of your face. Then I heard a scream and Peter was gone. I knew he'd fallen into a crevasse.'

'What happened to my father?'

'I lost him and Lazar in the blizzard, but I really didn't care. I just wanted to get off that mountain and back here.' Vogel held up his frostbitten hand. 'It took me four hours and cost me my fingers and half my nose, but I was lucky to be alive.'

They came to the bottom of the steps. At the far end of the basement room was a door. They heard the Dobermans barking in the upstairs hall, followed by a human scream, then four shots rang out. Vogel gave a distraught cry. 'My dogs . . . they're shooting my dogs!'

'We'll be next if we don't get out of here.' McCaul handed Jennifer the Beretta. 'Have you ever fired a handgun like this before?'

'No.'

'If anyone comes down the stairs just point it and squeeze the trigger, just as you did with the machine pistol you fired on the train, but remember you've only got one round left.' McCaul lifted the door latch. 'Keep your voices down, both of you. I'll be back as quick as I can.'

'Where are you going?'

'To take a look outside.'

The blond and his accomplice opened the front door and moved inside. They had barely taken a step when two snarling black Dobermans leaped at them out of nowhere. The man with the machine pistol screamed as one of the dogs sank his teeth into his arm, forcing him to drop his weapon.

The blond fired two rapid shots, hitting the other dog in midair and sending its body reeling, then he turned and pumped two more rounds into the Doberman mauling his accomplice's arm, killing the animal instantly. The hall was quickly awash with blood and the injured intruder clasped his wound in agony.

The blond handed him back his weapon in disgust. 'Idiot! Go round the back. You know what to do,' he ordered.

His accomplice exited the hall and ran towards the back of the house. The blond levelled his weapon and moved into the hall.

58

The sound of gunfire died and suddenly the silence in the house was overpowering. Jennifer was certain that the men were moving about upstairs but she couldn't hear anything. She clutched the Beretta, not knowing whether she could kill again if she had to. Her alarm increased when a full minute passed and McCaul didn't return. Vogel was still distraught. 'Those bastards killed my dogs. They killed Ferdie and Hans . . .'

'Please, Herr Vogel, keep your voice down.'

'You're mad if you think we can escape alive. They'll find us and kill us . . .'

'Why didn't you tell the police what happened to your brother?' Jennifer spoke in a fierce whisper.

Vogel looked at her as if she were crazy. 'How could I? It was easier to tell the locals that Peter had gone to live in Zurich. Otherwise, I'd be cutting my own throat.'

'What do you mean?'

'Years ago Lazar hired me as a courier for his mafia friends. Every few months, I'd cross the Wasenhorn into Italy to pick up a package and then I'd hike back across the glacier. But I never should have become involved with the bastard.'

'What kind of package?'

'It was always a big rucksack full of money. Lazar's friends would take the money to a bank in Zurich where it was cleaned. I knew what I did was illegal, but I didn't care, the Russians paid me too well.'

'What do you mean by cleaned? Laundered?'

'Of course. That's what Lazar told me.'

'Was my father part of this conspiracy?'

'How should I know? All I knew was there were two desperate men trying to escape with a fortune.'

'What do you mean by that?'

'As we made our way up to the glacier Lazar told us that he and your father had stolen a fortune from the Russian mafia. He said that Peter and I would be paid generously for our help but that we'd have to keep our mouths shut. But we had the feeling that once we helped them over the border they would murder us. That's why I fled when I had the chance.'

Jennifer heard a floorboard creak upstairs. How long could it be before the men found the basement? Her heart pounded. She was confused by Vogel's revelation. 'You said that my father looked afraid that night. What exactly did you mean?'

'Anxious. That's how he looked to me. Both of them were scared, but him especially.'

'Did you speak with him?'

'No. Lazar did all the talking.'

Jennifer heard another noise, the sound of a shoe scraping on floorboards. The men were searching the rooms. They *had* to find the basement door soon. 'Herr Vogel, I need to know if my father could have survived the blizzard.'

'Impossible. The snowdrifts were metres high. He and Lazar couldn't have found their way out of treacherous weather like that.'

'But *you* did.'

'Only by a miracle.'

'Didn't you go back to look for their bodies?'

'*Ja*, six weeks later, when I was well enough. But there was no sign of the bodies and I'm not surprised. They probably fell into a crevasse and perished, as Peter did.'

'You're wrong. One of them survived and reached the Crown of Thorns monastery five days later.'

'*Impossible!* No one could have stayed alive in those snowdrifts for five days.'

'There's a mountain hut near by where they could have found shelter.'

Vogel didn't look convinced. 'Believe me, you are clinging to a vain hope. Your father would have frozen to death. But I can't offer you a body as proof, if that's what you're looking for, because I never found one.'

304

Vogel suddenly fell silent. Jennifer's pulse raced as the door-knob rattled at the top of the stairs. Then she heard another noise and spun round. The door leading to the outside began to open slowly. She raised the Beretta and prepared to fire.

'It's me,' a familiar voice whispered, as McCaul appeared.

'They're upstairs, Frank. They're trying to open the door.'

Sweat beaded McCaul's face as the doorknob rattled again at the top of the stairs. 'Then we're in the shit. There's a guy with a machine gun covering the back of the house and he's coming our way.'

59

Mark pressed his foot hard on the accelerator. They were speeding along the road east from Murnau and Kelso was frantically checking the map. Grimes and Fellows were following. Narrow country tracks veined off on either side, but every one of them looked the same. Mark felt hopelessly lost. 'Which way now?'

'Left at the next turn.'

Mark hung a sharp left at the next junction, and they bumped down a muddied track until they came to a dead end, a bank of thick fir trees blocking their path. 'There isn't a house or property in sight, Kelso. You're sure we're on the right road?'

Kelso quickly checked the map again. '*Shit.*'

'We're lost, aren't we?'

'The farm's got to be around here somewhere, for Christ's sake. Go back the way we came.'

Jennifer heard the knob rattle again on the landing and then a creak of wood. *Someone's trying the door.* They were trapped from both sides with nowhere to turn, and she was panic stricken. 'Isn't there another way out of here?'

'If there was I would have taken it by now.' Vogel's voice trembled. 'We're finished, don't you understand? What chance do we have against machine guns . . . ?'

'Both of you get back against the wall, and for Christ's sake don't make a sound,' McCaul ordered.

'What are you going to do?'

'Just do as I say, Jennifer.' McCaul took the Maglite torch from his pocket, flicked it on, and stepped over to the light bulb in the centre of the room. He raised himself on his toes, using his coat sleeve to grip and loosen the bulb. The room was plunged into darkness, except for the weak glimmer from the torch, which was just enough to see by.

Jennifer and Vogel pressed their backs against the wall and McCaul put a finger to his lips for them to be silent, then he picked up a heavy log from the wood pile, stepped back behind the door and flicked off the torch.

They heard the noises on the landing grow louder, and then came muffled voices. Seconds later, the basement door creaked open. Daylight trickled into the room and the barrel of a gun appeared. The door opened wider and one of the intruders entered in a crouched position, clutching his machine pistol. Just then the door rattled on the landing above and he looked up in alarm. 'Dimitri?' the man called out softly, his accent Russian.

McCaul lunged out of the shadows wielding the log and struck the man a blow across the arms. He yelped and dropped the machine pistol and McCaul struck him again, this time across the back of the neck. The man gave a muffled cry and slumped to the floor.

As McCaul grabbed the machine pistol, the blond appeared. Vogel panicked and bolted towards the far door, shoving past Jennifer as he begged desperately, 'Please, don't kill me!' He had reached the doorway when the blond fired his pistol from the top of the stairs hitting him in the back. McCaul raised the machine pistol and fired in reply, a rapid burst that gouged plaster and chipped the landing walls. The blond was outgunned and tried to back out of the door but McCaul fired again, stitching the wall above the man's head.

'Put your gun on the floor!' McCaul screamed. 'Put it down or you're dead.' The blond dropped his gun. McCaul was up the stairs in an instant. He grabbed the man by the coat and pushed him down the stairs. The blond staggered halfway down before he lost his footing and landed in a heap on the floor. He was dazed as McCaul reached him. 'Get up.'

The blond got to his feet, and McCaul searched him for weapons. Jennifer looked around. The assailant McCaul had struck was still unconscious, crumpled in a heap near the door. An overpowering smell of cordite filled the basement, and Vogel's bullet-ridden body lay slumped on the floor.

She went to feel for Vogel's pulse but there was none. She felt numb.

McCaul spun their captive round to face the stairs. 'I don't know who the hell you are, buddy, but you've got some questions to answer. Now take a walk back upstairs and do it one step at a time.'

McCaul pulled up a kitchen chair and pushed the blond on to the seat. 'Let's start with who exactly you are, Dimitri.'

'Go fuck yourself,' the man answered.

'Why are you trying to kill me?' Jennifer asked.

'If I had wanted to, I could have killed you long before now, you stupid bitch.'

Jennifer persisted. 'Who are you working for and what do you want from me?'

The man sneered at McCaul. 'Go ahead and shoot, but that's all you'll get out of me.'

McCaul lost his patience, grabbed the man by his lapels and hauled him to his feet. 'She asked you a question.'

The blond remained defiantly silent. McCaul's anger got the better of him. He struck him a blow to the jaw, then another, punching him hard. As he made to strike him again, Jennifer grabbed his arm. 'No, Frank!'

McCaul let the man go. He collapsed into the chair, barely conscious, and his head lolled to one side, blood trickling from his mouth. 'This guy's not going to talk. We're wasting our time.'

He searched the man's clothes and found another cell phone and a set of car keys, then crossed the room and ripped out the wires to Vogel's telephone.

'Why did you do that?'

'I want to make sure our friend here can't call for help when he comes to his senses.' McCaul took her by the arm and led her down to the basement, where he searched through the second assailant's pockets. The man was still unconscious. McCaul found his wallet and stuffed it into Jennifer's tote bag, then he removed the man's trouser belt and tied his hands behind his back, before crossing to Vogel's body. His eyes were open and McCaul knelt and placed two fingers on the lids and eased them shut. 'The poor bastard didn't stand a chance. We're done. Now let's get out to the car.'

Three minutes later the blond came to. He massaged his face and staggered towards the window. He saw that the Volkswagen was gone, then he checked his pockets and discovered that his keys were missing. He stumbled down the basement stairs, out the door and over to the garaged Mercedes. He saw the keys in the ignition, slid into the driver's seat, started the engine and reversed over to the basement door. He undid the belt tying his comrade's hands. The man was barely conscious as he bundled him into the rear of the Mercedes. Then he slipped back into the driver's seat, gunned the engine and drove towards Murnau. Two miles farther on, doing sixty kilometres an hour, he barely noticed an Opel and a Volkswagen swish pass him at high speed, travelling in the opposite direction.

60

A gas station lay ahead and McCaul slowed and pulled in. His shoulder had started to throb. He removed his jacket and Jennifer examined the wound. The bleeding had stopped but the flesh was raw and angry. 'We ought to find a doctor, Frank.'

'Forget it. I visit a surgery with a gunshot wound, first thing you know the cops will turn up. The wound's pretty clean. We'll find a drug store later and dress it properly.'

'Are you always so stubborn?'

'It's a family flaw. Now how about we see what we've got in that bag of yours?'

They searched through the assailants' wallets and found an assortment of Swiss and European currency, but no forms of ID.

'They must have learned from the last mistake. There's nothing to betray their identities, false or otherwise.' McCaul examined the assailant's cell phone. 'Same thing as last time. It's got a password code.' He tossed the phone down in frustration. 'If you ask me, we've reached a dead end here, and a dangerous one at that. Have you still got your passport?'

'In my bag. Why?'

'The trail's gone cold and all we've got is the stuff Vogel told us. I think we ought to hop on the first plane home and try to find out what happened to your father's security box. I've got a feeling that whatever's inside may be the key we're looking for. And maybe we'll learn who's been pulling those guys' strings.'

Jennifer knew that McCaul was right. 'What if they have the airports watched?'

McCaul consulted the map. 'If we head west to Geneva we can try and grab a flight stateside. We're ahead of the game right now, so we might catch them off guard before Blondie sets off alarm bells. But you know what's got me stumped? If you believe it when he said they're not out to kill you just yet, then what's their motive? I know you've tried, but you've got to try and think again. Think really hard. They've got to be after *something*, Jennifer. Did you ever hear your father mention the Russian mafia?'

'No, never.' Jennifer had no answer. She was as confused as ever, and felt she'd reached breaking point. The endless killings and the trauma of being hunted by brutal and sinister men, and for no valid reason she could think of, were finally taking their toll. *If all this doesn't stop soon I really think I'm going to go out of my mind.* She felt close to despair and put her head in her hands.

McCaul touched her shoulder. 'I think it's time we got ourselves back home.'

Mark noticed the silence as soon as Kelso killed the engine. The farmhouse wasn't just quiet, it was *eerily* quiet. A black BMW 530 with Swiss registration plates was parked on the gravel. The barn and garage looked deserted, the front door of the house was ajar, and the place was as hushed as a grave.

Grimes and Fellows joined them as they stepped out of the Opel, and Kelso said cautiously, 'Ryan and I will cover the front. You two go in from the back. And for Chrissakes be careful.'

Grimes moved to the rear of the house with his weapon drawn, and Fellows covered him. Kelso cocked his pistol and Mark did the same as they waited uneasily by the car. Minutes seemed like an eternity, until Grimes finally appeared in the front door, his handgun by his side, his face impassive. 'You'd better take a look.'

61

'I'd take a guess that he's been dead less than an hour. Looks like he was heading towards the door when he took five rounds in the back.'

Mark knelt beside the dead man and examined his wounds. He had already decided that the victim didn't look remotely like McCaul, but Kelso squatted down to take a closer look. Their first shock had been the bullet-ridden Dobermans and the entrance hallway drenched with blood. Mark had grimaced as they stepped past the dogs and Grimes led them through a shattered door that had been smashed off its hinges. When they descended a broken stairwell to a basement, they saw the body sprawled by the door. Kelso finished examining the corpse and stood to address Fellows. 'Did you take a look upstairs?'

'It's empty. From the personal items we found in one of the bedrooms it looks like the dead guy lived alone.'

'What personal items, for Christ sakes?'

'Photographs, bills, clothes. Grimes found this in one of the bedroom closets.' Fellows showed them a driving licence bearing the dead man's photograph and the name Heinrich Vogel. 'And there was some other stuff lying around.'

'Like what?'

'Correspondence. Letterheads. Seems our friend Vogel here was a ski instructor and mountain guide.'

Kelso examined the licence before he stuffed it in his pocket. 'I'll have Langley run a check. Not that I think it's going to turn up much, but I'd take a bet we may have found our mule.'

'Did you find anything else?' Mark asked Fellows.

'Over a dozen spent nine-mil cartridges in the basement and on the landing.'

'Any signs that Jennifer and McCaul were here?'

'No. But we found a small amount of blood on the kitchen floor.'

'Go examine the BMW,' Kelso ordered. 'See if you can find out if it belonged to this guy Vogel.'

Mark was tortured with worry as Fellows and Grimes left. 'Where is she, Kelso?'

Kelso studied the blood-spattered floor and the bullet holes in the walls. 'I'm not a psychic, Ryan. But it looks to me like we've got all the hallmarks of another blood bath, and I'm not exactly hopeful.'

Mark charged across the room and grabbed him, pushing him back against the wall. 'Why the hell couldn't you have told Jennifer the truth from the beginning? You had to play your stupid games and put her in jeopardy. This is all your fault, Kelso. *All of it*. But I can promise you one thing. The first chance I get I'm going to blow this thing wide open. I'm going to nail your ass for what you've done. Nail you and your goddamned CIA.'

Kelso turned ashen. 'I wouldn't advise that, or you could find yourself in deeper shit than you could ever imagine.'

'Is that a fact? We'll see about that when the time comes.'

'Get your goddamned hands off me.'

Mark released his grip, still livid, and crossed the room to examine the blood trails. Kelso saw him follow the trails out into the yard, then look up towards the roof and frown. He stepped back inside the basement and headed towards the stairs, Kelso behind him. 'What the *fuck* do you think you're doing, Ryan?'

'Saying my prayers.'

'*What?*'

But Mark was barely listening as he raced up the stairs.

Kelso followed him into the kitchen. 'Care to tell me what you're up to, Ryan? Or do I keep talking to myself?'

'I told you, saying my prayers.' Mark started to follow the electric leads from the back of the TV security monitor as the penny suddenly dropped for Kelso. 'There's a camera out front,' Mark told him. 'And another camera on the roof. The way they're pointed, they're covering every angle at the front and rear of the house. If the cameras are working, they either have a live video feed with no playback, or else the feed's recorded. I'm praying it's the type that's recorded, because that means there's a chance we might learn something about what happened here.'

Mark followed the wires down to the back of a cupboard near the sink and yanked open the cupboard door. '*Bingo.*'

Inside, nestling on a shelf, was a video recorder with a tape running in the slot.

Geneva

The city was dazzling in the spring sunshine, the giant Jet d'Eau fountain out in the lake spewing water into the air which cascaded down like a million cut diamonds. Trams trundled past luxury shops, and in the cobbled streets elegant cafés and expensive jewellery stores gave a feeling of solid Swiss respectability. It seemed so normal to Jennifer after all the bloodshed that she found it hard to take in what had just happened.

McCaul drove along the lake shore and the Rue Versonnex until he pulled up outside the magnificent Hôtel du Lac, the most luxurious in Geneva.

'Why stop here?'

McCaul pointed to a plush-looking travel office next door to the hotel. 'We'll need plane tickets and I figure it's better to buy them here than hang around in a queue at the airport ticket desk. That way, if anyone's watching the terminal they'll have less chance of spotting us.'

'Just so long as we can get out of Switzerland.'

McCaul emptied the assailants' wallets and counted out their cash, which came to over five thousand in US dollars. 'This ought to cover our ticket expenses, and maybe even a business-class upgrade if we're lucky. Keep your fingers crossed there's a flight to somewhere stateside.'

He disappeared inside the travel office and came out fifteen minutes later.

'Well?' Jennifer asked as he climbed in beside her.

'Here's the bummer. There's no direct flight to New York until tomorrow. But there's one to New York via Paris with Air France, leaving Geneva in just over an hour.' He waved a wad of airline tickets. 'If we hurry, we might make it.'

62

Berg Edelweiss

They watched the tape and saw Jennifer and McCaul arrive out front, and later depart by the track at the rear of the house. They saw the two armed assailants step out of the BMW and advance towards the house, then later the blond drag his comrade out to the Mercedes and speed away. The entire episode lasted no more than twenty minutes, from the arrival of Jennifer and McCaul to the departure of the wounded assailants. From the time display on the tape, Mark calculated that Jennifer and McCaul had left in the Volkswagen only fifteen minutes before they'd arrived.

Kelso studied the two assailants. 'I've never seen either of those guys before, but I'll have Langley run an ID check from the tape. Rewind it, Ryan, and let's get going.'

The next hour was a frantic blur to Mark. They sped towards Murnau, hoping to spot Jennifer's Volkswagen, but they were out of luck. They scoured the streets for half an hour, then headed north towards Zurich, still desperately trying to get a bead on the Volkswagen, until Kelso gave up in frustration. He took out his cell phone and ordered Fellows to pull into an autobahn gas station while he made an urgent call to Langley.

Geneva

McCaul abandoned the car in the Geneva airport lot. They stopped off at a line of concession shops in the terminal. At a pharmacy, Jennifer bought antiseptic cream, sticking plaster and a roll of gauze, and a pair of cheap, non-prescription reading glasses and some toiletries. In a gift store next door they purchased two overnight bags, a Tyrolean hat, a pair of sunglasses, and a baseball cap and a woollen scarf. Their disguises were paltry, but all they could manage with only thirty-five minutes before the aircraft departed. As McCaul donned the hat and reading glasses, Jennifer said, 'Shouldn't we dress your arm?'

'There isn't time. I'll take care of it after we board. If they're watching the terminal they'll be looking for a couple. Stay near me, but not so close that it might look like we're together. When we get to the ticket desks we'll check in separately.'

McCaul handed over her tickets. Jennifer slipped on the sunglasses and the baseball cap and wrapped the scarf around the bottom half of her face. 'Have we got a plan if we run into trouble again?'

'Scream and run like hell while I try to fend them off.'

'That's *it*?'

'I ditched the pistols in the car so there's not much else we can do. But I'd take a guess they're not going to try to grab you in a crowded airport with security around. Though I could be wrong after what happened on the train.'

'Thanks, McCaul.'

'You OK?'

'Sure, I'm having a ball.'

'Keep about ten paces in front of me and let's try not to look like we're a couple of jail-breakers on the run.'

As they walked towards the Air France ticket desk, Jennifer's heart pounded furiously. She had a gnawing dread that every step they took they were being watched by unseen eyes, but they checked in without a hitch and immediately headed towards the security aisles and the boarding gates. Fifteen minutes later, to her relief, she and McCaul started to board the Air France flight to Paris, with an onward connection to JFK, New York.

Forty kilometres away, travelling at high speed on the main A21 autobahn to Geneva, Mark was agitated and tried to keep from looking at his watch. The Opel was hurtling along at over a hundred kilometres an hour as Kelso talked on his cell phone to

CIA headquarters in Langley. According to Langley's computer wizards, at precisely six minutes past noon an international airline booking computer in Paris had recorded that a Frank McCaul and a Jennifer March had purchased two tickets from a Geneva travel agent. The tickets were for an Air France shuttle to Paris, departing from Geneva airport at 12.45, with an onward connection to New York.

Kelso finally switched off his phone. 'It's done. I'll have undercover agents tagging them the moment they land at JFK.'

Mark was still strung out with worry after seeing the carnage at the farm. 'You're assuming they'll get safely aboard the flight. But what if the airport's being watched? What if they get to them before they board?'

'That's our blind spot,' Kelso agreed, 'so we'd better pray their luck doesn't run out. Langley's trying to hack into the airline computer and we'll know the moment they board. After that, my people in Paris will take it from there.'

'*What* people in Paris?'

Kelso's voice was hoarse with excitement. 'I'm convinced they've discovered something important, otherwise why would they be in such a damned big hurry to get back home? So I've arranged for three more undercover agents from our Paris station to board their flight at Charles de Gaulle and babysit them until they reach New York.'

'So what do *we* do? Sit on our asses until the next available flight?'

Kelso consulted his watch. 'Jennifer and McCaul ought to be on the ground in Paris for at least an hour before their connection departs, so Langley's booked us on a private jet to New York. With luck, we could be waiting at JFK when Jennifer arrives.'

'And then what?'

'Maybe you were right, Ryan,' Kelso confessed. 'Maybe it's time we dropped this whole charade and told her exactly what's going on.'

PART FIVE

63

New York

Lou Garuda arrived at NYPD headquarters on Police Plaza at ten and took the elevator up to the thirteenth floor. Danny Flynn was a grizzled, cigar-chomping detective with the Organised Crime Investigation Division, and he met Garuda in the hall and showed him into his office. 'Take a seat. The fuck brings you here, Lou? I figure it ain't a social call?'

'I need some info on the Red Mafia. I'm a little out of touch, so I thought I'd ask an expert. Have the reds got much of an operation going in New York?'

Flynn took a packet of peanuts from his desk, popped a kernel in his mouth and munched. 'Which fucking planet are you on, Lou? The Red Mafia operate fucking *everywhere*. They're the big boys of crime and into everything. Prostitution, tax fraud, computer fraud, drug running, you name it.'

'You ever hear of the Moscaya clan?'

Flynn raised his bushy grey eyebrows before he answered. 'Why the questions? Organised crime ain't your territory.'

'I need some details on the Moscayas. Who the head honchos are, what businesses they're into, that sort of shit.'

Flynn shook his head, dropped the pack of nuts on his desk and dusted his hands. 'We don't give out detailed stuff like that to anyone outside the division, unless they're involved in a specific case. You ought to know that, Lou.'

'But this is in confidence, friend to friend, you got my word, Danny . . .'

'No buts. Those are the rules.' Flynn stood and scratched his backside, then turned to a metal filing cabinet behind him, searched through some files and plucked out a thick one. He laid it on the desk in front of Garuda. 'I'm going to grab myself a cup of coffee. I'll lock the door and be back in twenty minutes. The fact you might read through that file while I'm away is something I'm totally fucking ignorant of, OK?'

'I owe you one, Danny boy.'

'You mind me asking what in the name of bejesus you're up to?'

'Just as soon as I've figured that out, I'll let you know.'

64

The Air France 747 climbed above the rain clouds over Paris and when it reached cruising altitude levelled out to begin its eight-hour flight across the Atlantic. For the first time in forty-eight hours, Jennifer felt she could relax. They had made their Paris connection without any hitches and now that they were safely on the last stage of the homeward journey her feeling of relief was overwhelming.

Twenty minutes after take-off, McCaul winced and put a hand on his arm.

'What's the matter?' Jennifer asked.

'The wound's starting to hurt. I'd better go fix on a dressing.'

'Do you want me to help?'

'No need, I'll be fine. At least the bleeding hasn't started again. Why don't you try and grab some rest while you can?'

Jennifer was exhausted, and felt on edge again. 'You're right. I'll try.'

McCaul stood, touched her shoulder. 'You can relax now, Jennifer. We're at thirty-five thousand feet. We're completely safe.'

The next five hours were a blank to Jennifer as she settled into a deep sleep. When she woke and stretched they were only two hours out from New York. McCaul was beside her and wide awake, sipping a Coke. 'How'd you sleep?'

'Like a two-year-old. How's your arm?'

'It could be worse, but I think I spoke too soon about us being safe.'

'What are you talking about?'

323

McCaul was uneasy. 'We're being watched by three passengers and I'll bet you a hundred bucks they're tails.'

'Which three?'

'Don't look now, but two of them are guys, seated together, eight rows ahead. One's red-haired, wearing a grey business suit, and the other's dressed casually in a navy blue windbreaker and glasses. The third's a blonde woman in a charcoal two-piece, a dozen seats behind us, in row thirty-six.'

'How can you be sure they're tails?'

'Two of them passed our aisle while you were asleep. They tried to make it appear innocent, but I know an appraising look when I see one. They're professionals, make no mistake, Jennifer.'

'Why didn't you tell me this before now?'

'I didn't want to get you worried.'

'You're worrying me now.'

'Don't fret, they won't try anything while we're aboard. Walk to the washroom and take a look at the two guys. On the way back, go to the end galley and ask the stewardess for a drink. You'll see the woman on your way, but don't make it obvious by making eye contact with any of them. I don't want them to know we've marked their cards.'

Jennifer stepped out into the aisle and walked to the washroom. As she passed row sixteen she didn't dare look back, but she caught a side-on glimpse of the man in the grey business suit. He was about forty, muscular, with thinning red hair, and he looked as if he spent every free hour in the gym.

The washroom was vacant and she ran the cold tap and threw water on her face. When she came out three minutes later, her legs felt like jelly as she passed the two men face on. The red-haired guy in the business suit didn't look up, but the man seated next to him did. He wore a navy blue windbreaker and a checked cotton shirt and glasses, his hair cropped close to his skull, military style. He looked more like a backpacker than a business-class passenger. He gave her a casual glance as she walked towards the end galley.

As she approached row thirty-six Jennifer noticed the woman in the charcoal two-piece with the short blonde hair. She was flicking through a magazine. Jennifer saw her glance up in her direction for just an instant, but it was enough. *McCaul is right. She's watching me.*

Her stomach was a knot of anxiety as she got a glass of water from the galley and rejoined McCaul. 'How could they have known we boarded *this* flight? And *this* connection.'

'I can't figure that one out. But they're good, I'll give them that. In future you'd better keep your sunglasses on, so they can't tell if you're observing them. And as soon as we land, stick right beside me.'

'How are we going to lose them?'

'I've been trying to figure that one out, too. But this time maybe I've got an idea.' McCaul pressed the call button and a few moments later a stewardess came down the aisle.

'*Monsieur?*'

'Does the aircraft have a satellite telephone system on board?'

'*Oui*. But only in first-class.'

'You'd better lead me to it. This is a personal emergency.'

65

Thirty minutes behind the Air France 747, the chartered Gulfstream G450 business jet cruised at 41,000 feet above the Atlantic. Mark sat up near the front of the cramped cabin beside Kelso, who had spent the last fifteen minutes on the aircraft's satellite phone, planning their next move.

'We're on schedule to arrive at JFK at five p.m.,' Kelso explained. 'Which puts us almost thirty-five minutes behind their flight. And I've fixed it so that we won't be bothered by Immigration or Customs once we land.'

'What happens to Jennifer and McCaul after they touch down?'

'As soon as they enter the arrivals area they'll be taken under our protection, by force if necessary, and held in custody until we arrive.'

'Then what?'

'I tell Jennifer everything and try to find out what she's turned up. But your job's done, Ryan. Once we land your involvement comes to an end.'

'Listen, Kelso, I want to be there when you meet with Jennifer face to face.'

'Forget it. Those are my instructions and they're not negotiable.'

Jennifer braced herself as the wheels of the Air France Jumbo bit JFK's runway. Ten minutes later the aircraft taxied to the apron and the seat belt chime sounded. McCaul grabbed their bags from the overhead locker as the aircraft's exit door yawned open and the passengers began to line the aisles to depart.

As she stepped out into the aisle, Jennifer wore her sunglasses. She saw the two men retrieve their hand luggage from overhead and noticed the red-haired man glance at her slyly before he filed towards the exit. She suddenly felt fearful.

'Stick close to me,' McCaul whispered, and he took her arm and guided her towards the door.

With no luggage to retrieve, they were the first in the queue for Immigration. Once their passports had been scrutinised, they headed towards the Customs lanes, but halfway there McCaul suddenly diverted Jennifer towards the restrooms. 'Wait here and pretend you're searching in your bag.'

'What are you up to?'

'Just trust me and do as I say.'

Jennifer pretended to rummage in her tote bag. To her left there was a solid steel door with a security keypad off to one side. A sign on the door said: 'ID PERMIT HOLDERS ONLY. NO UNAUTHORISED PERSONNEL BEYOND THIS POINT'. She glanced right and saw a couple of armed uniformed police standing near the Customs lanes. Then she spotted the three passengers lingering near a pillar: the blonde woman was nearest, the two men a couple of paces behind her, all of them trying to appear inconspicuous. Jennifer heard the panic in her own voice. 'They're fifty yards behind us, Frank.'

'I see them. My guess is that with the cops around they won't try anything until we're in arrivals. Except this is where we're going we lose them.'

'*How?*'

McCaul indicated the steel security door. 'Through there.'

Jennifer was puzzled. They would need the code to open the door. 'You mind telling me how we're going to do that?'

'With inside help.' McCaul punched a number into his cell phone and spoke. 'Where the hell are you, Marty? We're waiting right where you told me, by the staff entrance. You'd better move it, buddy. Trouble's right on our tail and we haven't got all day.'

As McCaul flicked off his phone, Jennifer looked at him, perplexed. 'Who were you talking to?'

'I'll tell you later.'

327

'Has this got anything to do with the call you made on board?'

But McCaul was preoccupied and looked past her. 'I think they may try to make their move on us any minute now.'

She followed his gaze. The two men and the woman were still waiting by the pillar. They seemed to suspect that something was amiss but looked unsure about what they should do next.

Jennifer's heart jumped when she heard a sudden noise. She looked round as the security door burst open. An overweight man with a bushy black moustache stood inside. He wore an airport official's uniform with a peaked cap and carried a clipboard in his hand, a staff photo-ID dangling from a chain around his neck. The name on the ID identified him as Marty Summers.

'The hell kept you, Marty?'

'Got here as quick as I could. We've got to do this thing real damned *fast*, so move it, pal.'

The man spoke in a Bronx accent. He ushered them inside and the next thing Jennifer knew she was being propelled through the door by McCaul. She looked back and glimpsed the two men and the blonde woman running towards the door but they were too late and it slammed in their faces.

'I think you just saved our asses, Marty.'

Marty grinned behind his moustache. 'Hey, McCaul, one good turn deserves another. Now let's shift it.'

66

As Marty led them along a corridor, Jennifer heard banging on the door but she didn't look back. She was astounded that they had managed to escape so easily.

'Marty works for airport security,' McCaul explained. 'Lucky for us he owed me a favour. I once caught his wife in bed with a guy who worked at the Hertz desk and got the photographs to prove it. Didn't I, Marty?'

'Sure did. The slut was sleeping with half the frigging airport. Best thing I ever did, saying adios to that bitch. Who were the assholes following you?'

'A long story. What about the car?'

Marty handed McCaul a set of car keys. 'It's parked in lot three, as you come out of the elevator on level four. A blue Chevy Impala.'

'You're a sweetheart.'

'And I'd like it back in one piece, Frank. No fucking dents or scratches, man. I still owe two years' repayments, so drive gently, you hear?'

'That's a promise.' They turned into another corridor and McCaul said, 'When do we get out of this maze?'

'Loosen up, we're almost there.'

The Gulfstream touched down thirty minutes behind the Air France 747 and Kelso was the first off. As they raced down the stairs on to the tarmac his cell phone sounded. When he answered the call, Kelso turned instantly hostile, his voice hoarse with anger. 'You've got to be kidding me? *How the Christ did that happen?* I want the airport scoured, every entrance and exit watched. Just find them, do you hear me? Of course I'll stay on the damned line.'

'What's wrong?' Mark asked.

Kelso was livid as he cradled the cell phone to his ear. 'I don't believe this. Some morons fucked up, that's what's wrong. Jennifer and McCaul must have suspected they were being watched and they've given my people the slip.'

'Your mean you *lost* them?'

'They breached airport security. As of now, they've completely vanished.'

Jennifer felt completely disoriented. The maze of corridors seemed to go on for ever. Finally they came to another security door with a keypad. Marty punched in a number, the door snapped open, and suddenly there was daylight outside. Jennifer figured that they were somewhere on the far side of the arrivals building.

'You can't miss the parking lot. Hang a right and it's straight in front. Nice meeting you, ma'am. Good luck, Frank.'

'Marty, we owe you, big time.'

'Sure. Just be careful with my damn Chevy.'

The man named Marty watched from the doorway as McCaul and Jennifer headed towards the parking lot. He grinned, removed his uniform cap and tossed it into a garbage bin by the door. Then he punched his cell phone keypad and a voice answered. 'What's the story?'

The Bronx accent was gone – Marty sounded like a different man. 'They're heading towards the Chevy.'

'How'd it go?'

'She fell for the double act. Nick and me played it along, stuck to the script, and everything went real smooth. No hitches.'

'Perfect. Now let's finish the job.'

67

Lou Garuda's next visit was to a suite of offices in downtown Manhattan. He took the elevator to the sixth floor and found the room he was looking for at the end of a corridor. The sign in scratched gold lettering said: Frank McCaul, Private Investigator.

Garuda knocked, and when he got no reply he wandered down the hall to another office. The door was open. A middle-aged woman sat behind a desktop computer, typing away. A sign on her door said: *Carole Lippman Secretarial Services*. The woman looked up and smiled. 'Can I help you?'

'Frank McCaul, the PI down the hall. He ain't around right now?'

'He left for Switzerland a couple of days ago. I'm afraid his son had a tragic accident in the Alps.'

'Gee, I'm real sorry to hear that. You know Frank well?'

'Sure, he's had his office here for quite a few years. I do most of his secretarial work. Were you thinking of hiring him?'

Garuda smiled, flashed his badge. 'No, I'm with the Long Beach Police Department. You mind if I ask you a couple of questions about Mr McCaul?'

An hour later Garuda turned off the highway in Hempstead, Long Island. He came to a peaceful-looking neighbourhood and found the address at the end of a cul-de-sac; Frank McCaul's home was painted grey and butter-cream, with a garage off to the side and a basketball net affixed to the gable wall. He noticed a bunch of teenage kids skateboarding at the far end of the cul-de-sac, and a guy tending his lawn in a garden across the street, but neither paid him much attention. He locked his car, strolled up to McCaul's veranda and rang the bell. No answer. He hit the buzzer for ten seconds to be certain, and heard its hollow ring deep inside the house. Zilch.

The house was protected by a thick row of hedge and no one could see him from the street. He turned back, rapped on the door and called out: 'Anybody home?'

No answer. *The place is empty.* Garuda opened his wallet and took out a penknife with an array of filed blades. He'd confiscated the tool years ago from a house burglar. He slipped one of the ultra-slim blades into the lock, fiddled it around until he felt the tumblers click and the lock sprang open as if by magic. *OK, let's see what we can find out about Mr Frank McCaul.*

Garuda wandered along a hallway, past a comfortable lounge, to a large kitchen at the back. He rummaged in a couple of the kitchen-unit drawers, but found only cutlery and a bunch of old utility bills, so he moved into the lounge. *Nothing fucking remarkable here, that's for sure.* A TV and video, a hi-fi unit, books on the shelves, some on forensics and police procedures.

He spotted a bunch of photographs on the walls, mostly of a guy he assumed was McCaul, some of them taken with a young boy: pics of the boy as a kid, then a teenager, then a young man. In several, the kid wore climbing gear and a helmet, and there were mountains in the background. There was no sign of a woman in any of the shots. Garuda pocketed one of the photographs, then wandered upstairs to a narrow landing where he found three bedrooms, one of them full of junk and used as a storeroom. He was about to search the other two bedrooms when he heard footsteps in the hallway below and then the stairs creaked.

He wrenched out his Glock and stepped on to the landing.

68

A guy was coming up the stairs. Middle aged, balding.

'Hold it right there, pal.' Garuda recognised the neighbour he'd seen tending his lawn across the street. The guy carried a pair of leather gardening gloves in one hand and he looked alarmed when he saw a stranger holding a Glock. He took a couple of steps backwards down the stairs and Garuda flashed his badge. 'Police. The frig are you doing in here?'

The man's fear vaporised when he saw the badge. 'Hey, I could ask you the same question, Officer.'

'Who's asking?'

'Name's Norrie Sinclair. I live across the street. Saw you come in here and didn't know what the hell was going on. We've got a damned good neighbourhood watch programme around here, I'll have you know.'

'Glad to hear it.' Garuda put his gun away. He didn't have to explain diddly to this guy, which was just as well, because he had no search warrant and technically he had committed a criminal act by breaking and entering. *But that's another day's worry.* 'Frank McCaul lives here, right?'

'Sure. I usually keep an eye on the place when Frank's away.'

'Yeah? When did you see him last, Mr Sinclair?'

'A few days back. He had to travel abroad. His son, Chuck, died, you know.'

'So I heard. When exactly did Frank leave?'

'On Sunday afternoon he flew directly to Zurich. He was pretty cut up, and could barely hold himself together. Some people came to pick him up. I guess to take him to the airport. Look, what's going on here, are you a friend of his or something . . . ?'

Garuda frowned. 'You said Sunday. You're sure about that? He flew direct to Zurich?'

'Of course I'm sure. He also told me he had to identify Chuck's body.' The neighbour stared at Garuda as if he'd lost his marbles. 'Why, what's the problem here, Officer?'

Garuda frowned again. *No problem, except that, according to Mark, Frank McCaul arrived in Switzerland on Tuesday. It sounded like the guy was missing for a day.*

'You're positive you're not mistaken? It was definitely Sunday?'

'Sure.'

'Who came to pick him up?'

'Two guys in a dark Buick sedan.'

'You saw them?'

'No, but my wife Thelma did. She saw Frank leave with them. We haven't seen him since. Guess he's going to be away for a little while longer.'

'Did Thelma ever see the two guys before?'

'No, she didn't, as a matter of fact.'

'And this was on Sunday afternoon?'

'Are you deaf? How many times do I have to say it?'

'Did she maybe happen to get the licence number of the Buick, Mr Sinclair?'

The neighbour looked suspiciously at Garuda. 'Why should she? You mind me asking how you got in here?'

'The front door was open.'

The neighbour looked back at the porch and scratched his head. 'Hey, that's weird. When I checked yesterday it was locked. What did you say your name was, Officer?'

Garuda headed down the stairs and out the door. 'Detective Smith. Hey, thanks a bunch for talking.'

69

Mark stood outside the JFK arrivals terminal, watching Kelso have a heated argument with three strangers, a blonde woman dressed in a charcoal two-piece and two men; one red haired, the other sporting a crew cut and glasses. Mark reckoned the strangers were CIA, and even though he couldn't hear what was being said, it was obvious that Kelso was lambasting them. Then he barked a bunch of orders, the group dispersed into the terminal, and he strode over and said bitterly to Mark, 'Some guy opened a security door in the Customs hall and they got clean away.'

'*What* guy?'

Kelso ground his teeth in frustration. 'How the hell should I know? No one saw his face. He could be anyone, some dumb-assed airport employee, or someone who deliberately helped them escape.'

'Are they still in the building?'

'We don't know, but they couldn't have gone far. We'll have to search the terminal.'

Grimes and Fellows suddenly appeared and Kelso beckoned them. 'Take the parking lots. The others will search the terminal and the public transport queues. I'll take the car-hire and limo desks. Give it fifteen minutes, max, and we meet back here.'

As the two men raced away, Kelso said to Mark, 'Take the bars, restaurants and the men's restrooms. They may have tried to disguise themselves, so be vigilant. If you haven't spotted them within fifteen minutes the same applies, you shift your ass back here.'

'What if they've already left the airport?'

Kelso was red faced. 'Don't vex me, Ryan. My blood pressure's up to ninety as it is.'

Mark took the escalator to the mezzanine and passed between the busy restaurant tables. Families having snacks, transit passengers and business executives grabbing a quick cup of coffee, but not a sign of anyone who looked remotely like Jennifer or McCaul. Next, he tried the bar, then the mens' restrooms near by and the coffee dock, but without any luck.

As he passed a payphone he noticed a man with his back to him, hunched over the telephone receiver. He wore a black hat and had the same build as McCaul, but when the guy turned round Mark saw that he was in his sixties, wore a priest's collar, and sported a grey beard. Disguise or not, it wasn't McCaul. *Where have he and Jennifer disappeared to?*

A hundred yards across the mezzanine he spotted the blonde woman and her red-haired companion, frantically searching a sea of passengers. By the look of it, they weren't having much luck either. As he turned back, Mark saw the priest replace the receiver and walk away. He realised that this was the first chance he'd had in the last twenty-four hours to make a private call to Garuda. He stepped over to the payphone and rummaged in his pocket for some change.

Garuda answered his cell phone on the second ring. 'Jesus, where the frig are you, Mark? You were supposed to call me back.'

'I'm in JFK arrivals. I just got in twenty minutes ago and things have been kind of crazy, so listen up, I may not have much time. Did you get the lowdown on the Moscaya clan like I asked?'

'Yeah, I had a talk with Danny Flynn. The Moscayas are just like you said. Very low key and they operate mainly offshore.'

'I'm listening.'

'Then I did some digging into McCaul's background like you asked. Got his mug shots from his PI registration and driving licence, and called out to his address on Long Island. It all looks pretty legit, but there's something just a little fishy that I don't understand.'

'*What's* fishy?'

'Not on the phone, Mark. I'll tell you when we meet. I've got some questions of my own that need answering, and we really need to talk.'

'Lou, *please* . . .' Mark said desperately. 'You don't understand.'

'Damned right I don't, so when do I get an explanation? All the digging I've been doing for you, I think I've earned it. And let's not forget who worked the fucking case to begin with.'

'I'll try to explain soon, but please, Lou, just tell me what's fishy. I really need to know.'

Garuda sighed. 'You said McCaul flew into Switzerland on Tuesday last.'

'What about it?'

'According to one of his neighbours, McCaul left for the airport on Sunday after he was picked up at home by a couple of guys in a dark Buick. Which meant he should have arrived in Switzerland on Monday morning at the latest, but he doesn't get there until Tuesday, so there's a whole day missing from his schedule. Does that make any kind of sense?'

'No.'

'It doesn't to me, either. Whoever picked him up could have been friends of his, I guess, but there's a secretarial service down the hall from McCaul's office and the woman there said that McCaul had definitely booked to fly direct to Zurich on Sunday evening. So I had a lady friend of mine over at JFK check the passenger bookings. McCaul's ticket for the Sunday evening flight was cancelled an hour before he was due to travel, and rebooked for the flight the following night, which means he did arrive in Zurich on Tuesday morning. Something sounds a little out of kilter here.'

Mark's mind was working overtime. 'It's beginning to seem that way. Is that everything?'

'That's it,' said Garuda. 'So how about telling me now what the fuck's going on?'

Mark suddenly saw the blonde woman and Red-hair come up the escalator, followed by Grimes, scanning the faces of everyone they passed. 'Listen, I've got to go, Lou.'

'Hey, wait a sec, that ain't good enough, for Christ sakes,' Garuda protested. 'And here's me beginning to think we were working together. Just as well I've been doing some investigating of my own. And you know what? I think I've finally got a lead on the March case.'

'What lead?'

'Something us dumb cops never figured at the time. Prime was owned by a Cayman Island shell company that smells of dirty money. East European mafia dirty money to be precise. That's the angle you're sniffing around, isn't it? You're thinking that maybe it had something to do with Paul March's disappearance. That it had something to do with these Moscaya Red Mafia guys. Though what the hell this private dick McCaul has got to do with all of this, I'm fucked if I know.'

Mark was silent, then he said, 'Lou, I really can't talk about this.'

He heard the anger in Garuda's voice. 'You know what? Maybe it's time I started working this case for myself. Because you sure aren't being much of a help, that's for sure. So screw you.'

Garuda hung up. Mark saw that Grimes and the others had moved off in the opposite direction, still scanning the faces of passers-by. Had they spotted him?

He thought: *How did Garuda figure out the Cayman angle?* And the information about McCaul disturbed him deeply. He was sweating, confused, caught in the middle of a nightmarish puzzle, and he felt an insane desire to run away. He suddenly realised how drained he was, emotionally and physically, but he knew he had to find Jennifer. No matter what, he *had* to find her. But right now Kelso had some explaining to do. In a fit of mounting anger, Mark started down the escalator towards the exit.

70

McCaul switched on the headlights. It was five o'clock in the afternoon, but the sun was buried somewhere behind a mass of clouds that scudded overhead. They had been driving for half an hour. Jennifer saw the towering skyline as they approached Manhattan. She could hardly believe she was back in New York, and still couldn't get over how lucky they had been to escape. Every few minutes since they left JFK she had checked over her shoulder, but in the heavy evening traffic it was impossible to know whether they were being followed.

'Stop worrying, Jennifer. This time we've given them the slip.'

'How can you be so sure? They found us everywhere else we went.'

'I've been watching the rear-view mirror. There's no one on our backs.'

Jennifer hoped he was right. The sky grew darker, and from the look of the clouds New York was in for a storm. 'Why are we going this way?'

'I thought it was the quickest route to Long Beach.'

'Frank, I need to see Bobby first. I haven't seen him in days and I need to know if he's OK. The Cauldwell's only a ten-minute detour. Please.'

McCaul sighed with sudden impatience. 'OK, but do you think you could do the driving?'

'How come?'

'I need to do some figuring out, and I've got a call to make.'

'To who?'

'A friend of mine.' He pulled in, got out of the car, and Jennifer slid into the driver's seat. McCaul climbed into the passenger

339

side. As Jennifer prepared to drive off he opened the glove compartment. The internal light came on, and she saw an automatic pistol and a cell phone stashed inside. McCaul took out the pistol, laid it on his lap, and punched in a number on the cell phone.

Jennifer stared at the pistol. 'Why . . . why is there a gun in there?'

'Shut up a minute.'

'I don't under—'

'I said shut up.' McCaul sweated and looked under pressure as he cradled the phone to his ear. Jennifer heard the faint click at the other end of the line, but she couldn't hear who McCaul spoke to. 'It's me. I'm heading for Cove End. Meet me there in half an hour.'

He flicked off the phone and Jennifer stared at him, perplexed. She had a premonition that something was terribly wrong because McCaul was suddenly a different man. There was a cold edge to his tone as he picked up the gun. 'Start the car.'

'Frank? Frank, what's going on?'

'And you can stop calling me Frank. Now do as I say. Start the car and drive towards Long Beach.'

71

Mark found Kelso already waiting outside arrivals. He was talking on his cell phone as a black limo driven by Fellows suddenly screeched out of the traffic and drew up at the kerb. Kelso flicked off his phone, strode over to Mark and said bitterly, 'We're wasting our time here, there's no sign of them. Get in the limo. The others are going to stay here and continue the search, just in case.'

'I thought you told me that you had Frank McCaul checked out?'

Kelso heard the anger in Mark's voice and his eyes sparked with caution. 'So I did. What about it?'

'I did my own investigating and there's something not right about McCaul. Either you lied to me, Kelso, or else you made a grievous mistake.'

Kelso frowned. 'What the hell's this about? Who have you been talking to?'

Mark was livid. 'That's irrelevant. There's something seriously weird going down here and I'd like to know what it is. *Right now.*'

At that moment Grimes rushed out of the arrivals building just in time to witness the altercation. Fellows got out of the limo. Both men looked unsure about what to do as passers-by began to stop and stare. Kelso was embarrassed, and said to Mark, 'This isn't the place to have this conversation, so keep your voice down. If you want to talk, get in the damned car.'

'I'm going nowhere until I get the truth,' Mark yelled. 'And I *mean* the truth. Not a load of bullshit, not a bunch of lies, but the honest truth. And I want it right now. What are you and the CIA really up to, Kelso?'

Kelso said furiously, '*Get in the car.*'

'Screw you. I'm not going anywhere until I get an explanation.'

It happened quickly: Kelso gave a nod and his two men over-powered Mark. Fellows cupped a hand over his mouth as Grimes grabbed him in an arm lock. Kelso opened the rear door and Mark was forced into the limo. As Grimes restrained him on the back seat, he saw Kelso hold an ID up to the pavement audience. 'Police. This man is in our custody. Now get on your way, there's nothing more to see here.'

Kelso climbed into the back, balled his fist and struck Mark a blow to the face. 'You *idiot*. That's for shooting your mouth off in public. You know something, Ryan? I could cheerfully put a bullet in you this minute, and without a shred of remorse.'

Mark's jaw was on fire as he struggled with Grimes, then Fellows climbed in the front to start the engine and the limo screeched away from the kerb.

Kelso continued, enraged. 'When will you get it into your thick skull that our job is to protect Jennifer? Your behaviour's done nothing but slow our pursuit. Don't you see that, or are you just completely dumb?' He nodded to Grimes. 'Cuff him.'

Grimes produced a pair of handcuffs and snapped them on to Mark's wrists.

'Now,' said Kelso, 'I want to know what the hell you meant about McCaul. And then I want to know who you called from the airport.'

72

The sky opened up and it began to pour; a cold, icy sleet that beat against the windscreen, sounding like tiny drums gone mad. They were on the highway, driving east on Long Island. Jennifer had the wipers on. She kept her speed below fifty. 'Who are you?'

'You can call me Nick Staves.'

'Why . . . why did you impersonate McCaul?'

Staves tucked the gun inside his jacket. 'So I could get close to you. Protect you from the people who intend to kill you once they get what they want.'

'*Who* intends to kill me and what do they want?'

'We'll talk about it when we get to Cove End.'

Jennifer's head spun. A second later she lost her grip on the steering wheel and the Chevy started to veer off the road. Staves grabbed the wheel and pulled them back on track. 'Hey, steady on. I didn't come this far for us both to get totalled in an auto accident. Keep your eyes on the road, for Christ sakes.'

But Jennifer found it impossible to concentrate; she felt she was going to break down. 'I can't take any more . . . I . . . can't take any more of not knowing what's going on. I don't understand *any* of this.'

'You will, Jennifer. Now start driving.'

Kelso's two men were no longer restraining Mark. He put a hand to his jaw and felt a walnut-sized bump. 'Where are you taking me?'

Kelso said, 'You're pissing me off, Ryan. Grimes spotted you on a payphone in the terminal. So you'd better tell me who you called, and *fast*.'

Mark's anger fuelled his frustration. 'You can't do this, Kelso. You're breaking the law by holding me against my will. It's kidnapping.'

'Right now I *am* the law. Now tell me who you called or else you're going to find yourself in a shitload of trouble.'

Mark felt confused, angry, helpless. 'I don't get it, Kelso. Why lie to me about McCaul?'

Kelso's eyes sparked with hostility, and for a second Mark thought the man was going to lash out again with his fist, but instead he just sat there, seething, his temper at breaking point. 'I wasn't lying. And I haven't the faintest idea what you're talking about. Now answer the damned questions.'

'First, how about you take these cuffs off as a gesture of trust?'

Kelso nodded to Grimes. 'Take them off.'

Grimes unlocked the handcuffs, and Mark rubbed his wrists. 'I had a friend of mine run a background check on McCaul.'

'Why?'

'Because I didn't trust you, and because you kept holding back on me.'

'Is that what the phone call from your hotel room in Brig was about?'

Mark nodded. 'My friend called at McCaul's address on Long Island and discovered something odd.'

Kelso raised an eyebrow. 'What?'

'You told me McCaul flew to Switzerland on Tuesday. According to McCaul's neighbour, he left Sunday and was picked up by two men in a dark Buick.'

Kelso stiffened. He removed the envelope containing the photograph of McCaul from his pocket and flicked on the interior light. 'Take a look again at McCaul's mug shot.'

As Mark studied the photograph, Kelso said, 'Are you still sure this is the guy you saw?'

'It's a lousy photo but I'm as sure as I can be. But remember, I only got a brief look at him.'

'You mean you could be wrong?'

344

'I could be, but both men had the same general appearance, the same hairstyle, the same hair colour . . .'

Kelso shook his head, his face tight with concern. 'That means nothing, Ryan. A haircut and a cheap bottle of hair dye would take care of that.'

'I told you, I only got a brief look at the guy . . .'

'To tell the truth, the more I thought about McCaul's presence at the scene of Jennifer's accident, the more it seemed just a mite too convenient. It could have been a set-up, and McCaul may not be who he says he is. That's obvious now.'

Mark's face drained. '*You're* the one who said his background checked out.'

'His *background*, Ryan. But unless we can identify him in the flesh we can't be a hundred per cent certain.'

'Then if he isn't McCaul, who the hell is he?'

73

'I work for the CIA.'

Jennifer stared at the man named Nick Staves. '*What?*'

'The Central Intelligence Agency in Langley, Virginia.'

'I *know* what the CIA is. What happened to the real Frank McCaul?'

'We moved him somewhere secure while I borrowed his identity.'

'Moved him where?'

'McCaul's being looked after at a safe house outside New York. We needed to keep him out of the way until this was over. You believe me, don't you, Jennifer?'

'I . . . I don't know. Who intends to kill me?'

'A man named Jack Kelso. He once told you he was a friend of your father's, but that was a lie.'

Jennifer was stunned. 'Go on.'

'Seeing as you didn't know what Spiderweb meant, let me start with that. Kelso works for the CIA, and a couple of years back he ran a covert CIA operation by the same code name. The target of the operation was Prime International Securities.'

'*Why?*'

'It was owned by an offshore company run by the Moscayas, a Russian mafia clan. Their fortune was invested in the US from illegal offshore accounts, which is why the CIA became involved. Spiderweb was meant to shut down their business, permanently.'

'The Russian mafia *owned* Prime?'

Staves nodded. 'They used it to launder their dirty money. Your father had no idea that the company he worked for was involved in criminal activity, until Kelso appears, tells him the truth, and convinces him to help get the paper evidence the CIA needed to nail Prime's owners.'

'Why would my father agree to do that?'

'For one, Kelso knew he had a secret.' For the next mile, Staves explained about her father's past and his prison record. 'Kelso had all his court and prison records destroyed as part of the deal. Fixed it so that Joseph Delgado never existed. That's why the cops hit a brick wall with the name.'

Jennifer's mind was reeling. She was devastated to learn of her father's criminal past. But despite her horror, she felt certain in her heart that he was a good man who had been driven to bad behaviour. And the mention of Joseph Delgado made her realise why her father had hit her that one time. She felt tears start to roll down her cheeks, but struggled to hold them back. 'What was my father doing in Switzerland?'

'He was given instructions to withdraw fifty million from a Zurich bank used by Prime, and hand it over to a Moscaya gangster named Karl Lazar. Except it was all a set-up. Kelso had spun a web of deceit.'

'What do you mean?'

'He and a couple of his corrupt CIA buddies had struck a secret deal with Karl Lazar to steal the fifty million between them, and frame your father for the theft. They meant to kill him, get rid of his body, and make it look like he'd disappeared, so that the blame would fall solely on Paul March.'

'But why?'

'Greed, pure and simple. Had the plan worked it could have made them a fortune. Karl Lazar would force your father at gunpoint to cross over the Wasenhorn with him, where he planned to murder him along with the Vogels, dump their bodies into a crevasse, then later share the stash with Kelso and his people. But then the storm blew up and the whole thing went haywire. The rest you know.'

'Why . . . why didn't you tell me before now? Why did you put me through all this?'

347

'I was under CIA orders. The less you knew the better, at least until we found the disk and nailed Kelso. The CIA sanctioned his present operation but we've had our suspicions that Kelso was crooked. Except we couldn't make Kelso's team aware of that, in case he got to hear of it. And to tell the truth, some of it we only figured out in the last couple of days.'

'*We?*'

'The guy who helped us escape from the airport is one of my team. They've got orders to stay in the background until we need them, but they're only a phone call away.'

Jennifer's mind was in turmoil. There were so many unanswered questions. 'Who killed my mother?'

'Kelso. He meant the attack on your family to appear as if it was all part of some game plan that your father had concocted before he vanished, to make him look even more guilty.'

'What . . . what happened to my father?'

'He probably died the night of the storm and his body's still somewhere up on the mountain, and that's being realistic, Jennifer.'

'But *someone* survived . . .'

'We don't know that for certain. The guy who turned up at the monastery could have been anyone.'

'It was my father. It *had* to be.'

'You're torturing yourself, Jennifer. He couldn't have survived. Not in a blizzard like that.'

A surge of grief overwhelmed her, so intense that she couldn't focus on the road. She pulled in and laid her head on the steering wheel. Sobbing racked her body. Staves put a hand gently on her shoulder. 'I'm sorry. I can imagine how you must feel . . .'

'No, you can't. You've no idea . . .'

'You do believe me, Jennifer, don't you?'

She wiped her eyes. 'Right this minute, I don't know what to believe.'

'That's understandable. There's a lot coming at you all at once.' Staves took away his hand, reached into his pocket and removed an ID wallet. He opened the flap and Jennifer saw the CIA logo on one side, and an embossed photograph on the other. It was of the man seated next to her. The ID said his name was Nicolas Staves and the document looked authentic.

'I just wanted you to believe me. You've heard enough lies from Kelso.'

Jennifer was shaking as she handed back the ID. 'I'd like to believe you.'

'How about you let me drive from here on? You're in no fit state. And then I'll explain what Mark Ryan and Kelso have been up to during all this.'

'*Mark?* Been up to? What are you talking about?'

'Let me tell you what I know.'

74

The limo was heading towards Manhattan. It had started to rain, a torrent of icy water hammering on the roof.

Kelso said, 'Who *exactly* did you call, Ryan?'

'That isn't significant, not when Jennifer's gone missing with someone who may want to kill her . . .'

Kelso persisted. 'I want the *name* of the person you called.'

'You'll get it when this is over. But right now it's enough for you to know that I didn't mention a word about your operation.'

'Seeing that we've now got some semblance of trust, Ryan, are there any other enquiries you made that I should know about?'

'No.'

'You're sure?'

'Certain. Now how about telling me what we're going to do to find Jennifer?'

'We'll come to that.'

'And there's something else bothering me that maybe you could clear up.'

'What's that?

'You never explained how the Moscayas found out about the disk.'

'That's right, I never did.' Kelso smiled thinly, then turned round in his seat. 'Pull in, Fellows.'

Fellows did so. Rain beat against the limo's roof as Kelso took out a pistol, screwed on a silencer and levelled the weapon at Mark. 'I sure hope you're telling me the truth.'

Mark paled. 'What the hell are you doing?'

Even Grimes looked uneasy, and said to Kelso, 'I could ask the same thing, sir.'

'I'm afraid this is where things take an unpleasant turn.'

Mark was stunned as Kelso suddenly swivelled the Glock. It coughed once. The bullet hit Grimes in the chest, killing him instantly, sending him sprawling across the seat.

'What in the name of *Jes* . . .' Fellows said as he turned in his seat, confusion on his face. Kelso fired again, hitting him in the head, and his body jerked and collapsed against the steering wheel.

Mark was in shock, not understanding any of it. Instinct made him try to defend himself and he attempted to lunge at Kelso, but the Glock was suddenly pointed at his chest again. 'Don't be a dumb asshole.'

'Are you insane, Kelso?'

'You're starting to bug me, Ryan, so just do as you're told.' Kelso slid across the seat and felt Grimes' wrist, then rolled his body on to the floor and stepped out of the car. 'Get out. Put Fellows' body in the back and lie him on the floor.'

Mark did as he was told, while Kelso kept him covered with the gun. He dragged Fellows' bloodied corpse from the driver's seat and slid him into the back of the limo, rolling him on to the floor to join Grimes.

'Now get in the front seat and drive,' Kelso ordered, slamming the rear door.

Mark was drenched as he slid into the driver's seat. Kelso kept the Glock pointed at him, jumped into the passenger side and pulled the door shut.

'What the hell's going on? Why did you kill the others and not me?'

'Because from now on you're a hostage to fortune.'

'Whose?'

'Mine.'

75

Staves turned on to the highway for Long Beach. Jennifer peered beyond the rain-lashed windscreen. The storm was getting worse. For the last three miles her mind had been reeling as the pieces of the puzzle started to fall into place. Staves said, 'You were right about seeing Mark in Turin. He'd been tailing you on Kelso's orders.'

Jennifer was still in shock, and upset that Mark would betray her by going behind her back and following her. But it made her realise how deeply he must have cared about her, and that realisation caused her to question her own feelings. If she were honest with herself, didn't she feel deeply for him in return? But where did her feelings for Nick Staves figure in all this? Right now she couldn't answer that question, but her attraction to him was still there, despite her shock. 'How did you know all this?'

'We bugged Mark's home. He and Kelso have been following you since you landed in Switzerland.'

'*Why?*'

'Kelso needed someone close to you in case you discovered any evidence of his involvement. And I bet I know how he intended to use Mark.'

'How?'

'Right after you went to identify the body he probably intended to have Mark make his presence known to you, by telling you he'd followed you to Europe out of concern. After that he would have stuck with you, which would have kept Kelso on the inside track, but then I entered the picture and messed up his plans. Mark thinks Kelso's out to protect you.'

'What does Kelso want?'

'At first, he just wanted to protect his own ass and find out what happened to his share of the money, but now he knows the disk exists he'll want it. He probably intends to sell it to the Moscayas, and make up for the loss of his share of the fifty million. We also think he had Chuck McCaul murdered.'

'For what reason?'

'Kelso was on uncertain ground once the body was discovered on the glacier, and he was desperate to know if any evidence was found that might reveal his complicity. We believe he or one of his people met with Chuck McCaul to try to find out what evidence he'd found in the rucksack. Then he was murdered, probably to cover his tracks.'

Jennifer felt in a trance, and was fraught with worry. She looked back at Nick Staves. *What if everything he's told me is lies? What if I'm in danger from him?* She wanted to believe everything he had said, wanted to trust him and feel safe with him again, but she could not be certain.

'What's wrong, Jennifer?'

'N . . . nothing.'

'You said you didn't know where your father hid the box. But you've *got* to think again, and think very, very hard, Jennifer. If there's a chance it might still be somewhere in the house, or if your father left some clue as to where else he might have hidden it, we have to find it before Kelso does. You understand that, don't you?'

'Y . . . yes.'

'He'll want the disk badly. And make no mistake, he'll have hired help, most likely professionals, the best money can buy.'

'What . . . what about your men?'

'I'll give them a call. They'll be right behind us all the way.' Staves took out his cell phone and punched several buttons, then listened and frowned with concern.

Jennifer said, 'What is it?'

'The service is down. Don't worry, I'll try again in a minute.'

'I am worried. If I'm to believe what you've told me about Kelso, he's capable of anything. Even blocking your calls.'

'I doubt that's the case,' Staves reassured her. 'It's probably just a technical glitch because of the storm. Listen to me, Jennifer, we'll have this thing over and done with before you know it. Then we can settle our score with Kelso. But right now it's imperative we find out where your father hid the box. Don't you think it might be worth searching your parents' house? I'm sure you know places where it could be hidden.'

'I . . . I guess so.'

As he drove, Staves reached across and gently touched her hand. 'Will you help me?'

'Yes . . .'

The rain was pelting down as they turned in towards Cove End. The house was in darkness and the gate unlocked. Staves drove the Chevy inside and parked on the gravel. They had arrived.

76

Five miles from Long Beach, the limo was touching eighty as it sped along the highway. Rain lashed the windscreen and the tension was unbearable as Mark tried to keep his eyes on the wet road.

Kelso said, 'Take the next turn for Long Beach and head for Cove End.'

'Why there?'

'You ask a lot of questions, Ryan.'

'Is that where Jennifer is, at her parents' house? This all has to do with the disk, hasn't it?'

Kelso gave a tiny smirk. 'What are you looking for, Ryan, help in joining the dots? Just take the next exit.'

'I want some answers here, Kelso. You were behind Paul March's death, weren't you? You set him up in some way.'

Kelso's smirk became a grin. 'I guess it's all falling into place.'

'You made it look like March stole the fifty million but *you* took it.'

'Close. It was me *and* Lazar. We did a deal, except the fifty million vanished on the Wasenhorn when he and March perished. For all I know it's probably so far down a fucking crevasse it'll never be found. Just like the bodies of March and Lazar.'

'That wasn't the way it was supposed to pan out, was it?'

Kelso shook his head. 'Not completely. Lazar was meant to walk away with the fifty million, I'd get half, and March would wind up dead, along with the Vogels, their bodies pushed down some bottomless crevasse.'

'Didn't you search for the fifty million afterwards?'

Kelso's mouth tightened. 'That was the weak part of the plan.

Lazar never told me where exactly he intended to cross the border. I left that decision entirely up to him, which was my big mistake. Until March's body turned up, I had no idea where to look, or what the hell had happened to Lazar.'

Mark said, 'The explosion at the morgue, Caruso's murder, the killings at the monastery . . . That was all your doing. You pretended someone else was responsible but you were just making sure that no evidence of your involvement in Paul March's death ever showed up.'

'You're brighter than I thought.'

'You even spun a tale to make it look as if it might be the Red Mafia, or even Lazar or March, that they might have survived and were attempting to hamper the investigation. But it was all part of your act, Kelso. You were trying to deflect any suspicion, and making sure your CIA superiors had no inkling of what you were up to.'

'I'm impressed. You're good, Ryan. Maybe even Langley material.'

'Why do it? Was it just to cover your tracks?'

'Have you got any idea what the disk is worth? We're talking at least another fifty million. The Moscaya clan will have no problem paying that much to keep themselves out of prison.'

'Don't tell me – and then you vanish, permanently?'

Kelso nodded. 'No one's ever going to find me, not even Langley.'

'I wouldn't take a bet on that.'

'Believe me, Ryan, after almost thirty years with the CIA I know exactly how to cover my tracks.'

'Why are you doing this, Kelso?'

'If you're fishing for motive, I could give you lots. Disaffection. Envy. Greed. Try those for starters. You get so tired of seeing assholes like the Moscayas pocket millions while the rest of us play at being good guys and put our lives on the line but don't turn a nickel's profit. And at the end of it, all you've got to look forward to is a lousy gold watch and a shitty pension plan. You get to thinking that maybe it's time you put to good use all those nasty dirty tricks that the CIA taught you. That answer it for you?'

'So where's the disk?'

Kelso grinned again. 'I've got a feeling Jennifer may be able to help me answer that question, once I use a little leverage to jog her memory.'

'What kind of leverage?'

'You're about to find out.'

77

Leroy Brown had never seen the two white guys before, but the ID badges they showed him said they were NYPD detectives. One of them was blond and had a bruised jaw. As Leroy led him and his buddy down a corridor in the Cauldwell he said, 'So how come you need to see Bobby?'

The blond had a look of concern on his face as he walked beside Leroy. 'His sister Jenny's been hurt in a car smash on the freeway. The good news is she'll live, the bad news is she's cut up pretty bad.'

'*What?* When did this happen?'

'Late this afternoon. She just got in off a flight and the cab she was travelling in was involved in an accident.'

'*Jeez*, that's lousy news. Jenny's the only family that Bobby's got. Hey, it's going to upset him to hear the news, don't you think?'

'Sorry, we're only doing our job. And the kid will have to come with us. Jenny's asking to see him.'

'Hey, I don't know about that, Officer. Bobby's had a lot of upset recently, and I ain't got no authority to hand him over to your custody.' Leroy halted outside a windowed door.

The men looked in and saw Bobby sitting in a wheelchair by the window, doodling on some paper. 'That him?'

'Yeah, that's Bobby. But like I said, I ain't got the authority to let you take him . . .'

'I got all the authority you want right here.' The blond pulled out a pistol and struck Leroy a blow across the temple. The big nurse was dazed, but he was powerfully built and he wasn't going down easily, not until his companion stepped in and slammed a cosh hard across the top of his skull and he passed out.

The two men dragged his unconscious body across the floor. One of them opened a janitor's closet and they dumped him inside and locked the door. 'Let's go get the kid.'

Lou Garuda was pissed off, big time. He'd gone back to his apartment late that afternoon to find Angelina waiting for him, lying on the bed, a devilish smile on her face, her naked body splayed on the sheets, ready to offer him the comfort she figured he needed. 'I've been waiting for you all afternoon. Get over here, Lou.'

He'd been irritated by Ryan, the man not helping him at all, getting him angry, so he joined Angelina in the bed and fooled around for a while. Except his heart wasn't in it and halfway through the act he sighed, slid off Angelina's thighs, and lit a cigarette.

'The fuck's wrong, Lou?'

Garuda drew angrily on his cigarette. 'Everything's fucking wrong. The case I told you about, the body in the ice.'

'What about it?'

'Something's weird, Angelina. Something is *very* weird and I can't make out what the *fuck's* going on.'

Angelina saw that faraway look in his eyes which meant he was preoccupied. There were beads of sweat on his forehead. 'Jesus, Lou, you're stressed out. Can't you forget about work for five minutes, for Christ sakes? I'm just here for the sex, remember? And I'm not getting much of that any more.'

'I know, honey. But this is cracking my skull.'

Angelina ran a hand across his back, then skilfully slid her fingers round to grip him and giggled. 'Why don't you come back down here and I'll do that thing you like with my tongue. The thing you said makes your eyeballs roll. Maybe that'll help make you forget?'

But Garuda was already stubbing out his cigarette, dragging on his clothes, making a beeline for the door. 'Honey, I've got to go. Call you later, OK.'

'Going *where*?'

'Love you, babe.'

'*Lou . . . !*'

The noise sounded like someone was having sex – lots of groaning going on – but Garuda didn't really know whether the groaning sounds conveyed pleasure or pain. The way it started, he'd climbed into his car and just driven, trying to clear his mind, trying to figure out what the fuck was going on and what he might do next, when he decided to drive over to the Cauldwell, for three reasons.

One, to make sure the kid was OK; two, in case Mark Ryan had decided to call by and see Bobby – if he did, Garuda wanted to continue the conversation with him, face to face – and three, to tell the truth, he really wanted to talk to Bobby again. He didn't know why exactly, and it was probably dumb to ask the kid whether he'd ever heard his old man discuss the Red Mafia or anything about the offshore owners of Prime, but he figured it was worth the long shot because he had fuck all else to go on.

But he sure didn't expect what happened next.

As he walked down the hall towards Bobby's room he heard someone moaning. The sounds came from a janitor's closet. *The fuck's going on?* Maybe a couple of the staff were having a little horizontal exercise during their break? Or one of the patients had locked themselves in and was hurt or scared? Whichever it was, the moaning intensified as Garuda paused outside the closet; now it sounded as if someone was in some *serious* pain.

'Hey, who's in there?' Garuda called out.

In reply, he heard some more moaning, deep and masculine. Garuda grabbed the handle but the door was locked, and then he saw a key lying on the floor, across the hall. He picked it up, inserted it in the lock, opened the closet and saw Leroy slumped in the tiny space, blood streaming from a deep gash in his skull, the whites of his eyes looking like a couple of golf balls in the dark recess of the closet. 'The *fuck* happened to you?'

Leroy groaned, holding his head and sounding as if he'd been crushed by a brick wall. 'Cops . . . hit me.'

'*What?*'

'*Jesus*, man, feels like an elephant stomped on my head. Get me a doctor.'

It took Garuda a couple more seconds to get the gist of Leroy's story, a couple of valuable seconds lost, and then he said, 'Shit,' and raced back down the hall. He was running past an open fire exit that led out to the gardens when, a hundred yards across the parking lot, he saw two guys bundling Bobby into the back of a dark blue Buick and then drive off.

Shit.

Garuda wasn't carrying his service weapon – he'd left the damned thing in his car, along with his cell phone – so all he could do was watch the Buick speed down the driveway and disappear through the exit gates, leaving behind a plume of grey exhaust fumes. He didn't even have time to see the damned licence number.

But one thing was for sure, he needed to get in touch with Mark, pronto. Sweating, he ran towards his car.

78

Jennifer stepped out of the Chevy into the teeming rain. Nick Staves shone the torch as he led the way. They were both drenched when they reached the veranda. 'You'd better give me the key.'

Jennifer fumbled in her tote bag, handed him the key, and Staves unlocked the front door. The alarm sounded as they stepped into the hallway, and Jennifer went to turn on the lights. 'No, it might be better to leave them off for now.' Staves wiped rain from his face. 'Go silence the alarm, Jennifer.'

As he directed the torch, Jennifer punched in the security number on the alarm keypad, and the buzzer died. 'What about your men?'

Staves tried his cell phone again and frowned.

'What's wrong?'

'The service is still down. I don't understand it.'

'Can't you contact them any other way?'

'Does the house still have a phone line?'

'No, it's been disconnected.'

Staves' jaw tightened with concern. 'Don't worry, my men aren't far away, and I told them to meet us here. But I'll keep trying.'

A burst of lightning lit up the windows and bathed the hallway in electric blue light. In the desolate silence that followed, Jennifer froze, couldn't take another step. The house was suddenly a forbidding place in the raging storm, and it brought back a flood of anguished memories. She thought: *I don't know if I can do this.*

Staves seemed to sense her fear and reached out to touch her arm. 'There's nothing to be scared of, Jennifer. Where do you think we should search?'

'Maybe the study first, then the attic and basement. If need be, we'll look in the boathouse last.'

The study was in darkness as Jennifer stepped inside. The bay was being lashed by a screaming wind, and the French windows were lit up by violent flashes of lightning. She fumbled to find the light switch and flicked it on.

'You take the desk and I'll try the shelves,' Staves told her.

The room was almost as Jennifer remembered, with her father's apple-wood desk and his leather chair, but his books, his personal belongings, his photographs were no longer there. *Ghosts. There are ghosts everywhere in this house.* She forced herself to rifle the drawers while Staves went to work on the empty shelves, searching for a hidden recess, but after ten minutes he gave up. 'It's no good. We'll try the other rooms. But we'd better move quickly. When we disappeared at the airport, Kelso probably reckoned this would be one of the places we might head.'

'What do you mean?'

'For all I know, he might have figured out what we're up to and he's already on his way over here.'

They searched the attic and then the basement, but when they found nothing they wasted no more time and moved into the kitchen. Staves unlocked the back door and a powerful gale swept into the room, almost knocking them off their feet. A split second later the lights went out and the kitchen was plunged into darkness.

Staves flicked on the torch. 'The storm must have knocked out the power lines.'

Jennifer saw that the gardens were deluged, trees waving angrily, the night sky crackling with lightning, ferocious waves pounding the boathouse dock. 'We could both be killed if we go out there.'

'You'd better stay beside me and don't let go of my hand. I don't want you being swept out to sea. Ready?'

'I think so.'

Staves pulled up his coat collar and ushered Jennifer out into the storm.

'Pull in here,' said Kelso.

Mark pulled into the kerb, two hundred yards from Cove End. Across the street he saw his parents' house, the lights extinguished. Not that he'd get very far if he tried to escape; Kelso still had the pistol aimed at him. 'Leave the engine running but turn off the headlights. Hurry it up, Ryan, or I'm liable to get impatient and put a bullet into that skull of yours.'

Mark obeyed, and Kelso said, 'Now drive forward, very slowly.'

Mark did as he was told, keeping his speed to a crawl, and when he was within fifty yards of Cove End Kelso said, 'Stop right here and kill the engine.'

Mark halted and turned off the ignition. A moment's silence followed, and then he heard the roar of the storm as a violent gust of wind shook the car.

Kelso studied Cove End. The house was bathed in darkness. He checked his watch. 'We're early.'

'What's that supposed to mean?'

'We wait.'

'For what?'

'A phone call to tell us it's time to make our grand entrance.'

'I don't get it.'

'You will, Ryan.'

79

The boardwalk was in darkness. Waves lashed the dock, and Jennifer was drenched as Staves forced open the boathouse door. He shone the torch over the motorboat and the shelves of engine parts and rusting tools. 'Get in the boat, Jennifer. Search every nook and cranny.'

Jennifer stepped into the boat and began to search the tiny cabin and wheelhouse, while Staves played the torchlight into the engine compartments and felt around with his hands. When he found nothing, he went to search the shelves, tearing down tools and motor parts. There was a dangerous look in his eyes that frightened Jennifer. When he'd emptied the shelves he suddenly kicked out savagely at the boat. 'Where the fuck is the box? *Think, Jennifer!* Where could it be? *Where?*'

She moved out of the boat and without warning Staves turned on her and grabbed her by the hair, twisting it viciously, before he struck her a stinging blow across the face, sending her staggering against the wall. 'I asked you a fucking question.'

Jennifer was too stunned by the outburst to reply. She trembled as she straightened herself up. Something was terribly wrong, she realised that now. Her jaw was on fire and she was so shocked she couldn't speak, but Staves was in a frenzy now, rage in his voice as he came to stand next to her. 'You're holding back on me. The box has got to be *somewhere* in the house. *Now where the fuck is it?*'

'I . . . I told you, I don't know.'

Some instinct made Jennifer rush for the door, but Staves came after her and grabbed her by the wrist. 'Where the fuck do you think you're going?'

There was a crazed look on his face, and at that moment Jennifer had no doubt he was capable of anything. 'You're . . . you're hurting me. Please . . .'

He dragged her from the boathouse and out across the flooded lawn towards the kitchen, ignoring her protest. 'Keep your fucking mouth shut.'

When they reached the kitchen door, Staves wiped rainwater from his face, took out his cell phone and punched in a number. 'It's me. I want him in here *now*. This fucking minute. Bring him round to the back of the house.'

He finished the call and seconds later Jennifer saw headlights sweep into the driveway. A car braked to a halt and an over-weight man with a black moustache struggled out. Jennifer recognised him as the man named Marty from the airport. His companion climbed out of the rear and she got another shock; it was the blond assailant from Vogel's farm. They bundled someone out of the back of the car but in the downpour Jennifer couldn't see the person's face. The men hauled their captive towards the house, his head slumped, his legs dragging on the gravel. Suddenly Jennifer recognised who it was . . .

'*Bobby . . . !* '

She started to move towards her brother but Staves grabbed her savagely by the hair. 'Get him inside,' he ordered the men, and held on to Jennifer as he made another call, shouting into his cell phone, 'I gave it one last shot and it didn't fucking work, Kelso. *Nothing's worked.* The bitch doesn't know where the box is. What do you want me to do now? OK, but I don't want this dragging on all fucking night.'

He finished his call and stared into Jennifer's face. 'I think it's time we all had a little talk, don't you?'

80

Mark was sitting at the wheel of the limo as Kelso's phone rang. He listened for a moment, his mouth twisted with frustration, and then said angrily to the caller, 'Wait there, I'm coming in. I've got Ryan with me.'

His features were tight with anger as he ended the call. He pointed his gun at Mark. 'Get out of the car.'

'Why?'

Kelso gestured with the gun, indicating the pathway up to Cove End. 'Don't ask questions. Just walk towards the back of the house.'

'It's OK, Bobby, I'm here. It's OK. Are you hurt? Tell me if you're hurt.'

The two men had dragged Bobby into the kitchen and sat him next to Jennifer at the table. His eyes were swollen from crying and there was an angry bruise on his left cheek.

As Jennifer clutched him, his body was racked by a sudden fit of sobbing, and she felt a powerful urge to protect him. 'Nod if you're OK. Do it for me, Bobby, please. I need to know if you're hurt or if you're OK.'

She couldn't tell whether he was upset out of fear or pain or both. He looked like a confused child, but as she dabbed his eyes with her sleeve he finally gave an uncertain nod. 'You're sure you're all right?'

Bobby nodded again, but with a puzzled look, and she realised that he didn't have a clue what was going on.

'Your kid brother's doing fine, aren't you, Bobby?'

'You bastard! He's been hurt . . .'

'Big fucking deal.' Staves' face twisted in a sneer and he jerked a thumb at his two accomplices. 'Kelso's on his way, and he's got company. One of you get out front and stay in the car and keep watch. The other had better stay in the back yard. Don't leave your posts unless you're told.'

Jennifer tried to comfort Bobby as the men went out. Moments later their car started up and reversed down the driveway. Staves searched the kitchen drawers, as if looking for something, but when he found that the drawers were empty he pulled up a chair, spun it round and sat. He was calm again, but Jennifer was afraid he might resort to violence at any second.

'Who are you? Why are you doing this to me?' she asked. A second later she heard footsteps outside the door.

Staves grinned. 'Relax, you're about to get the answer to everything.'

81

Jennifer heard more footsteps and then the kitchen door opened again and Mark stepped in, followed by Kelso, who held a gun to his back. Mark had a look of grim determination on his face as their eyes locked. He came towards her, but Kelso prodded him with the gun. 'Sit at the table.'

He pushed Mark into a seat, then slammed the door and said to Jennifer, 'I see you've met my partner in crime. Nick's quite an actor, I think you'll agree. He's always been one of the Agency's best when it comes to deception.'

Staves smirked. 'So, what did you think of the performance? I figure I made only one big mistake. I misjudged how slowly your brake fluid would leak away when I loosened your jeep's hosepipe. I had it all figured out that you'd have brake problems soon after you left the hotel and would have to stop, and I'd play the white knight and come to the rescue. Then I'd get you to trust me straight away with that bullshit story about someone trying to kill you. But you sure got me worried when I had to follow you up the mountain, and ended up having to crash into you to save your neck. Except I guess it all worked out in the end.'

Mark said to Jennifer, 'The bombing of the morgue, the deaths of Caruso and his wife, the monastery killings – it was all their handwork, a set-up. They wanted to make sure that no evidence was found of their involvement in your father's death.' Then he turned to Kelso. 'Your motive's nothing more than greed. What about him? I assume he's not McCaul?'

'You're right. His name's Staves and he's CIA. And if you want his motive, let's just say he liked my pension plan better than Uncle Sam's.' Kelso grinned, and turned to Jennifer. 'Your friend's good, I'll give him that. He's got it all about right.'

'What about the other men, including the two who abducted Bobby, who are they?' Jennifer asked.

'Guns for hire, nothing more. One of the fringe benefits of working for the CIA is that you get to know the best. Professionals who'll do whatever's asked of them, so long as you pay them handsomely. Unfortunately for the one you killed on the train, he was only meant to frighten you, but he probably played his role a little too earnestly. He should have been more careful.'

Mark looked at Kelso angrily. '*Why?* Why pretend to hunt Jennifer down and at the same time have Staves act like he's protecting her?'

'An old Agency tactic. If you put someone in danger, and then make it look like you've helped them out of that danger, then bingo, you find they'll entrust you with their life, maybe even enough to tell you all their secrets.' Kelso smiled, pulled up a chair and sat down. 'That was the plan. Once she trusted Staves, Jennifer would see him as her protector and confidant while she was under threat. The deception even got us a bonus when we got a lead to Vogel. And best of all, we found out what happened to Lazar and March, and about the security box. To tell you the truth, it was a terrific plan, if I say so myself.'

'And where did I fit into your plan?' Mark asked.

Kelso's smile became a grin. 'You were our back-up, our insurance in case Jennifer didn't take to Staves. In fact, our original idea was that you'd travel with her and get close to her, maybe screw her, and then perhaps, if we had to, we'd kill you in front of her just to make a point, so she'd be putty in our hands, and terrified enough to tell us anything we wanted to know. But when Jennifer didn't want you to come with her, we moved to plan B, which meant that once you were in Europe you became our insurance. She even thought she was being tailed by your Opel, so you started to frighten her as well. Like I said, it was all a neat plan.'

Jennifer stared vehemently at Kelso as all the pieces fell into place. 'What happened to Frank McCaul?'

'Oh, he's dead, I'm afraid. Like young mountain-climbing Chuck, whose death played no small part in helping our deception.'

'You're a heartless, evil bastard, Kelso.'

'Who may be about to become very rich.'

'You killed my mother. You shot Bobby.'

Kelso glanced at Nick Staves, and raised an eyebrow. 'You told her?'

Staves nodded. 'Even the part about us and Lazar setting up her old man.'

'Unfortunately, it's all true,' Kelso said calmly to Jennifer. 'There was nothing personal, it was just business, something that had to be done.'

At that moment Jennifer wanted to kill Kelso. In a fit of anger she lunged at him, but he caught her wrist, twisted it behind her back. Mark jumped to his feet and made a grab at Kelso but Staves was quicker and in an instant he had his gun pointed at Mark's head. 'Wouldn't do that if I were you.'

Wide eyed with fear, Bobby began to cry.

Kelso said to Jennifer, 'Not the cleverest thing to do. See, you've gone and upset your brother. Now stay seated until I tell you otherwise.' He shoved her into her chair, and she turned and held on to Bobby. 'Give me the key,' Kelso ordered.

Jennifer opened her bag and handed over the silver key. Kelso stared at it, tossed it in his palm, then slapped it on the table in front of him. 'Hard to believe that a little thing like this could cause so much trouble.'

Jennifer said defiantly, 'What do you want from me? I don't know where the box is.'

Kelso smiled as he removed his pistol from his pocket, produced a black metal silencer and screwed it on to the barrel. 'If that's the case, then I'm afraid we've nothing more to say to each other.'

82

Kelso pointed the silenced pistol at Jennifer's head. 'Of course, I had thought maybe you were holding out on me. But every trick we've used to try to loosen your tongue hasn't worked, so I figure you must be telling me the truth.'

Kelso smiled thinly, then carefully laid the pistol down on the kitchen counter and sat back. 'However, I still think the box may be somewhere on this property. You know why I think that? Two years ago I had every bank in New York State surveyed to see if your parents had a safety deposit box in any of them. They didn't. Now, what does that tell you? Either your father got rid of the box, or else he hid it. If it was me, and I had something that valuable, I know I'd hide it somewhere it's going to be real safe, and probably somewhere close by. What do you think, Jennifer? You agree?'

'I already told you I don't know where—'

Kelso slammed a fist down hard on the table and Jennifer fell silent. 'Sure, you told me. But remember what Staves said about racking your brains? Well, you'd better start racking again, because after this little talk, if you don't come up with some ideas, *fast*, I'll kill Ryan. Then I'll kill Bobby. Pop him one in the head. Then I'll kill you. Three pops and it's all over. But you help me find the box, who knows? Maybe you, Bobby and Ryan here will live to see another day. Clear?'

'That's a lie. You'll kill us all anyway.'

Kelso gave a tight, humourless smile and picked up his pistol. 'Then the choice will be between a protracted, painful death and a very quick one. It's your call. I'm sure you don't want Bobby to suffer.'

Bobby gave a cry of alarm and Jennifer pulled him close in an attempt to calm him. She felt helpless, sick with fear, and she knew that her brother was on the verge of breaking down. Kelso's cobalt-blue eyes had a callous look in them, and she knew he meant what he said, she hadn't the slightest doubt about that.

'Have I made myself clear?'

'Yes.'

Kelso got to his feet. 'Good. See, there's one important thing that occurred to me and that everyone's forgetting in all of this. Something that everyone's overlooked up to now. Go ahead and ask me what it is.'

'What is it?' said Jennifer.

Kelso grinned, then deliberately pointed his pistol at Bobby's head. 'No one's ever asked your brother here if he knows what happened to the box. What do you think? You think Bobby might know something?'

Bobby squirmed from Kelso's aim, retreating into Jennifer's arms. 'Please, don't harm him . . .' she begged.

Kelso pursed his lips in thought. 'Tell you what I'm going to do. I want you all to put your heads together, have a good think about it, and try and come up with some answers. Though I reckon Bobby here might respond more favourably if he didn't feel threatened, so Nick and I will leave you all alone to have your chinwag. That sound like a good idea?'

'Y . . . yes.'

'Glad we agree. Oh, and there's one loose end that I almost forgot. I'm talking to you, Ryan. Who'd you call from the airport?'

Mark didn't reply, and Kelso said, 'You really want me to hurt the kid, just to prove that I mean business? You decide.'

Mark said reluctantly, 'A cop named Lou Garuda.'

'Why?'

'He worked on the Paul March case two years ago with the Long Beach Police Department.'

'And what does this Garuda know about what's happening now?'

'Very little.'

'We'll see about that, but all in good time.' Kelso let the gun fall to his side and turned to Staves. 'Where's her cell phone?'

'Lost.'

'Is the house phone working?'

'No.'

'Any kitchen knives in the drawers?'

'No, I checked. The drawers are empty.'

'Good.' Kelso nodded to Staves, who lit a cigarette before he opened the kitchen door. A gust of wind raged into the room, and Staves went out. They saw him through the window, his collar pulled up as he paced up and down in the storm, dragging fiercely on his cigarette as he glanced at them through the glass.

Kelso walked over to the internal door, but as he opened it he looked back at them with a threatening stare. 'Nick's going to keep an eye on you from the garden. Me, I'll be out in the hall. A few words of warning. It's obvious we have the front and back of the house covered, so there's no way out of here. You're to stay put at the table and not to move. Try to run and escape, or call for help, put up a fight, scream or shout, and you're dead. Do I make myself completely clear?' Kelso checked his watch. 'You've got ten minutes to come up with answers, and not a second more. After that, if I haven't got the box, I kill each and every fucking one of you, starting with Bobby.'

83

The only sound was the wind raging beyond the kitchen door. Jennifer saw the trees in the garden being tossed about fiercely – the storm was showing no sign of abating. Kelso had stepped out of the room, slamming the door, and she saw Nick Staves looking frozen as he paced about the garden beyond the kitchen window. Every few seconds he glanced in through the glass at them before he continued his guard duty, keeping the blond assailant company.

Mark said, 'I'm sorry, Jennifer, I thought I was helping.'

He started to speak again, but Jennifer put a finger to his lips. 'Don't say any more about it, Mark.'

'But I should have been more wary of Kelso—'

'Let's not talk about it. Please. It's not important right now.'

Mark studied the kitchen. 'Was Staves right about the knives in the drawers? Is there nothing here I can use as a weapon?'

'No. I had all the kitchen utensils thrown out a couple of months after—' She was about to say *after Kelso murdered my mother*, but she faltered, bit back her anger. Her rage was white hot, her hatred of Kelso so intense that she felt physically sick. '. . . after Mom died.'

Mark noticed a small red domestic fire extinguisher hanging on the wall, then pointed to a door off to its right. 'Where does the door lead?'

'To a pantry. It's not an exit. Just a cupboard.'

He said, 'The extinguisher's too cumbersome to hide. I need something smaller. Something sharp I can use to stab with.'

'There's nothing I can think of.' Jennifer felt Bobby grip her hand. He looked so lost and confused, so utterly helpless. She knew that he was on the verge of tears again, and if she were being honest, so was she. And as she looked into Bobby's face, she thought: *What kind of man could shoot a child? What kind of man could turn a beautiful, normal young boy into a cripple, shoot him in the back, and without a shred of remorse? What kind of man could destroy an entire family because of greed?* If someone had put a gun in her hand at that moment, she would have killed both Kelso and Staves, and without a second thought.

Her eyes were wet as Mark touched her shoulder. 'Jenny.'

She was barely listening, was so caught up in her hatred of Kelso that she barely heard what Mark said next. 'Jenny, Bobby's trying to tell you something.'

She came out of her reverie, and saw Bobby's hands signing to her. She'd been so caught up in her anguish that she'd just been staring at him blankly, hadn't even noticed his hands moving. She frowned at her brother. 'I don't understand. Say it again.'

Bobby repeated his message and this time Jennifer deciphered the meaning.

'What's he saying?' Mark asked impatiently.

'That he's a little scared.'

'Only a little?'

Bobby made another sign. Jennifer said, 'No, a lot.'

'Join the club,' Mark said, and put a hand on Bobby's shoulder.

Bobby's eyes were red from crying. Jennifer said to him, 'I know now what happened to Dad and the reason why Mom was killed. I want you to know, I want to tell you everything, Bobby, but right now it would take too long to explain and we don't have the time. But you know that the men you saw here are bad, you realise that, don't you, Bobby?'

Bobby nodded. He made a sign with his hands. *Did they kill Mom and Dad?* Jennifer inwardly recoiled from the question, but she knew she had to answer. 'Yes.'

Bobby's hands went limp.

Jennifer said, 'Did you understand what the men said? That they mean to kill us if we don't tell them where the box is?'

Bobby nodded again. Jennifer found it difficult to control her own emotions as she wiped his eyes. 'Do you know the box I'm talking about, Bobby? It's a security box that belonged to Dad.'

Bobby frowned. Instinct told Jennifer that her brother didn't know what the hell she was talking about. He had probably never even seen the box. In response, he signed some more, his hands working slowly, deliberately. Jennifer frowned and looked towards the refrigerator.

'What is it?' Mark asked. 'What's he saying?'

'He says he thinks there's a kitchen knife wedged under the freezer.'

'How the hell does he know that?'

'He says it got lodged there years ago, and Mom couldn't remove it. He thinks it may still be there.'

Mark shot a glance at the refrigerator, then at the window. Staves was still on the move. For a second he glanced in and their eyes met before he continued on his patrol, smoking his cigarette.

'A knife's good, but a gun would be better. Did your mom or dad keep a gun?' Mark was sweating now, his mind feverish at the prospect of getting his hands on some kind of weapon.

'No,' Jennifer answered. 'Both of them hated guns.'

'If only we could get across the street there's a good chance there's a thirty-eight revolver in my folks' house. My old man always kept one in a writing bureau near his bed. Unless one of my family moved the gun, it ought still to be there . . .'

Mark hesitated just as Bobby made another rapid hand sign, and Jennifer paled. 'You're *sure*, Bobby?'

'What the hell's he saying?' Mark asked.

'He says he thinks he knows where the box is.'

84

A thought suddenly struck Garuda as he climbed into his Porsche in the Cauldwell's parking lot, right after the men drove away with Bobby: it was dumb of him to think he could phone Mark. He didn't have a cell phone number for him. Mark hadn't given him one.

Dumb.

So dumb, in fact, that it got Garuda angry, and he put his foot down hard on the 944's accelerator as he exited the Cauldwell, his engine snarling like a wild animal as he skidded out through the gates and on to the main road, turning right and joining the flow of one-way traffic. He sweated as he drove east for half a mile, cursing when there was no sign of the dark blue Buick, doing a hundred on the open strech until – *Hallelujah* – he spotted the Buick with the two guys, the blond in front, driving, his moustachioed companion in the back with Bobby.

There was only one fucking problem. *What do I do next?*

Garuda sweated as he approached the Buick and he reached for his cell phone, but then he saw that the car's licence plate was covered in mud and totally unreadable. He decided not to call for police back-up just yet; he needed to see where these two assholes were headed. Better to wait and see how it panned out – at least he knew what he was dealing with. But one thing was certain: the act of kidnapping a crippled kid in broad daylight had desperation written all over it, which got Garuda thinking: *I'll take a bet it's got something to do with the Red Mafia.*

It had started to rain heavily, storm clouds crackling overhead as he followed the Buick, dropping back a hundred yards, happy in the knowledge that the Porsche could tear the ass out of a four-door sedan any fucking day . . . Happy in the knowledge, that is, until halfway along Reardon Avenue the Buick drove across a junction. Almost immediately the lights turned red. Garuda kicked down hard on the accelerator, but he was too late. The opposing set of lights shifted to green and a delivery truck drove across Garuda's path, cutting off his view.

He slammed his foot to the floor and skidded across the road, braking just in time to avoid being crushed by the truck. The driver blared his horn in protest but Garuda gave him the finger. 'Asshole!'

Then he waited in a lather of sweat until the traffic had passed and the lights turned green again. When they did, he gritted his teeth and swore out loud as he stared at the wet, empty street ahead . . .

Fuck.

He'd lost the Buick.

85

Jennifer waited until Bobby had finished signing and then she looked at him in amazement. 'You're sure about this, Bobby?'

He nodded his reply and Mark said impatiently, 'Where is the box?'

'A week before Dad disappeared, Bobby was asleep in his bedroom when he was woken by a noise. It was just after dawn and he looked out of his window and saw Dad pacing the boardwalk.'

'So?'

'He was carrying a grey metal box.'

'Are you *sure* of that, Bobby?' Mark asked.

Bobby nodded.

'Go on.'

Jennifer said, 'Dad looked as if he didn't know what to do, as if he was trying to decide whether to hide the box or get rid of it.'

Mark frowned. 'What *did* your father do?'

'Bobby says he went into the boathouse and then came out again with a black plastic bag. It was tied up with a length of blue nylon rope and there appeared to be something heavy inside, as if he'd put the box in the bag. Then he climbed down the boardwalk ladder to the water, until Bobby couldn't see him. But when Dad climbed up again a couple of minutes later he didn't have the black bag.'

'Did he throw it in the water?'

'Bobby doesn't know.'

'Are you sure, Bobby?'

Bobby nodded again. Mark was frustrated. 'If your father meant to throw it in the water, why did he have to go down the ladder? Why not just toss it in the sea?'

Jennifer thought about it and shook her head. 'I don't know. Maybe he didn't want anyone to hear the splash. Or maybe he had the motorboat tied up at the bottom of the boardwalk ladder, and he meant to dump the bag out at sea.'

'*Did* he have the boat tied up there?'

'Bobby didn't see. He says it could have been tied up, because Dad often went fishing that early in the morning, but he's not certain because he went back to sleep. Afterwards, he never bothered to ask Dad what he was doing.'

Mark shook his head. 'If the disk was inside the box, I don't buy it that your father would get rid of it. The disk was too important, so it's likely he meant to hide it, but where?'

Jennifer looked towards the window, stuck for an answer. Staves was distracting her: he was pacing like a restless animal. He'd walk away from the window in the direction of the boardwalk for about a dozen paces, then he'd turn back to check on them. Jennifer shifted her gaze towards the turbulent, dark sea, then she turned back to answer Mark. 'About a hundred yards out in the bay there are some plastic marker buoys. They warn fishermen of the danger of jagged rocks near the water's surface.'

'What are you suggesting?'

'If Dad dumped the bag overboard, he could have used one of the buoys as a marker to tell him where it was.'

'I guess it's a possibility.' But Mark didn't look convinced. He watched Staves retreat from the window.

Jennifer said, 'What's wrong?'

Mark whispered, 'We can't just sit here waiting for Kelso to return. We have to do something. Keep an eye on Staves, Jennifer. If he spots me on the move let me know.'

'What are you going to do?'

'See if I can find the knife.'

'Be careful, Mark.'

'Sure.' He waited until Staves was approaching the boardwalk, then knelt and shoved his hand under left-hand side of the refrigerator and felt around.

'Can you feel anything?' Jennifer asked.

'No.'

'Try the other side.'

Mark slid his hand deep into the gap, skinning his flesh as he shifted his hand to the right. 'I can't feel a thing . . .'

'Quick! Staves is turning back!' Jennifer warned.

A second later Mark felt something slim and metallic. He heaved his shoulder against the refrigerator, raising it slightly, and dug his fingertips in as far as he could until he managed to nudge the object out. It wasn't a knife, but a rusted potato peeler.

'Mark . . . for God's sake hurry!'

He crawled back to the table and stuffed the blade in his pocket just as Staves came over to peer in through the glass.

'Look as if we're deep in conversation.' Jennifer caught sight of Staves out of the corner of her eye. He seemed unsure as he stared in at them, but after a couple of seconds he went back to pacing.

Mark let out a sigh. 'Let's hope he didn't see what I was up to.'

Jennifer watched Staves retreat in the direction of the board-walk to join the blond. A thought struck her like a bolt of electricity. 'What if the box is still out on the boardwalk?'

'What do you mean?'

'What if Dad secured it underneath the walkway, or tied it below the waterline? He could have attached the bag to one of the wooden support beams. It's exactly the kind of place you'd never think of looking.'

Mark studied the walkway. Every now and then a wall of water was driven by the squalls of wind to crash over it. 'Assuming the box didn't get washed away in a storm, it sounds like a good hiding place. How much time have we left?'

Jennifer consulted her watch. 'About a minute.'

They heard footsteps behind the internal door. It sounded as if Kelso was about to return. Mark thought frantically, then shot a look at the red fire extinguisher before he whispered, 'The question is, do we tell them about the box? I've got an idea that may buy us some time, but you'll both have to play it exactly as I tell you.'

'What's the idea?'

Mark explained, and Jennifer said, 'But Kelso will kill us if we don't tell him.'

'He's going to kill us if we do.'

86

The door burst open and Kelso entered the room. He had the gun in his hand. Right on cue, Staves entered from the yard. He looked frozen as he slammed the back door against the growling wind.

Kelso said, 'Well, did they behave themselves?'

Staves looked unsure and gestured at Mark with his pistol. 'I may be wrong but I've got a feeling Ryan moved out of his chair.'

Kelso raised an eyebrow. 'What do you say to that, Ryan?'

'I don't know what he's talking about.'

'Search him,' Kelso ordered.

Staves pulled Mark to his feet, then shoved him up against the wall, rummaged through his pockets and did a thorough body search. He found the rusted peeler and held it up for Kelso to see. 'Well, well. Someone's been a naughty boy.'

Kelso's jaw tightened in an expression of fury. 'You thought you were being smart, Ryan, didn't you?'

'Not as it turned out.'

Kelso lashed out with his fist, hitting Mark on the jaw, drawing blood. As he staggered back, Staves kicked him in the stomach. Mark let out a groan as the air went out of him and he collapsed on to the floor.

'Get up.'

Mark struggled to his feet, clutching his stomach, blood streaming from his mouth. Kelso stepped over, aimed the pistol at his temple and said to Jennifer, 'Has anyone else got any more surprises up their sleeves? I ought to warn you that if Staves searches you and it turns out any one of you has lied, Ryan here gets a bullet, pronto. Well, any more surprises?'

'No,' Jennifer promised.

Kelso addressed Mark. 'You lied to me, Ryan. Maybe I should just make an example of you and kill you right here and now.'

His finger tightened on the trigger, but without warning he swung the barrel round to point it at Bobby. He stared at Jennifer. 'Or maybe it ought to be Bobby first? Let you know that I really mean business. Well, what do you have to say about the box? Your time's up.'

'I . . . I think I know where it might be,' Jennifer answered.

There was a moment's silence, and then Kelso's eyes sparked with triumph. 'OK, let's have it. Start talking.'

Garuda spent ten minutes trying to find the Buick again. The storm had turned nasty, forked lightning exploding overhead. He drove all the way down Reardon Avenue but saw no sign of the car, or its occupants.

Shit.

It didn't help that he could barely see out past the wipers given the rivers of water lashing the windscreen, and now and then he had to roll down his window to get a clearer look. He reckoned the kidnappers must have turned off one of the side streets, or maybe even driven into an underground parking lot. He tried three of the side streets, then doubled back each time to the main road, keeping his eye out for an underground lot, but he saw none. He was drenched by the heavy rain flailing through his open window, and after ten minutes he figured there was really nothing for it but to call for back-up. But on a night like tonight he knew he was only kidding himself – he didn't hold out much hope of his fellow cops getting a quick lead on the Buick.

He didn't even have the fucking licence number, and he had to face it, the car could be anywhere by now. To make things worse, he couldn't even let Mark know about Bobby's predicament. Still, he figured he had to do something.

He pulled into the kerb and punched a number on his cell phone.

87

'You're telling me the box may be somewhere out in the bay, weighed down near one of the marker buoys? I don't fucking believe it.'

Kelso was enraged as he stared at the bay from the kitchen window. Jennifer doubted that he could see very far in the dark – the storm was building to its climax now, the weather so fierce that the swaying trees looked as if they would snap with the savage force of the wind. Kelso turned back from the window in frustration and went to stand over Bobby. 'You'd better be telling the truth.'

'He's not lying,' Jennifer assured him. 'He said he's told you everything he knows.'

'I'm not talking to you.' Kelso skewered her with a dangerous look, then turned back to Bobby. 'It better be the truth, you hear me?'

Bobby nodded.

Kelso said to Jennifer, 'If it isn't the truth, then I'm going to enjoy doing something I never got to finish.' There was a look of malice on his face as he tore open the top buttons on his shirt, pulled aside his tie and revealed the stitched flesh of a jagged knife wound below his neck. 'Remember this? Sure you do. I was lucky you didn't kill me that night.'

Jennifer regarded Kelso with unconcealed hatred, but he ignored her and crossed to the window again. 'Is your father's boat in working order?'

'I don't know,' Jennifer said defiantly.

'I don't want fucking don't know. Is it, yes or no?'

'The boat hasn't been used in years, so I can't say.'

Staves said to Kelso in disbelief, 'You're going out in a boat in that fucking weather? It's like a hurricane out there.'

Kelso gestured at Mark with his pistol. 'It won't be us, it'll be Ryan, but we'll have to wait until the storm dies down. At a guess, I'd say it's going to be a couple more hours before he can check out the marker buoys, see if the black bag's tied to one of them.'

'What the fuck are we supposed to do in the meantime?' Staves asked.

Kelso glanced out at the garden before he replied. 'Tell our friend out there to come inside before he freezes to death. Then take Ryan out to the boathouse and see if the motorboat is seaworthy. If it needs gas we'll have to siphon some from the car, but make sure the engine is in working order. If not, we'll have to come up with a plan B. And if Ryan tries to get smart, don't even think about it, just kill him.'

Staves pulled an electric torch from his pocket and opened the back door. A squall of wind raged into the room. He flashed the light towards the garden, beckoning the blond, and when the man had stepped into the kitchen he said, 'You stay here for now. Ryan, you get a fucking move on.'

Staves pushed Mark out into the yard. Another wind squall blasted into the room, and when the door closed Jennifer observed them both through the window as they struggled towards the boardwalk, their heads down against the powerful gusts. A few moments later they disappeared into the stormy darkness.

Staves kept the gun prodding into his back. The first thing Mark felt was the intense cold. The icy salt air slashed at his face like a razor. The dock was pounded by violent waves. When they reached the boathouse, Mark pushed open the door. They moved inside. Staves flicked on the overhead light and indicated the motorboat. 'Check it out. But just remember, fuck with me and I'll kill you.'

Mark wiped rain from his face. 'Let me ask you something, Staves. Do you really trust Kelso? Don't you know he'll kill you, just like he killed Grimes and Fellows? The man's got to be psychotic, he can't be trusted.'

'Are you trying to cut a deal, Ryan?'

'What do you think?'

In response, Staves raised his pistol and struck Mark across the face. 'You've got your answer. Now get to work.'

It was obvious to Mark after five minutes of examination that the boat wasn't seaworthy. A small amount of reserve fuel slopped around in the tank but the boat hadn't been maintained and the engine appeared to be seized. To make matters worse the wood had splintered in places. 'It's a waste of time. I'd sink before I got ten yards. It's not safe.'

Staves kicked at the hull, his anger seething. '*Fuck it.*'

'I've got a proposition, Staves, and I think you'd better hear it.'

Staves said angrily, 'I thought I warned you already.'

'This is important. I'm giving you a chance to get the box before Kelso does. You want to hear me out or not?'

'What are you talking about?' Staves was wary.

'There's something Bobby neglected to mention, something that may form the basis of a deal between us.'

'What kind of a deal?'

'In return for letting us go, you get the box.'

Staves' eyes sparked with caution. 'Spit out exactly what you've got to say.'

'The box may not be attached to one of the marker buoys. It may be elsewhere.'

'*Where?*'

'Under the boardwalk.'

When Mark explained, he saw a furious look erupt on Staves' face. 'You held back on us.'

'Wouldn't you if you were in my position? I figured I might stand a better chance of helping Jennifer and Bobby walk away from this alive if I dealt only with you. I sure as hell wouldn't stand a chance with Kelso. I don't think you do, either. My instinct tells me you're not part of his final pension plan. My deal is, you get the box, if it's there, and you let us go, unharmed. That way, you don't have to share it with Kelso.'

387

Staves hesitated, considering before he replied. 'That's a big if. What if it isn't there? What if it's out there tied to one of the buoys like you said?'

'We do the same deal.'

Staves pursed his lips, looking unsure. 'We'll see.'

'I need more than that, Staves.'

'I said we'd see.' Staves grabbed an orange nylon rope from the motorboat and tossed it to Mark. 'Here, tie that round your waist, make sure it's secure.'

'What for?'

'You're going to take a look under the boardwalk to check it out, and I don't want you washed away.' Staves grinned. 'At least, not until we find what we're looking for.'

Mark felt the crash of a powerful wave and the boathouse shook. 'But you heard Kelso, we need to wait until the storm dies down. It'd be suicide going into the sea in this weather.'

'There's been a change of plan. Now you do it my way.'

Danny Flynn was chewing a cigar butt and working his way through a mound of paperwork when his desk phone rang. He flicked the call to the speaker intercom. 'Flynn here.'

There was a hail of rain outside his window. Manhattan was being lashed by a violent thunderstorm, flashes of forked electricity sizzling on the horizon every few minutes, and Flynn wondered whether the power lines would hold out for the evening or whether he'd have an excuse to go home early for a change. The background noise on the line was so bad that he had difficulty hearing his caller, but he recognised Lou Garuda's voice and heard pretty much all of what he said, which was why he was now scowling. 'Have you been drinking, Lou?'

'I'm as sober as a fucking saint. You heard what I just said?'

'I heard. You're sure that these two goons you saw abducting the kid were Red Mafia?'

'Danny, I'm sure of nothing except that I'm sitting in my car on Long Island being pissed on, and a cop I know named Mark Ryan wanted me to check out the Moscayas for him. Sure, I saw the kid being abducted, but the two guys who did it could be fucking aliens for all I know. But there's some weird shit going down, Danny. You've got to believe me. Some very weird shit, man.'

'You got any idea what's it to do with?'

'A bizarre case from a couple of years back. A guy named Paul March vanished, and his wife was murdered. You remember it?'

'Naw, but what the fuck do you want *me* to do, for Christ sakes?'

'I followed the Buick to Reardon Avenue, then I lost it.'

'So?'

'So I got a favour to ask.'

'Not another? What's the favour this time?'

'A big one, Danny. A very fucking big one.'

Jennifer heard a banshee scream beyond the kitchen door. It was impossible to see Mark or Staves out on the boardwalk, the wind-lashed darkness as black as tar. She was fraught with worry. What if Mark's plan didn't work and Staves killed him? Or what if he drowned trying to find the box? And what if she and Bobby died because of what they were about to attempt? She knew that the next five minutes, and how they carried out the plan, would decide the fate of all three of them, meant the difference between life and death. She tried to bury her fear and stroked Bobby's hair as he clung to her. There were so many things she wanted to say to him – he had a right to know the truth, to know why Kelso had murdered their parents – but this wasn't the time. *Maybe I'll never have time.*

Every shred of reason told her that she and Bobby were going to die, no matter what she and Mark did. But she forced herself to stay focused, her hatred of Kelso building inside her until it was almost ready to explode. *Stick to the plan,* Mark had said. She thought: *But what if it doesn't work?*

She looked at her watch – Mark had been gone exactly three minutes. It was time. She squeezed Bobby's hand, made a signal with her fingers so that he'd understand that things were about to begin. *Ready?*

His fingers moved in reply. '*Ready.*'

Kelso turned back from the window, saw Bobby's gesture and frowned. 'What the fuck's he doing?'

'He . . . says he needs his medication.'

'What medication?'

'He doesn't feel well. He needs Dilantin, to stop him having an epileptic fit. It can happen if he's under stress.'

'Forget it. He'll do without.'

Jennifer said bitterly, 'My brother may die if he doesn't have his pills, but maybe you're so cold hearted you don't care about that. Remember that Bobby's the last person who saw the box, and we haven't found it yet.'

Kelso considered. 'Where's the fucking medication?'

'I think I've got a spare bottle of pills in my bag, out in the car.'

'You *think*?'

'I always keep some in case of an emergency. They should still be in my bag.'

Kelso tucked his pistol inside his waistband and said to the blond, 'Shoot them both if they try anything dumb.' He stepped out and banged the kitchen door after him.

The blond pulled up a chair and sat down, resting his pistol lazily across his lap. Jennifer remembered exactly what Mark had told her and Bobby to do, and she started praying that the plan would work, but they were playing for high stakes. *Shoot them both if they try anything . . .*

But it was too late now. Bobby suddenly started to shake, his body racked by convulsions, and he collapsed in a heap on the floor. Jennifer panicked and moved to kneel beside him, but the blond pulled her away. 'What the fuck's wrong with him?'

'He's having a seizure. Please, I need a towel. Let me find one—'

Jennifer turned towards the sink but the blond pushed her back and said warily, 'You fucking stay there. I'll get it.'

He crossed to the sink and at that moment Jennifer took her chance. She reached out and grabbed the fire extinguisher from the pantry wall. As the blond turned back with a dish towel in his hand, Jennifer aimed the nozzle at his face and squeezed the firing handle.

Nothing happened.

Oh God . . . This wasn't the way she had planned it. She meant for the foam to blind the man, but there wasn't even a trickle. And then she realised why: in her panic she'd forgotten to pull out the handle's safety pin. *This isn't happening.*

The blond was enraged. 'You fucking bitch . . . !'

As he dropped the towel and pulled out his gun, Jennifer swung the fire extinguisher in an arc and struck him across the jaw. There was an almighty clang of metal and he grunted with pain, blood spurting from a cut in his jaw as he staggered back and fell to the floor. But he was still conscious and he clapped a hand to his face, and with the other he reached out blindly to grab at Jennifer. This time she brought the extinguisher down hard on his head. There was a sickening thud and a sound like bone splintering. The man grunted and then lay still.

Jennifer recoiled in horror at what she'd just done, and it was a moment before she went to pick up the man's gun. Bobby had stopped acting – he'd done exactly as Mark had suggested – but he was deathly pale and Jennifer sensed that the violence he'd just witnessed had distressed him.

'Please, Bobby, we don't have time to get upset, so you have to do exactly as Mark said.' She indicated the pantry. 'Stay in there until . . .' She was about to say *until I get back*, but who was she kidding? She didn't know whether she *would* get back. It all depended on luck, on how fast she could run, and the answer to the question she dreaded asking herself: *Can I do what I have to do in time, before Kelso kills us all?* 'Stay in there until you think it's safe to come out. But leave it as long as you can.'

She turned the knob on the cupboard door and revealed a tight space surrounded by wooden shelves, with barely enough room to stand up in. 'You can't move, or make a sound. I know that's going to be scary, especially if you hear shooting, but *please* do as I tell you. If you make a noise, or let Kelso and his men know where you are, it could ruin everything.'

Perspiration beaded Jennifer's face as she helped Bobby move inside the tiny space and sat him on the floor. He looked like a child again; so helpless, fear in his eyes as he stared up at her, his body trembling. She wanted to kneel down and hug him, but there was no time for goodbyes, and she was frantic, knowing Kelso would return any second now – there was no medication in her bag – and she had to get out of the room *fast* before Staves came back. She would head out to the hallway and let herself out through the front door. 'Promise me you won't move?'

Bobby nodded.

'Close your eyes. Try and imagine how you used to hide in there when we were kids. Remember?'

Bobby nodded again and shut his eyes tightly.

'I'm going to close the door now, Bobby. Try not to be afraid, please.'

She closed the pantry door and the lock clicked. Then a thought suddenly occurred to her. If the blond had another cell phone, she could call 911, right away. Frantically, she stepped over, searched the man's pockets, and found a cell phone . . .

Thank God.

She switched it on, and after what seemed like an endless wait the screen lit up. She punched in 911 and hit the dial key. *Please answer* . . . Almost immediately, a female voice came on the line. 'Police operator one-one-eight-four. What is your emergency? What borough?'

'Please . . .' Jennifer blurted out. 'My name's Jennifer March. Some men are trying to kill my brother and me . . .'

Before she could utter another word she heard footsteps outside the kitchen and she panicked. She dropped the phone. It clattered to the tiled floor and came apart, the battery pack separating from the phone. *Oh God.*

Kelso was returning. She knew she had to leave the room now, *this second.*

The door handle began to turn.

She was too late.

90

'It's too dangerous, Staves.' Mark finished tying the nylon rope around his waist, having secured it to a rung on the boardwalk ladder. He had counted the period between each wave crest and it was barely seven seconds. The wood creaked under the force of the water, and he was doubtful that he could make it very far down the ladder without being pounded against the boardwalk or swallowed up by the waves.

Staves pointed his gun at him and handed over the torch. 'Too bad. Lower yourself down and take a good look under the walkway.'

'But I told you . . .'

'Shut the fuck up and do what you're told. Now *go*.'

The torch had a grip string and Mark slipped it on to his wrist. He flicked on the light and waited until the next wave struck and began to recede. As he began his perilous descent down the ladder the sea looked terrifying. 'This is crazy, Staves,' he shouted back.

'Keep going,' Staves roared, the noise of the ocean almost drowning out his words.

Mark had reached the sixth rung when another wave crashed into the boardwalk. Ice-cold water hammered his body and he held tightly on to the rungs, but as the wave subsided he was swung like a pendulum by the sucking force of the receding water. He slipped, lost his footing, grabbed the rope to save himself and barely managed to pull himself back on to the ladder.

He was already drenched to the skin when another wave hit him four steps later. This time he succeeded in maintaining his footing. He was low enough now to see a criss-cross of thick wooden beams under the boardwalk. But it was dark, and even in the light of the torch almost impossible to see as the swells of water thrashed the wooden beams. He waited until the swell had subsided, and just before an incoming wave was due shone the torchlight into a recess in the beams.

Empty.

He probed another recess.

Nothing.

A wave smashed him against the ladder like a rag doll. He held on to the rope grimly, waited again as the wave buffeted him in the angry swell, and when it had washed away again shone the torch. Nothing. But a second later the torchlight reflected from something. His heart leaped when he saw a black bag tied to one of the cross-beams, the plastic slick with a sheen of salt water.

Mark's heart pounded as he struggled back up the ladder and on to the boardwalk. He was frozen. He coughed up a lungful of salt water, barely able to hear above the roar of the waves and wind as Staves shouted at him. 'Well?'

'It's . . . down there. I found a black bag tied to one of the beams.'

Staves' face lit up with excitement. 'Why didn't you bring the fucking thing up?'

'Because I can't – it's tied to a cross-beam and I'll need something to cut the rope. A knife or box cutters . . .'

Water dripped from Staves' face as he fumbled in his pocket and took out a Swiss Army knife. He opened a blade. As he handed over the knife there was animal caution in his eyes and he pointed his pistol at Mark's head. 'A word of warning, Ryan. Try getting fucking smart with the blade and I kill you. Got that? Now fetch the bag.'

Jennifer hid behind the kitchen door as the knob began to turn. Her heart pounded as she gripped the gun in both hands. Her plan had been to race to Mark's house and use the phone, but she didn't have time. She readied herself. She knew she had to shoot Kelso dead. It was the only way. In the space of a second or two, a dozen thoughts seemed to race through her mind.

Hold the pistol steady as you aim, then squeeze the trigger, she told herself. But her hands shook with fear. Could she again shoot someone dead, up close, but in cold blood? She wanted her revenge, wanted Kelso to pay the price for destroying her family, but what she was about to do would bring her down to Kelso's level, and that angered her.

Kelso stepped into the room. Jennifer found herself staring at the back of his head. She had a split second to act and she aimed at a point just above the base of his skull.

Please God, please let me kill him with the first shot . . .

She closed her eyes, squeezed the trigger, and the gun exploded in her hands.

91

Everything seemed to happen slowly. As the sound of the gunshot died, Jennifer snapped open her eyes and saw Kelso being punched forward by the force of the bullet.

Her heart pounded and her body shook from the trauma of what she had just done. Kelso was slammed into the kitchen worktop, then fell to the floor, shock on his face, but he was still alive and he clapped a hand to his neck, blood oozing between his fingers. Almost without thinking, Jennifer again aimed at his head and squeezed the trigger.

The pistol exploded with a powerful recoil and this time the shot hit Kelso's hand, slicing through a finger, severing the knuckle joint, the digit barely held on by a sinewy tendon.

Kelso let out a scream but by now he was moving, already rolling towards the kitchen door, his shock replaced by rage. Jennifer had the terrifying feeling that she had managed only to graze his neck – and so she aimed at his torso and fired again. Her shot went wide. Suddenly Kelso struggled to his feet and backed out through the kitchen door. His gun appeared in his hand and he fired two rapid shots, then two more, the rounds smacking into the plaster above Jennifer's head.

'You bitch!' he screamed, then fired again. 'You fucking bitch!'

Jennifer desperately sought cover as a bullet grazed her arm. It felt as if a red-hot poker were searing her skin, and she yelled and dropped the pistol. There was no time to pick it up again, everything was happening too rapidly, and she knew she had to get out of the room fast before a ricochet drilled through the pantry door and killed Bobby. Kelso fired again and a bullet zinged above her head. She darted out into the hallway and within seconds had reached the front door.

She knew now there was no going back. She had to stick to Mark's plan: *Get over to my parents' house and call 911. There's a chance that the gun is in the chest of drawers . . .*

It was the only real option she had left, she had to take the risk – and yet she was desperately afraid of leaving Bobby behind.

Please God, keep Bobby safe. Let him live.

She hoped he stayed hidden in the cupboard, but he'd be terrified after hearing the shots, and she felt as if she were abandoning him . . .

There isn't time for soul searching.

She ran across the lawns in the pelting rain. Halfway across the street, her lungs on fire, she dared to look back and saw Kelso stagger out through the front door, clutching his neck. For a split second their eyes locked.

Then Kelso ran after her with a burst of speed.

Danny Flynn was having a lousy night. It didn't look as if he was going to get home early after all, not since Lou Garuda had begged him to pull out all the stops to try to find the March kid.

Flynn had authorised one of his senior detectives to put out a bulletin – every patrol car on duty in New York was to be alerted to the navy blue Buick with the two men and an abducted seventeen-year-old named Bobby March. But Flynn didn't hold out much hope, at least not until ten minutes later when he got an urgent call from the detective.

'Danny? Something came in you ought to hear about. A woman just called 911 from a cell phone. She said her name was Jennifer March and that some men were trying to kill her and her brother. Soon as I heard the name March, I figured I'd better tell you . . .'

Flynn frantically grabbed a notepad. 'What else did she say?'

'Nothing. The line went dead.'

'Gimme the details again.' Twenty seconds later, Flynn

slammed down his phone and immediately made another call, this time to Garuda. 'Lou, it's Danny. Where the fuck are you?'

'Still driving near Reardon Avenue trying to spot the fucking Buick. Where else?'

'Listen, I got some good news, and some bad. We got a 911 a couple of minutes ago from a woman using a cell phone. She claimed her name was Jennifer March and she sounded panicked, and said that some men were trying to kill her and her brother. Then the cell phone went completely dead.'

Garuda immediately slammed on his brakes. *'Where is she, Danny?'*

'We don't know. She was on the line for less than nine seconds, and that's about the minimum we need to get a fix. The cell phone provider's trying to trace the call from their end, but they say the phone she used has gone dead. If we want a precise location fix we'll have to pray that she calls again.'

'That may never fucking happen, Danny!'

'That's the bad news.'

Mark knew he was going to drown. He sucked in mouthfuls of salty air as the waves slammed into his body and clung defiantly to the rope, Staves still up on the boardwalk covering him with the gun. Mark knew now he had little chance of escape. He'd hoped to get close enough to Staves to push him or trip him into the sea, but Staves had been careful and kept his distance. Mark knew that cutting himself free from the rope and trying to swim away wasn't an option: the sea was too violent, and he'd drown before he got twenty yards. But somehow he had to make his move once he got back up on the boardwalk.

He had cut the rope holding the black bag to the cross-beam, but he kept Staves' penknife clutched in his hand. The bag felt heavy, with something rectangular inside that might be a box, and he grasped it to his chest and struggled up the ladder, the icy sea water drenching him in endless salty waves.

Staves roared, 'Toss the knife up first. Then get back up here. Don't lose the fucking bag.'

Damn. Mark's hope that Staves' excitement might make him forget about the knife even briefly was dashed.

'Toss it up, Ryan,' Staves repeated.

Mark tossed the knife on to the boardwalk. Staves began to reel in the rope, pulling Mark up. When he reached the top of the ladder, he knelt on the boardwalk, exhausted. His only chance now was to rush Staves and risk being shot. Dangerous, but what choice had he got?

Staves bent to pick up the bag. Mark braced himself to rush him, but suddenly a shot rang out. The noise was faint in the storm, but then came another shot, and another, a chorus of gunfire.

It came from the house. *Jennifer . . . Bobby.* Frantically Mark tried to get up but in an instant Staves grabbed the bag and kicked him back into the water. 'So long, sucker.'

Staves fired once as Mark fell into the boiling sea, his body swallowed up by the waves, and then Staves turned and ran like a madman towards the house.

92

Rain lashed against Jennifer's face and she ran as fast as her legs would carry her. She had forty yards to go before she reached the Ryan house and she could just about make out through the downpour the white door, the steps leading up to the veranda, the dark porch. The sky exploded with thunder and light, and her heart pounded as she dared to look back. Kelso was racing across the street. *Oh God . . . ! He's going to kill me!*

Thirty yards to the door.

Twenty.

Fifteen.

Rain cut into her eyes. She was too afraid now to glance back, certain that Kelso would soon catch up with her.

Ten yards.

She raced up the veranda steps, knocked over the flower pot and found the spare key underneath, exactly where Mark had said it would be. She fumbled the key into the lock and pushed open the front door. As she stepped into the hallway, she flicked on the light switch and the hall blazed with light. She saw the stairs ahead. Without a second's hesitation she ran towards them.

Kelso reached the hallway seconds later. He was drenched with sweat and rain, and as he clutched his wounded neck he looked deranged, like a wild animal scenting blood. He noticed the wet footprints on the stairs and gritted his teeth. 'You bitch, I'm coming for you!'

Then he bounded up the stairs.

★

Which is the master bedroom? Jennifer faced six doors. The landing didn't resemble that in her parents' house, all the doors were closed, and she didn't know which room to pick.

Pick the nearest.

She opened the door and found herself in a boxroom, one that had probably once belonged to Mark or one of his brothers. She moved on to the next room and pushed open the door. This bedroom was bigger than the last, overlooking the rear garden, but it wasn't the master. She heard a noise in the hall down-stairs, the sound of heavy panting as someone clattered on to the patio.

Kelso.

In desperation, she flung open the next door and darted inside a large room, but didn't turn on the light switch. She heard foot-steps on the stairs. Kelso was racing after her.

She looked around the room in panic. The curtains were open, flashes of blue lightning drenching the walls. She saw a dark-wood writing bureau with a chair, framed family photographs and a phone on top. She was in the master bedroom. No time to use the phone. She had to find the gun.

Kelso's footsteps were coming closer, racing up the stairs.

She ran to the bureau and pulled away the chair. Six drawers. Which one held the revolver? Left or right? Top or bottom? Mark had said he wasn't even certain that the gun was still there. *What if it isn't?* She dreaded even contemplating that possibility and yanked open the top left drawer.

Empty.

She tried the top right.

Empty.

Kelso was on the landing . . . she heard him trying one of the doors, then a few seconds later heard him push open another door.

Please God, help me find the gun . . .

She tried the next drawer. A wood smell wafted out. She fumbled madly, but there was no gun inside, only a jumble of erasers and paper clips . . .

She heard a noise and looked round. Was it her imagination, or was the bedroom door handle starting to turn?

In a frenzy she tried the next drawer.

She found only a stapling machine.

And the next drawer.

Empty.

She had tried every drawer but the gun wasn't there . . .

Maybe she had missed it?

She started to search again, but a split second later the bedroom door burst open.

93

Bright light exploded into the bedroom from the landing, and Kelso was framed in the doorway. His face was in shadow, but Jennifer heard his laboured breathing, his voice angry with pain. 'Well, well. If it isn't the bitch who shot and knifed me.'

Jennifer stepped back against the bureau, and her breath came in short, rapid throbs. She was petrified, riveted to the spot.

'It wouldn't do any good if you were thinking of using the phone. I'd be long gone before the police ever got here.' Kelso stepped forward, a self-satisfied look on his face as it materialised out of the shadow. He put a hand to his neck, then took it away to stare at crimson fingers, one of them almost severed at the knuckle, and his eyes flashed with rage. 'It seems you have a bad habit of doing me harm. Where's Bobby?'

Jennifer didn't reply. Kelso shot her a look of malice as he flicked on the light and stepped closer. 'Don't worry, I'll find him. But first, you and I have some unfinished business.'

Jennifer was paralysed with fear. Kelso was two feet away and she could smell his sour breath. A flash of lightning flooded the bedroom.

'Please . . . please don't . . .' she begged.

'What? Rape you?' Kelso grinned. 'The thing of it is, I got to enjoy it the last time. And now that it's time to teach you a lesson, I confess I'm pretty much looking forward to it.'

Kelso brushed her cheek with the back of his hand. 'You know what else? Afterwards you're going to tell me exactly where Bobby is. Do that, and maybe I'll try and make it a quick death for him, with as little pain as possible. Otherwise, if I've got to find him myself, your kid brother's going to suffer. Have you got that?'

Jennifer pressed her back against the bureau, and in desperation twisted her right hand behind her and again fumbled in one of the drawers. She felt some papers . . . but no gun.

Mark was wrong about the gun, and I'm going to die.

Kelso inched closer. Jennifer had nowhere to retreat to as his hand crawled over her breast, then came up suddenly and grasped her throat. Jennifer struggled but he tightened his grip. 'Stay still!'

She recoiled in horror as Kelso's mouth came closer and he whispered, 'Don't struggle, or I'll fucking hurt you.'

Jennifer felt desperately in the next drawer. More paper clips, a notepad . . . and then her fingers felt something hard, metallic. Blunt at one end, stiletto sharp at the other.

Not a gun, but a letter opener or scissors? What did it matter, so long as it could be used as a weapon.

Kelso's face was right up against hers, his sour breath on her skin, and as he leaned close enough to kiss her he said hoarsely, 'Maybe this time you'll enjoy it too? What do you think, Jennifer?'

'I think you're going to hell, Kelso.'

His grin vanished as Jennifer brought up her free hand and he gaped in horror at the brass letter opener before she plunged it like a dagger into his chest. His body jolted and he lurched backward, dropping his gun, his eyes wild as he clutched at his wound. Jennifer grabbed his pistol from the floor, aimed and squeezed the trigger.

The shot tore into Kelso's chest and he flopped sideways like a puppet whose strings had been cut. Jennifer fired again, and again, hammering Kelso's body against the wall, and then he crumpled to the floor. She kept firing until the weapon gave an empty *click*, and then she fell to her knees, fighting back tears, her pent-up fear and anger finally bursting like a dam inside her head.

Then she heard the noise. A hoarse gurgling sound.

Kelso was still breathing. *He's still alive.* Most of her shots had struck his body, but they hadn't been enough to kill him.

A second later, she heard footsteps on the stairs.

94

Jennifer looked round just as a figure stepped into the doorway. Was it Mark? Or the police? Oh God . . . It was Staves, and he held a gun in one hand, a wet black plastic bag in the other. Jennifer panicked, raised her pistol and squeezed the trigger.

Click.

She had forgotten the gun was empty. A grin spread over Staves' face, and he glanced at Kelso's body. 'I guess I don't have to share, after all.' He raised his gun, preparing to shoot. 'It's nothing personal, honey, just something that's got to be done.'

The howl of a police siren sounded in the distance and Staves hesitated. For a brief second, Jennifer wondered whether someone was coming to save her, but she knew now it was too late. She was about to shut her eyes and wait for the bullet that would surely kill her when a shadow appeared on the landing. Someone was moving out there in the hallway behind Staves. Then there was a crack of thunder and a second later a flash of lightning exploded, and she saw Mark, his figure outlined in the hallway, inching forward. His clothes were drenched and he had a nylon rope tied around his waist and a pistol clutched in both hands.

She saw the anger on his face, heard it in his voice as he shouted, 'Staves!'

To Jennifer, everything seemed to happen in slow motion. Staves ducked as he spun round, caught off guard, and as he went to aim, Mark fired. The single shot hit Staves in the heart, and Mark fired rapidly again and again, hitting Staves twice in the head, killing him instantly.

95

It was 8 p.m. and the rain had stopped, the sky no longer bruised and black, the stars silver bright. Jennifer had comforted Bobby, had told the police everything she knew, and when she could take no more she told them she wanted to be alone and walked down to the boardwalk.

The storm had moved on, the black clouds driven away by icy Atlantic winds. She sat on the edge of the walkway. A little later a uniformed officer came by and put a rain cape around her shoulders and told her he didn't want her to freeze to death. It was a cold night, he said, and asked whether he could take her back up to the house, but she said no, she wanted to stay a little longer, and so he left her sitting there and walked away.

She felt the breeze on her face, heard the water lapping beneath her feet, a swell still there, and at that moment she knew she had reached the end and was suddenly more tired than she had ever been in her life. She heard the footsteps but didn't look round.

'You'll catch cold out here.' Mark came to sit beside her and slid his legs over the jetty's edge. He had told her everything: how Staves' shot had missed him as he had hit the water, how the rope around his waist, still tied to the ladder, had saved him from being swallowed by the waves. After he'd struggled out of the water he'd made it to the front of the house and seen another of Kelso's men, the one named Marty, heading towards the veranda at his folks' place. That was when Garuda's Porsche and two black-and-whites arrived, the police alerted by a neighbour's report of gunshots, and Kelso's man was confronted. He had tossed down his pistol and given himself up; Mark had grabbed the weapon and pursued Staves into the house.

'I've still got a lot of explaining to do to Garuda. But what about you? How are you coping?'

She wiped her eyes. 'I'll be fine.'

'Bobby's doing OK. He's confused, sure, but he'll come through. Right now he's wondering where you are and wanted me to come and find you.'

'I just needed a little time to myself. Can you understand, Mark?'

'Sure. I just thought you'd want to know that Kelso didn't make it. He died on the way to the operating theatre.'

Jennifer nodded but didn't reply. Mark put his arm around her shoulder and she leaned into his chest. At that moment she felt safe with him. And as he held her close, stroking her hair, something struck her: she realised that she hadn't been able to move on because she was waiting for her father to come back and hold her, the way Mark wanted to hold her. 'I can see that for now you just need to be on your own,' he said.

She didn't want him to let her go, didn't want to lose the secure feeling that he gave to her, but he seemed to sense that she needed to clear her head. His arm fell away but he held her hand as she said, 'For a little while longer. What about the Moscayas?'

'They're not going to be interested in you and Bobby. Now that the Organised Crime Division has the disk, they'll have their own worries trying to run for cover from criminal charges that are going to tear their organisation apart.'

She bit her lip and brushed a strand of hair from her face. 'I knew my father would never have hurt us. I knew he'd never have deliberately put us in jeopardy. I knew that all along. But you know what I keep thinking? I don't want him to lie cold and forgotten on a faraway mountain. I don't want that.'

Mark squeezed her hand. 'I'll do everything I can to make sure they try to find his body. That's a promise.'

Jennifer nodded silently, knowing that he meant it. 'There's someone else I keep thinking about.'

'Who?'

'The young woman at the airport, Nadia Fedov.'

'What about her?'

'Seeing as the Moscayas are going to be busy in court, they mightn't care so much about her.'

'What are you saying, Jenny?'

'If I can convince her to turn federal witness, would you try to help her stay out of prison?'

A smile flickered across Mark's face. 'You don't give up, do you? And let's face it, you've kind of got me at a tender moment.'

'She's an innocent, Mark. She doesn't deserve to pay for a crime that she was forced to commit.'

'I'll talk to the federal prosecutor's office, see if I can convince them to go for it. But on one condition.'

'What?'

'If I ever get into trouble, I want you for my attorney. Deal?'

'It's a deal. Will you do one last thing for me, Mark?'

'What?'

'Will you bring Bobby down here? There's something I need to say to him.'

'You're sure you want to talk to him here?'

Jennifer nodded. 'It's where we used to come to sit with our father.'

'I'll try and get a chair from the paramedics.' Mark slowly let go of her hand, stood and looked down at her face. 'I don't give up either, you know.'

'I know.'

'If you feel you need a shoulder to lean on, or someone to listen, don't be afraid to phone.'

She heard the words, wasn't immune to them. 'You're always the first person I call. I've a funny feeling you always will be, Mark.'

He nodded. Before he left he said, 'There's a lot more to say. But we'll talk again.'

Jennifer heard his footsteps as he walked away, the way her father used to walk away. She still missed him. Missed his voice, missed him coming up the path and running to his arms. Missed so

409

many things about him. The ache had never gone away and she knew it never would.

In her heart she knew that it was impossible, but someday, somehow, she had to learn to live in peace with the demons that haunted her soul. She was forever trapped in her past, bound by its chains. The memories still haunted her and she knew why. Sometimes dreams were all she had. All she had to remember the life she had shared and lost with her father and mother, and the sacredness of their lives together.

A little later she heard a noise behind her and turned. Mark stood there, behind Bobby's wheelchair. He nodded silently to her then turned and was gone, back towards the house, leaving them alone.

Jennifer crossed to her brother, knelt and looked into his face. He still seemed confused and lost as he rocked back and forth in the chair. A breeze blew in from across the bay and ruffled his hair, and she patted it down. 'Remember how we used to come and sit here some nights and talk with Dad?'

Bobby nodded.

Jennifer took his hand. 'There's going to come a time very soon when *we* have to talk, Bobby. Not just about tonight but about everything that's happened. About all the things we never got to discuss because they were too painful. You know that, don't you? You know it's the only way we can try to put the past to rest and move on with our lives.'

Bobby nodded again, and she squeezed his hand. 'You're sure?'

She wanted to say so much more, to reassure him it would be OK, that no matter what they would always have each other, that they were tied together, the same flesh and blood, but she knew that Bobby knew this already. She hugged him. Suddenly he started to cry. She pulled him close, his cheek against her shoulder, and they clung tightly to each other, swayed together in the cold Atlantic wind, as if the other was all either of them had in the world, and they would never let each other go.

WATERFORD CITY AND COUNTY

WITHDRAWN

LIBRARIES